The Magician's Guide
Book 1: Faces in the Stones

By

Robert E. Gelinas

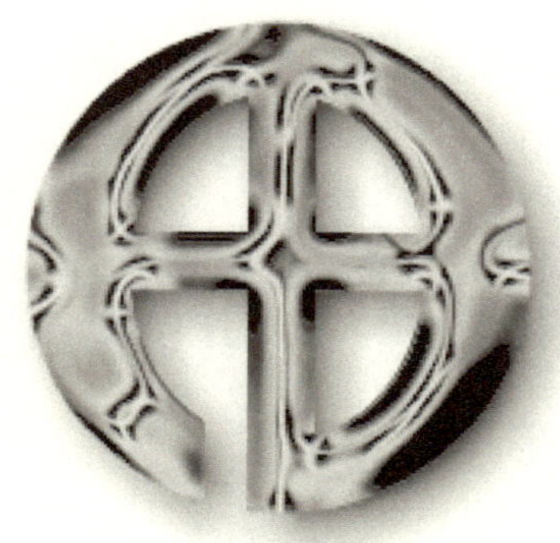

ArcheBooks Publishing

THE MAGICIAN'S GUIDE
BOOK 1: FACES IN THE STONES

A Novel By

ROBERT E. GELINAS

ISBN 10: 1-59507-267-5
ISBN 13: 978-1-59507-267-2

Published by
ARCHEBOOKS PUBLISHING

www.archebooks.com

Trade Paperback First Edition: 2015

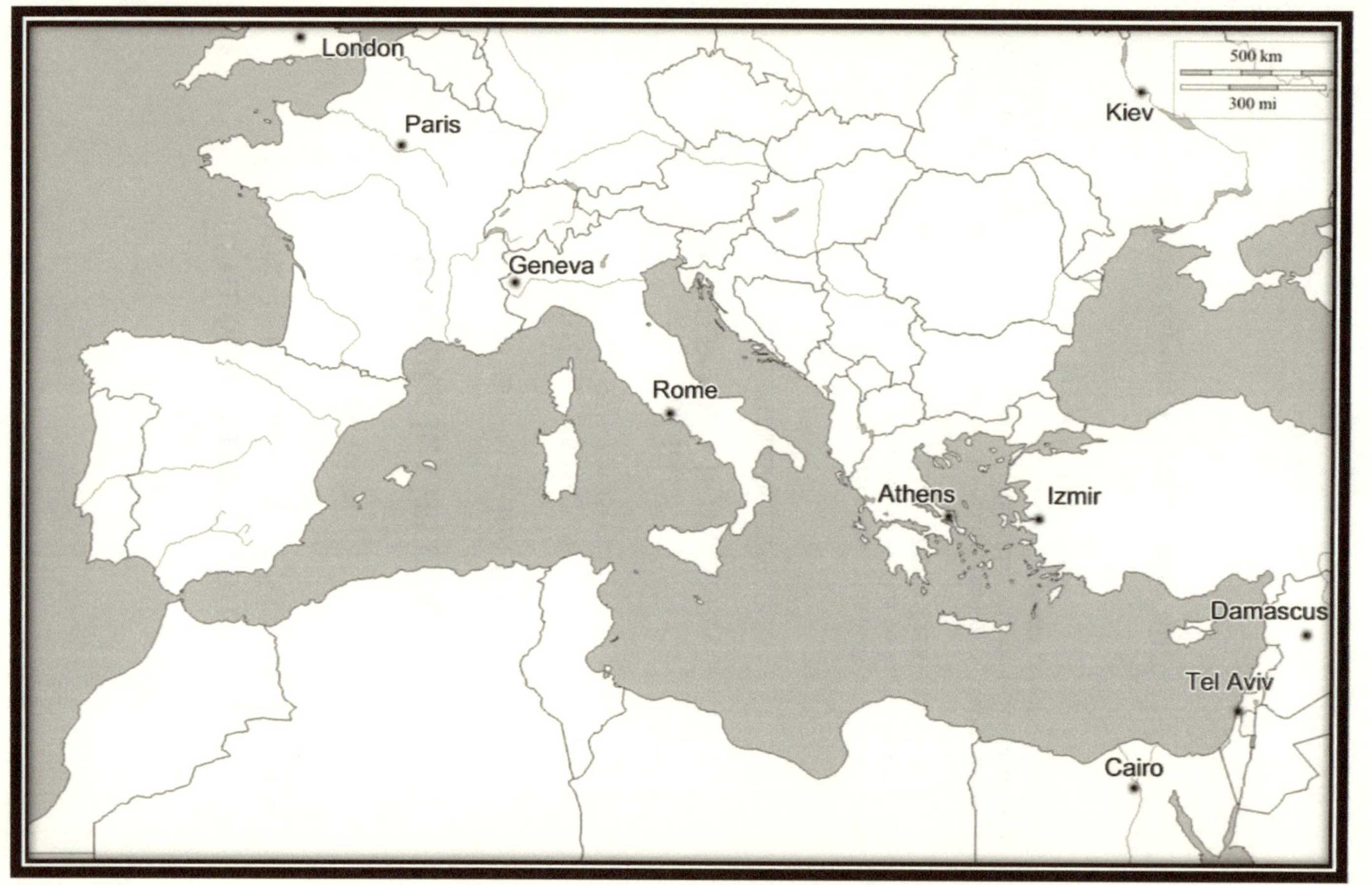
London
Paris
Geneva
Rome
Athens
Izmir
Kiev
500 km
300 mi
Damascus
Tel Aviv
Cairo

Dedication

To all of the true Magicians I've had the pleasure and honor to have known and experienced in my life,

To all who've nurtured their Magic in the cradle of their iMAGInations, and used it to give birth to all manner of creative arts and selfless acts of love.

Thank you.

You are true Magic.

Robert E. Gelinas

Other Books by Robert E. Gelinas

The Mustard Seed

Touch of a Stranger

Dead Man's Run

Dead of Night

Players

Anticipation

TABLE OF CONTENTS

Author's Note

This fictionalized novel was based upon the discovery of "The Journal of William Turner," portions of which have been excerpted for inclusion in this story. During the period of the events of this story, Dr. Turner was a world-renowned physicist, an expert in the field of quantum mechanics. Thus, much of his writing documented herein tends to be a bit technical in nature. However, if you can bear through his intricate explanations, opinions, firsthand observations, anecdotes, and conclusions, he has a lot to offer in terms of wisdom and insight on the topic of Magic and its inner workings.

Our heartfelt thanks go to his daughter, Alexandra Turner, for her generosity and support in allowing us unrestricted access to the Journal for the development of this book. Her goal is for her father's words and eye-witness testimony to be made public, and, in turn, be of benefit to all. But her greatest desire is for her father's name to be forever cleared and the truth about his involvement in matters documented in this book to finally be known and properly understood in historical context.

A Letter of Introduction to The Journal of William Turner

Magic is real.

Unfortunately, far too few souls genuinely understand the true meaning of the word "Magic" any longer.

At best, mortal folk mistakenly confuse Magic with vain illusions or clever prestidigitation; or, at worst, consider it nothing short of outright delusion or some aberrant psychopathy. Fewer still comprehend its primal origins and natural utility – ignorant of the Creative power of its Light, or the genuine Dangers of its Darkness.

Despite its universal ubiquity, a scarce remnant of humanity these days are Magic's few remaining crude practitioners, mired more in rote habits of ritual and contrived traditions than in the achievement of any objective efficacy. I regret to report, Magic's true high-level Masters are mostly remembered only in ancient legends and bygone myth. Although, if a living Master were to be encountered by mortal folk in today's world, it would be exceedingly rare if there were any recognition of the event.

It is how the Magi wish it to be.

It is how it must be for both high-level Magic and the Magi themselves to survive. At least that's how it was explained to me by my Master.

Now, my Master personally did not agree with that seminal axiom regarding universal Magi secrecy. Oh no, quite to the contrary. He held a most unique vision of Magic to be used for the benefit of all of mankind, or at least for a vast multitude of mortal folk, such that one day many souls would eagerly embrace the awesome power of practicing high Magic as the norm and not the exception, and thereby utterly transform the fortunes and destiny of all humanity.

Naturally, his peers all thought him mad.

Ages of history had taught the Magi all too well the often tragic and frequently lethal repercussions of fearful and ignorant mortal folk when exposed to any idea outside their small, finite domains of understanding and knowledge. Candidly, and much to my own chagrin, I too thought my Master to be insane at first.

With my background, how could I believe otherwise?

Not coincidentally, the very concept of learning not to fear Magic, i.e. parting the veil of fear and banishing the darkness of ignorance with the light of empirical truth instead of superstition, was one of the very first lessons he taught me regarding the true nature of Magic.

Like all Magi, I was instructed to be most wary of all those who superstitiously label anything outside their comfort zones of comprehension or tribal ideologies as magical. Likewise, I would admonish you, too, dear Reader, to also avoid all those who pejoratively brand all forms of Magic as witchcraft, or sorcery, or alchemy, the conjuring up of enchantments, or the casting of spells, hexes, and curses.

So much of that is such nonsense, fiction and folly.

For example, did you know that during the Salem Witch Trials at the end of the seventeenth century, a woman was once put on trial for making an apple turnover? It's true. No one could figure out how she got the apple inside the pastry, so it was deemed a demonic act of witchcraft. She would have been convicted and burned at the stake had she not demonstrated to the court her recipe and technique. So even that which is not high Magic at all, but perfectly normal activity, through ignorance, can also be disparaged and condemned as the evils of Magic.

Now it is irrefutably true for most of mankind, at least culturally speaking, that Magic of any kind is commonly associated with pure malevolence and evil intent. Guilt by association, you see. However, on rare occasion, should a manifestation of Magic ever have any positive connotation, then it might be labelled a "miracle," a "sign," an "omen," a "wonder" – or more commonly, merely swept from the light of day, cast under the rug in the most benign of terms: a "mystery."

No matter. Disbelief, superstitions and fears can never negate what is tangibly real and what is irrefutably true.

Magic is real, and its existence is true.

I confess, I myself came by this understanding of Magic's truth and its manifestations in physical reality somewhat gradually, as the byproduct of a most arduous process of learning and training, not via a birthright, natural talent, some instantaneous epiphany or external anointing. In truth, true Magic is quite hard to master and a most difficult form of power to wield. Sorry, but that is just the reality of how it works. And it is why I have taken the time to put ink to paper to record and preserve in these pages what must be done in order for a greater number of mortal folks to be empowered and educated to fulfil what is now both my own as well as my Master's dream.

I pray whoever finds this Journal will take the time to read it, and at a minimum, do so with an open mind and heart.

It is understood that what I have seen and experienced over the last several years and now deign to share with you herein shall, at first, surely be interpreted as utterly preposterous nonsense. Some may understandably also deem me to be mad. So be it. All I ask is that I be given a fair hearing, but better still, permit me a trial by evidence.

Indeed, what you are about to learn isn't a compendium of mere myth and lore, but a wealth of ancient secrets revealed, magical methods and techniques detailed, and true wonders explained. However, the proof of my words lies not in my testimony alone, dear Reader, but rather in the observance and replication of my instructions and thus believing the witness of your own eyes as to what comes of your own preparation and actions.

Rest assured, I understand the risks of what I am asking. Yes, there are indeed potential dangers involved in what I'm about to share with you. But all exploration involves risk. For even as I write this, I also know that there are vastly greater dangers than Magic for men to face – dangers that must be confronted and defeated.

So read on and learn, but be mindful to do so at your own risk.

For you see, there is an incomparable manifestation of wickedness coming not many days hence. And without true Magic alive and active in the hands of at least a remnant of souls, then the era of men may very well pass into the ash heap of history. This must be my gravest of warnings to all who behold this journal and refuse to heed its wisdom and exhortations.

Prepare. Train. Learn. Endure.

Explore and find the power within you, and then strive to master it and release it.

It can be done. I am evidence of that.

Hear me one and all, and all who have an ear to hear: A dark storm is coming, and without the protection and power of high Magic, the hands of mortal folk will be naively unprepared and wholly insufficient to meet the ferocity of its challenge and the devastating carnage and unimaginable slaughter and suffering that awaits in its path.

Magic is your only hope.

Most Sincerely,

William Turner

William Turner, Ph.D.
Managing Director, Large Hadron Collider (LHC)
Conseil Européen pour la Recherche Nucléaire (CERN)
European Organization for Nuclear Research
Geneva, Switzerland

PART 1

THE CONFLUENCE

There are more things in heaven and earth, Horatio,
Than are dreamt of in your philosophy.

Shakespeare
Hamlet (1.5.166)

The Confluence of the Rhone and Arve Rivers, Geneva, Switzerland

CHAPTER 1
ALEXANDRA

AUSTIN, TX

"I'm so very sorry, Miss Turner."

Sasha Turner couldn't speak. The lump in her throat was about to choke her. A thousand precious memories welled in her eyes and were about to roll down her cheeks. The visage of the kindly man sitting before her began to blur – that of her father's long-time friend and attorney, Marvin Gonzalez.

Arrested?

Gonzalez's office was spacious and well appointed. Marvin was one of the most highly sought-after attorneys in all of Austin, and the same could be said for the entire State of Texas for that matter. His large desk was a uniquely-carved and ornately inlaid rustic wood antique, said to have once belonged to Sam Houston himself when he served at Texas' first president in 1836. Houston won Texas' first presidential election as a free and independent nation, running against Stephen F. Austin, for whom the Capital of Texas itself is named.

Committed?

Directly behind the attorney stood a tall built-in cherry wood bookshelf stocked full with volumes of law library books, each bound in tan leather with thick red and black horizontal stripes on each spine. The entire floor of the private sixteen foot by twenty foot office was covered with a single Persian carpet, intricately woven in rich scarlet and gold threads. A faint toasty scent in the air told Sasha that Mr. Gonzalez was fond of enjoying an occasional fine cigar in the privacy of his office – despite this being a non-smoking building.

Not a surprise; with prosperity comes privilege.

Sasha managed to whisper, "But that's impossible. I just spoke with him a couple of months ago. He was completely fine. And I can promise you, he sounded perfectly lucid."

The elderly lawyer leaned forward and folded his hands on the rich burgundy leather ink blotter on his desk. "I know it's a shock, my dear, but I'm afraid it's true. As I said, I've been advised his arrest took place two days ago. The Swiss authorities sent him to the Geneva University Psychiatric Hospital for an in-depth psychiatric evaluation. And under the circumstances I believe that was very fortunate for him."

"Why?" she asked.

"Because it's the headquarters for the World Psychiatric Association. It's the best facility there is. He was evaluated by the best doctors on the planet. Unfortunately, as I said, they're saying he was found to be completely delusional, clearly suffering from the most bizarre hallucinations, and worse, apparently the victim of a complete psychotic break."

Sasha shook her head in utter disbelief, her hastily-scrunched midnight black ponytail swishing back and forth furiously. She insisted, "*Impossible*! Mr. Gonzalez, my father is one of the world's top quantum physicists. A leading scientist. A Nobel prize winner. A Max Planck medal recipient. He sits on numerous boards and international standards committees. He has one of the most incredible scientific minds in the entire world. Everyone knows that!"

"I know," the portly man responded, wiping a bead of perspiration off his temple and nervously stroking his thin salt-and-pepper moustache. "It makes no sense to me either. I've known William for almost twenty years. Perhaps the pressure of his responsibilities got to him. He's been working at CERN for many years now, exploring the true nature of the universe and unlocking its secrets. I can't begin to imagine the stresses he may have been under."

"Wait, wait," Sasha stopped him. "Go back. You're leaving something big out of the story here. Why in the world was he arrested in the first place and sent to a psychiatric hospital?"

Gonzalez paused for a moment before matter-of-factly telling her, "Yes, you are right. I'm sorry. That part is even more preposterous to accept than his incarceration. But what I'm being told is – and bear in mind I was just informed about this a few hours ago– that…it is being *alleged* he was arrested because he stands accused of murdering some high ranking government official."

"*What?*" Her delicate chin came forward and her dark eyes squinted in appall. "*Who* is he supposed to have murdered?"

"I believe it was some banking minister from France. Uh…" He glanced at his notes before him. "A man by the name of…a…Monsieur Vincent Delacroix. They say they've got surveillance video as well as full media coverage of the entire incident."

"What did he supposedly do?" she asked.

He answered, "I'm told shortly after your father shook this fellow's hand in a receiving line at some big fancy symposium dinner, the minister went into immediate respiratory distress, collapsed, and eventually suffered full cardiac arrest. The local authorities are saying they believe his death may have been due to some kind of synthetic poison discretely administered by your father. They're running toxicology screens right now to determine precisely."

"Designer poisons? You've *got* to be kidding me."

This was too much. Sasha looked out the sixth floor window at the stately rotunda of the Capital of Texas building only a few blocks away, desperately trying to calm herself with slow, deliberate breaths in and out. These accusations were the only things she could truly believe were pure insanity. Despite him being her own father whom she loved very much, the world-renowned Dr. William Turner was the most rational, thoughtful, logical, and open-minded man she'd ever known in her entire life.

Sasha's hands were shaking, so much so she held onto the knees of her jeans. She wore jeans most days with a comfortable top, and could always be found in either shorts or sweats at home. Sasha Turner simply wasn't a skirts and dresses kind of woman, unless, of course, some formal occasion demanded it.

Makeup wasn't a big priority for her either. Then again, Sasha didn't really need much help to look presentable. Even though she was soon approaching her thirtieth birthday, her features were strikingly beautiful and she could have easily chosen modelling or some public role in the entertainment industry as a serious career path. That is, she could have had she not been such a hardcore academic, earning her master's and doctorate degrees in anthropology and ancient linguistics and was now teaching at the University of Texas. For the most part, Sasha's life was neatly structured, disciplined, routine and ordered, if not boringly mundane at times, and basically normal, just as she liked it – and just like her father's. There was no easy way to process this horrible news.

A psychotic break?

Sasha hadn't known what to expect when she got the urgent text that morning at the university, immediately summoning her to the law office in downtown Austin. But it wasn't terribly inconvenient to go there considering the University of Texas's primary campus is also located in the heart of downtown Austin. She had her teaching assistant, Travis Gardner, take over all her afternoon classes.

Fearing the worst about her father's well-being, she didn't know if what she was now hearing about her father's incarceration and aberrant mental diagnosis was any easier news to comprehend and accept than learning whether or not her father was dead or alive.

"So *where* exactly is he now?" she asked.

The man leaned back with a peculiar look on his face. "Well, that's just it. No one knows. Have you heard from him?"

"No, I haven't. Why? What's happened to him?" Her brows knit together in confusion.

"He's disappeared. Somehow he's escaped. Vanished. He was confined under heavy guard. But, inexplicably, he got out of a maximum security facility and vanished without a trace. Due to the extreme high level of security at that particular psychiatric facility the authorities believe it had to be done with some inside help. That's not out of the realm of possibility. He was certainly very well regarded in many high circles, so it's not a completely implausible scenario to believe he had friends who might be willing to help him."

"And no one's *else* has heard from him?"

"No. And certainly not *me*," the lawyer defensively insisted. "I'm told Interpol is on the lookout for him all over Europe. But it looks as though he's gone completely off the grid. No credit card or ATM transactions. No calls on his phone. No travel reservations. No hits on surveillance cameras. Nothing. Just gone, like a ghost."

"So then why am I *really* here?" Sasha was more puzzled than ever, and growing all the more frustrated in no small measure. "You could have told me all of this over the phone. I'm getting the feeling that my being here is more than just to tell me of the situation. Mr. Gonzalez, is there something you need me to do to help him?"

The lawyer opened a lower drawer in his desk and pulled out a small, gray, brushed-metal attaché case and slid it across the desk toward Sasha, explaining, "Your woman's intuition serves you very well, Miss Turner. I received this case from your father about a month ago. It came with a very brief cryptic note saying that something very serious was about to happen, and if anything were to happen to him, anything *at all*, that I was to give this to you. No other explanation." He nodded and pointed at the case. "Something *has* happened to him. So that's why you're really here. For me to give this to you."

Her dark eyes scanned the case. "What's in it?"

Gonzalez shrugged, "I have no idea. But maybe it's something that will tell us where he might be and what's really going on."

Sasha looked at the combination locks on the front edge. "What's the combination?"

He shrugged again. "He didn't provide it. So I'm thinking he was pretty confident you would be able to figure it out."

Sasha frowned, "Mr. Gonzalez, I'm a professor of anthropology and a linguistic researcher over at UT, not a cryptographer. What am I supposed to do with this thing?"

He gave her a wan smile. "Maybe call a locksmith?"

She rolled her eyes and reached for the case's handle.

"Sign here." The lawyer pushed a release receipt toward her and extended a pen.

Sasha took the pen and quickly signed her name: Alexandra Turner.

Chapter 2
Daniel

La Défense
Paris, France

"It's happened again."

Monsieur Daniel DuMonde turned from the computer monitor sitting on his very own massive antique Louis XIV styled credenza to look across the matching ornately carved walnut desk and saw a familiar face standing before him. It was Stephan Burke.

Daniel bade Burke take a seat in one of the two matching ornately upholstered winged-backed crest chairs positioned opposite his desk.

As usual, Stephan Burke was impeccably dressed in a dark blue tailored suit from Saville Row. He stood only a few inches over five-feet tall, and definitely suffered from a severe case of "Short Man's Disease" or sometimes referred to as a "Napoleon Complex." With a round face and slightly balding, he wore a neatly-trimmed full beard and heavy-framed glasses, all of which served to make him look more like an academic than a multimillionaire businessman, not to mention one of the leading members of the Inner Circle.

Daniel DuMonde, on the other hand, was a very tall and imposing figure of a man, with long, light-brown hair generously peppered with gray, and deep, piecing green eyes. His facial features were somewhat gaunt: high cheekbones, a sharp brow, thin nose. Daniel was the high leader of the Inner Circle.

"Who?" DuMonde asked in English, a courtesy to his British guest.

Burke's countenance was grim. "Sir Peter Blanchard."

"Where?"

"At his estate in Suffolk."

"How?" DuMonde settled his elbows on the arms of his high-backed hand-tooled leather chair and steepled his index fingers under his chin, symmetrically stroking the fine gray whiskers of his Vandyke beard.

Daniel DuMonde's office in Paris was far more opulent than any A-List lawyer's in Austin, Texas. Daniel was a billionaire, and he liked everyone around him to know it. This particular high-rise top-floor Parisian penthouse office featured an entire wall of floor-to-ceiling windows (mind you, a twenty foot tall ceiling) offering a breathtaking panoramic view of the entire Avenue des Champs-Élysées, down to the Arc De Triomphe.

The office itself was larger than most residential apartments and many average single-family homes, with over 200 square meters of floor space. In addition to featuring a large sitting group and formal dining area, it also offered a private bath, sauna, gentleman's closet and dressing room, along with a well-equipped exercise room. A thirty-six square meter alcove was lined with shelves and stocked full of Daniel's private library.

"It was the exact same execution method as was used with Delacroix in Geneva. Acute asphyxia. Cardiac trauma."

"Which means he must now be in England."

Burke nodded. "So it would appear."

"Who knows about this?"

"All in the Inner Circle are being notified as we speak. All face-to-face, no electronic communications permitted for security sake. I'm sure you understand."

"*Oui.*"

Burke stood, approached the desk, and opened the lid of a fine-grain burl wood humidor sitting on Daniel's desktop. He shot DuMonde a deferential glance. DuMonde nodded his approval and Burke removed a choice Cuban cigar, one of his favorite *Partagas Lusitanias*.

As Burke withdrew a guillotine-styled cigar cutter from his pocket he added, "We were also able to curtail any undue publicity thus far. We don't want the two events connected in any way and tied to us. Blanchard was seventy-three. It will be construed as a natural death."

"Of course." DuMonde's hands slid up and momentarily rubbed his tired eyes, taking in a deep breath and letting it out slowly, forcing himself to calm down.

He gave voice to the obvious: "So we are now being hunted. By none other than one of our very own, *Docteur* Guillaume Turner, a previously well-trusted, highly influential, and powerful fellow member of our circle. And one of no small measure of advanced skill and talent. This is could be a significant problem for us."

Burke snipped off the end of the cigar over a wide lead-crystal ashtray next to the humidor. "So it would appear."

Daniel DuMonde looked deeply into the eyes of his guest, with brows furrowed. "Then we have no choice. We must find him and stop him before he finds all of us."

"Indeed. All of our resources are being dedicated to this very task."

"*Tres bien.*"

Burke smiled and pointed to the unlit end of his cigar. "Do you mind?"

DuMonde obliged. With a soft flourish of his fingers and glance at the cigar, the tip illuminated for a few seconds with a harsh blue, almost white light, gently dimming to a warm orange glow as a tendril of smoke wound upward toward the ceiling of the palatial office.

Burke nodded his thanks as he put the cigar to his lips.

CHAPTER 3
TRAVIS

THE UNIVERSITY OF TEXAS
AUSTIN, TX

"Class dismissed."

All of the undergraduate students rose from their seats and began to file out of the lecture hall, and without exception all of them shuffled along, heads down, mindlessly staring at their phones or tablets, checking for new texts and emails, Facebook, Twitter and Instagram postings.

The smartphone zombie brigade.

There were only a few days left before the Spring semester ended and Summer break began, so everyone was urgently preoccupied with cramming for finals and getting in any last minute extra credit work. A week from now the campus would be like a ghost town.

Travis Gardner exited out of his presentation on the Sumerian creation mythology of the sky gods and closed his laptop. As he disconnected the HDMI cable from his computer perched on the lectern, his iPhone chirped the three marimba tones indicating the arrival of a new text.

It was from Sasha: Meet me at my house. ASAP. Emergency

He tapped back: What's up?

The ellipses flickered and then: Will explain when you get here.

He tapped back: See you in a few.

Travis grabbed his backpack and headed for the door.

•

Travis Gardner had been Dr. Sasha Turner's TA (Teaching Assistant) for four consecutive semesters now. He was finishing his senior year and due to graduate in December. He hadn't decided yet if he was going to stay for grad school, or just try to blast out a zillion résumés and see if he could find a job. The current job market royally sucked – especially for someone with a bachelor's degree in anthropology and sociology – so the idea of staying in school and getting a master's degree, maybe in business or finance, was looking *pretty attractive* these days.

He smiled to himself with the familiar thought that Dr. Sasha Turner was also looking *pretty attractive* to him these days, and every other day he'd known her.

He couldn't help it. Sure, part of him felt that Sasha was *way* out of his league – in beauty alone if nothing else. Her big brown eyes could melt you with a single glance. She kept her dancer's caliber body incredibly fit and lean. But she was also one of the most brilliant people he'd ever known as well. She made learning about different cultures, societies, and belief systems interesting and relevant. As an ancient languages linguist, she also did most of her own original source research, gaining incredibly unique insights and unlocking secrets that many others, if not almost all in their field, failed to observe.

As far as Travis assessed himself as boyfriend material, he knew he was a reasonably attractive and personable guy, had a good sense of humor, and was fun to be around (if he did say so himself). But, admittedly, like most young men his age, he was more into playing music, video gaming, and weather permitting, renting a paddle board on Lady Bird Lake every now and then rather than going to the gym or running for an hour every morning like Sasha did all the time. Then again, at his age, he could eat pretty much anything he wanted and never gain a pound.

Travis was right at six feet tall, with more of a swimmer's build, i.e. a long musculature and well-toned, not bulked up like a football player or a wrestler. He'd worn braces in junior high, so his Hollywood smile was what most people typically noticed about him first. Or, if not his dazzling countenance, then definitely people noticed the unique tattoo on the inside of this right forearm.

Geometrically speaking, it was a circle inside of a square inside of a triangle inside of another circle. He picked it at the tattoo parlor mainly just because he thought it looked cool, although the tattoo artist down on 6th Street told him it was a symbol that stood for "Squaring the Circle," meaning being able to do the impossible.

There might have been a shred of truth in that explanation, but Travis was oblivious to the fact that it was, in reality, the ancient symbol for the Alchemists, representing all the various elements and forces needed to work their transformational magic. Sasha told him on more than one occasion that she thought it looked cool, so that's all that really mattered to him.

Professionally speaking, Sasha Turner was a very popular teacher at the University of Texas, an associate professor no less, who was very likely to get a full professorship and tenure in a few years. Travis was still just a student. But, hey, as far as he was concerned, legally, they were both adults. So what, if he was twenty-two and she was twenty-nine. Not that far apart in his mind.

She certainly wasn't dating anyone right now. Oh no, Dr. Sasha Turner was always way far too busy for any kind of a social life outside of academia and her research projects. And by happy coincidence, he wasn't currently seeing anyone either.

Although, despite his sincere attraction to her, and being her TA, Travis inwardly feared she may only have thought of him like just another one of her students; or worse, like a little brother hovering around all the time; or worst of all, just one of "the help." Of course she was always 100% professional and courteous in their relationship and had never indicated any type of personal feelings whatsoever toward him nor to the contrary. But that didn't prove feelings didn't exist, or couldn't exist, maybe somewhere deep down inside. Right?

Okay, in all fairness there were some differences to consider.

He'd been raised in a very conservative Baptist home and church in Monroe, Louisiana. From what he knew about Sasha and her family, she'd been brought up in the Catholic church, growing up in Massachusetts, somewhere in the Boston area.

No biggie. Neither of them were very religious.

So, yes, it was true that she was a Yankee and he was a Southerner. He was certain that wasn't a total show-stopper. It just made for more lively discussions about their favorite sports teams, the right way to cook food, the correct name for carbonated beverages, the precise pronunciation of "pecan," proper recreational activities involving bodies of water, the proper amount of deference one observes with respect to the 2nd Amendment of the Constitution – okay, a lot of things.

However, one area where they were in violent agreement was when it came to music. Both of them loved live music with a wide range of tastes from Red Dirt Road Country (a hallmark of the Austin sound) to good old head-banging Rock-and-Roll. Sasha was especially into classic rock, seventies and eighties hair bands, and a little bit of metal. Now, Travis and Sasha and never once been on an official "date" in the four years he'd known her and two years he'd worked for her, but they'd been to quite a few shows in town to hear their favorite groups play.

All right, okay – *fine* – there were a few other minor differences between them of note.

Yes, Sasha did come from money and apparently had a pretty fat trust fund. Travis had a wealth of student loans and a part-time weekend job at a vintage vinyl record store on South Congress. She drove a new Mercedes. Travis drove a used Toyota badly in need of new tires and an air-conditioner repair (which really sucked in Texas in the summertime!).

Sasha's father was some famous scientist who had been living and working over in Europe for many years, and was also a widower. Sadly, Sasha told him her mother had passed away when Sasha was around nine or ten. Fortunately, Travis still had both of his parents, who still lived in Louisiana, and were of very modest means. But they were still together after twenty-five years of marriage, loved each other very much, raised four great kids, were in good health, and overall did all right. Truly, he was very thankful to have grown up in a very stable and loving home, along with his two sisters and younger brother.

So, all things considered, he reasoned (rationalized?) it could theoretically work out between him and Sasha someday.

Why not?

Okay, there was this one other little, teensy-weensy, tiny, superficial difference between them: Despite the long dark hair and dark smoldering brown eyes, in Travis' opinion, Sasha Turner was about as white as white gets among the Caucasian variety of the human species.

Him, not so much.

Travis' father was of mixed race. That is, on his father's side, his grandfather was black and his grandmother was French Creole. On his mother's side, his mother was born in Trinidad and Tobago with a generous dash of Dutch mixed in there somewhere in her lineage and perhaps a pinch or two of Spaniard. So, one could say that yes, *technically* Travis Gardner was considered "a person of color" or "black," as he filled out the requisite form fields for demographics and statistics, but his actual skin tone was more of a light caramel/butterscotch hue, which created a certain air of mystery as to exactly what his heritage really was, and thus he personally chose to think of himself as more...*exotic.*

One thing was certain, Travis Gardner was clearly not a product of modern urban African-American culture, and socially speaking, didn't particularly care for anything remotely related to trendy Hip-Hop or Rap style. Although, despite it personally not being his cup of tea, to get a degree in anthropology and sociology, he had studied urban culture extensively in school and had convinced himself he understood it well. He didn't dislike it, per se; it just wasn't his thing.

That notwithstanding, his personal taste in music, as well as his personal fashion sense, tended to lean much more toward the stylings of your basic Bruce Springsteen/Lenny Kravitz type classic rock artists and aficionados. Said another way, in Austin, he blended in well with the skinny-jean hipsters.

As a musician himself, Travis had played the guitar since he was ten years old, and was pretty good at it. He'd been in a couple of college and local bar bands off and on over the last few years, but most of Austin's better musicians wanted to gig in the bars and clubs three or four nights a week. While he sincerely loved playing, he just wasn't into music to the degree of forsaking all else going on in his life to do that. He was determined to get his college degree and start a career that didn't involve the phrase "starving artist."

All in all, Travis' upbringing was most heavily influenced by the fact that his father had served a full twenty year career in the US Army, and consequently, his family had moved around quite a bit when he was a kid, changing schools every year or two. That was a mixed blessing. It sucked uprooting and leaving all your friends behind every so often, but the military brat lifestyle also brought you to new places where you made more and more new friends.

Travis Gardner was very adept at making friends.

As a result, he thankfully never fell in with a bad crowd, which was an aspect of his life strictly policed by his parents. He knew they had to approve of anyone he wanted to hang out with or even talk on the phone to for more than a few minutes. That policy hurt his feelings on occasion, but as he got older he grew to appreciate how much they looked out after him throughout his childhood and kept him on the straight and narrow road.

Travis' father's Army career also got Travis used to the concept of self-discipline: wearing his hair closely shorn, being clean-shaven, enunciating his words clearly, speaking in complete sentences, observing the "yes, sir, no, sir – yes, ma'am, no ma'am – please and thank you" protocols of proper manners and civility, and always dressing extremely neat and professional, even when attempting to be hip and stylish. Travis would be the first one to admit that prior to going to college, at first glance, many people would have taken him for a nerd who clearly belonged to both the math and the chess clubs. In his freshman year of college, while taking one of her classes, it was actually Sasha that got him to ditch the heavy, black-framed Buddy Holly glasses and begin wearing contacts. It always warmed his heart whenever she complimented his appearance.

•

Travis broke his reverie and analysis of his romantic relationship prospects with Sasha as he pulled into her driveway. She didn't live too far from the UT campus, just south of the Colorado River that flowed west to east through downtown Austin, just off Riverside Drive, in the posh area between South Congress (aka So-Co) and Interstate-35. It was a nice area, in an older section of town, but was in the process of being gentrified by the influx of all the nouveau-riche, high-tech entrepreneurs, and Silicon Valley transplants from Apple, eBay, PayPal, et al, as well as the up and coming young professional hipsters of Austin. If he had pick a category, socioeconomically speaking, Travis considered Sasha Turner to be more in the traditional "just came from money" class.

Her house wasn't terribly huge, maybe a little over two-thousand square feet, but it was very nice, contemporary in style with quartz countertops, travertine tile in the entry and baths, hardwoods in the kitchen and dining room, plush carpet in the living room and bedrooms, and all professionally decorated to the nines. Sasha also like to cook, so the kitchen was a full gourmet layout of top-of-the-line stainless steel professional chef-quality appliances.

Travis rang the bell and waited politely until he heard a hasty, "Come on in. It's open." He could hear a *Def Leppard* album playing in the background.

His smile came out on autopilot as he saw Sasha seated at her dining table playing with a small metal briefcase. He set his backpack on the far end of the dining table and asked, "So what's the big emergency?"

"Well, let's see..." Sasha broke her gaze from the small case and gave him a frazzled look as she wiped a lock of her raven's wing black hair out of her eyes and enumerated each of her pronouncements on her fingers, "One, I just learned that my father was arrested for murder. Two, he was also declared insane. Three, he escaped from an insane asylum and is currently at large and being hunted. And four, he sent me this." She pointed at the metal case.

"Whoa!" Travis held up both hands. "Seriously?" He frowned. "Or is this like a...*test* of some kind?"

Sasha gestured to the case again. "No, God's honest truth. My father's lawyer briefed me on it all about an hour ago and then gave me this mysterious case. He said my father sent it to him about a month ago with some weird instructions to give it to me if anything ever happened to him. So here it is."

Travis slid a nearby dining chair out and took a seat next to Sasha, carefully peering closer at the case. His eyes glanced to the side at her. "What's in it?"

"I don't know," she shrugged, "I don't know how to open it."

"You don't know the combo?" Before she could reply in an outburst of boiling-over frustration, he raised a hand in defense and mimed a "stop" gesture. "Of course you don't have it. No. Otherwise it would already be open."

"So...any idea how to get one of these things open if you don't happen to have the combination handy?" she asked. "I mean, can't we just call the manufacturer and see if there's a master code or something that the TSA uses at the airport?"

"You could," he replied, turning it around to inspect it from various angles. "Or you can just try a few guesses first."

"Like what?"

He pulled that attaché towards him once more. "What's your birthday again?"

She frowned, "January twenty-seventh."

"Right. 0-1-2-7. Got it." He rotated the four digit dials on each side to those four numbers and then pulled on the latches.

The case popped open.

Sasha narrowed her eyes, "That was luck! Pure luck!"

Travis laughed. "So let's take a look."

It was Sasha's turn to pull the case toward her. But first she picked up her phone and paused the Pandora One channel playing on her Bluetooth connected Bose player sitting atop the sofa table between themselves and the couch. In silence, the room suddenly felt tense and uneasy.

Sasha lifted the case lid very slowly, as if something malevolent might unexpectedly leap out and attack, not really knowing exactly why she felt such a sudden cloud of apprehension.

Nothing happened.

They both shared an anxious glance. Travis nodded, and Sasha opened the lid all the way. As it came fully open they both stared at what was resting inside. It was a single object, rectangular in shape, a couple of inches in height, covered in a heavy muslin cloth and bound with several strands of a straw-colored twine. Sasha pulled the object out and set it down before her, gently untied the twine, and then carefully unwrapped the object's cloth shroud.

"Okay..." Travis leaned closer as it became obvious what it was. "It's a book."

The heavy leather-bound volume had no visible writing on its cover or spine. It looked like it could have been a single volume from a set of encyclopedias, or perhaps a library-sized dictionary or giant print old family Bible. But, no, that wasn't what it was.

Sasha carefully opened the thick, leather cover. In her father's neatly printed script handwriting on the first page was inscribed a title:

A Letter of Introduction to
The Journal of William Turner

Just below the title, also written by hand by her father. The first line riveted her attention:

Magic is real.

CHAPTER 4

FROM THE JOURNAL OF WILLIAM TURNER

FIRST PRINCIPLES

I am tempted to spend a great deal of time recounting the extraordinary circumstance by which my Master and I first crossed paths. But that would waste your time, dear Reader, as well as mine – and time is something very precious to us both at this point. Suffice it to say that he sought me out. That's how it works amongst the Magi – they find you, not the other way around.

I recall him telling me that "I had been chosen." He said it with a laugh advising me to forget any melodrama associated with his statement. The choosing had been done by him, and no "higher power." He was somehow familiar with a great deal of my work in quantum physics at CERN, had read several of my published papers, and considered me to be of sufficient intellectual aptitude to learn what he had to teach me.

It turns out, I was a very apt pupil.

On the very first day of my training in magic he and I sat alone on a riverbank in a spot called the Confluence, which soon became one of my favorite places in the entire world. It's located at the juncture of the Rhone and Arve rivers, at the tip of the largest lake in Europe, Lake Geneva (aka Lac Léman). It's quite a sight, the Rhone being so dark blue and clear as it comes out of the lake and from running through southeastern France, whereas the Arve was milky and muddy coming down from glaciers of the Chamonix valley. It was quite the apt symbol for two completely diverse universes of thought and experiences merging into one.

Such was to be my life from that moment forward.

My Master's first discourse with me must have taken hours, but it felt like only moments. I will endeavor to recount for you all of the main points he made, but please realize that I am paraphrasing and summarizing not directly quoting unless indicated otherwise where it's important to distinguish.

The first point he made to me regarding the reality of Magic was just how common it really is, yet for the most part it is virtually invisible and taken for granted by most mortal folk. To properly grasp this point it is essential that we have a common working definition of what Magic really is. It certainly is not a predefined cookbook of herbal recipes of mystical incantations, hexes and spells, each designed to produce some metaphysical response or condition. Far from it.

Magic is:

- It is the deliberate process whereby sentient energy is manifested into the physical world.

- It is the evidence of things hoped (willed) for.

- It is the (new) substance of things not (before) seen.

Yes, in many theological/religious contexts Magic's closest synonym is the literal and pragmatic meaning of the word "faith" – but not merely representing a specific belief system or creed, rather "faith" being used like a muscle, an active power with tangible efficacy. With faith it is said that you can move mountains or heal the sick. Such miraculous examples could also rightly be deemed manifestations of high-level Magic.

As I am a scientist by trade, and a physicist in particular, and certainly not a theologian per se, my proper understanding of Magic was best achieved by my Master using familiar terms and concepts I already understood well. So, for your sake, my dear Reader, I shall endeavor to offer you the same courtesy and therefore confine my various analogies and examples to familiar physical objects and principles which are more easily comprehended. I apologize if some of this is still a bit too technical sounding, but I shall do my best.

To begin with, each human being (and most other living creatures) possesses a small modicum of Magic in his or her everyday life, evidenced by the existence of voluntary motion. When you reach for an object, or take a step, consider what must be involved for that task to be accomplished. It is true, your body is equipped with some reflexive actions that are predetermined and instinctual, as well as autonomous activity such as your heart continuously beating, lungs breathing, and the continuous process of digestion and so forth, but think about all of your voluntary actions for a moment.

Voluntary movement originates by virtue of specific thoughts, a choice of "will," you might say. I shall pick up that glass of water. And your arm and hand obey. I shall walk over to my bookshelf. And your legs obey. Your arms and legs are responding to a command. Their obedience is a biomechanical reaction resulting from a communication your limbs receive as an order for action. And it is not random action, but a precise series of motions designed to comply with the full intent of the order.

Thus, this begs the all-important question: Where does that order to move come from?

Your mind? Yes. But how does a thought become the catalyst for mindless flesh to become its servant and physically obey?

For many people they are content to say "it's all a mystery," or liken it to something of a supernatural, metaphysical or of a more spiritual nature. Unfortunately, that perspective would be in error.

Fundamentally, thoughts are actually "electrical" in nature. But not in the direct current versus alternating current (DC/AC) sense of electricity. No, thoughts are a pure form of energy operating at defined frequencies and measurable levels of power. To be more specific, a "thought" is an element of "sentient" energy, meaning energy originating from a unique organism's will, desire, and perceived needs.

The process of converting the sentient energy of will into a physical catalyst in the physical world is what is properly called "Magic."

At this juncture I interrupted my Master and inquired as to whether this notion of sentient energy were not merely a description of the human psyche. He laughed at me again and admonished me to brush up on my Greek. To assuage my puzzlement and to answer my question he told me that, yes, properly understood, the human psyche is in fact what we were talking about. But the word "psyche" is but a different label. A distinction without a difference.

He explained that the word "psyche" is, in fact, the Greek root word for "soul" or the "essence of life" itself. It literally comes from a Greek root word that means "breath" or "spirit." It was sometimes used to refer to a "ghost." This is an important concept to grasp – i.e. how much Magic has to do with breath and breathing, spirit and inspiration.

So, again, without waxing theological, and to perhaps boil this point down a bit, what I refer to as sentient energy, what the Greeks called the psyche (or "breath of life"), and what major religions call the immortal soul are all one and the same thing – they are the real you, distinct from your intellect and physical body. Said another way, and to bring it all full circle, Magic is the mechanism that allows your soul to obtain whatever it wants, or more precisely, whatever it is strong enough to obtain.

Let's move on.

Next, you must come to realize and appreciate the fact that all forms of creativity are a manifestation of Magic. Creativity itself is the product of one's imagination.

Now look at that word:

i-**MAGI**-nation.

The very root of imagination is MAGI (i.e. Magic).

Imagination is what conjures something into existence that heretofore didn't previously exist: a new idea, a new song, a poem, a novel, a play, a film, a painting, a sculpture, a culinary creation, a product, a service, a software program, an architecture, a kingdom, a planet, a moon, a star. All creativity is, in fact, defined as the process of converting the imagination into reality.

This is the core of true Magic.

Ergo, many mortal folk use Magic every day in their lives and are obliviously ignorant to that fact. And this is also why it is eternally true that those souls who most intimately embrace the creative arts live the most magical lives.

It's true. Living a magical life is a literal truth, not a metaphorical one. Magic begets magic. Magic, in a very real sense, is an energy source, the purest energy source of all. And the more Magic that is concentrated in one place, or more importantly, within one individual, yields a logarithmic and cumulative effect whereby that person's will, desires, passions, wants and needs more intensely influence the physical world, bending it to their satisfaction.

There have been many great Magi living in the midst of mortal folk throughout history, those whom virtually everyone were oblivious to the true nature of what they really were, although everyone richly loved the fruits of their Magic. And please note that I'm not referring to the heroic characters of mythology such as Merlin of the Arthur legends or Gandalf the Gray of Tolkien's fictions, but rather, renowned men and women of great wisdom and creative achievement such as Leonardo Da Vinci, Joan of Arc, Michelangelo, Mozart, Madame Marie Curie, Benjamin Franklin, Thomas Edison, Nikola Tesla, and even Walt Disney, to name but a few.

Magi one and all.

So where does Magic come from? How is it obtained?

Here's a fact about Magic that my Master taught me that surprised me. Please recall my mention of that small modicum of Magic that each person possesses, which is needed to do the voluntary motions of life. Where does that Magic come from?

It comes from what you eat.

Yes, all creatures capable of voluntary motion are imbued with some small degree of life force energy, energy which is necessary to harness for the most basic level of the practice of Magic. This energy exists down on a cellular level. Just as each cell produces microscopic elements (such as Adenosine Triphosphate, or ATP) necessary for the production and movement of physical energy for the body's various functions, the energy source for the operation of base level Magic is generated in parallel. It is then primarily moved and stored in the brain for operation.

And this truth makes perfect sense. For the acquisition and eating of food requires voluntary motion. If your body lacked the Magic to be able to physically participate in the act of eating, you'd starve and die. It is no exaggeration to say, you need Magic for your very survival.

However, as you might very well surmise, the objective quantity of energy derived from food intake used to enable the body's basic voluntary functions is for the most part limited to only that level of functionality. Your basic energy levels are meticulously regulated within the body so as to maintain a state of equilibrium whereby there is never too little energy, thus limiting motion, nor too much, and have it not used and therefore wasted.

As a side note on nutrition, i.e. as it relates to your development of power to use Magic, the fresher and more natural (i.e. organic, not chemically processed) your food is, the more life force energy it contains. If you eat fruits and vegetables from your own garden, they are the best for you. And that's not vegetarian propaganda, that's a biochemical fact.

Likewise, if you have a butcher cut fresh pieces of meat for you from animals not long ago slaughtered, the life force energy within them are at the highest levels. The same is true for fresh fish. Eat the fish you catch and scale yourself for the best results.

Now when it comes to beverages, the purest of water is always preferred, not so much for what's in it, but for what's not. Toxins and pollutants require your body to filter and neutralize those things, and all biological tasks require some degree of energy.

Energy saved is not energy wasted.

If you're curious about the consumption of alcohol, I give you a caution and encouragement to highly respect and value moderation. There are actually good nutrients and antioxidants in many wines and fine spirits. Beer can help keep your kidneys flushed clean. But also realize that ethyl alcohol has the effect of dulling and impairing your senses. When abused, it can even impair the collection of memories. A Magi needs all his mental faculties to achieve the best results. But with all that said, I would readily admit that for a hard-working adult, tipping a pint at the end of a long day to relax can be most welcome and enjoyable.

Use some common sense when it comes to food and drink, and you'll be fine. Just be sensitive to the fact that what you ingest truly does have a direct impact on what you physically are and have the capacity to do.

However, with that said, to manifest Magic at much higher levels of functionality, from simple acts of artistic creativity to the practical reality of ..."moving mountains"... the energy for that Magic must come, not from food alone, but from elsewhere, from other key energy sources. And there are many of them for you to learn about.

In a very genuine sense, higher energy levels must actually be cultivated and harvested like a crop. And this requisite skill is what you, too, must soon learn in order to open the door to higher level Magic in your own life. Exactly how one begins to do that is what my Master and I discussed the next time he and I went to the Confluence of the great rivers.

It was there he first opened my eyes to the Faces in the Stones.

Chapter 5
Penelope

Roma, Italy

Piazza Di Spagna

On that particular Saturday morning, as usual, the Piazza Di Spagna was teeming with unwashed masses. Hundreds, perhaps thousands, of sweating bodies from all over the world flowed like a rushing river up and down the wide staircase leading up to the Trinità dei Monti Church. It was just past noon and the sun was especially harsh and cruel on that summer day.

Penelope Angelucci sat alone at the small wrought-iron outdoor table of the trattoria, waiting and watching. She was tastefully dressed in a simple white blouse, knee-length navy skirt and sensible heels, the type of outfit that she typically wore beneath her white coat at the hospital. Well, that is, it was the type of outfit she would wear when she was making rounds or in consultations or meetings. When she was working she'd be clad in teal blue surgical scrubs, booties, a hairnet, a facemask, goggles and latex gloves – usually covered with blood. The scarf and dark sunglasses that day were more for discretion.

The air smelled heavy with vehicle fumes and uncollected trash, occasionally interrupted with the pleasant whiffs of delectable cooking, but all too often quickly eclipsed by the aroma of pungent humans. Pigeons and other scavenger birds toddled, bobbed and hopped about on the sidewalk in desperate search of a discarded crumb or scrap of food. The din around her of the dense throng of the engines and horns of cars, trucks, and swarms of mopeds was near deafening, but with a little concentration, it would meld into a general cacophonous white noise.

Penelope didn't really care to mingle with the mobs of tourists and the colorful menagerie of locals, but sometimes the very best place to hide was in plain sight. Most cold-blooded murderers preferred to do their dark deeds in private – at least she hoped that was true, for her sake.

On the other hand, there would be no hiding from him.

He'd called her after such a long, long time and requested to have a brief conversation. She tried to explain to him that she would have preferred to do it over the phone.

He demanded the face-to-face meeting.

After another sip of chianti she set her glass down with slightly trembling fingers. A brief flash winked in her peripheral vision. That was odd. She wondered who needed a flash camera to take a picture in this blinding sunlight.

Penelope heard his voice before actually seeing him. A chill ran up her spine. He'd somehow managed to approach her discretely from behind. But how was that even possible? There was nothing behind her, save a dark niche and a metal door that she would have heard if it had opened.

Was this a fatal mistake?

He sounded chipper. "Penelope, my dear, so good to see you again. You're looking quite lovely today. You haven't changed a bit."

Penelope gracefully rose and dutifully exchanged butterfly kisses of welcome on both cheeks. She was surprised to see how long his once sandy brown beard had grown and turned completely gray, almost white. His formerly dirty blond hair was completely gray now as well. And it was much longer, too, a lot longer than the last time she'd seen him. He kept his hair pulled behind him in a long ponytail tied with a small strand of leather. He was dressed casually like most of the other tourists around them in khaki slacks and a loose fitting white polo shirt. The expensive

Stefano Bemer Italian loafers looked new. It made her smile to see that the Raymond Weil watch he still wore was the one she'd given him so many long years ago.

Penelope extended a polite invitation, "Have a seat. Please."

"I can't stay very long," he said. "But what I have to discuss with you shouldn't take long."

"I know," she gestured once more to a wrought-iron companion chair at the small bistro table. "Please. It's been a long time."

He cautiously looked around then took a seat.

A waiter appeared. "*Signore?*"

"*Barbaresco, per favore,*" he responded without taking his eyes off the beautiful woman seated next to him.

It was a warm and admiring look. Penelope liked that look – especially coming from him, or these days from anyone else for that matter. His warm expression caused her to actually believe for a moment that she just might live to see the sunset that day.

Penelope was in her mid-fifties but knew she could still easily pass for thirty. She remembered life a lot more fondly back when she was in her thirties – young enough to still look amazing, but mature enough to be taken seriously. She adjusted the colorful Hermes silk headscarf covering her long dark tresses. He looked puzzled, or perhaps conflicted. Could he have changed his mind? Did he still have any feelings for her?

No matter. If it was her time, it was time. Best to just get it over with and pray the suffering would be minimal.

"I am told by some of our mutual friends that you've been...*busy,*" she quipped, adjusting her sunglasses on her nose.

He smiled. "You could say that. We all have our To-Do lists."

"Of course." She took another sip of her wine as the waiter placed a full glass of the select red wine in front of her guest.

"*Grazie,*" he thanked the server.

Penelope carefully returned her glass to the table, the ripple in the surface of the wine betraying how much her hand was still shaking. She looked him directly in the eye and said, "That's why I agreed to talk to you today. I don't want to be on your list. And I'd really like to hear you tell me that you're not here to take my breath away and break my heart."

He paused in thought before saying, "Well, I guess that's really up to you, my dear. What exactly are you willing to do?"

"What *must* I do?" She tried not to sound like she was pleading.

"I think you know," he replied.

Penelope sighed. "If I betray them, they'll put me on *their* list. So where does that leave me?"

He said with a smile, "With a very full dance card, it seems."

She let a slight note of desperation slip into her voice. "*Exactly*. And even if I said yes to you, what possible good am I to you against so many of them?"

He reached over and covered her hand with his own, prompting a small flinch and all her muscles going rigid. He shook his head and said, "It's okay. Don't worry. Today we're only talking. Nothing more."

She visibly relaxed a bit.

He leaned over to her ear and said, "I know you've grown much stronger, my dear. A *lot* stronger. Do they know just how much?"

Penelope swallowed with some difficulty as he sat back. "I would like to pretend I don't know what you're talking about, but it wasn't my intent to antagonize you in any way. And I fear lying to you, which you would instantly be able to read, wouldn't be in my best interest. Truthfully, I don't know exactly how much they know about me anymore, or even care to know. I try to keep our interactions to a minimum."

"And that's my point," he replied. "And why I'm here to talk to you. If you agree to help me, there's a possibility we might both get to live to a ripe old age. You said it yourself, the alternative isn't good. And personally speaking, my dear Penelope, all things considered, I'd prefer that you not stay on my list."

Penelope felt her cheeks flush for a second. Her eyes returned to the ebb and flow of the crowds around them. She didn't want to admit it, but it was an almost daily challenge to prevent him from intruding into her thoughts, even if but for a second or two. After so many years – what was it? twenty now? – thinking of him was never far away.

She did her best to sound incredulous. "I know you fully intend to do what you wish to do. And I don't question your reasoning why. But how can you possibly entertain the fantasy that you can stop what's coming?"

He shrugged. "Maybe I can't. Maybe *we* can't. But maybe we, and perhaps with the help of others, *can*."

Her eyes returned to his. "What others?"

His smile was back, "There will be others. I've seen to that. And soon. We just need to take a few of the Inner Circle's key players off the chess board, destabilize their operations, which will force them to spend a great deal of valuable time reinforcing and backtracking, time we need to fortify our own capabilities and stop the madness they're contemplating."

"That's your plan?"

He lifted his glass and savored a long sip of his wine. "Yes it is, in a nutshell. With perhaps one or two little contingency wrinkles thrown in the mix for a rainy day."

She was almost afraid to ask. "My dearest Guglielmo, just how strong have *you* become?"

He patted her hand and assured her, "I can tell you that they greatly miscalculated and seemingly forgot that for many years now I have had continuous access to the world's largest super-collider, with unlimited availability of energy, energy that's literally beyond human imagination. And I've learned how to harness such vast amounts of energy. If it comes to it, to quote Dr. Oppenheimer, I can become death itself, a destroyer of worlds. Come and help me, Penelope, and let us both pray it never comes to that."

After a frozen moment of fearful silence, she looked him in the eye and hesitantly nodded her assent, trembling from head to toe in complete terror, knowing deep down in her soul he was telling her the absolute truth.

CHAPTER 6
ALLISTER

GENEVA UNIVERSITY PSYCHIATRIC HOSPITAL
GENEVA, SWITZERLAND

"It must be an error with the system. A malfunction." Captain Paul Duvall chided the technician sitting before the computer monitor. "Play it again."

Chief Inspector Allister McKenzie from Interpol folded his arms and watched the flat-screen monitor in silence one more time with the other two people gathered in the video surveillance monitoring room, Captain Duvall and a security technician.

Professionally speaking, Allister was nearing retirement. Now in his late sixties, he'd well-earned all the sparse white hair and wrinkles and curmudgeon demeanor. He had grown up in Glasgow, Scotland, having started his career in law enforcement almost forty-five years ago. His record was good enough to earn him a top position at Scotland Yard working in London for much of the first half of his career. The last half had been spent working in The New Scotland Yard, almost exclusively with Interpol on behalf of Her Majesty's government on a very specialized task force with no name.

This organization was more secretive and discrete than MI-6, made up of specialists from many different countries. It operated across any border, off budget and at any expense. Its mission was to solve the unsolvable. To thwart the impossible. To make sense of and foil the unbelievable. And, indeed, Allister had seen so much of the unbelievable over the last twenty years or so, he was surprised he hadn't been admitted as a guest in this august facility a long time ago, having gone completely mad.

The technician hit his keyboard and the scene replayed from the beginning. The camera was a full color, 1080p Hi-Def unit positioned high in one corner of the prisoner's cell. Using a wide-angle lens, the entire six by eight foot room was visible, inclusive of its heavy steel door, all three adjacent windowless concrete walls, the low-frame bed, and the metal toilet and sink. The prisoner wore the standard issue white tunic, pants, and slippers as did all the patients in the CID (Criminally Insane & Dangerous) wing at the world-renowned psychiatric hospital.

The video they were watching was a two minute edit from a four hour segment of raw surveillance footage. Every four hours the video security system would automatically transfer and archive its most recent file to a server cluster in their data center and begin recording a new file.

On the screen, the man with long graying hair and full white beard just sat on the edge of the bed with his eyes closed, seemingly meditating, praying, or possibly chanting something softly to himself. The video included an audio track, but the man's words were spoken too softly to be discernable. About a minute into the scene, something could distinctly be heard: a high pitch whine of a single frequency, very faint, but clear. The shrill sonic frequency sounded almost electrical in nature.

The man stood and then remained motionless for almost ten seconds.

And then it happened.

FLASH!

Allister McKenzie thought it looked a bit like a camera flash. Just one bright strobe of light, almost instantaneous in duration.

And then the cell was empty – and completely silent.

"Stop it there," Capt. Duvall commanded. "Go back frame by frame through the entire sequence."

The technician complied.

Allister nodded with a feeling of recognition when it was revealed the flash was only recorded on a single frame. In the prior frame: the prisoner was standing by his bed, absolutely still.

Next frame: the blinding flash, the screen going almost completely white.

Next frame: the empty cell.

Allister asked, "Might it be possible that the video feed was interrupted at that point, and after the prisoner made his escape, however he managed it, the recording was restarted again? Wouldn't that explain what we're seeing?"

Capt. Duvall nodded, "It would."

The technician spoke up. "If that's what happened, then whoever these guys are that did this are way more sophisticated than I've ever seen – hacking a secure fiber-optic feed, spontaneous frame duplication, lossless editing. I don't really think than can be done with our system. Sorry, but that's impossible."

"Why do you believe that?" Allister asked.

The young man replied, "Because of the time stamps on the frames. They're continuous. There's no lost time. If the camera was stopped and then restarted, then there should be a gap for the duration of the stoppage and there isn't one. Any gap would have had to have been filled, and done in a way that's completely undetectable. And the full master archive file is a full four hours long. We checked it. No missing time, not a single second. And that file was in synch with the following archive files. No missing time between this scene's master file and the next file in line."

"So what are you saying?" Allister leaned closer to peer at the monitor screen.

The technician gestured toward the screen "I'm saying that however this guy got out, it took no time."

"What?" Capt. Duvall was visibly perplexed.

"Well," the technician conceded, "It happened within one frame, which at thirty frames per second, is one-thirtieth of a second. I'd say that's almost no time."

"That *is* impossible!" the captain fumed.

Allister chuckled, "Not if one happens to be personally gifted with the art of teleportation."

"Right," the technician laughed. "Just beam me up, Scotty!"

Capt. Duvall just shook his head at the joke.

Allister McKenzie was the only one in the room who knew he wasn't joking.

CHAPTER 7
ALEXEY

KIEV, UKRAINE

The Mother Motherland Statue, Kiev, Ukraine

The morning hours were abnormally cool for the summertime. The rains had stopped hours ago, but a damp mist still hung in the air. Alexey Borochenko strolled casually through the World War II memorial sculptures near the Mother Motherland statue overlooking the Dnieper River. Alexey was thin, with a light complexion, a prominent brow, high cheekbones and bright blue eyes. He didn't wear a beard, but perpetually bore a five o'clock shadow, and wore his hair buzzed down close to the scalp.

He spoke calmly into his cell phone. "No, I have not been able to reach her in Rome."

Daniel DuMonde sounded more angry than usual. "Nor I. She's not returning any of my messages. And that's not like her."

Alexey watched some tourists taking pictures of the more than 200 foot tall stainless steel statue of a woman looking over the river toward the east holding a sword and shield aloft. He gave voice to his theory: "I think she surely must know about the deaths of Vincent and Peter by now. So I suspect she may have merely gone underground until he's caught and neutralized."

"Those weren't her orders," DuMonde seethed. "All of us must work together to find him. No exceptions."

"Understood," Alexey replied. "But I must ask you, Daniel, what if Vil'hel'm can't be captured and neutralized exactly as we wish?"

"What the devil are you talking about?" His voice was incredulous. "The Swiss authorities were able to catch him quite handily, right after his attack on Vincent. He put up no resistance. He's *not* invincible. They do have guns."

Alexey had a dark thought. "What if his getting caught the first time was intentional?"

"Explain," came the curious voice on the line.

Alexey remained silent for a moment as a young couple strolled by arm-in-arm. When he felt they were out of earshot, he continued. "What I mean is, had he assailed Vincent just as he did with Peter, in private, in his home, it might have been thought to be a natural death. With such a public display, there was no doubt. Certainly not with us. And when he took out Peter, it was confirmed that he's after all of us."

"So his first attack was to send us a message? A declaration of war?"

"Possibly," Alexey replied. "It got *my* attention. Plus, he certainly proved that he couldn't be held captive by any normal means."

"*Oui, mon ami.*" Daniel DuMonde paused, lost in thought for a moment. "And so perhaps you believe his antics got Penelope's attention as well?"

"Let us hope so. The most unpleasant alternative might be that he's already paid her a little visit as well…and her body is yet to be found."

DuMonde let out a frustrated sigh. "I really don't wish to contemplate that possibility just yet. We need Penelope for the operation. Besides, if Guillaume has been to see her, how is he able to move from Switzerland to England to Italy so quickly without being detected in any way? Our data intelligence network and analytical resources are second to none. If he moves in any detectible way, he *will* be found."

"A private jet?" Alexey offered.

"Which, if so, means Guillaume has at least one other very resourceful and discreet ally." Daniel laughed, "Either that, or our old friend has learned to fly all by himself."

Alexey frowned. "I wasn't aware he owned a jet. And if he did have one or rented one, there would be an audit trail."

Daniel DuMonde quipped, "That isn't what I meant."

Alexey was puzzled for second, then understood, laughing softly to himself. "Who knows? But I'm fairly confident our Dr. Vil'hel'm Turner is *not* Superman. However, I don't counsel that any of us should ever underestimate the good doctor. Look, Daniel, I'll keep trying to contact Penelope, and will let you know if I make any progress."

"As will I. *Bonjour*," was the last thing DuMonde said before ending the call.

Alexey looked up at the massive steel sculpture once more, wondering: *Flying hundreds of miles? Are such things even possible?*

CHAPTER 8

FROM THE JOURNAL OF WILLIAM TURNER

CAPACITANCE

Higher levels of Magic, i.e. Magic that goes far beyond volitional physical movement, requires increased levels of energy. This energy is channeled through the Magi, as directed by thought and will, to its intended purpose.

However, energy transfer is not a one-for-one linear process. The Magi isn't simply a conduit, a "wire" if you will, for simple energy transfer going in one end and coming out the other. Rather, using our analogy of electronics, the Magi is more like a "capacitor," a component which stores energy until it is released. And the more practiced the Magi becomes at exercising this process of collecting and storing higher-level energy, the larger capacitance capability for Magic is obtained.

This is how one grows in strength with Magic.

As a Novice, I was taught to open my senses and to allow energy to be appropriated, literally breathing it in, if you will, and breathing it out. Always note how important respiration is. Pay close attention to it.

My Master taught me that the training process to become a true Magi begins with the Faces in the Stones. Becoming sensitive to acquiring their Magic is the secret door to all that lies ahead for you in developing your own Magic.

Now, Rule #1 for this process is as follows: if you deliberately look for the faces, it invalidates the process. Intentionally seeking them out puts the imagination in gear and it becomes easy to deceive yourself, rather than allowing the authentic faces and their spirits to manifest themselves of their own accord. They want to be seen, and they will readily appear to a true Magi, or to mortal folk with magical aptitude.

The exercise is quite simple.

You merely need a textured surface – floor tiles, a textured wall, an abstract print, a natural stone outcropping, anything of the sort will do.

I confess, seeing the faces occurred more often in my case whilst using the restroom. It's true. I would be sitting there relaxed, daydreaming and glancing down at the tiled floor when the faces would slowly appear before me. Not always in the same places, and most of the time only once, not to ever be recognized there again, even if I was looking in the exact same place on another occasion.

As I said, you can't search for them. Your mind needs to be still, in a peaceful place, relaxed, not really focused upon anything in particular. And that's when they will come to you. Quite reflexively, your eyes will see their features emerge: eyes, nose, mouth, chin, the outline shape of the face and whatnot. The variations are endless: wearing a hat or not, clean-shaven or with beards, long-haired or short-haired, male and female, young and old, of any ethnicity.

However, when a face appears, it is then time to breathe in slowly and deeply, and do so as calmly and in as relaxed a manner as possible. Take at least seven breaths in through your nose, holding each one as long as you can each time, and then exhaling slowly and deliberately out through the mouth until all the air within your lungs is released and there is no more. At some point the image will begin to fade a bit. When it does, you are finished harvesting energy with that one.

Resist the urge to doubt what you are doing when you see the face, and especially do not doubt when you are ingesting its energy. The first time may feel a bit silly, but it's not. It's gravely serious work necessary for your preparation with Magic.

You may be wondering what the faces are – or better still, you would be more correct to ask "who" they are. The answer may be a bit shocking, but nonetheless true. They are the sentient energy and life force of others who have passed on from the physical realm into the ethereal. I will share a wee bit more about them later, but suffice it to say for now, they still have the ability to interact with the physical world, and in this capacity, to help young Magi grow in personal energy capacitance.

Your next exercise is designed to heighten your senses, and actually open up new levels of magical sensitivity you don't even know exist. For this second lesson my Master took me to a broad meadow covered with flowers of every imaginable shape and hue. And it was there he said I must learn to hear Flos Canticum, the Songs of the Flowers.

This was a most pleasant revelation to me. For the truth is, each type of flower sings its own unique song. But they do so within a frequency range not normally heard by the narrow audible range of the human ear, which has a maximum range of approximately 20,000 hertz. In fact, it is flower song that is used by the bees to locate the specific varieties of flowers that they symbiotically pollenate and collect to make their honey. Likewise, hummingbirds hear it too, and use it to navigate.

Scientists have long known plants emit different types of measurable energy waves, which can vary and respond to different stimulus. Thus, some refer to this energy as the plant's "feelings." It is, in reality, music. And a flower will sing its song until its petals fade.

Thus, the exercise is straightforward.

After you have inhaled the energy of the Faces in the Stone, go pick a flower, bring it up near your ear, relax and quiet your mind. This is best done in a very quiet place, free from other distractions and competing sounds. At first you will hear nothing. This is when you must tap into the energy you've gleaned from the Faces in the Stones. If you've omitted the first step of ingesting the inspiration of the stones, you must go back and do that first.

If that energy is indeed within you, in the quietness of your mind, your focus thought that you must concentrate on is: "Sing for me."

And then wait.

It usually doesn't take terribly long. Perhaps a few seconds or a minute or two the very first time. But when it comes, you will know it. A song will begin to play in your head, softly at first, perhaps a little disjointed and fragmented, like when people used to try and tune in an analog radio station manually with a knob and weren't quite centered on the correct frequency setting. But when you finally find it, it is most pleasant, and is truly addicting, in fact.

Rose song is my personal favorite, followed by lilies. For what it's worth, I find that I don't especially care for hibiscus song; it's too dissonant for my tastes. Now, if I were a musician I suppose I would attempt to recreate the more pleasant melodies in a form of song humans could appreciate, transposing it down into the audible listening range. But sadly, I confess, I'm not a musician.

As an aside, should you ever see someone holding a flower along their jawline close to the earlobe for an extended period of time, you're looking at a fellow Magi. So, unless you wish to give yourself away, enjoy your flower song in private. Or, mask your public displays of flower song in the form of a boutonniere or corsage. The Hawaiian custom of the floral lei worn around the neck, or a flower placed behind the ear is a historic legacy of Polynesian Magi.

As you might suspect, flower song is also an abundant source of life force energy. As you listen to flower song, breathe in deeply and exhale slowly, just as with the Faces in the Stone.

With at least a week's worth of faces and flower energy absorption you shall be ready to begin basic manipulations of Magic, and work forward developing your magical skills from that point.

A side note, worthy of mention: human hair is important factor in Magic, specifically hair on the head in closest proximity to the brain – i.e. long hair for both men and women, and also facial hair for men. It enhances energy absorption. Think of it almost like antennae, improving the strength of reception the longer it gets. You see, hair follicles are a natural receptor to life force energy. The longer the hair, the greater the energy absorption.

Think about it: Art has classically and universally depicted Wizards with long hair and long beards. Now you know why.

Not coincidentally, that's exactly how God has been usually depicted in art as well over the centuries. That is also no coincidence.

There are, likewise, many other forms of energy sources you must become aware of and make use of as well. One of the most common is energy absorbed from pets, most commonly dogs and cats.

The love of a dear pet contains amazing amounts of available life force energy. And naturally, this energy is most readily conveyed by means of simple touch and embrace. Curling up by the fire with a dog or cat may be a loving and pleasurable experience for the animal, but it is enriching in terms of energy supplies for you. This is also why dogs and cats sleep so much. Sleep helps them recharge their own energy after they have given so much of it to you.

It is a myth that witches have a "familiar," i.e. a pet such as black cats, to harbor unclean spirits. They have them to feed upon their energy. That's also why wizards are extremely partial to dogs.

In general the larger mammals have abundant energy available. Surprisingly, despite their typically small size relative to humans, birds contain abundant energy reserves. In terms of house pets types to consider, rodents tend to have less energy available, and reptiles and amphibians near none. The same is true for fish, insects, and arachnids.

This same principle of energy transfer is also true for other human beings as well. Physical touch always instigates an energy transfer. Most of the time it is a mutual transfer and quite benign, and therefore of no quantitative net gain for the Magi. But that is not always the case. Each Magi possesses the ability to deliberately take energy from just about any sentient form of life.

It is a function known as Percipio Cantamen, or "Harvesting Spell," usually just referred to as a Harvesting.

It's quite common for a Magi to simply shake hands with mortal folk or embrace someone in a warm hug and the mortal may feel a strange, unfamiliar sensation, and nothing more – but at the end of the day, feel unusually tired. So there's no harm done in casual Harvesting.

But beware!

Harm is certainly possible if the Harvesting is overdone, or done maliciously with intent to do harm and inflict injury. It is technically possible to harvest all of the energy and basic life force out of another being, whether it is animal or human, leaving behind nothing but a desiccated pile of ashes and dust.

I was surprised to also learn that kinetic, mechanical, and even magnetic energy can also be Harvested by a Magi. One only needs to be physically within the perimeter of an active energy field to consciously ingest the power, breathing it in and absorbing it like the very oxygen in the atmosphere needed to survive.

Be most wary of ingesting non-sentient forms of energy, especially in the X-ray and gamma ray frequency spectrums. They can be extremely dangerous, even in small quantities and can do a great deal of damage to both your physical cell structure and your capacitance for Magic.

CHAPTER 9
SASHA AND TRAVIS

AUSTIN, TX

"...can be extremely dangerous, even in small quantities and can do a great deal of damage to both your physical cell structure and your capacitance for Magic."

Sasha slammed the journal shut, put it down, and stared slack-jawed in silence at Travis for nearly a full minute, rarely blinking. Her hands were trembling. She had been reading aloud, but couldn't go any further.

They were both still gathered at Sasha's house, but no longer seated at the dining table. They had migrated to the living room to be more comfortable on her dark brown leather couch. Sasha had also fired up her Pandora One account again, this time on her Smart-TV, and selected a smooth jazz station to fill the room with a little more relaxing background music. It felt more appropriate at the moment than a playlist of *Stevie Ray Vaughn, Kiss,* and *Cheap Trick.*

Sasha's cat, Alamo, was curled up in a matching leather club chair across from them, fast asleep – which was his primary activity for most of the day and night. He was a twenty-five pound black alley cat that Sasha had rescued from a local animal shelter a little over five years ago. Alamo was relatively well-behaved and low maintenance. Plus, as long as Sasha fed him regularly, he was good for an affectionate snuggle or two each day. For some reason Sasha always felt better, both emotionally and physically, after a good kitty-snuggle. Naturally, at night he slept either in the small of Sasha's back, or behind her knees. On cold nights, Sasha really appreciated her living space-heater; in the summer months, not so much.

Travis' eyes were as wide as her own, but Sasha couldn't tell if it was from excitement or fear, or a little of both.

He took in a deep breath and swallowed with visible difficulty. "Do you believe...*any* of it?"

With Sasha's chin quivering with emotion, she insisted "My father is *not* insane."

Much to Travis' surprise, Sasha suddenly burst into tears and threw herself into his arms, sobbing against his neck. He caught her and held her close for several moments, tenderly patting her back and telling her it was all going to be okay until her sobs subsided and she calmed a bit.

Alamo lifted his head, saw that his mistress was in good hands, and promptly laid his head back down and closed his eyes.

Travis leaned Sasha back and looked deeply into her eyes. "Sasha. I know it all *sounds* completely crazy. And I agree." He glanced down at the thick leather-bound book sitting on the coffee table, pausing to work up the nerve to say what he was thinking. "But have you considered the remote possibility of what if...I mean, *what if*....it's all *not* so crazy? What if it's all true?"

Sasha leaned back fully, her expression going from a look of pained despair to one of genuine astonishment and appall, "If you think my father has become some kind of a wizard or sorcerer, then you're the one that's insane."

He pointed out, "As an anthropologist, you of all people can't deny that cultures from all over the world, from the beginnings of recorded history to this day, all have some pretty universal beliefs when it comes to the reality of magic."

Sasha cocked her head, arguing, "Travis Gardner, you should know better than that. Of course, every culture seeks to explain what isn't understood behind the veil of superstitions. It's but one of several major social organizing principles that all social communities embrace in order to provide a sense of order and organization. Without all of our superstitions, ideologies, politics, religions, arbitrary laws, regulations and authoritarian structures we'd be living in complete barbarism and anarchy."

"Spoken like a true academic anthropology professor," he shot back.

"I *am* a professor of anthropology."

"Right, Professor. And I'm just asking you to take off that hat for a moment and consider for just a second – *what if* there is another realm of human existence out there that goes beyond three-dimensional space? Is that so hard to imagine?"

She rolled her eyes then shot him a scolding stare. "You're serious?"

He shrugged, "Hey, it's just like the journal asked us to do. All I'm saying is that I'm willing to approach it all with an open mind."

Her brow furrowed in realization. "No. That's not it. Is it? This isn't an issue of academic or scientific inquiry for you. You actually want to give it a try. Don't you?"

His eyes fell as he sheepishly confessed, "Um. Sort'a. Maybe? I don't know. Aren't you even a little bit curious?"

Sasha glanced down at the journal again. "Travis, I've researched hundreds of books, parchments, scrolls, stelas, you name it, on magic from cultures all over the world, some dating back to the Sumerians, Akkadians, and Egyptians. Most of them are all just tedious cookbooks of superstition. Love potions. Poisons, curses and spells. Aphrodisiacs and intoxicants. About the only tangible merit we've ever discovered in any of them are from the few that managed to come up with herbal remedies that really did provide some medical benefit."

Travis nodded, "Exactly! That's just the point. Yesteryear's shaman, or witch doctor, or village wizard was the scientist or pharmacist of their day. Scientists work to expand our body of knowledge, and they often do so by venturing bravely into the unknown. Your father wrote that in his understanding, magic isn't something spooky or some mysterious type of voodoo, rather it's just a specialized electrical brain function, a manifestation of energy that's part of a uniquely acquired skill set. As one of the world's most renowned scientists in quantum physics, he just might know what he's talking about."

Sasha protectively folded her arms across her chest. "So you just want to try all of this out as a *scientific* experiment?"

He smiled and then confessed, "Okay, you got me. I just want to see if it's for real. Who hasn't wanted to be able to cast lightning bolts, or levitate objects, or turn someone into a newt?"

That made her laugh. Instantly Sasha adopted a bad English accent and mimicked John Cleese from *Monty Python and the Holy Grail*: "She turned me into a newt!" A pause. "Well...I got better."

"There you go." Travis pointed at her. "See?"

Her smile faded. "Travis, forget it. I'm cool with the teaching gig. I don't really want to become a witch."

He pointed at Alamo. "You've already got the cat!"

"Funny," she shot back.

He argued, "Well, if there's nothing to it, then you can't become something that doesn't exist. Right? Besides, not all witches are hags. Remember Elizabeth Montgomery on Bewitched? She was hot."

Sasha feigned a look of surprise. "Oh, is that your off-hand way of telling me you think I'm hot?"

He blushed, "No, of course not! That's not what I meant."

"Oh, so you *don't* think I look nice," she pretended to be offended.

"Of course I do," he stammered. "But that...um...I mean, what I meant was—"

"*Kidding*!" She let him off the hook with a playful smack on the hand and then added, "They used to burn witches, you know."

Travis nodded, "Which only proves that a lot of people used to believe they were real."

"Public executions did *not* prove the women they burned were really witches," she said.

He thought for a moment and then asked her, "You believe the Bible, don't you?"

She folded her arms. "What does the Bible have to do with this?"

He pointed out, "Well, when Moses went before pharaoh, one of the signs he performed in order to prove he had truly been sent by God was to turn his staff into a serpent."

She conceded, "Yes, but that was God's doing. Not Moses."

"Perhaps. But then it says pharaoh's *magicians* also turned their staffs into serpents as well. Magicians! That wasn't an act of God, but acts of biblically documented magic, performing a physical transmutation of an inanimate object into a living creature. That's not card tricks or sawing the pretty assistant in half!"

"I don't know," Sasha was starting to question her own thinking.

"Or what about the Witch of Endor whom King Saul sought out? A witch! A witch whom Saul forced to perform an act of necromancy to bring back the soul of the dead prophet Samuel to advise him."

She shook her head, "Man, you must have really paid a lot of attention in Sunday School."

Travis haughtily tilted his head left and right in jest, "As a matter of fact, I did. Gold stars and everything."

"Okay, Bible scholar," she replied, "but doesn't the Bible condemn witchcraft? Doesn't it say you shall not permit a witch to live?"

He paused for a moment, then admitted, "Yes, it does," then quickly appended, "but it doesn't say that about *wizards*!"

"You're impossible," she chuckled. "You're not going to let this go until you try it, are you?"

Travis grew serious. "Probably not. But hey, it may be the only way to know for sure if your dad is still sane or not."

CHAPTER 10
ALLISTER

INTERPOL FIELD OFFICE
LONDON, ENGLAND

Allister McKenzie compared the two autopsy reports sitting on the desk in front of him. The detailed information wasn't quite an exact match to much of what the public was being told about the deaths of a high ranking government official from France and a prominent English industrialist. Both men, Vincent Delacroix and Peter Blanchard, both ultimately died of severe heart ruptures, brought on amid acute asphyxiation from collapsed lungs. The trauma of the asphyxiation was most unique.

He pushed the stack of graphic color photos away and glanced around his office. It was small and Spartan, but utilitarian. At five stories underground it was also windowless. A single gray metal desk and chair was all the furniture he had been issued, other than a row of matching gray metal filing cabinets. The harsh florescent lights above him didn't make the claustrophobic atmosphere any more charming.

Allister took a sip of cold coffee out of a Styrofoam cup and cringed.

He spat the sip back in the cup with a scowl on his face and then tried to scrape the bitter taste off his tongue by rubbing it against the bottom of his front teeth as he returned to his homicide analysis.

Neither man had been strangled or smothered. No ligature marks. No defensive wounds. Rather, it was as if their lungs shriveled up like grapes into raisins almost instantaneously. There might have been desperate attempts to gasp for breath, for such frantic gasps are the normal spasms of the diaphragm when someone can't breathe, desperate for oxygen. However, that would have been totally futile as the shriveled lungs left no room for incoming air. He could well imagine that death, or at least unconsciousness, came rather swiftly, especially after the massive heart rupture.

He picked up one of the photos again. In the case of both men their hearts had been torn almost in two, cleaved evenly, not torn, as if it were done with surgical precision.

And the only stimulus for this was a handshake? Impressive.

Well, that was still the official explanation.

Allister recalled the tales of Indian fakirs who were said to be able to pull the still-beating hearts out of their victim's chests. Now, extracting a human heart from a person's chest cavity was certainly physically possible to do, as every heart surgeon is well aware; but in those old stories, the hearts were completely removed, and yet the victims still lived as zombie-like slaves. Clearly that wasn't what happened here. The chest cavities were still intact, as were the sternums. Whatever cut through these men's hearts happened on the inside but left no trace of itself.

This was all too familiar.

He lifted another report and adjusted his reading glasses. It was the toxicology results. He wondered if anyone would believe some type of acid collapsed the lungs. But there was nothing to be found. No heavy metals, no neurotoxins, nothing. Absolutely clean.

There was no good alternative explanation.

Nevertheless, the simple fact that he was looking at two men found murdered in the exact same way dismissed any notion of some freakish biological anomaly. No, this was clearly a deliberate and methodical act – and that fact disturbed him.

Conclusions would be drawn that weren't helpful.

Allister lifted the phone receiver near him and dialed an extension. "Stewart, I want to see the telephone records for both of the victims for the last ninety days. How soon can you get me that information? Ah, good lad."

He hung up the phone. He'd have what he wanted within the hour.

Allister knew these two men were connected, but that connection wouldn't be immediately obvious to a casual observer. He took another look at the bio files. Vincent Delacroix was a finance minister from Paris, France. He was responsible for currency regulation and oversight of the international wire systems. A money-mover. Sir Peter Blanchard was an English industrialist. It wasn't a well-kept secret, but among his many lines of business, he was also a major arms dealer. So that fact might easily explain his connection to a French money man.

Allister continued to peruse his files for over half an hour, until his laptop notified him he'd received an email from Stewart Turley, one of his younger associates on the Interpol task force. He clicked on one of the two spreadsheet attachments.

The call list for M. Vincent Delacroix was long. Apparently, he spoke to a lot of people by phone on a regular basis. The file was currently listed chronologically from most recent call to the oldest. Allister resorted the file by destination telephone number, i.e. from most frequent party called to the least. The resulting list was much more helpful. At the top of the list was one particular party to whom Delacroix had spoken with on almost a daily basis.

He muttered to himself, "Ah, Daniel DuMonde. In Paris."

I knew it.

Chapter 11
William and Gerhardt

On the Autobahn
Near Garmisch-Partenkirchen, Germany

The Ferrari accelerated to just over 180 miles per hour. He still had plenty of pedal left. The drive from Munich had not taken long. The snow-crested Alps loomed ahead in the distance as the rolling hills and forests of Bavaria blurred by on either side of the sports car. Dr. Gerhardt Mueller sat nervously in the passenger's seat, tightly clutching the shoulder strap of his seatbelt with both hands pressed against his wide chest. He could feel his own rapidly beating heart.

The car only slowed to 120 miles per hour when the road began to wind its way up into the foothills and dip into the valleys beyond. Whenever the road straightened out, even for just a kilometer or two, the precision Italian engine would climb back toward the 200 mph mark.

It was for this reason the large man used all of his available energy to cast a Protection Spell over his own body. The Protection Spell probably wouldn't do much to prevent his death in the event of a crash at these speeds—i.e. inertia, velocity, and the physical mass of his body all still had to obey the laws of physics—but at least his magic could serve to keep the driver of the car from Icing him, Reading him, Harvesting him, or worst case, applying a Death Spell. He was reasonably certain about the first three types of spells, but not a hundred percent positive about being safe from the last one.

Mueller said, "While I've always sincerely enjoyed your company as well as lovely drives in the country, Wilhelm, if your intention is to kill me, too, I'd prefer that you would have just been done with it back in the city."

Dr. William Turner laughed, "Gerhardt, if it was truly my intention to kill you straightaway, you would already be dead. I picked you up this afternoon at your club for the sole reason of us having a little polite conversation. Just a little chat."

The German nuclear physicist nervously spat, "After what I hear that you've done to Vincent and Peter, *and* I'm told perhaps to Penelope too, how can you possibly expect me to trust you?"

"You shouldn't," retorted Dr. Turner. "I'm not asking for your trust. As always, I am only a seeker of the truth. And I believe you have information that is very important to me."

Mueller sighed, "And what is it that you believe that I know?"

William answered, "I believe you know when and how the delivery is to be made to Syria."

The heavy-set man huffed, "And of what possible value is that information to you?"

William down-shifted the transmission with the paddle shifters at his fingertips and passed several more cars ahead of him with ease. "Don't play games, my friend. We both know that as soon as the device finds its way into unfriendly hands, the Armageddon clock starts ticking. Within days, if not hours, the conflagration begins."

Mueller turned his gaze out his passenger-side window, watching the picturesque scenery fly by. "It doesn't really matter, does it? They'll either get one from us, or from someone else. In any case it will still happen. So what difference does it make if we are the ones enriched by it?"

Dr. Turner pressed the accelerator even harder. The speedometer crept past the 200/320 mph/kph mark. "You are a greedy fool, Gerhardt. You don't realize that Daniel and the others care very little for the acquisition of more and more riches. They've enjoyed king's fortunes beyond the realms of avarice for generations. Their real intent is to exterminate over half the world's population in a matter of a few days, starting at the cradle of civilization and radiating out from there, if you'll pardon the pun."

"That is *not* what will happen," the fat man insisted. Despite the cool temperature of driving in the mountains and the superb air conditioning of the elite sports car, he was starting to sweat. "The device is purely for propaganda purposes. A status symbol for sexually frustrated and angry boys who wish to thought of as brave men. It is but an escalation of sabers rattled. And, of course, for us, it is the catalyst of *sales*. Don't you understand that? Once the Syrians and their new Iraqi masters have acquired one device, Iran will then break out and make one or buy one, and then Saudi Arabia will have to have one or more, and then all of the emirates and the whole of the Middle East and North Africa will join the game. They will all demand to have one or more of our products, and every one of them we sell is worth untold billions of dollars to us."

"You're not listening," William snapped. "This isn't about *money*. It's about mass annihilation. During the Cold War the United States and the Soviets achieved a successful détente via the threat of M.A.D. – Mutually Assured Destruction. No one wanted to die. The religious fanatics of the Middle East don't mind unleashing death on a catastrophic scale. They pray for it. Their apocalypse scenario requires it before their savior can return to vanquish all remaining infidels, and only then can everyone live happily ever after – except, of course, that doesn't apply to women, gays, and any other non-members of the club."

The German grunted again, "I tell you, you worry like an old woman, Wilhelm. Look, we know North Korea has at least one weapon, if not several, they've tested them. Pakistan we know has several. These are crazy nations, too, and they've not seen fit to destroy the world. It will be the same. I am certain of this."

"Sorry, old boy, I'm not too keen on giving these murderous barbarians Daniel wants to do business with the benefit of the doubt. I'm going to do everything in my power that I can to stop this insanity. And you're going to help me by telling me when the shipment leaves Athens."

Gerhardt spun his gaze to face William Turner. "How do you know about Athens?"

William knew no one would suspect anything Penelope may have told him yet. "Don't worry about it. I know. I just don't know when the package is due to arrive there from Pakistan, and when it is scheduled to depart for Damascus."

"You have no idea of the enormity of the security arrangements. After what you've done, you would be killed on sight. Daniel is overseeing all of the operation personally. I would wager that you'll not be able to get within a hundred kilometers of the device."

William countered, "Okay, if that's true, then I really don't see why you would have any reservations whatsoever about telling me the day and the hour. Unless, of course, you are *that* worried about my personal safety. Would you miss me, Gerhardt?"

"And what do I get in return for my cooperation?" A faint smile started to cross the big man's lips. "As I said, knowing when it will happen won't do you any good, but if you are intent on committing suicide, why should I not make a little profit? A man has to eat, *nicht war*?"

William returned a warm smile. "Ah, yes, my friend. You are, to be sure, if nothing else, a man of substantial material means and great appetites. All right, how about this idea? Do you like this car? It's brand new. Less than a thousand kilometers on it. Without any of its options and upgrades it lists for well over five-hundred thousand American dollars."

Mueller was now admiring the custom leather and electronic appointments of the Ferrari much more closely. Clearly it was a top performance vehicle and vastly superior to the Porsche he currently drove. "Very well. Take me back to *München* in *my* new car and I believe we have a deal."

"Doesn't work that way, old friend. Tell me what I want to know first and then you get your prize."

Mueller smiled broadly. "Fine, Wilhelm. If you are so eager to meet your own dark fate, the itinerary is as follows. The package arrives in Athens in nine days. Coming by military submarine. After I certify it as operational, it gets flown three days later to Cairo, and then put on a truck traveling through Jordan and on into Syria. The transfer to the Syrians will be two weeks from tomorrow, at noon, in Raqqa."

The Ferrari was high into the alpine roads by now, carving turns through the twisting and snaking switch-backs. William turned to his companion and thanked him. "Gerhardt, you can be a difficult man to deal with sometimes. But I do appreciate and thank you for your assistance with this matter. I mean that."

"You will take me back to the *stadt* now?"

Turner shook his head. "You can manage that yourself."

Mueller looked puzzled for a moment. His eyes squinted at the sudden sound of a high pitched whine. It was grating on his nerves and his back teeth began to hurt. Even his skin started to itch all over. He could feel all the hairs on his body start to stand on end.

The car accelerated toward a sharp hairpin turn, and just beyond it, loomed a thousand foot plunge into a gorge and its jagged rocks below.

Turner smiled and said, "It's time for me to go, old boy. It has been a pleasure doing business with you. The car is all yours. Do drive safely. *Auf wiedersehen, mein freund.*"

And then it happened.

FLASH!

A bright white light momentarily flashed inside the car, just moments before it ploughed headlong over the guardrail and sailed down into the great crevasse with a large man inside screaming continuously in pure horror until the plummeting car met the rocks below, exploding in a massive red, yellow and orange fireball, which plumed upward into a thick black cloud curling up within itself back up into the afternoon sky.

CHAPTER 12
SASHA AND TRAVIS

AUSTIN, TX

It had been over two hours and nothing had happened yet. Travis Gardner sat cross-legged on the back patio of Sasha's house, trying to meditate, relax, and quiet his mind. That was a near impossible task – especially with Alamo rubbing against him, purring with his eyes closed, and insisting on getting all of Travis' attention.

Dr. Turner's journal presented him with a genuine dilemma. How can you attempt to see something, but are cautioned that if you deliberately look for it, then you can't find it? Was that a trick question?

•

Sasha was still inside the house. Every few minutes, she'd peek out the sliding glass door and make sure Travis and Alamo were all right. In fact, she was looking out at Travis the very moment when nature called. She excused herself into her master bathroom and sat down on the toilet.

She was worried about Travis. To her, he seemed to be rushing into all of this in a very naïve and foolhardy way. What if there were dangers? If magic really *did* exist, wouldn't it kind of be like playing with fire? What were the rules? What do you need to avoid? Before they went much further she knew they needed to read a lot more of her father's journal.

And that's when it happened.

Her eyes were absently looking down at the floor, which was covered with an intricate Italian tile she'd picked out when remodeling the house two years prior. There in the swirls and natural discolorations of the tile was the clear shape of a face: eyes, nose, mouth, chin, jawline. It looked like a young woman. It was a sad face. However, the more she stared at it, the clearer it became. Her breath stilled when she could have sworn that the eyes tilted toward her.

Perhaps by instinct, Sasha began to breathe in deeply through her nose, hold the breath for several seconds, and then slowly release it though her mouth. A second time, a third, fourth, fifth, sixth, and finally a seventh time. As she released the last long breath, her eyes felt tired and blurred for a moment. She rubbed them with her fingers and then looked down again. She couldn't find the woman's face.

It was gone.

As she washed her hands, she looked at her own face in the mirror. She couldn't quite identify exactly what it was she saw, but something was different. Something *felt* different. Maybe it was something in her eyes. Her dark brown irises seemed a little brighter. Or maybe it was nothing. She dismissed the thought with a shake of her head and returned to the living room.

Standing just inside the sliding glass door was Travis, breathing hard. He looked at her and exclaimed, "I did it."

Sasha apprehensively asked, "Did what?"

"I saw a face," he said.

"Where?"

"On the wall. In the stucco." He came into the living room and sat down on her couch. "I was about to give up on it all, and then I started petting Alamo, daydreaming about fixing something for lunch, and then there it was."

Sasha sat down with him on the couch once more. "What did it look like?"

Travis described for her, "Like an old man. Very old, wrinkled. At first it wasn't so clear, but as I remembered to breathe in and out like the journal said, it got a lot clearer."

"And after the seventh breath?" she asked. "Did your eyes blur for a second?"

"Yes," he frowned. "But how could you possibly know that?"

"Because—" she began.

"You saw it too," he interrupted. "Didn't you?"

Sasha nodded. "I did. But mine was a woman."

Travis shook his head, "Do you think it was real? Or just our imaginations showing us what we wanted to see?"

"Maybe it was a little of both." She wasn't sure. "Didn't the journal say magic is the very root of imagination?"

"Okay, so how do we know for sure?" he asked.

"I know how." Sasha jumped off the couch, grabbed Travis by the hand, and pulled him back outside in her backyard.

Lining the rear of Sasha's home were lovely flower beds, neatly landscaped and bordered with large blocks of limestone. She picked two geraniums and handed one to Travis, announcing, "And now we listen."

He smiled at her as he took his flower and held it up to his right ear. After a few seconds he said, "I don't hear anything."

Sasha was holding her flower against her earlobe. "Give it time. It said the first time might take a while. Quiet your mind. And remember to breathe. And use the focus thought of 'Sing to me'."

Travis closed his eyes and began taking long cleansing breaths, focusing on repeating the words over and over: *Sing to me.*

And that's when it happened.

It was very faint at first.

Travis' eyes came open with genuine surprise, and then closed again tightly as he strained to hear what he thought he was hearing. What was that sound? Was it like a violin? A voice? A bird? Or something never heard before? He wasn't sure. But there was something playing softly in his hearing. It was ethereal, enchanting. As he relaxed and continued to breathe, it grew stronger.

"Oh my," he heard Sasha exclaim.

Travis opened his eyes to see Sasha slowly swaying back and forth to some invisible rhythm. He smiled and said, "So did you get the Beach Boys on yours?"

She laughed out loud. "No. More like Yanni. But with less synthesizer and more angelic choir."

He nodded, "Yeah, I'm on that station too."

"You know what this means, don't you?" she asked.

"That our whole world just got a lot more beautiful?" he replied.

It was Sasha's eyes that were wide now. "It means it's all real."

CHAPTER 13
DANIEL AND BURKE

IN THE SEA OF CRETE
APPROXIMATELY 150 NAUTICAL MILES
SOUTH OF ATHENS, GREECE

"It can't be a coincidence," Daniel DuMonde insisted.

Stephan Burke stood at the wet bar on the upper deck of the two-hundred and twenty foot long, five story tall yacht, which was christened *The Libertine*, refilling his drink. "It wasn't like the other two executions. It was a car accident."

DuMonde stood at the rail, his eyes trained on the open sea as his ship sailed north towards their destination. He was glad to be aboard his yacht once again. The short flight from Paris to Marseilles, where he routinely kept his ship docked, took very little time. The leisurely cruise down the western coast of Italy, around the Isle of Sicily, and across the Ionian Sea, past the southern tip of Greece was delightfully pleasant at that time of year. Although, recent events had spoiled much of the joy of travel for Daniel DuMonde.

"It was *no* accident," Daniel insisted. "There was absolutely no reason for Gerhardt to be driving in the mountains alone in a sports car he didn't even own. He would never be that reckless or careless. He knew his mission in Athens with us was critical."

"Was the car tampered with?" Burke asked.

"Impossible to determine," DuMonde replied. "The reports I received said the car was virtually disintegrated. Based on the trajectory of where it left the road to the impact site, I'm told it had to be moving well over three-hundred kilometers per hour. Just charred bits and pieces left on the floor of a deep gorge. The only way Gerhardt could even be identified was from a few dental fragments and DNA samples of tissue bits they were able to find."

"But he was alone in the car, yes?"

"So it would seem." DuMonde walked over and sat down at the white marble-topped dining table positioned at the rear of the upper deck. He took a long breath of the brisk air, letting the sweet salty breeze blow through his long, graying locks.

Burke asked, "So whose car was it?"

"It was stolen from the home of some hedge fund manager in Munich. He was not even aware that it wasn't still parked in his garage with the rest of his amazing car collection until the German *Polizei* arrived at his door yesterday to inquire about the incident."

Burke took a sip of his gin and tonic. "So, somehow we are to believe that Dr. Turner manages to undetectably transport himself, presumably from either Italy or England, to Germany. He steals an expensive sports car from a total stranger without being noticed. He then kidnaps Dr. Mueller. Drives him high into the Bavarian Alps, and somehow escapes unscathed himself from a car moving at ridiculously high speeds, leaving the good doctor to plunge off a cliff alone to his death."

DuMonde smiled. "I admit, it does sound rather farcical when you say it like that. But what other possible explanation could there be? Did Gerhardt steal the car himself? Did he get drunk and careless? Was he suddenly stricken with remorse and decided to end it all? No! None of it makes sense."

Burke set his Waterford lead crystal glass on the table and stirred his ice around with a thin, black cocktail straw. "But the level of power that would be needed to accomplish the 'farcical scenario' is unthinkable, far beyond anything even *you* are capable of doing."

Daniel DuMonde stoked the whiskers on his chin and nervously said, "I know. That is what concerns me. We have no way to know for certain just how powerful our Guillaume has become or what he is truly capable of doing."

"But powerful or not, he's still just one man," Burke pointed out. "And we still have superior numbers."

DuMonde forced a smile. "Oh, but he's clearly become much more than *just* a man, Stephan. Nevertheless, he still thinks with the mind of a man. And men are vulnerable to mistakes. When he makes one, we must be prepared to take action."

"We don't even know where William is."

DuMonde nodded. "No, we don't. But we can at least assume he spoke to Gerhardt. And if he did, and if he now knows what Gerhardt knew, then we have a good idea of where he will be going. In fact, I would not be surprised if we don't cross paths with him just ahead, right here in Athens. That would be his next logical step, if he is so adamantly intent on trying to stop us."

"But how can we proceed in Athens without Gerhardt?"

Daniel shrugged. "We will have to find a substitute for the operational certification. We still have a little over a week before the package arrives. I will make some calls. It can be done. Yes, Gerhardt was important to us, but not irreplaceable. In fact, Nancy is flying in from New York with the others next week. She may have the proper background we need for this task. I'll talk to her first."

Burke added, "I would also strongly recommend, especially in light of what's happened to Gerhardt, that we alter the entire operational schedule somewhat. That is, I think it may be a mistake to attempt the hand-off of the device here in Athens as planned. We could, instead, reroute it to a more discrete port in Turkey, just across the Aegean. The operation is too important to risk having William show up uninvited and interrupt it. If Nancy does have the right skills we need, then send her there to meet the package in Turkey."

Daniel DuMonde began to smile. "Excellent idea, Stephan. I like it. But I think we must do both. We shall indeed reroute the shipment to Turkey for the next leg of its journey. However, we ourselves shall also continue on to Athens, just as planned, so William is none the wiser that our plans have changed. This may be our one opportunity to find the great Dr. Guillaume Turner before he finds any more of us and picks us off one at a time."

"But how will you stop him, if indeed he's grown so powerful?" Burke finished his drink with one long sip.

"I will gather several others of the Inner Circle, as well as you and I. Together we will all unify our strength. We need only an opportune moment of surprise to strike. And then we shall finally destroy Dr. Guillaume Turner, once and for all."

CHAPTER 14

FROM THE JOURNAL OF WILLIAM TURNER

WORKING MAGIC

In the science of physics the simplest definition for the word "energy" is "the ability to do work." Likewise, the ability to do work is the same purpose of Magic, for it too is a form of energy exerted by conscious will upon the physical world.

Magic exists for a very distinct and defined purpose, and that purpose is to equip the practitioner, the Magi (or Magician if you prefer), to accomplish work that rightly needs to be done. It is properly thought of as a tool, not a finished product. It is a means to an end, not the end unto itself.

It is the journey, not the destination.

This truth opens the door to a most profound and imperative realization: Magic can be used for either good or evil. But Magic itself is neither good nor evil.

Magi practicing good Magic use their powers to help those in need, the sick, the helpless, the subjugated, the hungry, the weak, the poor, the lost, the meek, the lonely. Magi practicing evil Magic use their powers primarily for the benefit of themselves and to subjugate others, to satisfy their avaricious appetites for wealth, power, fame, and for the experience of all manner of carnal gratifications.

So be careful to use your Magic for the service of good, and you will live a long and happy life. But if you use Magic with evil or selfish intent you can expect all manner of danger and calamity to ultimately be your fate, even if you are able to enjoy dominion over others, material success and temporal pleasures for a season.

Let us also take a moment to clear up a little semantical confusion. There are many terms used to refer to practitioners of Magic, some words which are very benign, almost clinical sounding, and some words that sound quite pejorative. These are words such as Magi, Mage, Magician, Wizard, Sorcerer, Witch, Warlock, and so forth. Don't let these terms confuse you. These words all represent those who use Magic, and are used so interchangeably in the vernacular that any distinctions between them are more epistemological trivia than useful information.

But if you're curios: Magi, Mage, and Magician are all variants of the same root word, which refers to those who have acquired and perfected their magical arts through study and practice.

The word Magi is actually of Persian origin, and was used in the New Testament to refer to the three "Wise Men from the East" who brought gifts to Jesus upon occasion of his birth. So the idea of "Magi" contains a foundation of the idea of "wisdom" gained through study.

The idea of "wisdom" is also the derivation of the word "Wizard." It too comes from a root word that refers to that which is "wise." So the only real difference between the words Magi (and its variants Mage and Magician), which are from a more eastern or Persian language origin, and the word Wizard, which comes from a more Anglo-Saxon origin, is semantics. Magi and Wizards are essentially the exact same thing, and may be used to refer to either males or females.

Now the term "Sorcerer" is more of a creation of exaggeration, legend and lore. That is, Sorcerers are believed to have come by their magical powers, not through arduous study, but completely naturally – born with all the talents, skills, and power of a Master Magi. I can't say with a hundred percent certainty that they don't exist, or have ever existed, I can only say that as a Master Magician myself and well-versed in high-level Magic, I have never personally encountered one or anyone claiming to be one. On the other hand, what is very plausible for me to believe is that there could be a Master Magician, whose head is so inflated with personal ego and selfish power that he has no remorse whatsoever telling the souls he subjugates that he was born as powerful as he represents himself to be.

Therefore, what is called a Sorcerer may also be another distinction without a difference. If you are battling an evil Master Magi, or one claiming to be a Sorcerer, what difference does it really make? They're both bad news and potentially very dangerous.

The labels Witches and Warlocks typically have a gender-specific association, i.e. Witches are female, Warlocks are male. But not always. Some males may call themselves Witches. However, in my experience, those Magi who prefer to be known as either Witches and Warlocks do so as a means of demonstrably associating themselves with the dark or evil side of Magic. On the other hand, is there such a thing as a good witch, such as Glenda in Frank L. Baum's tale of the Wizard of Oz? Presumably so, but I would be most curious to learn why any female Magi would choose to refer to herself as such, or a male for that matter.

The terms "Enchanter" and "Enchantress" are again typically gender-specific terms equivalent to Warlock and Witch, but with a somewhat of a less dark and evil connotation.

Furthermore, you may hear of pagan groups, such as the Wiccans, who consider themselves a type of religion and call themselves Witches. Yet if they have no true Magic, they are little more than a club.

Here's the long and short of it: Regardless of which fancy or intimidating titles a Magician may wish to bestow upon themselves, when it comes to the Art of actually practicing Magic itself, they are all either a Novice Magi, a Practicing Magi, or most powerful or all, a Master Magi.

Those three levels of power are the only distinctions that matter.

Let us move on.

If you have been bold and courageous enough to experiment with the two elementary exercises I have discussed with you thus far – i.e. you've seen the Faces in the Stone, ingested their energy, and have used it to hear the flowers sing, and have faithfully done so every day for at least one week, then you are likely ready to at last take the next steps in your journey to discovering and nurturing your own magical power and at last using it creatively and productively.

Chele Cantamen

The next fundamental exercise I have designed to teach you is the Chele Cantamen, which is Latin for a "Trigger Spell".

A Trigger Spell is quite literally a catalyst of action. In the most basic way possible to understand this concept, a Trigger is a means to instigate an event, which could be something as simple as changing the flight path of an insect (that might be bothering you), to kicking that first pebble that starts an avalanche.

As your power grows, you will find many different and more challenging Trigger exercises on your own, beyond the simple examples I ask you to try. You should endeavor to continuously create and practice various Trigger Spells, to begin developing your outbound senses and work to strengthen them.

The first trigger I would suggest you attempt are traffic lights.

When you stop at a red light, and without looking at the traffic light on the cross street and seeing when it turns to yellow and thereby knowing your red light is about to become green, decide when you want your red light to switch to green. Snap your fingers when you are ready. If you are dispatching your power correctly, your energy of will shall trigger the light's timing mechanism to obey your will and the light will change on your command.

Your focus thought is: "Time is up. Time to go." Snap your fingers on the word "Go" in your mind.

It will take a few tries to master it, but this capability comes quite easily when applied to a simple electromechanical device within a range of less than fifty yards. Just don't be astonished when it happens. In fact, your mind must expect your will to be obeyed. And when it isn't obeyed, then you have a solemn responsibility to deduce why not.

Normally, when any magical command fails, it is primarily due to a lack of power. The other common cause of failure is a lack of focus. This is the importance of having a focus thought. If you aren't really serious and you don't sincerely believe yourself that your Magic will produce the desired outcome, there is little chance it will work on its intended target.

Less common, but noteworthy, is the reality that some magic can fail when a stronger magician wishes it to fail.

Listen to this very carefully:

Magic can be stopped. But only with greater Magic.

The next exercise I would like you to attempt shall be your first spell involving the influence of another human being. This technique is extremely helpful, especially in busy or chaotic situations.

Tractoria Catamen

Tractoria Catamen is a "Summons Spell."

It works exactly as it sounds. It is the ability to command the attention of someone else wordlessly over distance.

Imagine you are standing in a crowded square and across the way you see someone you wish to speak with. Let's say, unfortunately, they don't see you, or are perhaps busy with their own affairs, or maybe in a conversation with someone else. You lay your eyes directly upon them, and release your energy at them with the focus thought of: "See me."

If you know the person's name, that can strengthen the effect. If it is working properly, you should command their attention.

If you wish for that person to come over to you, after your successful focus thought of, "See me," add the focus thought of, "Come to me." As you grow in power, so will the frequency and degree of obedience of those to whom you direct your focus thoughts.

You'll find this technique to be extremely handy in restaurants or shops when you need prompt service. You can even use it at home when summoning a person from another room. Just bear in mind that it does have physical limits in terms of range, predicated on your total level of accumulated power.

Virgula Diuina

And now a note on Virgula Diuina, which is Latin for "Magic Wand," but covers all manner of Intermediate Objects (IO).

Some Magi prefer both to "direct" their powers, in the sense of aiming, and additionally, to better "focus" their powers, in terms of strength, by means of employing the use of a familiar object. Most commonly used objects are wooden staffs or small wands. Please note that the object itself has absolutely no power whatsoever. Those who believe otherwise are simply ignorant or mistaken.

Think of the intermediate object functioning akin to the barrel of a gun. The longer the barrel of a gun, the more accurate the bullet. Short barrel guns are notoriously inaccurate. When the energy behind a bullet is focused for a longer period of time in a specifically aimed direction, the bullet tends to remain true to that direction. The energy disbursement characteristics of Magic possess similar properties. It's analogous to the difference between using a shotgun or a rifle.

Intermediate objects such as staffs or wands are by no means required in order for you to practice your Magic. However, in some instances they can be of some assistance.

Personally, I believe IOs tend to become a crutch for some Magi, trusting more in the efficacy of an inanimate wand of hickory or an oaken staff rather than in their own personal capabilities. But, if the touch or feel of something familiar helps instill a greater degree of confidence, then there is no harm done.

CHAPTER 15
DANIEL AND ALLISTER

ABOARD THE LIBERTINE
ATHENS, GREECE

The small motor launch wound its way out into the bay, slowing as it reached the stern of the vast yacht anchored about a few hundred yards offshore.

Its passenger appeared to be an elderly man, not quite dressed appropriately for spending time at sea; rather, he looked as if he would have been much more comfortable in a library, or hectoring students in a final exam. One of the uniformed stewards met him at the stern swim platform and assisted him safely aboard.

Daniel DuMonde was most curious to meet with his new guest. His telephone call the day prior had insisted with great urgency the necessity of a face-to-face meeting – even if it involved having the gentleman flying from London to Athens by private charter. Daniel rose and extended his hand when the steward entered the luxuriously appointed salon on the second deck of *The Libertine* and presented his charge.

DuMonde offered a firm handshake. "*Bonjour, Monsieur...McKenzie?* Is that right?"

Allister McKenzie grasped Daniel's hand and pumped it twice. "Yes, quite right. Chief Inspector McKenzie, Interpol, London office. Thank you so much, Monsieur DuMonde for agreeing to see me. It is of the greatest import that we chat."

Daniel gestured to a deck chair. "Please, please, take a seat and be comfortable. Can we get you anything?"

Allister glanced back at the young steward, and held his thumb and forefinger about an inch apart. "Perhaps just a wee bit of water and ice, if it's not too much trouble?" He found it curious that the young man wore a holstered semiautomatic sidearm.

The young man smiled, nodded, and disappeared.

"So what is so urgent that has brought you all this way to see me so urgently?" Daniel asked with genuine seriousness.

"Monsieur DuMonde, as I told you on the phone I work for a special task force at Interpol. And as such we are seeking to recapture the dangerous fugitive, one Dr. William Turner, a man whom we believe you are well acquainted."

"*D'accord*," concurred DuMonde. "Dr. Turner was conducting several key research projects for our research foundation. We have been funding his research for the last couple of years, both in the US and also at the CERN laboratories in Geneva."

"Then can I assume you are well aware of his alleged involvement in the deaths of Monsieur Vincent Delacroix in Switzerland and Sir Peter Blanchard in England?"

DuMonde nodded, "Sadly, I am afraid that I am." He wondered why there was no mention of Dr. Gerhardt Mueller.

Had they not made that connection yet?

"And can you tell me in what way, precisely, were you acquainted with these two individuals?" Allister asked.

"Vincent worked in the ministry of finance in Paris, which is where I live and make my base of operations for several of my business ventures. Many of my investment deals involve large sums of money, and therefore necessitate government oversight and regulation, and in some cases high-level approvals. It was therefore critical for me and my key executives to establish a relationship with Vincent's office, and in time, he and I became good friends and have been for several years. I was very saddened to hear of this tragedy."

"I see," Allister nodded, as he took a notebook and pen out of his worn leather satchel and began to take notes. "And what of your involvement with Sir Peter?"

The young, armed steward returned with Allister's glass of ice water and placed it on the table before him, earning him a polite nod of thanks.

He unobtrusively exited the salon once again.

DuMonde waited until the steward had left before explaining, "Peter Blanchard was one of my suppliers, or...how do you say?...*vendors*, yes. I've done numerous transactions around the world that involved Peter's company's products and services."

"Arms and munitions perhaps?" Allister's bushy gray eyebrows rose in anticipation of the answer.

DuMonde only smiled, but after a brief pause for thought, said, "My business dealings with Peter over many years involved all manner of commercial and industrial materials and services. So naturally...*security elements* were commonplace."

"Yes, yes, indeed." Allister nodded and scrawled another note. It was time to move beyond the superficial and onto the meat of his mission. "Monsieur DuMonde, other than recognizing your own name, do any of the following names here mean anything to you?" He handed DuMonde an alphabetized and printed list:

Dr. Penelope Angelucci	Rome, Italy
Mr. Alexey Borochenko	Kiev, Ukraine
Mr. Stephan Burke	London, UK
Justice Frank Donaldson	San Francisco, CA
Daniel DuMonde	Paris, France
General Mohammed bin Faisal	Riyadh, Saudi Arabia
Dr. Gerhardt Mueller	Munich, Germany
Arch Bishop Renaldo Vasquez	Buenos Aires, ARG
Dr. Walter Stephens	Sydney, Australia
Dr. Nancy Thompson	New York City, NY

Daniel DuMonde's heart was pounding in his chest, but he dared not let it show on his face or interrupt his smile. This seemingly mild-mannered academic public servant had a list of all of the primary members and leaders of the Inner Circle – all twelve when including Vincent, Peter and himself!

Who *was* this man?

Allister noticed the slight break in inflection of the Frenchman's voice when Daniel answered. "Of course I know several of them. Again, mostly through business dealings. But *how—?*"

It was Allister's turn to offer a polite smile and said, "Data mining."

"*Quoi?*" DuMonde was confused for a second.

Allister waved a dismissive hand at him as he explained. "Of course you're keen to know, of all the thousands of people you must know, how could we possibly come up with this particular list of names. I'll admit it wasn't easy, but I tell you, the magic of computers and business intelligence analytics these days is most impressive. Interpol is as advanced today, if not more so, as is the NSA in the US.

"So, based upon the patterns of your two deceased colleagues' telephone calls, emails, texts, voicemails, travel itineraries, social media postings, search engine searches, and so forth over the last few years, and then correlating all of that data with Dr. Turner's data, the analytical reports document specific patterns and networked connections highlighting all of these individuals into a nexus, and that includes yourself. I mean this was just top ten names highlighted, excluding those already deceased, of course. The list could very well be much longer."

"I see," DuMonde felt most uncomfortable at the moment, actually a bit violated. *Could* the intelligence community so accurately pinpoint some of his most closely guarded secrets?

"And that brings me to the real reason of why I'm here today," Allister continued. "We don't know exactly *why* yet, but it is our belief that Dr. Turner means to systematically terminate all of these particular individuals, perhaps more, and each one of them is in grave danger."

For Daniel, this pronouncement wasn't exactly news. He assured his guest, "I take my personal security extremely seriously, Chief Inspector. I know to be on the lookout for Dr. Turner."

Allister smiled. "And pray tell me, Monsieur DuMonde, other than based upon my warning to you just now, and as his patron and benefactor as you've just explained, *how* exactly are you aware to be on the lookout for Dr. Turner?"

DuMonde's mind was racing. This old fool just bedeviled him into a corner. What plausible explanation could there be for how he would have known that the assassination of two other people in two different countries would have any connection to imperiling himself? He couldn't actually divulge the true nature of the Inner Circle and the global extent of their influence and power.

Allister just sat there patiently awaiting his response.

Daniel cleared his throat and said the first semi-plausible sounding thing that came into his head, "It was because I received a communication from Dr. Turner a few days ago, threatening me. And after what happened to Vincent and Peter, I believed him."

Allister looked astonished, "And to whom exactly might you have had occasion to report this threat?"

DuMonde shook his head. "To no one. I really don't have a great deal of trust for most of the French authorities. We've not always seen eye to eye on several matters. I can assure you, I easily tire of lining the pockets of everyone standing there with their hand out. Truly, so many of them are notoriously corrupt. So I elected to leave France immediately, and hence why we are at sea here in Greece."

"I see." More note scribbling. "But can you tell me, sir, do you have any idea what Dr. Turner's motivation might be? Why does he seem so keen on apparently targeting all of you on this list in particular?"

"That's simple," he lied. "We recently chose to terminate Dr. Turner's funding. It wasn't a personal decision, just a shift in our top funding priorities. But quite obviously he took our decision very personally, believes this will ruin him and his reputation, and is clearly now on some deranged vendetta spree."

"That explains *you* being on his hit list, but what about all the other individuals from around the world?"

The fictitious answer came quickly to him.

Daniel said, "Please forgive me, Inspector, I neglected to mention a moment ago that in addition to my various business dealings with some of the others you mentioned, several of them are also members of the Board of Directors of our research foundation. Others are key donors to the foundation. So they all, to one degree or another, had a bit of a say on the decision to cut off Dr. Turner's funding. And he is well-aware of who they all are."

"Unbelievable," Allister nodded, meaning that word literally. "I say, with his reputation and accomplishments, one would think he could have found numerous other organizations more than willing to back him and his work."

"*D'accord*," said Daniel. "Which is why it was so shocking to learn of the news reports of his psychotic breakdown. But there can be no doubt about what he has done. I mean, what happened to Vincent Delacroix in Geneva was all captured on video. The fact that this man is a cold-blooded murderer isn't in dispute."

"Indeed," agreed the Chief Inspector. "So tell me, please, have any of your colleagues on your foundation, or its major donors as you say, have any of them reported seeing or hearing from Dr. Turner? Or worse, are you aware of any of them gone missing?"

Daniel shrugged and said, "No, I'm sorry. Not that I'm personally aware of myself. But if you should learn of anything happening to any of them, I would sincerely appreciate a call from you."

Allister wrote that down. "I'll follow up and let you know. And, of course, you'll let us know should you yourself receive any further communications from Dr. Turner."

"Absolutely," Daniel assured him.

Allister stood and repacked his satchel. "Please feel free to pass along my most urgent warning to all of your other colleagues to be most wary and prepared for the worst." He was confident Daniel DuMonde would do exactly that, which would, in turn, give him the exact location of each of them. Virtually all of them had gone off the grid in recent days.

"Of course," Daniel rose to his feet as well.

With their meeting concluded, the young steward once again escorted Allister to the waiting motor launch to take him back to the mainland.

Daniel DuMonde stood at the rail and watched the small craft moving away. Yes, he would definitely be talking to most, if not all of the other members of the Inner Circle very soon as each of them individually arrived in Athens, prepared for whatever came next with respect to dealing with the most bothersome and clearly dangerous Dr. Guillaume Turner.

In fact, one important call he wanted to make right away.

He pulled his phone out of his pocket and dialed a Favorite.

The call was answered on the third ring. "*Allo*?"

"Penelope, my love, I finally caught you." He was genuinely pleased to finally hear her voice.

"Daniel?" she replied. "What is it? Are you all right? Is...something wrong?"

"I was getting very worried about you, my sweet," he said, detecting a slight trace of apprehension in her voice. "You haven't been retuning my calls."

"I'm sorry, Daniel. With the terrible news about Vincent and Peter, I've been laying low as much as possible."

"I understand. But you know our timetable. And I need you with all of the others here in Athens this week. How soon do you think you can get here?"

She said, "First thing in the morning shouldn't be a problem. There's a shuttle from Rome to Athens. It leaves every hour."

"Excellent," he said. "I want you to come straight to the ship as soon as you can get here."

"Why?" she asked.

"We need to talk," was all he said before he hung up.

CHAPTER 16
SASHA AND TRAVIS

AUSTIN, TX

Sasha's white Mercedes two-seat sports car slowed at a stoplight and came to a halt. Travis sat buckled into the passenger's seat beside her. He absolutely loved her car, he couldn't deny it. What was not to love? It was awesome, a symphony of leather and chrome, accented with fine hardwoods, along with an AMG racing engine under the hood. An old *Aerosmith* song was playing on the digital radio.

"Are you going to try it?" he asked her with a grin, as he turned down the Harmon-Kardon stereo from head-banger volume to a more suitable able-to-have-a-conversation level.

Sasha glanced at him for a second, then said, "I feel kind of stupid. I mean, messing with traffic lights? What does that accomplish?"

"It's just practice," Travis replied. "You know, like a golfer going to the driving range. It builds up muscle memory. Improves swing thoughts. That kind of stuff."

"Okay. Here goes. I just hope no one other than you is looking." Sasha bore her gaze into the red LED stoplight suspended directly across the intersection from her, and said with authority, "Time is up. Time to," and snapped her fingers as she said, "Go!"

The light instantly changed to green.

They both whipped their heads toward one another, gasped, and stared into each other's eyes in awe. The car behind them honked its horn. Sasha let off the brake and pulled forward.

"That could have *just* been a coincidence," she insisted, still feeling very skeptical.

"I don't know," Travis said. "We've been through that light many, many times. And I seem to recall it being one of the slower ones in town. We weren't stopped there very long at all."

"So let's continue the experiment," Sasha said as they came to a stop at the next red light. "Your turn."

"Me? Okay. Here goes nothing. Time is up. Time to Go." He snapped his fingers.

Nothing happened.

"Oh, *man*. A dud." He was clearly disappointed.

Sasha corrected him. "You did it wrong. You have to snap right on the word 'Go', not after. Do it again."

He broke his gaze with her, faced the light, and matter-of-factly said, "Time is up. Time to," and snapped right on, "Go."

The light turned green.

"No way!" he gasped.

"Yes, way..." she teased, as she pulled ahead.

Travis' voice still sounded doubtful and uneasy. "But I still think it's maybe just a coincidence. I mean, we've been through these lights so many times we may just have a preprogrammed sense for how long they take and when they're about to change anyway."

"Fine. Then we'll find one that can't work that way, and then we'll know for sure."

"How?" he asked.

"Like that one," Sasha nodded her head toward another light just up ahead that had just turned yellow. She stopped at the light just after it changed to red. "We don't wait. We do it right now."

"Who's going to do it?" he asked.

"Both of us. Together."

"Okay. You start it."

She turned to face the light. "Time is up." Travis chimed in on, "Time to," and they both snapped their fingers in unison on the word, "Go!"

The light turned green.

"Go, go, go!" Travis exclaimed with his palms smashed against both of his cheeks. "This is totally insane. Let's get out of here!"

•

Twenty-five minutes later Sasha and Travis were sitting in a booth at a popular brew pub in North Austin, finishing an appetizer of chicken casadias and sipping a house-made beer.

A country musician with an acoustic guitar, complete with cowboy hat and boots, played on a small stage in the corner. He played a sad country song Sasha had never heard before. It could very well have been one of the musician's own originals compositions, or just an obscure cover song. Listening to new or nostalgic songs from a singer-songwriter was a pretty common experience in Austin.

"We're becoming quite the magic act," Travis announced, not taking any great pains to hide his sarcasm. "We can misconstrue ordinary pattern recognition as faces in rough textured surfaces. We can pretend we hear music coming out of flowers. And now we can get where we're going faster and not waste so much time stuck at lights. *Amazing*."

Sasha laughed. "Yep. We're not exactly great and powerful wizards yet, are we?"

Travis noted, "Maybe that's why all the wizards you see in the movies are always depicted as really old guys. It must take decades to really master it all."

"That's a depressing thought," she said. "I was sort of hoping we'd get to do some cooler tricks sooner rather than later."

"Me too," he agreed. "But I get the feeling there aren't many shortcuts available to mastering the critical elements of the magic arts. You just have to go through the whole process and learn and get stronger a little at a time. No pain, no gain."

"Right," she nodded, noting her empty glass, then looking around the crowded dining room. "Where our waitress? I could use another beer."

"There she is," he pointed. "She's over there at the order terminal by the kitchen."

"Got it." She waited several seconds before pointing her finger at the waitress and whispering, "See me."

The girl across the room looked up from the terminal, as though she'd heard an unfamiliar sound nearby and was looking back and forth to determine its cause.

Sasha remembered the girl's name tag and did it again, only this time said, "*Carla*, see me."

The waitress turned around and stared directly at Sasha.

Sasha gave her a little wave, and then under her breath whispered, "Come to me."

The girl immediately made a bee line to their booth. "What can I get for you, honey?"

Sasha held up her empty glass. "Another blond ale, please?"

"Sure." She looked over at Travis and his half-finished beer. "And how about you? You okay for now?"

"I'm good. Thank you," he said as the overly perky and cheerful blonde spun around and departed. Travis looked into Sasha's eyes. "You do realize that that was just out-and-out spooky."

Sasha shrugged, "Hey, the book said a *Tractoria*, or Summons, could come in real handy. Especially at restaurants."

"Right," he acknowledged, but then pointed out, "but I'm thinking ordering a beer wasn't that particular function's *primary* purpose."

"I'm sure you're right," Sasha conceded. "But like you said, it's all just practice. To get good at *Chele*, the Triggers."

Travis said, "*And*...the book also said that we would be able to come up with our own Trigger ideas. And I think I've got one that might be interesting to try."

"What is it?" she asked.

"Well," he explained, "we've seen that we can change a single traffic light. But what if we can change many of them all at once?"

"How?"

"By triggering the ambulance strobe sensor," he replied.

She tilted her head and asked, "What are you talking about?"

Travis explained, "On many of the busier city streets with traffic lights on every block, in an emergency, when an ambulance needs to get somewhere fast, it turns on a strobe light on the top of the cab, mounted by the other emergency lights and sirens. If you've ever noticed what looks like a small white cylinder mounted on the light posts aimed down at the intersection—"

"Yeah, I've seen those," she interjected.

He continued, "They're sensors, waiting to detect the ambulance's strobe light. And when they do detect it, they turn a whole series of traffic lights green on an entire route so the ambulance can get through faster without stopping for cross traffic."

"So how do you think you could trigger that strobe function with magic?" Travis' idea initially sounded silly to her, but Sasha was actually getting curious now.

Travis said, "My guess is that since the sensor is looking for a sequence of light pulses, light is just a form of energy. As we've learned, magic is a just another form of energy. So we just focus on the strobe sensor instead of the traffic light's timer."

"And our focus thought is 'Ambulance Coming Through'?" she joked.

He chuckled. "Why not? Sounds good to me."

Sasha grabbed her purse and pulled out her wallet. "Okay! Let's go try it. See if you can get the waitress' attention this time and I'll get our check."

Travis softly commanded, "Carla, come to me."

Less than five seconds later the cheery waitress appeared again. "Y'all need anything else?"

Sasha held out her credit card, "Yes. You can forget that other beer for me. Unfortunately, we found out we have to go. We just need our check, please."

Carla smiled, "I'll take care of that right away for you."

As she walked away, Travis said under his breath, "Man, I could have really used that trick in high school."

Sasha laughed out loud.

CHAPTER 17
WILLIAM AND PENELOPE

HOTEL GRANDE BRETAGNE
ATHENS, GREECE

FLASH!

Penelope Angelucci startled at the brief flash of light that came from the main salon of the Presidential suite, reflected in her dressing mirror. Until that moment she had been alone in the elegant master bath touching up her makeup.

Now, she was no longer alone.

Dr. William Turner appeared in the doorway. He wore a tasteful black custom tailored suit, with black shirt and no tie. His long gray hair was pulled tight behind his head, flowing down between his shoulder blades, cinched with a thin strand of leather. "I'm back."

Penelope looked at him and shook her head in amazement. "How the devil do you *do* that? Just popping in and out like that."

"How do *you* prefer to travel? By broomstick or magic carpet?" He grinned at her.

"I fly commercial, albeit first class, thank you very much." She blotted her lipstick on a tissue, then turned her back to him and pointed at her unzipped gown.

"Do you really want to know?" he asked, pointing his finger at the small zipper tab, and with a gentle raise of his hand it zipped its own way up to the neckline of the elegant Oscar De La Renta original. The dark blue silken bodice was form fitting and the skirt gracefully cascaded down to mid-calf. He thought she really did look quite amazing in it.

"Would I even understand if you did?" Penelope walked past him into the master bedroom and found her shoes.

"You might," William replied. "Are you familiar with the Double Slit experiment, sometimes called Young's experiment? It was first done back in 1801. Or the main ideas of the Heisenberg Uncertainty Principle?"

"You're already over my head. Sorry, love. I'm a thoracic surgeon, simple blood and guts, knives and saws, not a physicist. Remember?" One elegant Jimmy Choo shoe was done. She put her toe in the second one.

William tried to explain, "Well, my somewhat unconventional mode of travel is based on the concept of an energy wave or particle being able to be in two places in space and time simultaneously. At the point of a singularity, one instance of the particle is completely destroyed while the other instance of it is recreated complete and intact."

"What's a singularity?" she asked.

"In this quantum space-time context, it is literally the application of my own magic. The point to grasp is, I don't actually travel from one place to another in the context of motion or movement. Rather, I simply cease to exist in one place and then I become me again and exist anew in another place in the very same instant of time. And when I say 'instant' I mean the exact moment of the actual execution of the spell. Whereas, it takes me at least ten seconds or more to summon the energy needed to actually do it. Which I guess you can think of that as like needing to get a running start. Only it involves breathing, powering up, not running."

"How can that possibly be true?" she asked. "You cease to exist and then re-exist? I don't believe it."

"It's basic quantum mechanics, my dear. What was theorized for years and finally observed at the subatomic quantum level, I have managed to apply at the physical macro level." He took a little bow.

"And how exactly did you figure this out without killing yourself or destroying the world or something?" Penelope did a little presentation spin for him, awaiting his approval. "Passable?"

He obliged, "Perfection, as always. A vision. Absolutely stunning."

"Thank you," she said. "So, you were saying about your phenomenal discovery…?"

"Ah yes," he continued. "It's nothing so terribly complicated or grand. I merely tested a theory which proved to be true."

"And what theory might that be?" she asked as she handed him a gold necklace, then turned around and lifted her long black hair.

William dutifully clasped her necklace for her, manually, and not by magic. He could smell her perfume. It was a familiar smell he'd not encountered in many years – a light fragrance, very close to the actual scent of a red rose. An ever so slight pang of regret echoed in his gut.

With a slight shudder William blinked away his momentary distraction and further explained, "The most basic axiom in magic states that with enough energy—and the *quantity* of energy is absolutely the governing element here—anything imagined can be made a reality."

Penelope concluded, "And since you thoroughly understand all of the quantum principles so well, you could easily imagine yourself as the quantum particle in the formula."

He nodded, "Exactly. That's *exactly* how it works."

Penelope picked up a couple of rings and a gold bracelet from the dresser top. "How far can you go?"

He shrugged. "I'm not sure at this point. Hundreds of miles at a time have not been a problem for me. My assumption is that the amount of energy consumed is proportional to the objective. Sufficient energy completes the task. Insufficient energy, it fails. Honestly, I just get a sense about making a jump when I do it. If I have any doubts, I don't go. Theoretically, in a moment of Singularity, there should be no limit. But I'm just not quite ready to put that to the test just yet."

"So what would happen if you tried to go farther than your energy could sustain?" Penelope asked.

Dr. Turner shrugged, "My guess is that, worst case, I would successfully be destroyed at the point of origin, but fail to be created at the destination, and thus obliterated. Best case, I end up right back where I started from having accomplished nothing."

She shook her head. "The first one sounds really bad."

"Indeed," he agreed. "Which is why I am very careful."

She abruptly changed the subject. "So what, if anything, did you learn on your last little excursion to Bavaria?"

William recounted, "I discovered that not only is Daniel DuMonde right here in Athens, just as Gerhardt foretold, but most of the other Inner Circle members are going to be assembled here very soon as well, if they're not here already. Presumably he's gathering them here for the certification. I'm not completely sure. But with Gerhardt out of the picture, that's not likely to happen."

"Then why are they all still coming?" she asked, picking up her clutch purse. "He called me yesterday and asked me to come meet him here to brief me, as I am supposedly going to be escorting the device on its road trip after it reaches Cairo. The route we're going to be taking is a bit complex. However, when we met this morning Daniel didn't mention to me why everyone else needing to be here in attendance."

William opened the door of the suite for her. "Then that's what we have to find out as soon as we can. And it is also why we needed rooms at this particular hotel."

Penelope stopped in her tracks. "What? They're all staying right here in *this* hotel?"

"Not all of them. Daniel is still staying aboard his yacht anchored just offshore. But, according to Allister's digital computer spies, the rest of them all have reservations here in this hotel." William added, "Which could be either very convenient for us. Or very dangerous, depending on why they are all coming here."

Penelope took his arm as they headed for the elevators. "Any kind of speculation come to mind?"

William pressed the down button and said, "Circling the wagons would be my first guess. And, of course, preparing in some way to unite and try to stop me."

"Isn't all of them gathered together a problem for us?" she asked as the bell chimed and the gilded metal doors opened.

"Or it could be an ideal opportunity," he said as they stepped inside the elevator car, adding. "It's keenly important that we seek and find them individually with both of us together. Strength in numbers is key. We must always have superior numbers."

As the elevator car began to descend, Penelope said, "What if they also know this, and *that's* the reason why they're all here? To confront you as a group?"

William swallowed with some difficulty at that thought. The tips of his fingers tapped on the back of the elevator doors, emphasizing his next five words as he said, "*We—can't—let—that—happen.*"

Penelope whispered with a faint smile, "Of course not."

William gave her a disarming smile of his own and said, "Besides, we should be able to sense their energy signatures from a little distance away. If we pick up too strong a concentration, then it will be time to blink out to places far away."

"And just leave me behind?" she frowned.

"Oh, no," Turner chuckled. "My little trick isn't confined to my physical body alone. Within certain limits I can take anyone or anything with me wherever I wish. And that means if we need to hit the panic button, wherever I go, you can go too."

Penelope felt slightly relieved, but then asked, "Does it hurt?"

He cast her a sideways glance. "Only a little."

"You're kidding, right?" Penelope really wanted to know.

"It's doubtful it will ever be required," he said. "And if it is needed, it's over before you even have to think about it."

"All right. Enough. I don't want to think about all of this anymore. New topic. So where are you taking me for dinner tonight?" she asked.

He answered, "*Strofi*. It's a favorite place of mine. Not too far from the Parthenon. The car I hired is waiting outside."

"Excellent," she nodded.

When the elevator's bell chimed, announcing they had reached the ground floor, Penelope abruptly let go of William's arm and stepped quickly to the side, pressing her back tightly against the side wall of the elevator car.

William turned to her in confusion. "*What*... in the world are you doing? What's wrong?"

As the elevator door fully slid open, William Turner heard Penelope scream out, "*Now*!"

He turned his gaze back to the open door to behold the furious face of Daniel DuMonde standing there. And he wasn't alone.

PART 2

NOVICES, PRACTITIONERS & MASTERS

"Physical strength can never permanently withstand the impact of spiritual force."

Franklin D. Roosevelt
May 4, 1941

CHAPTER 18

FROM THE JOURNAL OF WILLIAM TURNER

THE HEALING ARTS OF MAGIC

From prehistoric times, Medicine Men, Shamans, Witch Doctors, the Warlocks and Witches, Sorcerers and Wizards, and all forms of Magi were centrally involved in treating the various infirmities of their own people, often using natural healing practices that were erroneously considered to be magical. There is much confusion in this area, confusion which we shall endeavor sort out here in a straightforward manner.

For you see, most healing practices – even to this day, administered by licensed medical practitioners – largely work as a function of stimulating the human body to heal itself. That is exactly how antibiotics and vaccines work. The medicines themselves do not vanquish disease directly; rather, they boost the body's own natural immune system to defeat the invading microorganisms.

A bandage on a wound doesn't cause any healing. It merely protects a wound from further damage and infection. Stitches hold cuts together such that they may heal properly, but the healing is not a function of the thread of the stitches but what the body does for itself.

Is this not a true Confluence between the natural and the supernatural?

Nevertheless, there are indeed pharmaceuticals, chemicals, plants, herbs, and even elements of certain foods that have true healing and restorative properties. While bicarbonate of soda mixed with water can indeed neutralize the excess acids of an upset stomach, or quiet a sour one, and while there is nothing inherently magical about that remedy, you can be certain that it was the Magicians of ancient times who discovered this to be true, along with millions of other practical treatments.

Did you know that common cayenne pepper in your kitchen can be used to stop bleeding in severe wounds? It's true. Its capsaicin speeds natural blood clotting.

In ages past, where malnutrition was more the norm than the exception, it was common for people to suffer from diet related infirmities – e.g. scurvy from a lack of Vitamin C, addressed by increasing a diet with more citrus fruits. This is how Englishmen came to be called "limies." Their sailors brought limes with them onboard to prevent their naval crews from getting scurvy.

Iron deficiencies, and magnesium deficiencies are to be expected in those peoples who barely have enough food to survive. And yet again, it was those ancient practitioners of the healing arts, who often times were also the practitioners of the magical arts, who were at the forefront of relieving human suffering.

Understandably, a tonic or potion containing much needed vitamins, minerals, or other nutrients that demonstrably helped the sick to become well could easily be considered miraculous and/or magical. As has been aptly noted, most of the time, the supernatural is only the natural not yet understood.

The same is true for Magic.

As has been said many times herein, Magic is just the impartation of a form of energy for the purpose of accomplishing a specific goal. So in a sense, Magic shouldn't be thought of as "supernatural" activity at all, but a perfectly natural function for all those who understand it and know how to use it.

It's therefore understandable for those who are ignorant of Magic to see it as something supernatural, but some people go far beyond merely confessing their lack of understanding, and instead consider Magic to be "Unnatural." Or they may go a step further, seeing Magic as something inherently "evil," and its practice the works of evil ones.

Fear is a natural emotion. And the natural response to anything that causes fear is either to flee it or fight it. And that is typically what the Magi must face throughout his or her entire existence. This is a travesty, and all I can encourage you to do is to help those whom you can with your Magic, and stay out of the way of those who would be fearful of you or wish to do you harm.

Curationum Cantamen, or Healing Spells

The art of healing itself, whether it be manifested by purely physical means, or purely with your Magic, or perhaps even with a little bit of both, should be approached from the minimalist view first and foremost, not the maximum approach.

Ideally, with healing you are searching for the optimum solution, not a maximum or a minimum. But in the case of administering a medicine or a cure of any type, the idea of starting with a small dose and observing a reaction before administering more is a far better approach than starting with an overdose and making the situation far worse. Adding more is far easier than trying to undo something that has already been done that can't be undone. And even turning to the use of Magic itself may be an exercise in overkill and/or wasted energy.

Let me give you an example.

Let's say that someone has suffered a common mosquito bite. A bump has arisen on the surface of the skin, and it itches terribly. If it's scratched it could cause an abscess and thus become an even bigger problem. While it is true that you could simply put your finger on the bump and command it away, there is a much easier way to heal the bite without having to needlessly squander any of your accumulated energy.

For healing a mosquito bite, all you have to do is take a metal soup spoon and run it under hot water (not too hot, just as hot as you can reasonably stand it without getting burned) for about a minute. Then take the hot spoon and place the bottom of the bowl, the round side, on the mosquito bite and hold it there for thirty seconds. This will achieve the same result as only using your Magic, but with no energy lost.

And there is a simple reason for why this works.

In both instances of healing, with or without Magic, the mosquito bump and the itching are caused by the injection of a particular protein by the mosquito when it was extracting your blood from you. The human body interprets this protein as an infection and responds to it with the swelling of the surrounding tissues, specifically in an attempt to apply greater heat to it and kill it. But the normal temperature of the human body isn't quite hot enough to destroy this protein quickly and this is why it takes many hours, if not a day or more to heal naturally. The protein also irritates subdermal nerve endings, hence the itching.

If the hot spoon provides around 130 degrees of heat or more to the bump, the protein inside it is destroyed in about thirty seconds. If you were to use your Magic to bring the protein to at least 130 degrees and destroy it, you will have expended a non-trivial amount of energy. And for what? To repair something that could have been treated with a little hot water and a spoon?

With either treatment for the mosquito bite, the Magicians of old can be thanked. Before biologists and biochemists discovered the protein of the mosquito as the culprit, the reaction to mosquito bites was believed to be anything from a venomous toxin to an unclean spirit, both of which were addressed by the application of heat.

Nevertheless, there are a vast number of infirmities that may afflict the human body which are not as conveniently accessible near the skin's surface, nor as easily healed by a hot spoon – rather, there are dire situations where your Magic is specifically going to be needed, and in some cases may be the victim's only hope of survival.

The most common method of energy transmission between human beings is via the act of physical touch. Every human being learns fairly early on in life that a hug, an arm over the shoulders, holding hands, and so forth brings a noticeable sensation of comfort and pleasure. This should be obvious. And, of course, human life itself is created as the result of the greatest levels of human intimacy.

Imposito Manuum

Many of the world's most populous religions include as part of their prayers for the sick the act of Imposito Manuum, or the "Laying on of Hands." While for many people this activity may be interpreted as an act of symbolism or tradition, it is in fact an actual form of practicing the healing arts when infused with Magic. For mortal folk to do it, it may accomplish no more than provide comfort and encouragement. For the Magi, it is a physical connection intended to provide a pathway or conduit for healing energy.

Once again the application of energy is the key here.

Think about it: natural healing within the human body, where damaged cells are removed and disposed of, where new cells are grown and put into service, where toxins are filtered and eliminated, where foreign invaders are attacked and destroyed – all of this requires energy to make that happen. And energy is finite at any particular moment in time within a human being. Thus, a body heals as fast as its own energy can fuel all the tasks that need to be accomplished.

So, just as some medicines help stimulate and accelerate the natural healing process, so can an application of Magic via the laying on of hands. And that must be your focus thought for the healing treatment, i.e. to amplify the recipient's own personal energy and allow them to use it to heal more rapidly. In some cases, this can be very rapid, as in a matter of seconds or minutes that otherwise might have taken days, weeks, or months to heal naturally, if at all.

As always, energy spent is energy gone. Use your energy prudently, and continually refuel you own energy supplies.

To put this in a more practical perspective, a Novice Magi can use his magic to accelerate healing of minor cuts and bruises, short term viral infections such as a cold or sore throat, and to help reduce pain in more serious physical wounds. Think: First-Aid kit level.

The Practicing Magi should have no trouble vanquishing most physical infirmities in himself, and heal all but the most severe cases of illness in others. Think: General Physician level.

The Master Magi, as long as his own body can still heal itself at all, is practically impervious to physical injury or disease, and can restore any human who has not passed completely from the physical realm. Think: Miracle Worker.

However, please note the exception of a Magi not being able to heal himself at all. There are special circumstances of injury where no amount of healing Magic will help, other than to provide symptomatic relief and comfort.

So use your power to heal generously, but wisely.

CHAPTER 19
ALEXEY AND NANCY

THE PORT OF IZMIR, TURKEY

"Has the package been transferred from the submarine?" Alexey Borochenko asked Stephan Burke. Alexey stood next to the black Jaguar sedan in which he had just arrived. His passenger remained inside the car.

"Yes." Burke stood with a heavily armed security contingent and several workers standing at one end of a forty-foot steel shipping container. It looked no different than the hundreds of other metal containers stacked in the remote seaport warehouse. Some containers were rusting, others appeared to be still serviceable. The air smelled of diesel fumes, mold, and decaying organic matter. Burke gestured and nodded to one of the workers standing near the container's door.

The worker unlatched the door and opened it wide.

A flurry of broad-beam flashlights came on inside the vast and dimly lit warehouse, illuminating the interior of the long metal shipping container. Its contents yielded a wooden crate, about the size of a small refrigerator. It was heavily chained and securely locked. The workers immediately set about their assigned tasks of unchaining and opening the inner box and displaying its cargo.

Burke glanced back at the darkened windows of the Jaguar. "Is that Dr. Thompson from New York?"

Alexey nodded. "Yes. Nancy was going to be delayed a day in arriving on time in Athens yesterday, so, due to you and Daniel changing our itinerary, her route was diverted straight here, just as mine was from Kiev. Luckily, we were able to confirm that she could perform all of Gerhardt's required tasks."

Burke nodded and said, "It is probably for the best you two weren't there yesterday."

While the men continued to unlock all the locks and remove all the chains from the wooden crate, Alexey drew close and cautiously asked Burke. "Were you there? Did you see what happened?"

Burke gave a terse nod. "I was."

After an awkward pause, Alexey prompted, "So *what* happened?"

Burke shook his head as if to forget an unpleasant memory. "To be honest, it was all kind of a blur. I don't know if I remember it all."

"Tell me what you *do* remember," Alexey said.

"Just as we planned, Daniel, Frank, Walter and I were waiting for him to reach the lobby in the elevator. The four of us were there waiting in the lobby. With Penelope, we were more than sufficient to the task." Burke glanced over Alexey's shoulder at the workmen still uncrating the payload of the shipping container. "When the elevator door opened, we were ready. Penelope delivered him to us just as she was instructed. He was clearly surprised to see us and we caught him completely off guard."

Alexey had a sudden sinking feeling in his gut. "Are you going to tell me you let him get away?"

"No, no, no," Burke shook his head firmly. "We didn't give him time for that. Although, we're sure he tried, which was how, I think, we were able to eventually dispatch him."

"Explain."

Burke continued, "Daniel's plan was a synchronized Harvesting. By all of us simultaneously. Drain him to dust, if possible. We all pushed forward. As Daniel was the strongest of us all, his role was simply to hit him with an Icing Spell and hold him, while Frank, Walter, Penelope and I drained him of his powers."

"Did it work?" Alexey implored him.

"It was like nothing I've ever seen or experienced. I've done my share of Harvesting to be sure, but this was like sticking your fingers in a light socket. I mean, all three of us were thrown back on first contact a good two meters. But Daniel kept him pinned tight, and so we had another go at him. And again, and again. It felt like it was taking hours, in what was probably just a few frantic moments. Our own energy was draining so fast, I couldn't believe it. I thought any minute we'd all collapse dead away."

"And then what?"

Burke's face betrayed a struggle to truly understand what he himself was recounting. "He...collapsed."

"He fell down?"

"No," Burke shook his head vigorously. "I mean collapsed like a flan in a cupboard, like the air going out of a balloon. His whole body quickly shriveled, wrinkled, shrank, twisted, becoming smaller and tighter, like balling up a piece of tin foil, or crushing an aluminum beer can in your fist. Tighter and tighter until it was a nothing but a ball no bigger than a tangerine. And then, amid a spray of sparks and rays of light, that too crushed down upon itself, vaporizing into smoldering dust. Seconds later it was completely gone."

"So he's...*gone?*" Alexey asked, although his words were half question, half hopeful statement.

"Daniel believes so," Burke said. "He's the expert who believes he is close to gaining full Master level. I am barely a Practicing Magi. He believes the magic Dr. Turner's uses to travel was also the magic of his own destruction."

"And you are confident Daniel is correct?" Alexey eyes were pleading.

Burke replied, "I am confident that Daniel believes it to be a fact."

"I see." Alexey didn't sound completely convinced.

One of the workman waved to Burke, who then turned to Alexey. "They're ready. You can bring Dr. Thompson now. Does she have all the equipment she needs to perform the certification?"

Alexey nodded. "*Da.*" He moved to the passenger's side of the sedan, opened the door and said, "Nancy, it is time."

A tall, statuesque redhead covered in a full-length Russian sable coat exited the vehicle and strode confidently toward the open shipping container.

•

Another unseen pair of eyes carefully watched the scene within the shipping container unfold, listening to every word spoken. Everything was transpiring just as anticipated.

CHAPTER 20
ALLISTER, SASHA AND TRAVIS

THE UNIVERSITY OF TEXAS
AUSTIN, TX

"Professor Turner, there's someone here to see you."

Sasha looked up from her desk, actually relieved to take a break from reading and grading student's final exam papers. She looked at her administrative assistant, Cynthia Mitchell, as she paused one of her favorite *Boston* songs playing on her laptop and pulled out her earbuds. "Who is it?"

Cynthia was not only Sasha's admin, but in many ways she also functioned as Sasha's surrogate mother, always full of good advice and wisdom. Cynthia was in her mid-forties, African-American, a little over five feet tall, and readily admitted she needed to lose several pounds, always blaming her figure on a sweet tooth.

She shrugged and adjusted her glasses on her nose. "It's a gentleman calling himself Chief Inspector McKenzie. He says he's with Interpol or something. From London. Sounds official. Do you want to see him?"

Sasha's heart sank. Had they finally found her father? Was he still alive?

"Okay, you can show him in," Sasha said, as Cynthia closed her door once more.

Sasha quickly scanned her small office, looking for anything in need of tidying up.

Uh oh!

Her eyes locked onto her father's journal sitting on her desk. It was hastily stashed in a desk drawer just as her door opened again and Cynthia bade an elderly gentleman carrying a worn leather satchel to enter. He wore a dark gray, wool suit with a thin black tie. Sasha couldn't imagine anyone wearing anything like that in Texas in the summertime. Although, he didn't appear to be overly perspiring or uncomfortable.

He graciously extended his hand with a warm smile. "A good morning to you, Miss Turner. My name is Allister McKenzie. I'm with Interpol."

With some apprehension Sasha rose and took his hand, bracing herself for the worst news. Yet in the moment she touched his hand, an oddly warm sensation ran up her spine.

"How do you do?" Sasha greeted him, but with an unexpected yawn she did her best to suppress. "How can I help you, sir? Is this about my father? Has he been found? Is he all right?"

Allister looked over his shoulder, ensuring Cynthia was gone and that the office door was securely closed before he looked back at Sasha and asked, "May I sit?"

"Of course," she said.

Sasha pointed toward one of her two guest chairs and took her own seat behind her desk once again. She steeled herself for what she was sure he was about to say to her, fearing the absolute worst.

She could not have been more wrong.

"I'm here today, my dear, because I very much need your help," was all he said.

"I'm sorry?" She was genuinely confused. "Help with what?"

The old man placed his satchel across his lap and folded his hands over it. "I need your help in *assisting* your father."

"He's alive? He's okay?" was all she wanted to know.

"I trust so," he nodded. "Although, I've not heard from him in a day or two. But even if he is still alive, and I pray he is, I'm afraid he might not be for very much longer. That is, if I can't get to him and bring him some much needed help."

"Help him with what?" she asked.

"His mission," the old man replied.

"What *mission?*" Sasha asked, looking at him askance.

Allister took a pair of wire-rimmed glasses out of his jacket breast pocket and put them on. "I suppose this would all make a lot more sense to you if I started at the beginning."

"Please." Sasha's head was spinning.

Allister smiled, opening his satchel and removing his notebook. "I trust by now that you know your father is not merely a brilliant physicist, but he is also a Master Magician."

Sasha audibly gasped.

Thus far, all the talk and experimentation with Travis into the art of magic seemed like just so much entertaining fun and games, parlor tricks, and such. Hearing such a matter-of-fact declaration regarding her father come out of this elderly stranger's mouth suddenly made all of the fantasy she'd been living seem so much more real—*frighteningly* real.

"How would *you* possibly know that?" It was more of a demand than a question.

Allister checked inside his satchel for a pen, as well as patting at each of his pockets for one, all to no avail. With a minor frown of frustration he reached forth his hand toward a ballpoint pen lying on Sasha's desk a few feet away.

The pen silently rose into the air and floated over to his hand.

Allister McKenzie chucked softly as he caught it, catching her shocked expression. "I know he's a Master Magician, my dear, because I trained him to be one. I chose him, and he has sent me to choose you."

•

"Back up and start over," Travis implored Sasha, as he retrieved the salt, pepper, garlic powder, cayenne, and smoked paprika out of her spice cabinet. He began seasoning one side of a couple of prime ribeye steaks they were planning to grill for dinner.

Alamo looked bored, sitting on his favorite chair and glaring at Travis until he became drowsy and nodded off.

As Sasha cleaned several baking potatoes with a bristle brush under the faucet, she said, "I know, right? It's completely insane. I'm still trying to get my head around all of it, thinking any second I'm going to wake up and realize all of this has just been one crazy weird dream. Or make that a nightmare."

Travis finished applying all of his favorite seasonings to one side of the steaks, flipped them over with a set of metal tongs, and continued seasoning the other side as he recapped, "Okay, so you said this old guy, who's come all the way from England, just shows up out of the blue claiming he works for Interpol, which may in fact just be his day job, but in reality is really a Master Magician, just like your father. And he not just any old storybook Master Magician, but he's your father's very own Master, his personal teacher, the actual guy from his journal."

"Right," Sasha nodded, carefully pricking the skins of the potatoes in a few places each with the point of a knife and then brushing them with some olive oil. "Apparently they've known each other for over ten years. He told me my father was part of an ancient group of Master Magicians located in Europe. But then about five years ago, they became aware of another group of rogue Magicians, some of whom were scattered all over the world, who were primarily using their magical powers to enrich themselves." She stopped prepping her potatoes and observed, "Apparently, I'm starting to get the distinct feeling that avarice is a lot more common in the Magicians' Guild than you'd think." She resumed brushing the potatoes. "Anyway, these particular guys are supposed to be some kind of evil magic oligarchy, if you will."

"And these are the same guys your dad's been after?" Travis asked, watching Sasha place the large baking potatoes directly on the middle rack of her preheated convection oven, not really noticing that she put in three of them.

"One and the same," she answered. "A couple of years ago, Allister – his name is Allister by the way – asked my father to use his credentials and reputation as a world-class scientist to try and covertly infiltrate this group. He was sent to fool them into believing he was really one of them. Initially, it was just to surveil them, to keep an eye on their activities, but eventually it became much more than that when he learned of what they were planning."

"What were they planning?" he asked.

"Apparently, it's World War Three level, end-of-life-as-we-know-it, extinction level event kind of stuff. So his first priority became to stop their plans, because if they were to succeed, it would initiate nothing short of a worldwide holocaust. And then secondarily, he was to...uh...*deal with* each of the individual members of the group, as opportune circumstances presented themselves. And I mean *deal with* as in the whole dispatch, eliminate, terminate, kill kind of thing."

"Okay. So your dad's really a Wizard Secret Agent with a license to kill, with or without the Walther PPK. Got it. So why is this guy *here*? What does he want with *you*?" Travis asked, taking a sip of his glass of iced sweet tea that was resting on Sasha's white quartz countertop.

"He says he's here seeking help, sent by my father." Sasha went to the built-in Sub-Zero fridge and pulled out a bag of fresh lettuce, a container of cherry tomatoes, a cucumber, and some baby carrots for their salads. She only wore a pair of jogging shorts and a faded *Lynyrd Skynyrd* tee-shirt, which was a serious distraction for Travis.

Travis concentrated on maintaining eye contact with Sasha, or else he quickly would lose his train of thought. "What *kind* of help?"

"*Magical* help," she said, feeling a chill run though her just saying it out loud. The lettuce leaves first went into a stainless steel colander and then under the faucet in the prep sink in her work island. She rinsed each leaf of the Romaine separately and laid them to dry on a stack of paper towels.

"I don't get it," Travis said. "By your father's own definition, you're a Novice. What can a Novice do to help him?"

Sasha could barely get the words out of her mouth. "What I can do is grow past being just a lowly Novice and actually become a full-fledged Practicing Magician with a substantial amount of power."

Travis shot back, "Oh, really? And, pardon the pun, but how do you plan to magically pull off that trick?"

Sasha folded her arms proudly with a cucumber in one hand and a chef's knife in the other. "He's going to teach us."

Travis caught his breath. "*Us*? You mean as in *both* of us, not just you? Us *plural*?"

Sasha nodded with a mischievous smile and a wiggle of her eyebrows as she began to slice the cucumber on a wooden cutting board, which was fashioned in the shape of the State of Texas. "He told me that he needs *two* assistants, working along with himself, in order to help my father complete his mission. And he wants us."

"And so we're just supposed to just drop everything in our lives and go with him back to Europe?" Now it was Travis' head that was spinning. He dutifully fetched two salad bowls from a nearby cabinet and laid them next to Sasha's salad prep.

"Exactly," she confirmed. "That's the plan. Only not just Europe. He said we're also going to the Middle East, Israel, perhaps even Egypt."

"Wonderful, but who's going to watch your fat cat while you're gone?" He glanced over at Alamo, who was already fast asleep, as usual.

Sasha said, "If I leave enough food and water out, he'll be fine for a few days, or even a week. If I'm gone longer than that, Judy next door has a key. I can get her to check on him."

"Okay, and so when is this magical mystery tour supposed to happen?" he asked.

"We leave a week from today," she said as she popped a piece of raw carrot in her mouth and crunched it between her back teeth.

"Wait a minute! So our entire training in magic is supposed to happen in less than a week?" Travis couldn't believe what he was hearing. He'd read a good bit of Dr. Turner's journal himself by now. And from the sheer complexity of everything he'd read about thus far he could not possibly imagine gaining any serious competence in the practice of high magic for many, many years. In a few days? Ridiculous!

He was absently shaking his head back and forth. "How is that even possible, Sasha?"

She shrugged, "Apparently, under the tutelage of a Master, good things can happen swiftly. Trust me, I asked him the same question myself, and he seems to think, if we're willing, we can do it. Oh, and would you please hand me one of the boiled eggs there in the fridge. They should be on the second shelf in a little plastic bowl."

"But why us?" he asked, finding the eggs in the bowl she wanted and grabbing one.

"One, because he knows I'll do anything to help my father. Two, I know you'll do it if I ask you..."

Travis started to blush.

"And three, he's well aware that we already believe in magic, and that gives us a head start over anyone else right now."

"Oh yes, we *do* believe in magic." Travis smiled as he held the boiled egg before his face with his thumb beneath its base and his index finger on its tip. He commanded it, "Go to Sasha."

The egg slowly floated forward in midair, moving toward Sasha in a straight line. A few inches from her face, Sasha snatched it out of the air and said with an approving grin, "Thank you. And four, obviously we *do* have *some* skills."

Sasha proceeded to peel the boiled egg under the running water in the prep sink.

"Well, as long as we don't have to move anything bigger than eggs, pencils, or car keys, we should be fine." Another thought occurred to Travis. "But what about all those other members of his Master Magician group in Europe you mentioned? Why can't they help him?"

She paused her peeling and then said. "I asked him about that, too."

"And?"

Her voice sounded genuinely sad. "And he said that he and my father are the last of their kind. They've all died off over the years, and haven't been replaced. There is no one else available to help him."

Sasha retrieved her egg-slicer from a drawer and set it down on the prep-island. She opened the wires of the egg slicer without touching it, rather by just a swipe in the air above it with her index finger to her left. She pointed at the now shell-free egg and with a snap of her fingers made it promptly fly itself over to the slicer and position itself perfectly in the recessed oval. She swiped the air once more with her index finger to her right and the slicer's wires cut through the egg.

"Nice trick." Travis chuckled to himself. "So I guess the bottom line is we're really going to get a chance to be the Sorcerer's apprentice!"

"Yes, but hopefully with no walking broomsticks and water pails." Sasha's voice grew serious. "Travis, we're about to go oppose an evil group of witches and warlocks and fight them with magic in order to save the world." Her jaw dropped as she muttered aloud, "And you better believe that I never in a million years ever thought I would say something like that out loud for real."

Travis' smile faded. "Okay, I'm in, of course. So, like, uh...when does all this advanced training start?"

Right on cue the doorbell rang.

Sasha raised her eyebrows. "Right now. Oh, and you're going to need to get me another salad bowl, and season up one more steak."

Chapter 21
Penelope

The Mena House Hotel
Cairo, Egypt

Penelope Angelucci stood on her room's balcony, sipping a full glass of extremely rare Bollinger champagne, which tasted absolutely divine. It perfectly complimented a magnificent summer sunset framed above by a cloudless royal blue sky dissolving into a burned orange horizon – all of which was layered over forty lush green acres of gardens in the shadow of the Great Pyramids of Egypt. She lifted her glass in a silent salute to the grandeur and beauty around her. She so loved breathing in the warm, relaxing air of the desert.

Her room was beyond opulent, embellished with intricate handcrafted furniture, original artworks and priceless antiques. It suited her well. While not considering herself a snob, per se, just someone of more refined tastes, Penelope so loved to be spoiled. She certainly didn't hesitate to spoil herself on any and every occasion possible. However, on this specific occasion she didn't have to. She was a most pampered and honored guest.

"You played your part perfectly," complimented her host.

Penelope turned around and saw him standing in the balcony doorway. He was dressed casually in tan slacks, a loose-fitting cotton pullover, and slip-on shoes with no socks.

She nodded to him with a slight shrug. "What's done is done."

"Indeed." He came to her side. "Any of that left?"

Penelope pointed down to the ornate silver ice bucket holding her bottle of champagne. "Help yourself."

He did so, grabbing a spare crystal flute from the serving table on the balcony and extracting the half-full bottle from the ice. As he started to pour, he asked her, "Did they all believe it?"

She threw her head back with a toss of her long, dark hair and let out a half-laugh. "For a moment there *I* believed it."

"Then that's all that matters. As long as I'm dead in their minds, then I am free to move and act."

"I still can't imagine how you did that," she said.

Dr. William Turner explained to her, "As I told you before. It was just a show. A five-layer Protection Spell was firmly in place shortly after we stepped into the elevator."

Penelope suddenly recalled his five firm taps on the back of the elevator door as they began to descend, commanding, "*We—can't—let—that—happen.*"

William noted, "Daniel's Icing spell had no effect whatsoever. Just wasted energy. The others' pitiful Harvesting attack completely discharged back on themselves. Did you see them get knocked back initially? I didn't do that. They did. Unbelievable."

"From where I was standing I could only see you," she said. "And when you started dematerializing, it was just too much to watch. I closed my eyes tight, just praying for it to be over."

He laughed heartily. "All they saw, you included, was an Illusion Spell. I had already teleported to the opposite side of the lobby and watched it all myself. Although, I had to finish it quickly otherwise Burke, Frank and Walter would have unwittingly Harvested each other into dust."

"Why didn't you let them?" she asked.

William sipped his glass, taking a brief moment to nod in appreciation for the deliciously smooth and rich flavor, then answered, "Because that would have terminated the operation right then and there, and without capturing the device. We have to see this through to the very end. You know that."

Penelope nodded and took another sip of her own glass, "Yes, and we shall. They still seem to trust me completely, so we'll always know their every move and decision."

"Exactly," he agreed.

"So what did you learn in Turkey?" she asked.

"I followed Burke to Izmir. Alexey was there from Kiev as well as Nancy Thompson from New York. And, as we surmised, she did pinch hit for Gerhardt on the certification work. So now we have confirmation that the device is already functionally operational. I also watched her go through the full arming sequence and explain to Stephan and Alexey the complete detonation procedure. Arming codes, everything."

"You were physically close enough to them to learn all that while all this was happening?" She couldn't imagine that.

"Yes, very. Arm's length, in fact," he said.

She didn't understand. "How, without them seeing you?"

William just smiled at her as his visage starting becoming transparent, and in a matter of seconds, completely disappearing. A crystal champagne flute hovered in mid-air before her.

Penelope gasped. "When did you learn to do that?"

His image faded back to normal. "Oh, I can do a great many things that few other living beings know about."

She nodded in admiration and little bit of fear. "I'm truly impressed, Guglielmo. While I may eclipse you in years of practice, you were always so much more gifted than I."

William graciously accepted the compliment with a slight nod of appreciation and steered their conversation back to the topic at hand. "And so, my dear, it was that little trick of an Invisibility Spell which allowed me to learn precisely what we need to know when the time comes to shut the thing down."

"When does the device arrive here in Cairo?" she asked.

"According to Alexey, he told Burke its flight arrives here sometime late tomorrow afternoon," he said. "They're going to put it on an Egyptian military cargo transport truck, allegedly with a load of waste management equipment bound for Amman, Jordan. The shipment should leave here the following morning. But don't worry. We'll keep a close eye on it."

"Why not just take it while it's here?" She finished her last sip and held her glass out for a refill.

William obliged, pouring her a fresh glass. "That's not the plan. We have to follow it all the way to Syria, or even into Iraq if need be. That way we get access to all of the major players, sellers and buyers. If we don't cut off the head of the snake, then it just happens over and over again."

"Just the two of us?" she asked. "We're enough to stop them all?"

He shook his head and said, "No. There will be three more of us. My own great Master plus two new Practicing Magi he's bringing with him. With five of us, I'm reasonably confident it will be enough."

Her brows rose skeptically, "Five Magi against nine?"

"No," he said. "We'll have two full Masters and three Practicing Magi against one foolhardy megalomaniacal Practicing Magi slash wannabe Master, three true Practicing Magi, and five Novices, one of whom is so talentless he couldn't start a campfire."

Penelope shrugged and smirked, "Burke. Yes, he won't be much of a problem. Okay, I guess that sounds like more of a fair fight."

He grinned, "Which is also why when the time comes, here and there along the way, we shall seize every opportunity we can to make the odds even greater in our favor."

Penelope took a fresh sip of her champagne, then asked, "So tell me, who are these two new Practicing Magi accompanying Allister?"

William looked almost proud. "Americans. Allister is in the States as we speak recruiting them. They are two of the most promising Magi, at least according to Allister, that he's ever seen. A young Texan from Austin named Travis Gardner. And..." he paused.

His hesitation was all it took. She instantly knew.

Penelope's eyes went wide. "No, no, heavens no, Guglielmo, oh please no! Not Alexandra! You *can't* bring our daughter into this!"

CHAPTER 22

FROM THE JOURNAL OF WILLIAM TURNER

OFFENSIVE AND DEFENSIVE MAGIC

As has been stated many times before, the benevolent purpose of true Magic is for the purpose of doing good. However, since Magic can be wielded by certain humans who are themselves neither good nor benevolent, then that means Magic, unfortunately, can also be used for evil.

That is why all good Magi are in danger from mortal folk, many of whom mistakenly believe that all Magic is evil and therefore to be feared; and the good Magi are likewise in danger from evil Magi who see them as a direct threat.

It is for these reasons that even the good Magi must learn the Magic Arts of Battle, and endeavor to use these skills and resources to protect themselves and others, whenever necessity calls. And it will call.

There are five primary spells, or perhaps categories of spells is a better way to characterize them due to so many possible variations, that every Magi must learn to wield with great skill and force in battle:

1) **Praesidium Cantamen, The Protection Spell**

2) **Glacio Cantamen, The Icing Spell**

3) **Valebunt Cantamen, The Levitation and Propulsion of Objects**

4) **Aggressus Cantamen, The Offensive Affliction Spells**

5) **Dispareo Cantamen, The Vanishing Spells**

There are many more spells available, to be sure, but these five spell types will be more than sufficient to give you a well-rounded foundation. Let us discuss each in turn, as well as a bit of elaboration on a few of them of note.

Praesidium Cantamen

The Protection Spell is exactly what it sounds like. The Latin root "praesidium" denotes the idea of a fortress. It is energy used defensively to thwart an attack or even access by a foe. It can be used in a circumstance as simple as barring a door and preventing entry, to shielding an entire village with an impenetrable dome of protection. As always, what I am describing represents a continuum of required energy.

More energy, more protection.

The Protection Spell, therefore, has "scope."

Therefore, the Magi must use a focus thought of quantifiable scope such as: "None shall pass through this door." Or, "Nothing may enter this house."

The application of the spell does, however, require physical touch to initiate it. The Magi must touch the object or person – and, yes, it can also apply to living things, including the Magi himself – while giving a verbal command regarding the institution of the Cantamen, or Spell.

The spell can also be magnified by multiple touches. Each additional application of touch adds a layer of energy. The more layers that are in place, the stronger the overall shield of protection. Please note: the total strength of the spell is key here, because Protection Spells can only be broken by the original Magi who cast the spell revoking it, or by a stronger Magi's Magic vanquishing it.

This may all sound quite metaphysical and supernatural, but it's really not. Like all manifestations of Magic there are objective scientific principles in play here, set in motion by sentient thought and will.

A Protection Spell operates in a very similar fashion to the behavior of two polarized magnets brought together with similar poles, either positive or negative, facing one another. If so, the magnets will repel one another. And unless a stronger force pushes them together, they will remain apart repelling one another indefinitely.

However, with a Protection Spell, the form of energy used isn't simple magnetic energy, rather it is comprised of a network of microscopic plasma tubes of energy. They follow the elliptic waveform of electromagnetics, but are a distinctly different animal. They are U-shaped, with both open ends of the tube facing outward from that which is being protected. Thus, any force coming against them is rerouted back from whence it came.

Please note, this is not a simple reflection, as with a mirror, but a re-routing of energy at a perfect 180 degree U-turn. This way the energy field of the spell itself is not absorbing any damage, as would a mirror if it were, let's say, hit with a hammer.

In a cultural, traditional, or perhaps even theological context, many belief systems incorporate the idea of "blessing" something, which is in many ways a form of asking for a kind of Protection Spell for safety. That can apply to anything from a motorcycle rally, to a shrimp fleet sailing off for a good catch and safe return, to an individual's safe journey. Just realize that this is the type of Magic that is really being sought.

Glacio Cantamen, The Icing Spell

This spell is, conceptually, a defensive spell, most often referred to as an "Icing," which counterintuitively results from an offensive disbursement of power. The energy of this spell is directed specifically at the spinal cord of a foe, with the expressed intent of temporarily paralyzing them for the duration of the spell. Think of this spell like an anesthesiologist administering an epidural – only it isn't chemically interrupting the nerve pathways from the waist down, it is electrically interrupting the spine from the neck down. Physical contact is not required to initiate this spell, but the target must be within clear eyesight.

Your focus thought is: "Be Still."

An Icing comes in very handy during escapes, when guards and attackers can be momentarily immobilized as you safely pass by. It can also be used during confrontational interrogations, in lieu of shackles and chains. The subject of the spell can still see and hear and speak, they just can't move any of their extremities, as if they were locked in complete bondage, or paralyzed from the neck down.

This spell necessitates a relatively low level of energy to cast, so strong Magi experience very little energy loss on momentary Icings, and can use it to subdue and hold a captive for extended periods of time, if need be, without fully exhausting themselves.

An Icing normally only lasts for as long as the Magi who cast the spell is physically present plus a few minutes as the energy of the spell dissipates. A more enduring Icing is possible, but as always, that requires much more energy, and at some point the energy will be expired and the spell broken. However, it is possible to create more perpetual Icings when the Icing Spell is augmented with certain chemicals, herbs, and sometimes toxins. This is a very dangerous practice and can run the risk of leaving the target seriously harmed and can even be fatal. It is not recommended, but has been known to be practiced by some evil Magi.

Valebunt Cantamen, The Levitation and Propulsion of Objects

This most common of tactical spells expands the idea of the energy characteristics of the basic Protection Spell, but adds a layer of vector mathematics to it.

Instead of a spell repelling anything coming from a specific direction back in the opposite direction, this spell is applied to an object – and that object can even include the Magi himself – and serves specifically to counteract the gravitational energy pull of the Earth.

However, much like flying a helicopter, the concepts of lift and altitude must be considered, followed then by a specific directional vector, all occurring simultaneously in three dimensions. But fear not, the Magi does not have to make all these calculations manually in minute detail; rather, he only need exercise his will on the desired final destination location of the levitated object. His Magic fills in all the intermediate factors, vectors and parameters.

Think of a pitcher throwing a baseball.

The pitcher gets the sign from his catcher to throw a fastball. The catcher positions his glove as a target. The pitcher's focus is to hurl the baseball with maximum velocity and accuracy at the target. He's not thinking about how many pounds per square inch of pressure must be applied to the ball, or the launch angle, delivery angle, or the angle and speed of rotation, and such. He just winds up and lets it rip – as a single thought. His volitional movement Magic makes all the calculations and communicates it to all the bones, muscles, sinews and tendons in his back, legs, arm and hand for him to successfully complete the task.

I would suggest you initially attempt the movement of objects in a small way at first, using very small objects: a cotton ball, a tissue, a pen or pencil. And for the Novice, short distances are perfectly acceptable. As your strength grows, so will your accuracy and distance.

From a combat perspective, this spell has many obvious applications: e.g. using nearby objects as projectiles, or summoning objects that can readily be used as weapons, landing a blow on an opponent from a distance, and so forth. Imagine being able to hurl an entire drawer full of sharp knives at a combat opponent, giving flight to all of them simultaneously. Perhaps your foe can manage to avoid or stop a few of them, but some may fly true and find their targets.

Furthermore, using this same type of practical application Magic, no form of bondage, save a superior Icing Spell (possibly even and Icing Spell augmented chemically), can ever hold you. For you will be able to use your Magic to untie any knot, open any shackle or lock, or open any door – i.e. doors without Protection Spells in place, lest you are strong enough to break them.

One of the great mysteries of antiquity has been to figure out exactly how so many great cities, temples, and other massive structures constructed in eons past were built of massive stones and monoliths, virtually impossible to move even with today's construction technology. How were the pyramids constructed? What about the great temples of the Inca? The

Temple of Baalbek in Lebanon? The Gateway of the Sun at Tiahuanaco?

The simple answer is, they were built by the magical powers of their Master Magi leaders. And now you know how it was done.

Your focus thought for levitation can vary dramatically. But basically it is going to boil down to a mental command, such as "Book come to me," or "Chair arise and move to that corner."

Think: Keep it simple, but be specific.

A common question that often arises in this discussion is: Can a Magi use this type of Magic to fly?

The simple answer is yes, but such application is rarely necessary outside of very limited tactical flight used to reach some object not easily accessible, or to rescue a living creature in peril and so forth. The magical art which addresses transportation will be discussed forthwith under the topic of the Dispareo Cantamen, or a Vanishing Spell, which we shall get to in our discussion due course.

Aggressus Cantamen, The Offensive Affliction Spells

These type of spells deal with the use of magical weaponry. They are to be used only when all defensive capabilities are exhausted and there is no other alternative but to defend yourself or others without engaging a foe and having no choice other than to vanquish them. Developing and perfecting these spells are analogous to carrying a loaded firearm, having a sword at your side, or being in possession of any other type of lethal weapon. These spells must be used judiciously, and always from a perspective of proportionality.

However, not all offensive spells are lethal. Some are only designed to inflict discomfort or disability, in an attempt to stave off an attack.

The first example of a non-lethal spell is a simple Exarmet Cantamen, or Disarming Spell.

Our example shall be something along the lines of a foe bearing a knife or gun or any other small hand weapon, threatening you. Using the skills developed in your training of Levitation and Propulsion of Objects, you could choose to knock the weapon out of the attacker's hand and ensure it is propelled far enough away that it is no longer a threat.

As an aside, a personal favorite of mine is the ability to engage the safety on any firearm that has one, rendering it incapable of firing, having it jam, or merely crushing the weapon rendering it permanently inoperable. You also might try simply destroying a firing pin, but that requires more energy and training to do satisfactorily.

Then there is the Unda Cantamen, or Wave Spell.

This spell is most appropriate to rebuff multiple attackers coming at you as a unit. This spell will be a combination of what you've learned in Praesidium (Protection Spells) and Valebunt (Levitation and Propulsion of Objects).

That is, with a sweeping wave of your arm, you are going to release a wave of plasma energy, but not stationary energy, rather energy propelled forward, radiating out like a wave. As such, it will be stronger and more focused nearest its point of origin, and weaker and more dispersed as it moves away from you in wave form, expanding its radius.

Your Focus Thought: "Be gone!"

Likewise, there is also the Pulsus Cantamen, or the Pulse Spell.

The Pulse Spell is roughly the same idea as the Unda (Wave Spell), i.e. launching a projectile of energy at a foe, but in this instance it isn't in a contiguous wave form, rather it is a concentrated pulse of energy. Imagine it like a snowball or a baseball in size relative to your hand.

The physical technique used here is to first start with your throwing hand in a loose fist, with your thumb extended, like the thumb's-up gesture, but tipped back such that your thumb just touches your chin as you breathe out warm air in the form of forceful energy into the palm of your cupped hand. The hand then comes forward, opening the fingers with a deliberate flourish, and rotating them – clockwise for a right-handed thrower, counterclockwise for a left-handed thrower.

Of special note here, the Focus Thought for a Pulse Spell is quite variable. Basically, you get to decide the intensity of the Energy Pulse you are about to throw.

Your focus thoughts might range from: "Knock Down," to "Stun," to "Break Bones," to "Destroy." Once again, the measure of energy you expend depletes the total energy store of what you currently possess at that moment. And it is also very important not to let base emotions dictate the ferocity of your pulses. You can end up wasting a lot of energy that way, and potentially causing much more harm than you intended.

I must confess, it is true that there are such things as Mors Cantamen, or Death Spells.

Death Spells should only ever be used in the most extreme of situations where no other alternative exists for safe egress or resolution of a situation, save taking a life.

There is nothing overly complicated about a Death Spell. The same principles of Magic apply:

- Will it.
- Expend the Energy to Accomplish it.
- It shall be done.

Applications of a Death Spell often involve conjuring the failure of a human target's internal organs. For mortal folk, they are extremely vulnerable to this form of attack. Magi are much more protected, especially regarding the brain.

Should you find yourself engaged in mortal combat against a strong Magi, it is strongly recommended that you focus on attacking the thoracic internal organs, such as the lungs or heart. Lungs may be easily crushed. The human heart, which is organized into four sections, is especially vulnerable to cleaving in two. Left atrium and left ventricle can be separated completely from the right atrium and right ventricle. The result is instantaneous heart stoppage. It also generates enough shock to the nervous system to cause the target to lose consciousness almost immediately.

From a "form of execution" perspective, while conceptually somewhat grotesque, the result of the technique is quite humane, as compared to crude manual beheadings, the electric chair, lethal injections, firing squads, hangings, burning at the stake, stoning, etc. The subject may momentarily feel the initial collapse of the lungs, the same way a drowning victim feels at the very outset, except their anguish only lasts a second or two before the heart is cleaved. From a level of pain standpoint, there is little to none because it's over so quickly.

This form of attack, used for centuries between various warring factions of Magi, has come to be colloquially called "Taking the breath away, and breaking a heart." So this act is a lot less of a romanticized metaphor and more of a euphemism for a literal function.

Lastly, such a Death Spell does require some form of physical contact to initiate the process and impart the requisite energy. Fortunately, Master Magi are typically the only ones who possess the power necessary to master such techniques. However, some Practicing Magi have successfully accomplished it on rare occasion.

Please note: our discussion of other Death Spell techniques henceforth is for reference purposes only.

That is, good Magi do not engage in the more gruesome forms of Mors Cantamen, or Death Spells, but evil Magicians have been known to do so with horrifying regularity. It is of no value for you to practice any of their techniques, but it is important for you to know of them and be prepared to defend yourselves against them.

One of the more common evil Death Spells is Incendium Cantamen, or Organic Combustion.

Literally, it is a spell that causes human flesh to erupt into flames.

The spell uses a variant form of the common electrolysis process, or the separating of oxygen from hydrogen in water, to transform the water content in the human body into a flammable form of released hydrogen and then igniting it. It is an extremely painful and horrible way to die, literally burning on the inside and the outside.

Another evil Death Spell is a Pestilentia Cantamen, or Pestilence Spell.

Any form of disease or pathogen can be conjured and inflicted upon a victim. The reality of this possibility highlights yet another reason why good Magi are sent forth to heal. Sometimes infirmity is of natural organic origin, and other times it can be the evil works of others.

Dispareo Cantamen, or The Vanishing Spells

Vanishing Spells are used to make a Magi visibly disappear. Why a Magi may wish to disappear is up to that particular Magi, but how he disappears determines his state.

You basically have three choices:

1) to simply not be seen, i.e. made invisible, although the Magi is still physically there;

2) to disappear and transport to a new location; or

3) to both disappear and transport to a new location, but create a lingering illusion in the original position to deceive an observer.

With the exception of a simple Invisibilis Cantamen, or Invisibility Spell, which all Practicing Magi can do, the other Vanishing Spells are primarily reserved for only the most powerful of Master Magi. And most Masters take a lifetime to master them, if ever. The reason for this has always been thought to be a function of talent or innate ability. I've discovered in my own experience that's only half true. What is of greater import in executing successful Dispareo Vanishing Spells is accessing super-levels of power.

The reason for this is because advanced Vanishing principles are also quantum mechanics principles. Vanishing deals with the recognition that all physical matter exists in terms of waves and particles at the quantum level, as well as the realization that even what are called particles are simply wave energy clusters.

All solid matter is really an illusion.

What we comprehend as solid objects are only intellectual constructs we create to keep us sane and to provide some sense of normalcy. In fact, there is far more empty space, i.e. true "nothingness" in between energy particles and waves than there is actual energy occupying space.

Think of it on the macro level in terms of the volume of all of outer space. Now think about the volume of space taken up by all physical stars and planets there are versus the vastness of empty space in the universe. As such, waves of energy can be manipulated from one form to another with Magic, irrespective of perceived size and mass.

Here are the family of Dispareo Cantamen, or Vanishing Spells. There are three Vanishing Spells in particular that we shall discuss:

1) Transvectio Cantamen, or Teleportation Spell

2) Invivibilis Cantamen, or Invisibility Spell

3) Immutatio Cantamen, or Transmutation Spell

Transvectio Cantamen, or Teleportation Spell

A Teleportation Spell is what is used to travel from any point A to any other point B instantaneously. It involves using a Master's Magic to create a "Singularity" event, which is a point in time where mass and energy are technically infinite. As such, all forms of energy can be manipulated, and are no longer constrained by three dimensional Newtonian physics, nor even by time itself.

Important Note: "Infinity" doesn't mean everything existing at once. It means "access" at once to everything and everywhere that "can" exist.

Not to belabor the technical mechanics of teleportation, the process of actually doing it is to first summon the requisite energy, which consists of at least five deep cleansing and energizing breaths, while at the same time picturing a specific destination in your mind. As your energy builds you will physically feel it. Every sense will sharpen. You shall hear a very high pitched frequency as time-space waveforms are aligning and coinciding, creating finely tuned harmonics. When that energy peaks, it shall be converted to pure light.

Your instantaneous focus thought is: "Go."

And then it happens in an instant.

The next thing you know, you shall be where you wished to be. The greater the distance of space and time that needs to be travelled takes more and more energy. So be mindful of the ranges of your capabilities. If you try to leap over a crevasse too far, you might not make it to the other side and plummet to your death.

Invisibilis Cantamen, or Invisibility Spell

This spell is primarily a defensive spell, providing the perfect form of camouflage. It not only cloaks you within the visible light spectrum, but a few others as well, such as the infrared and ultraviolet spectrums. Unfortunately, by itself, invisibility can't stop x-rays or gamma rays—or bullets, bladed weapons, or spears. It's simply a visual effect.

You may therefore be wondering if an Invisibility Spell and Protection Spell can be used simultaneously. The answer is yes, as long as you remember to cast them both separately. You can certainly bar a door with a Protection Spell, and should your foe come through the window, be hidden away from sight inside an Invisibility Spell. Applying a personal Protection Spell to yourself while inside a sphere of if invisibility is another option.

Invisibility is a mainstay of Master and Practicing Magi, used by some on almost a daily basis. The function of this spell is very easy to understand. Much like a basic Protection Spell, an Invisibility Spell involves the rerouting of energy waves, in this case, light waves.

When an invisibility spell is cast, it creates a perfect energy sphere around you. This sphere absorbs all light waves the instant they impact the perimeter of the energy sphere, and then retransmits those waves on the exact opposite side of the sphere, matching the wave's original velocity, direction vector, and frequency exactly, such that the effect is as though all light passed through you transparently – thus rendering you invisible.

Think of this function like one of those desk novelties where five steel balls are suspended from two wires each in a perfect row.

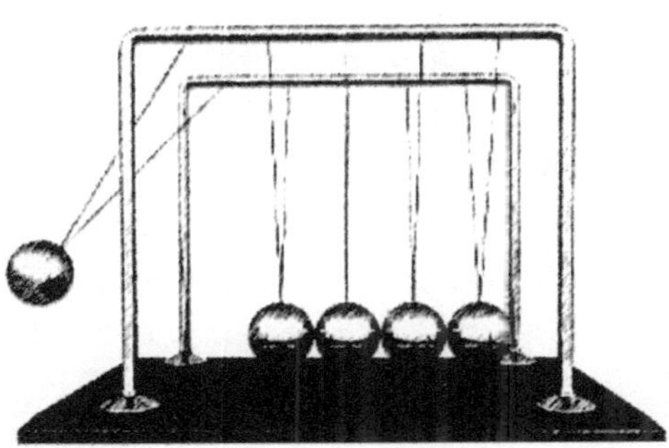

If the first ball is swung outward and released, it strikes the second ball, but only the fifth ball is sent flying outward on the opposite end of the row of balls. On the fifth ball's return fall, it strikes the fourth ball, and the first ball is sent flying again. And this exchange continues until all the energy is expended. And yet, balls two, three, and four never really move. But it's obvious that the energy from the first and fifth ball are passing through them. This is what the invisibility energy sphere does with waves of light.

Using an Invisibility Spell has two main practical applications: hiding and spying. It really serves no other useful purpose, but for those specific needs, it is most effective.

There is an important variant of the Invisibility Spell to be aware of as well. It is the Illusion Spell.

Praestrigiae Cantamen, or Illusion Spell

While invisibility is achieved by manipulation of light waves to achieve transparency, there can be visual exceptions deliberately created. That is, these same light waves can be manipulated akin to the pixels on a television screen to make appear any image or to conjure any animation of images the Magi desires. When several of these type of spells are combined in a sequence, it can achieve some remarkable effects and amazing illusions, such as a Magi transforming into a terrifying beast.

But note: it is only an illusion, not reality.

If the Magi really wanted to become something else, he would have to use a Transmutation Spell.

Immutatio Cantamen, or Transmutation Spell

This type of Magic is also sometimes referred to in modern parlance as "Shape-Shifting." It deals with a rearrangement of quantum waves to become coincident with alternate physical templates.

Please note, starting and finished size is meaningless. Since space-time inhabits over 99% of universal volume, as opposed to less than 1% the illusion of energy as mass, transmutations are limited only by the imagination of the Magi. And yes, that can include completely fictional creatures of myth and lore, not just existing ones.

Transmutation Spells are most often used by good Magi almost exclusively upon themselves, in order to hide in plain sight, or to spy – much like simple vanishing. They are more often used by evil Magi on mortal folk as a form of punishment or torture. So, yes, it is possible to transform a human being into virtually any form of animal – a chicken or perhaps a salamander, or even an insect that the Master Magi desires.

Just note that when a transmutation has occurred, while still retaining their own consciousness, magical skills, and energy, the target of the transmutation, is bound by the physical limitations of their newly reconstituted form.

On one hand, assuming the abilities of an alternate life form may be desirable – e.g. if a Magi wished to become an eagle or a hawk and then silently spy on an enemy camp, or track someone's movements from high on the wind currents with the sharpest eyes of any creature. Or perhaps even to become a mouse, if a very small opening is all that is available to gain access to an important objective.

On the other hand, the evil Magi have also often been known to use Transmutation Spells specifically for their own twisted forms of terrorism, intimidation, and frightening ignorant minds into submission. This is where most Leviathan (dragon), Nosferatu (vampire or living dead), and Lycanthrope (werewolf) legend comes from.

Therefore, be aware that flying, reptilian, fire-breathing dragons can indeed exist, and have throughout the ages. But at one point in their past they first possessed human form.

Of special note: evil Magi who take on alternate life forms on a regular basis run the risk of losing much, if not all, of their humanity, and in many ways physically becoming their alter-shape. This phenomenon can be so powerful that becoming human in form again, if they are still able to do so at all, is actually their disguise, not their true form.

Lastly, with respect to Transmutation Spells, let us now consider the scenarios of changing the inanimate into the animate, and vice versa.

Inanimate to animate transmutation with real Magic isn't exactly as it has been often portrayed in a great deal of prose and film.

It is, however, possible to turn someone into stone, just as the Gorgon Medusa did in Greek myth of the hero Perseus – and in doing so, thereby killing that person. This practice is really more of a Death Spell than a strict transmutation per se, akin to using a Combustion Spell to ultimately turn someone into a pile of ash.

Conversely, causing an inanimate object to become a living thing – not just a moving thing, nor an articulating thing – but to become a fully sentient being is not within a Magi's purview of powers. All creation of true sentient energy is a manifestation of Divine Providence, not man.

The exception to this truth would be a transmutation of a very basic organic source material such as wood or stone, being made into one of the lowest non-sentient lifeforms, such as an insect or worm or perhaps even a serpent, and decreeing it a modicum of the Magi's own life force energy to permit it to move. Thus, this is how a wooden staff may become a simple serpent.

However, please note that this type of transmutation Magic would not be applicable to wooden puppets who wish to become real boys. That is but a child's fairy tale. Although, it is very possible, and sometimes useful, to animate a puppet without strings for dramatic effect. But doing that is just simple Levitation and Propulsion of Objects.

CHAPTER 23
THE INNER CIRCLE

SALAH EL-DIN CITADEL
CAIRO, EGYPT

What remained of the Inner Circle's leadership sat as equals around the large circular table set in a private room in the Gawhara (Jewel) Palace. The palace was built by a renowned Ottoman army commander by the name of Mohammed Ali for his last wife. It was among the many intriguing structures, museums, gardens, and famous mosques located within the massive Salah El-Din Citadel complex, built in the late twelfth century by the great Saladin. He was the founder of the Ayyubid dynasty and the renowned warrior who fought against the European Crusaders.

Alexey Borochenko asked the question on everyone's minds. "What if the client should be so brazen as to actually *use* the device on a densely populated area?"

Daniel DuMonde threw up a hand in frustration. "Alexey, you know they would not dare to be so foolish and reckless. We've discussed this a hundred times. It would be like throwing a match on barn full of straw. They just want the power to blackmail and extort."

Alexey just shook his head in wonder, but did not respond.

"It's true," Burke added. "The retaliation would be nothing short of the beginning of a nuclear World War III. Millions would die in a matter of days."

"Perhaps billions," interjected his Excellency Archbishop Renaldo Vasquez from Argentina.

Vasquez was a large man, completely bald, with a large scar beneath his left eye trailing down to his jawline. The scar was earned in a knife fight decades ago, but was a daily reminder of his nefarious youth, in a time long before joining the priesthood. That day, he was dressed modestly in a business suit and without any of his formal priestly vestments. Despite being a high ranking prelate, he was steeped in Marxist-inspired Liberation Theology and well-known in the church and throughout South America for espousing many radical and controversial views.

He turned to Dr. Thompson and coyly asked, "Nancy, did not one of your country's founding fathers once say that the tree of liberty must be refreshed from time to time with the blood of patriots and tyrants?"

"Yes, Renaldo, that would be Thomas Jefferson, our second president." Nancy wore a loose fitting, floor-length gauze gown, which tastefully and modestly draped her elegant frame, complimented by a matching headscarf, in deference to the officials and local citizens in the Islamic section of Cairo, Egypt.

Archbishop Vasquez continued, "The Vatican and the Holy Father himself has been very clear of late on the state of affairs of this planet when it comes to the dire crisis of global warming. In the most recent encyclical, the church has taken a stand on the catastrophic warming of the planet. We've known since as long ago as 2009, as was officially declared at the Copenhagen climate conference, that this planet can't viably sustain a population of over one billion human beings. Something significant must be done."

Dr. Walter Stephens, a Kavali Prize winning astrophysicist and from Sydney, was a tall, thin man with light brown hair, a thin moustache, and deep-set blue eyes. He took the occasion of Vasquez's odd remark to speak up, his thick Australian accent taking a bit of the harsh edge off his comment. "So, right, Renaldo. Then, according to you, your church and your Pope, it's perfectly okay, then, if six billion people or so die?"

The Archbishop was smug. "Considering all the barbarous players currently on the field of battle, the world could potentially be much better off. Yes?"

"Gentlemen," DuMonde interrupted. "Enough of this. It's a strawman argument. Worldwide extinction of eighty-five percent of the world's population is *not* our goal."

Vasquez wouldn't let it go, saying with a thin smile, "But it could turn out to be a most beneficial byproduct. The Good Lord does move in mysterious ways. Does He not?"

DuMonde shot back, "*Mon Dieu!* Let's not have any more of that talk here. All right? We have much more important matters to discuss before the product departs for Damascus."

Walter threw out an idea. "How about this notion, just to make sure that nothing, shall we say...*untoward*..." he exaggerated that last word while glancing directly at the Archbishop, "...happens to the device. How about we do something to render it inoperable."

DuMonde shook his head. "Sorry, but we cannot. They will have their own scientists on hand ready to inspect it upon delivery, and if everything isn't working exactly as advertised, then the deal is off, and then it will be very unlikely we'll ever sell another one."

"I see," Stephens conceded.

"Personally," Nancy Thompson chimed in, "I think they absolutely *will* detonate it." She paused for effect, watching their eyes react – most in alarm, save the Archbishop's in satisfied pleasure. She continued, "They will surely do it in a widely publicized test, that is. Most likely an underground test in the middle of the Syrian or Iraqi desert, a demonstrable event that sets seismographs atwitter all over the world, to boldly announce on the world stage the level of their awesome new power, and their membership in the nuclear club. And they will then move quickly to buy another one."

DuMonde concurred, pointing at Nancy for emphasis, "*Exactly*, which is why the device *must* be able to work. And in turn, this is what will precipitate the rush by every other state in the entire region to similarly arm themselves as well. And this also means we must be fully ready to meet all that demand before any would-be competitor does."

General Mohammed bin Faisal had been content to watch and listen to the discussion up to this point. As was his custom, the general wore his khaki military uniform with dark gray epaulets which featured his rank insignia in gold. He was a barrel-chested man, with neatly trimmed black curly hair and a thick black moustache; although, he always looked in need of a shave day or night. His acne-scarred complexion was darkened by the sun, save the orbits of his eyes which stayed protected by a pair of designer sunglasses he wore whenever he was outside in the daylight.

The general spoke up on the point of weapon inventory, "Yes, but where can we get an adequate supply of this type of product? Pakistan will not completely disarm in a liquidation sale, even for a king's ransom. My kingdom will not be satisfied with buying only one. How is this seller's market we are creating going to sustain itself?"

DuMonde gestured to Alexey. "That's where Alexey comes in."

Alexey nodded. "I have contacts, very *high level* contacts, the *highest* you might say, in Russia. They have more than enough surplus stockpile from the Cold War arms race to incinerate the world many times over. They will be most cooperative and discrete in meeting our supply needs. And they prefer to deal with one primary wholesaler instead of selling them themselves retail."

"But why would they do this?" the general asked. "Is this not inviting an attack on themselves by NATO or thee Americans?"

Alexey replied, "I believe they will gladly accept the risk of serving this market because they have an economy built almost solely on oil and gas production, which is currently not producing the sky high returns of previous years, and so the country is now starving—literally—for cash."

Burke added, "And with international sanctions being lifted on Iran, their oil will begin flowing again on the world market, and it will then compete that much more with Russia's driving world oil prices down that much further. Russia must diversify their income streams."

The general wasn't satisfied. "Surely the Americans will know."

DuMonde conceded, "Of course they will. And they will rant and rave about the dangers of nuclear proliferation and the need for treaties and such. And then they will threaten sanctions – which only increases our coffers as intermediate merchants of other needed commodities – but one thing we know – they will do *nothing* to stop it. The United States has lost its taste for involvement in wet work that doesn't directly concern them. They have lost their will to be the world's guardian of peace."

"But surely they will take some forceful action if a close ally is threatened," the general insisted.

DuMonde laughed, "Do you mean the way in which they abandoned Israel these last few years? Or how they let Russia just take away parts of Ukraine? Or how they ignored Syria's slaughter? Or perhaps how they turned tail and ran from Iraq giving it up to the jihadists? Or how they cowered from the Chinese as they work to conquer the entire South Pacific unopposed and look to expand their fortunes even further?"

Dr. Nancy Thompson added, "It is true. The United States has lost its taste for foreign wars, and moves slowly to respond to the threats washing up on its own shores and breaching its borders. However, I have no doubt it will do all in its power to take care of its own when no other option is available to them. But in the end, as far as the rest of the world goes, it will do little more than send a little money and well wishes."

General bin Faisal gave her a stern look. "I sincerely hope and pray you are correct, Doctor."

Daniel DuMonde's eyes scanned his colleagues as he gave them all a stern word of caution: "But even if Nancy is right, and the US elects to stay on the sidelines, we cannot be naïve, nor blinded by avarice or presumptuousness. Pride goes before a fall. There will undoubtedly be forces aligned against us, intent on stopping us. We must be ever vigilant."

It was Judge Frank Donaldson's turn to speak up. Frank certainly looked the part of the typical well-to-do Bay Area Californian. Despite being in his early sixties, he strove to project the image of a much younger and more virile man with well-coifed and twice a month colored dark brown hair, a flawless tan, and a thirty-thousand dollar Da Vinci veneer smile. He was dressed in a dark blue Armani suit with matching tie and pocket square.

He wryly observed, "Well, at least we can be ever thankful that Dr. William Turner is no longer a problem. Right?"

That comment was greeted with a general murmur of laughter, hubris, and no small measure of relief.

The only other member of the Inner Circle's leadership who had remained completely silent throughout the entire meeting was Penelope Angelucci. She played her part well, and did not do anything she felt might expose her true loyalties with William Turner.

Although, one important event did occur in the meeting that greatly alarmed Penelope. Just as William's name was mentioned and everyone enthusiastically reacted, Penelope noticed how the whites of Nancy Thompson's eyes momentarily faded to a brilliant shade of yellow as the irises and pupils constricted from a perfect circle to the long vertical black slit of a reptile.

Penelope instantly realized that Dr. William Turner had no idea that one of his opponents was obviously not only a full Master, but she was also a dragon.

Chapter 24
Allister, Sasha and Travis

In the Texas Hill Country
Austin, TX

"You can put me down now, Travis."

Sasha Turner was hovering approximately three feet above the ground, her legs still in the cross-legged position she'd had while seated on the ground a little over two minutes ago. Travis sat on the ground a few feet away from her, just opposite her position, also cross-legged, with his hands raised chest-high, fingers wide.

Allister McKenzie, who leaned against a nearby live oak tree, was most pleased. His two new charges had taken to his instructions and leadership faster than any Novice Magi he had ever trained in his entire life, and that included Sasha's father.

"I can hold you a little longer," Travis panted, clearly winded.

"I'm over this," Sasha protested. "You're just going to exhaust all your energy. Put me down."

"Just a few more—" he began.

Sasha put her fist to her mouth, thumb to chin, breathed a measure of force into her palm and then hurled it at Travis, knocking him backward into a rolling backflip, covering him with dead grass and burs. Sasha instantly dropped to the ground, landing hard on her behind with a pronounced grunt.

"Hey!" Travis cried as he tumbled over. "Not cool!"

Sasha thumped into a heap herself, rolled over on all fours, clearly in a bit of pain and rubbing her backside. She got to her knees and then stood, brushing off her gray sweatpants and maroon *Van Halen* tee-shirt.

Travis struggled to his feet as well and saw her discomfort. "Serves you right! I would have put you down in a few more seconds."

Allister found this entire scene incredibly amusing, chuckling through the entire episode. He walked out to them, suddenly commanding Travis, "Protection Spell! Emergency! Sasha, hit him again, as hard as you can! Now! Now!"

Sasha's fist came to her mouth once again and blew hard into her palm just as Travis rapped his knuckles against his chest and commanded, "*Praesidieum*!" A gelatinous blur of the air about three inches thick radiated out from his hand and covered his entire body in an instant. The air around him shimmered and sparkled in the bright sunlight.

Sasha's right hand flew forward with great force spinning clockwise. The air blurred in a tight spiral about four inches in diameter, spanning from Sasha's outstretched hand and stopping about three inches before Travis's face. As it made hard impact against Travis' hasty Protection Spell a subsonic impact tremor rocked the ground beneath their feet and reverberated through the air like distant thunder. Each stood firm. Travis was not affected in the least by the force of Sasha's energy pulse.

They both started laughing.

Travis grinned and pointed at her. "You would have taken my head off. Wouldn't you?"

She folded her arms. "I had confidence you'd be ready."

"Excellent! Excellent!" Allister nodded with approval and clapped his hands. "You are both making great progress. But here. Take my hands. Recharge."

Allister reached out to them both and Travis grasped his left hand and Sasha his right, both of them breathing in deeply though their noses as he'd taught them, holding the breath for several seconds, and then letting the air out slowly through their mouths. In a few moments all the fatigue of the previous exercises faded away and a renewed sense of energy filled every fiber of their being.

That afternoon, as was usual in the early summer months, the air was hot and humid in the Texas Hill Country. Consequently, everyone was sweating profusely throughout the intense training session, Allister included. They were secreted away in a remote part of a small public park area on the north side of Lake Travis, where few people actually lived and complete privacy was easy to come by. Although, technically speaking, they weren't completely alone if consideration was paid to the white tail deer, rock squirrels and gray squirrels, an occasional coyote, rabbits, all manner of birds from gold finches to eagles, various lethal and nonlethal reptiles and amphibians, and insects without number. However, it was prudent avoidance of the many mounds of fire ants and a rattlesnake here and there that was of greatest concern.

The spectacularly hilly land was plentifully adorned with cedar, cyprus and live oak trees, interspersed with stands of several varieties of cactus, wisps of sagebrush, clusters of wild rosemary and tangles of weeds and thickets. None of the trees were very tall due to the dry, rocky terrain that limited root depth and access to water. But the beautiful hues of the wildflowers, highlighted by sprays of Texas bluebonnets made the landscape rustic and postcard picturesque – and for those with a magically discerning ear, filled with the joyous sounds of flower song.

"That's better," Allister said as he released their hands. "You are both doing splendidly. Absolutely brilliant!"

Both Sasha and Travis genuinely appreciated Allister's praise. For Sasha this was the adventure of a lifetime. She'd spent many years studying so many diverse cultures the world over, societies who talked about magic as commonplace in their lives as farming techniques and child rearing. It had never occurred to her at any point in her education that any of it was describing reality as opposed to superstition and the primitive fiction of legend, lore, and mythology. But now she knew that wasn't true.

Magic *was* real.

And better yet, she could *do* it. Once that simple fact was accepted as reality, the lessons didn't even feel that hard. She was eager to try each new exercise Allister challenged them with. And neither of them had failed a single test thus far.

Travis was like a hungry young dog turned loose all by himself at the meat market. He was in heaven. Not only was he gaining a wealth of practical wisdom along with phenomenal power, but he was doing it alongside the one person in the whole world that he really wanted to spend his time with and share any and all of his wonderful new experiences in life. His only regret was not yet knowing if any of his feelings about Sasha were requited. He'd still not worked up the courage to tell Sasha how he truly felt about her. It's hard sometimes to ask questions that you might not want to hear the answer to. But it was on his To-Do list. Someday.

They both grew serious and quiet when they saw Allister's expression grow grim and he said to them, "So now, class, it is time we move on to a new level."

Sasha and Travis traded anxious glances.

"There are some spells that only a true Master Magi can perform, and neither of you are at that level yet, and you may not be for many, many years hence. But a few key elements of metamorphosis are available to a rare special few Practicing Magicians, and I am hopeful that describes you, and if not now, then it will very soon."

That comment merited two eager smiles.

Allister rubbed his tired eyes, clearly lost in thought for a moment. "You are not yet ready to go from being in one place to being in another by sheer will and a collapsing and a reassembling of your being. This is the art of Teleportation. No, you two are not ready for that yet. So we'll forgo training in that particular spell for now."

Both Sasha and Travis looked confused and felt a little disappointed.

"But not to worry," he assured them. "Those lessons will come in time. But I do feel that there is a chance that you might be able to manipulate the flow of light, at least the small amount that touches you in a moment of time. And that's all we need in order to potentially save your life when faced with a moment of grave danger."

"The Invisibility Spell?" Travis asked, hoping Allister would say yes.

"Indeed," Allister pointed at his chest. "Well done, Travis. We'll make a Master Magi out of you yet."

Travis beamed with pride.

"A Vanishing," Sasha echoed, wiping the sweat off her glistening brow with the back of her hand. "You honestly think we're ready to give something like that a try?"

Allister nodded. "Trying it, yes. Succeeding? Well now, that remains to be seen." He added, "Or perhaps *unseen* as the case may be." He chuckled at his own joke.

"I'll try it," Travis stepped forward.

"Just tell us what to do," Sasha took a deep breath and stepped closer as well.

Allister took a long look at both of them, sizing them up, thinking it through. Yes, he was even more convinced now than he was the day before. They were going to work out just fine, he told himself.

Allister clapped his hands together and said, "Very well them. This spell requires a great deal of energy. Perhaps more than you have right now. We'll know that soon enough. But if you can summon it, your focus thought is: 'Do not see me.' Use your senses to feel the waves of light upon your body and consciously feel the light circumnavigating around you, like the currents of a river flowing around a large stone in its midst. You are that stone. All light energy is the water. But don't think of it as only flowing toward you from one direction and moving away from you in the opposite direction. See it in your mind's eye as coming from all directions at the same time, and leaving you on the other side of you flowing away. Do you understand?"

Allister received two affirmative nods in unison.

Yes, these two were amazingly gifted, and incredibly eager, and in many ways stronger than he had imagined they ever could be at this stage, but he was skeptical of the outcome of this test, knowing first-hand how difficult a task this was. It took him several frustrating and discouraging months to master it in his younger days. On the other hand, William took only a few weeks to grasp it, and that was remarkable.

It was time to see what they were really made of.

The truth be told, and Allister didn't really want to share this little detail with them, but a major part of the lesson at this point concerned how to deal with failure, setbacks, adversity and difficulty. Surely, in time, they would grasp a Vanishing. But everything up until now seemed to come so easily for them both. It was time for them to face something bigger than they were, and to commit their discouraged hearts to the task of overcoming the seemingly impossible.

He measured them both once more for few seconds and then asked. "Are you both ready to give it a try?"

Again, two nods in unison.

"Very well then," he said. "Close your eyes and—"

Allister suddenly found himself standing amidst the wildflowers and cactus all alone. He spun about, confused and perplexed.

Had they been taken? Had he done something wrong and accidentally vanquished them or banished them to some other realm?

Allister McKenzie stopped wondering when her heard the sound of mischievous giggling. With hands on hips he announced, "Oh, right! Now you're both just showing off!"

CHAPTER 25

THE ROAD TO DAMASCUS

William and Penelope had been on the road for many hours that day in the Range Rover. Penelope had rented the vehicle for them back in Cairo, playing her part as a member in good standing of the Inner Circle. Her assignment was to shadow the Egyptian military truck carrying the device all the way into Damascus, trailing it about five minutes behind, just in case it encountered any trouble along the way. Stephan Burke and Alexey Borochenko were driving it. Both they and she were able to stay in close communication via short-range walkie-talkies.

The route was arduous, crossing the full breadth of the Sanai peninsula, traveling east through Nekhel and on to the seaside town of Taba, just south of Eilat on the southernmost tip of Israel, which was also the northernmost tip of the Gulf of Aqaba. A ferry took them across the gulf and into Jordan, so as not having to cross the Israeli border. Once in Jordan, they headed northeast on the 15 highway to Ma'an. In Ma'an they got off the 15 and onto the 5 highway toward El Jafr. This route was very out of the way, but that was desirable, considering the secrecy and extreme risk of the cargo being transported.

Traveling further north, highway 5 connected to a spur, highway 30, which skirted just north of Amman where it rejoined highway 15, which became the M5 after it crossed the Syrian border, heading straight toward Damascus. However, once they entered Syria late in the afternoon they chose to keep to a winding series of two-lane, and sometimes single-lane, rural backroads and didn't take the more heavily travelled M5.

"You're certain she's a dragon?" William asked in disbelief.

"I literally saw it in her eyes," Penelope said. "She's been in the United States and, other than spending a great deal of time with Daniel, she's stayed away from the rest of us for a long time. *Apparently*, she's been growing much stronger, too. And changing."

"*Apparently*," he repeated, then adding, "and not for the better. She could be a big problem for us."

William turned his gaze out the passenger window.

The countryside going by was mostly a flat barren desert with rocky hills demarking the horizon off in the distance. Occasionally they would pass a cluster of stone or concrete buildings, most of them destroyed in the seemingly unending civil war. Burned out vehicles lay strewn on the sides of the road every few miles. What was noticeably absent was the sight of very many people on these rural roads. Again, considering the mission, that wasn't necessarily a bad thing. The Inner Circle was careful to avoid moving the device through major population centers – just in case. The weapon in the truck on the road five minutes ahead of them could eliminate an entire city in a matter of seconds.

For Penelope and William, crossing borders was no problem. Penelope had the physician's medical credentials of the United Nations and the World Health Organization. She was, in fact, a practicing thoracic surgeon from Italy. Doctors were almost always welcomed where suffering was the greatest. Papers were irrelevant to William. He could just vanish in the seat beside her and no one was the wiser. For that matter, he could have just teleported directly to Damascus from Cairo and waited for them to arrive. But no, he didn't want to lose track of the device, and he also wanted to have more time alone to talk privately with Penelope. Worst case, he could make the entire vehicle invisible and just drive right past any would-be obstacles.

Well, not all obstacles. At that very moment, their personal conversation was going to have to wait.

It was not uncommon for bandits, government opposition rebel groups, and even militant jihadists to set up roadblocks in Syria, robbing and/or kidnapping any foreigners they might encounter. The military truck carrying the device was an official Egyptian military vehicle with properly authorized paperwork, and was therefore unlikely to be stopped by anyone other than proper authorities. It was also being overseen by two Practicing Magi. On the other hand, an expensive European Range Rover being driven by a very beautiful Italian woman, seemingly alone, was an entirely different proposition.

Penelope just shook her head in dismay at what appeared in the road up ahead. Two badly beat-up light pickup trucks were parked across both lanes of the ragged two-lane road. Four armed men dressed all in black, including black balaclava masks, stood before them. One of them signaled for Penelope to stop. Another one had a Kalashnikov AK-47 shouldered and leveled at their windshield. A third held a Rocket Propelled Grenade (RPG) launcher at the ready.

"I don't think these guys just want to check your passport and see your papers, my dear," William said.

"We don't have time for this," Penelope seethed. "The truck will get too far ahead of us."

"Don't worry. I've got it," William assured her as he glanced down at his watch. "Stay put. I'll just be a minute."

The high-pitched whine filled the air.

FLASH!

William vanished.

Penelope saw him reappear standing directly behind the armed bandit aiming his assault weapon at her face. William touched the man on the back of the neck and he groaned, dropping his rifle and desperately clutching his hands to his chest. His three comrades turned in shock as their companion fell to the ground with collapsed lungs and a bifurcated heart.

Another one of the bandits quickly shouldered his weapon, preparing to fire. William thrust his palm in his direction. A bright red column of fire leapt out of Williams hand, crashed into the man's chest, causing the man to burst into roaring flames from head to toe. The remaining two men in black turned and ran away from the road as fast and they could.

William crossed his wrists before his face, hands in tight fists, holding his forearms in the shape of an "X." He shouted at them, "Run my little rabbits, run!"

FLASH!

The two fleeing men were instantly gone and one assault rifle and one RPG launcher clattered to the ground. Two frightened jackrabbits fled across open desert. William was confident a hungry predator would find them both soon enough.

With a spreading of his hands in the direction of the two pickup trucks, both of them tumbled to the sides of the road out of their way.

William chuckled to himself at the thought that these two trucks didn't look much different from the dozens of other abandoned and burned out ones they'd passed that day littering the roadsides. No one would think twice about two more. He also knew the burning pile of flesh that was once one of the bandits would be nothing but gray ash in just a few more minutes, driven into the desert sands by the night winds. However, the first bandit he dispatched was now just a corpse laying in the middle of the road.

William didn't like loose ends.

"The desert will take care of you, too, my friend," he said as he picked up the body of the man and hugged him close.

FLASH!

They both vanished, reappearing just as he envisioned it in his mind approximately a mile to the east in the midst of the open desert. William dropped the body on the ground. He was confident the avian scavengers would find it soon enough and dispose of it, leaving anything left to the six-legged creatures, scorpions and spiders.

William Turner took a deep breath and...

FLASH!

He appeared back inside the Range Rover sitting in the passenger's seat next to Penelope. He looked down at his watch once more and saw that he'd been gone less than one minute.

"Fifty-three seconds," was all he said.

She just shook her head at him. "Having fun?"

He shot her a smile. "You know, sometimes it is. It *really* is."

CHAPTER 26
THE ARCHBISHOP

TEHRAN, IRAN

The palatial offices of one of the Grand Ayatollah's foreign ministers and senior military attaché were exceedingly opulent even for the refined tastes of Archbishop Renaldo Vasquez. And that was saying something as he had served for several years in Rome. He quietly huffed to himself thinking, *I guess it really is good to be the king, or at least to be one of his most trusted lieutenants.*

Vasquez's host sat behind an enormous polished ebony desk arrayed in his formal robes and classic black headdress. His full beard was neatly trimmed. The only aspect of the man appearance that didn't appear as a traditional Islamic cleric was his western-styled Giorgio Armani eyeglasses and the gold Rolex on his wrist.

Conversely, on this day Archbishop Vasquez once again wore none of his official accoutrement; rather, as he was once more on foreign soil, he sported a conservative business suit and tie. Normally, a member of the Christian faith would never be allowed in the innermost sacred offices of Allah's highest servants – but desperate times sometimes necessitated desperate measures, and occasional exceptions.

"Is everything proceeding according to schedule?" the Mullah politely inquired, gesturing to a serving tray of hot tea. "Tea?"

"No thank you." Vasquez demurred politely. He was genuinely surprised how well the Persian spoke English. He himself spoke no Farsi, and this senior minister of the Islamic Republic spoke no Spanish or Italian. English was the only language they both knew in common.

Vasquez answered the man's first question: "But yes, I can assure you that all is going exactly according to plan. The Sunni militants in Syria and their colleagues in the Anbar province of Iraq believe that they will be receiving the device in Raqqa tomorrow. Instead, in Damascus tonight it will make a detour and come around, heading directly into Israel. I trust you have made all the necessary financial arrangements."

"We have done so, as agreed." The Persian nodded with understanding, then posed the following question to Vasquez: "And what new news is there on this unusual man...Walaam Turner, I hear is interfering in your work? I am told several of your comrades have been attacked and killed in recent days. Does he pose a significant threat to our mutual success?"

"Not at all," Vasquez brushed away the insinuation. "It *was* true, just as you have heard, in recent days there was a slight risk posed by this man, but I am happy to report that Dr. Turner was successfully dealt with several days ago in a direct confrontation in Athens. He is no longer a threat of any kind to anyone any longer."

The old man nodded with a broad smile of satisfaction on his face. "This is fantastic news, my friend. So the mightiest of all swords shall at last become ours. I know the Sunnis of Syria would have wanted to bring it personally right here to Tehran themselves and strike their own mighty blow against the Shi'a – using the very same sword that the Americans and Europeans have worked so hard to keep us from crafting for ourselves. But at long last we shall have it!"

"Indeed you shall," Vasquez said.

The Persian shook his finger, scolding an absent party, "The Sunni are like so many wild children. I know. I have been an Imam here in Tehran for most of my life. They fail to realize the irony in their ignorance of the fact that they will, on a great day very soon, get their way and most of us shall indeed be vanquished...right along with them. But to do that, the great sword must first be taken to smite the pestilence of the Little Satan. And when the west retaliates, as they will without fail, we shall then be martyred, just as prophesied, and only then shall your Christ return to help our 12th Imam, the Mahdi, defeat the False Messiah, that is, what you call your Antichrist, and only then rule for a thousand years."

Archbishop Vasquez just nodded and smiled in agreement.

He really did believe the old Persian to be completely mad, along with the rest of the governing theocracy. But that didn't matter. Lighting the fuse on the means to rid the planet of the majority of its dregs and return it to its more natural and beautiful origins was worth any price.

Vasquez was completely convinced that in the very beginning, God commanded Adam to subdue and replenish the earth. But within a few generations it became desperately evil and wicked, and so God destroyed man with a Great Flood, sparing only Noah and his family to give man a second chance to become good stewards of the planet. Unfortunately, mankind in this day and age had utterly overrun the earth, soiled it, and nearly ruined it and almost completely destroyed it. Yes, it was indeed time to wipe the earth completely clean and replenish it yet again.

Although, God did indeed promise Noah that never again would He destroy mankind with a flood.

Oh, no. God said that next time it would be with fire.

Yes, yes, if the Archbishop had to throw the switch himself, it would all be destroyed with fire and then earth's infestation of mankind would at long last be sanitized away.

To save the planet.

CHAPTER 27

FROM THE JOURNAL OF WILLIAM TURNER

TEMPTATIONS

Few Magi progress to the level of a true Master. This is primarily due to a lack of self-discipline, not from a lack of talent or desire. Not a lot of Magi realize this.

More Magi are destroyed by Magic itself than by any other cause. True Magic is very tempting to abuse. When you can enter any place on earth, why not a bank vault? When you can vanquish any of the mortal folk or weaker Magi, why not be a king?

The hardest test of being a Magi at any level is the daily challenge to remain the master of your Magic and not let it become your master. It is a test of character, of integrity, of maturity in knowing exactly who you are and remaining faithful to your core values.

Are you using your Magic to lift up the lives of others, to work to ease suffering, and to fight for good? Or are you using Magic to selfishly lift yourself up, to fill your own life with ease and comfort? Have you ever used Magic in a moment of anger as a weapon? For a good Magi, such things must be forbidden.

I recommend that each and every morning, your first call of duty is to take a few moments of solitude and quiet and take time to examine your own heart. Is it a heart filled with love and compassion for others? Or is it a selfish heart intent only on satisfying its own appetites and desires? What can you do each day to cleanse your heart, to keep your heart pure and not succumb to temptation?

If you are faithful to tend your own heart like a precious garden, your life will be filled with joy. But as with any garden, the weeds and pests are always a nuisance that must be dealt with on a regular basis. Pull the weeds. Kill the pests. Then you can richly enjoy the fruit and beauty of your own garden.

However, be forewarned, there will come a time in your life when you will soon learn that not all Magi abide by the doctrines, maxims and advice I've outlined above. Rather, an evil Magi can be a dangerous tyrant and a threat to all mortal folk as well as to inferior Magi.

It would be a simple task of avoidance regarding rogue Magi, who simply elect to use their Magic to acquire wealth and live a life of leisure, which you would be wise to avoid them. But for those devoted to destruction and oppression, there is little else to be done other than to eliminate them whenever possible. I know that judgement sounds severe. But it is what must be.

In Holy Writ there is a Divine command which says, "Thou shalt not suffer a witch to live." The word "witch" in that verse does not refer to all manifestations of Magic, nor its practitioners. How could it? For you now know that all sentient creatures with the ability to move by volitional will use Magic to do so. No, that passage of holy scripture refers specifically and exclusively to the evil Magi.

Once a Magi's heart has abandoned the sacred light of Creation and has completely darkened, there is little hope for that soul. The corruption within them will only grow until their hearts and minds shall be set continually on evil alone, and the result is a path of nothing but destruction and suffering for all who encounter them.

Thus, this is why they must be vanquished.

It was for this reason that my Master approached me about a special calling, "a necessary mission," he said.

My mission was to infiltrate a clandestine group of very influential rogue Magi calling themselves the Inner Circle. Their key members were based strategically around the world, chartered to influence key world events to the group's benefit.

For the most part the group was focused on the accumulation of great wealth, and was highly successful at it. It was only after I was able to join them here in Europe and be accepted by the group that I was taken into their confidence and learned that wealth alone wasn't their ultimate goal. No, their vast accumulation of great wealth was needed so that they might execute astronomical business transactions, mostly in terms of arms and war material.

You see, much like the great European financial houses of the last few centuries, the Inner Circle also worked to foment strife and violent conflicts around the globe, funding both sides of a war, and ultimately deciding the fate of one side or the other when funding was withheld from one side and not the other. But don't misunderstand, this group doesn't wish to merely rule the various countries and regions of the world. No, they wish to own them and plunder them – naturally, after installing their own puppet proxy managers to run them.

The endless sectarian strife of the modern Middle East is but one example of their latest handiwork. They funded the Iran-Iraq war for over a decade. Their money was what fueled the rise of terrorism in the Middle East, North Africa, and what is now being exported to Europe and North America and parts of Latin America. They fund all the aggression coming out of Russia toward its neighbors.

Do you ever wonder who pays for all those AK-47s and Rocket Propelled Grenades (RPG) you see on the nightly news in the hands of impoverished peasants? The cost of one of those assault rifles is more than most of those who wield them earn in a year. Nor is the seemingly unending supply of ammunition they indiscriminately fire into the air free of charge. Bullets are expensive. So are grenades and missiles. Someone is covering the costs. And that someone, I learned, is a many-headed beast known as the Inner Circle.

I formally left the Inner Circle a few months ago when I first learned of their intent to arm the jihadist radical militants in Syria and Iraq with a small yield nuclear device secretly purchased from Pakistan. I thought they were joking when I was first briefed in on the operation.

Their thinking was that instigating a nuclear arms race in the Middle East would enable the Inner Circle to dominate that oil rich part of the world, too. But by my reckoning that gambit was a bridge too far. There are just some things that are too dangerous and reckless to consider. Yes, an arms race potentially makes untold billions of dollars for the group, but it can also lead to billions of deaths. It was at that point that I knew that I had no choice but to start eliminating members of the Inner Circle and frustrating their plans.

There was simply no other way to stop them.

My Master concurred with my overall risk assessment and sanctioned my actions.

I also knew that I could no longer remain with the group when I accidentally discovered, much to my great surprise, that one of the remotely participating members of the Inner Circle was my ex-wife, Penelope. Talk about a small world. Nevertheless, I can say, candidly, while I hadn't seen her or spoken to her in twenty years, I really had no great desire to terminate her – but I knew in my heart that if she was in tight league with these insane plans of the others I might very well have to.

Penelope and I were married for almost eleven years. We'd first met in college while living in Boston. I was attending MIT. She was, at that same time, attending Harvard medical school. We had one child, a daughter, whom we named Alexandra, and lived the model life of a prosperous young family in New England. From my perspective, everything was just perfect. Well, that is, right up until the day discovered my wife was a witch.

Penelope tried to explain to me that she primarily used her Magic for healing, but I didn't (couldn't?) accept it. I didn't want to accept it. I didn't believe in Magic back then or understand it the way I do now. I wish I had known better at the time. Who knows, perhaps things might have been very, very different between us.

I think it was actually my innermost fear of Magic that made me seek full legal custody of my daughter, Sasha, after the divorce and then to flee to Texas with her. Penelope didn't try and stop us. She conceded that it might have been for the best to go our separate ways. She knew very well that close relationships between Magi and mortal folk are difficult at best. Besides, in her heart I knew she had really wanted to return to Italy where she was born. She had a big family and friends there.

I hated lying to my young daughter about her mother. But it was a lot easier for her to believe her mother was dead than to tell her the truth about what her mother really was. I regret that to this day. And I pray that one day Alexandra can find it in her heart to forgive me.

CHAPTER 28
SASHA AND TRAVIS

ON FLIGHT 768
SOMEWHERE OVER THE NORTH ATLANTIC OCEAN

"Are you crying?" Travis whispered to Sasha.

She closed her father's journal and set it on her lap. Tears ran down both cheeks, and her shoulders bobbed with quiet sobs. She whispered, "I just can't believe it."

"What is it?" he asked, suddenly worried about her.

She told him, "I just learned that I may have a mother who is alive and not dead."

"*What?*" Travis carefully set his near-empty plastic cup of soda on his tray table. "So is that a good thing or a bad thing? Are you happy crying or sad crying?"

Sasha wiped her eyes. "I don't know exactly. I guess a little bit of both. Of course, you know...I'm happy to learn that she didn't really die when I was nine. But it also means I missed out on having a real mother for the last twenty years."

Travis just nodded with a look of sympathy. He made a mental note to call his mother as soon as they landed and tell her that he loved her, and his father, too.

Sasha let more of her feelings out. "The tragic irony of it all is that they split up because of *magic*, because of *her* magic. Because of what she was, not over anything particular that she ever did to him or me or anyone else. He called her a witch!"

Travis whispered, "Do you really want to discuss this in public?"

She glanced around. "Everyone around us asleep. And I don't care. We won't see any of them again. They can think whatever they want. I'm upset about my parents splitting up, and I want to talk about it. Is that okay?"

"Yes, it's okay. But you might be going a little hard on your dad. Do you think he even understood what being a real witch even meant back then? Didn't he learn about magic himself a lot later in his life?"

"I don't know," she said. "All I know for sure was that my father was afraid of it all back then. He didn't understand it. I guess he thought it could somehow hurt me. But what she was back then is the very thing he's become, if not more so, and it's what we're becoming."

Travis covered her hand, which was resting on the end of armrest between them, with his own. "Yeah, that sucks."

"A part of me kind of understands his thinking. But in a very real way, I was lied to, and I guess...I guess I resent that." She glanced out the window at the tops of the clouds illuminated by the full moon. Far on the horizon a new sunrise was beginning to lighten the eastern sky.

"Well, what was he *supposed* to do?" Travis asked her. "Tell you that your mother was a Magi? You'd seen the Wizard of Oz. You knew what a witch was. Even at that age you probably would have thought they were both crazy. And if you'd ever mentioned it to anyone else, like a school teacher, then Child Protective Services would have swooped in and taken you away from both of them and put you in foster care. And then you would have lost them both." He saw the hurt look on her face and endeavored to lighten the mood. "And then maybe never went to college. And then you'd never have met me..."

That elicited a half smile and a playful elbow to the ribs.

Sasha shrugged. "You're probably right. The bottom line is I never had all those years to live with her and get to know her better. She was never there to see me graduate from high school or college. She wasn't there to ask questions about a first date, a first kiss, breakups, broken hearts, and just what it means to be a woman. I know deep down inside my father tried his best, but even a well-meaning father's perspective isn't the exact same thing as a mother's viewpoint in a young girl's life. I mean, God bless all those single parents out there, but I'm sorry, it just isn't the same. And who knows, with her, I might have discovered my own magic a lot earlier in life."

"Right," he half-laughed. "You could have had all those wonderful memories of making mother-daughter potions in the kitchen. 'Honey, will you hand me a little more eye of newt?' Or taken your broomsticks to the mall together to shop for pointy hats, have a wart removed, and get your ears pierced."

"Stop it," she playfully scolded.

"Look," he said, "your father did what he thought was right and best for you. That's all any parent can do."

"The funny thing is, based upon what I've read in the journal and from what Allister has told us, I can imagine that right now, due to my father's mission, they've had to reconnect to some degree. She's a part of this Inner Circle group he's trying to stop. The journal says so."

Sasha turned her hand over and interlaced her fingers with Travis'. He didn't seem to mind, and at that moment she just needed to feel some closeness and a connection with another human being.

She explained, "That would have to be the case. Wouldn't it? Them together again in some way?"

"Then that's probably true," Travis said. "We won't know until we get there and they fill us in."

Sasha had a troubling thought. "But what if she's just as bad as the rest of them? I hope he doesn't have to get rid of her. I can't imagine learning of her being alive and travelling half way around the world, only to find out that she's gone for real. Obviously, her practicing magic can't possibly be an issue now. And who knows? It might be a good thing to reconnect with her myself. We can't undo the past, but there's still the future. Right?"

Travis decided to steer the conversation in a more positive direction. "Why do you think your mother ever got involved in this kind of a sketchy group in the first place? You said she was some kind of a medical doctor, right?"

"Who knows?" Sasha leaned over and rested her cheek against Travis' shoulder and yawned. "Why does any magical wizard want to belong to an evil global cabal intent on world domination? Must be the perks."

That made Travis chuckle. "I hadn't really thought of it that way. Then again, I don't really run around in those globe-trotting circles of mega-players. I like to keep it real. You know?"

She huffed, "Yep. That's my Travis, just a regular boy next door."

Travis felt a pang in his heart. At that moment he sincerely wondered if that was the extent of what she really thought of him.

But then Sasha added in a weary voice, "...a regular boy who happens to be a powerful sorcerer who can kill you with a thought."

Travis kind of liked that description. A chill of excitement ran up his spine. He took one last sip of his soda and looked down at his empty cup. He wanted a refill. He glanced up the aisle of the aircraft and saw the flight attendant talking to a passenger seated near the front of the plane. He took a deep breath and thought: *See me. Come to me.*

The flight attendant immediately looked at him and began heading his way. Travis glanced down at Sasha and said, "I think you're right. It's definitely the perks. I just love that trick."

But Sasha didn't hear him. Her eyes were closed and she was fast asleep on his arm. He was content to let her sleep. They'd be landing at Heathrow in London in a little over an hour. Allister would be there to meet them for the connecting El Al flight to Tel Aviv.

CHAPTER 29
PENELOPE AND WILLIAM

DAMASCUS, SYRIA

"The warehouse is two more streets down, and then we make a left," Stephan Burke looked up from the map on his iPad.

Alexey Borochenko said nothing, just kept driving.

As they passed the intersection where Burke indicated they should turn to reach their destination, the truck kept going straight ahead.

Annoyed, Burke turned to Alexey and said, "That was your turn. Where are you going? Now you have to turn around."

Alexey shook his head, "No we don't. We're on the right road."

"What the devil are you talking about?" Burke demanded.

"There has been a…how do you say?…a little change in plans," the Ukrainian informed him.

"What change?" Burke was clearly agitated. He was the closest of all the leadership group to Daniel DuMonde, and Daniel was the high leader. If there had been any authorized changes approved, he felt he certainly would have been the first to know.

Alexey smiled and said, "*We* have a better buyer lined up than these barbaric militants here in Syria, someone willing to pay us a lot more."

Burke was incensed. "And who exactly is *we*?"

"The new leadership," Alexey replied.

"What on *earth* are you talking about?" Burke was shouting.

Alexey shrugged. "It is the way things are now, Stephan. You and Daniel want to play with all your little regional battles and make lots of money. That's all well and good. But you think too small. This device is destined for a much bigger destiny than a meaningless test in the desert for political brinkmanship purposes."

Burke shook his head in complete disbelief and dismay. "Wait. Are you telling me that you are actually thinking of *stealing* this weapon from the Inner Circle?"

Alexey pulled the truck to a stop on the deserted street. "No, my friend. I'm saying that it still very much belongs to the Inner Circle. It's just that there is going to be a much smaller Inner Circle now, and you and some of the others are no longer welcome in it."

Burke was too confused and openly outraged to even think about using a Protection Spell on himself. All he could think about was calling Daniel to protest this insolence and treasonous betrayal. He fumbled for his cell phone and didn't even see Alexey reach over and touch his cheek.

As Alexey made contact with his face, he whispered, "*Inshallah*..."

All Burke felt was the crushing moment of pain inside him as his hands flew to his chest.

•

"Stop! Stop the car!" William snapped.

Penelope slowed the Range Rover to a stop and looked down the darkened street. About a hundred yards ahead of them was the military transport truck carrying the device. It was inexplicably stopped on the side of the street, just idling.

"Something wrong," she said. "The truck was supposed to have been taken to a warehouse about a mile back. The militia representatives were to meet it there, guard it tonight, and then give it an armed escort to Raqqa in the morning for the formal delivery."

Penelope picked up the walkie-talkie and was about to depress the TALK button when they both saw the passenger door of the truck's cab open and a body unceremoniously fall out and land in a heap on the curb. The door reclosed and the truck quietly moved on its way.

Penelope cautiously drove forward as well, maintaining a generous and cautious following distance. As they slowly passed the body, William could see that it was that of Stephan Burke. A trickle of blood ran out of the side of his mouth.

He said aloud, "It's Burke."

Penelope said, "Well then, it certainly looks as if the rumors are true and the Inner Circle has decided to reconstitute itself."

William asked her, "Would Alexey dare to betray Daniel like that?"

She shook her head, "Not alone. There have always been tensions and petty squabbles among the members. But no one has ever tried to challenge Daniel's authority since he became high leader. Not like this. I can assure you that getting rid of Burke was no great loss to the group. He was weak and stupid. Daniel's errand boy. But Alexey daring to take the device all by himself is most curious. He surely knows I'm following him and will see what he's done."

"Maybe that's what he wants you to do," he said. "To see whose side you're on."

"That would be a surprise," she said. "I never really thought of Alexey as being that smart. But I would note that he hasn't bothered to call me either. I'm getting the distinct feeling he really doesn't want to talk to me right now."

She kept her distance from the truck, matching Alexey's speed.

William said, "You really do know and understand them all so well. Don't you?"

"Of course," she said. "I've been within the Inner Circle for over ten years now."

"How? And *why,*" William genuinely wanted to know. "When we split up in Boston you were barely a Practicing Magi. How did you get in? They wouldn't give me the time of day until I became a true Master, and a well-connected one at that in the global scientific community."

"It's true, I was only a Practicing Magi when I returned to Italy twenty years ago, and still am one, but a pretty good one if I say so myself. But I was in my mid-thirties back then, and working at one of the largest and best hospitals in all of Rome. I must admit that I was still very angry at you. I missed my Sasha. Perhaps you could say it was a rebound thing, but within two years I had remarried."

"I didn't know that." William felt strangely uneasy hearing this news.

"My husband was Antonio Angelucci," she explained. "He too was an active member of the Inner Circle, but that was long before your time with them. You would never have had an opportunity to meet him. Nevertheless, he was a very powerful Master. He continued to train me, and when he felt the time was right I was asked to join the Inner Circle."

"Wow. I just thought you changed your name to get rid of mine. So what happened to Antonio?" William wondered if he might still be in the picture somehow.

"He's dead," she replied. "He was Daniel's predecessor as the Inner Circle's high leader. You know very well that no one—well, no one before you, that is—ever quits the Inner Circle. It is a lifetime commitment, with the understanding that in the world of the Magi some lives don't have the same longevity as others."

He smiled. "Well, perhaps in my case, there's always a first time for everything."

"Not really," she disagreed. "They'll not stop until they find you and kill you. Which is why, when this mission is over with respect to stopping the weapon, if there are any of them left, and you have any concern for your own life, then you have to take care of them all."

"Present company excluded," he said.

Penelope gave him a little smile. "I appreciate that."

"So Daniel killed your husband?" he asked in disbelief.

She nodded. "In formal combat. Daniel challenged Antonio's leadership position. That's how we do it in our tradition, if you recall. Like a pride of lions, the younger male must defeat the elder male for the honor of leading the pride."

"But how?" William asked. "You said that Antonio was very powerful Master. Daniel doesn't have that kind of power. He didn't back then, and certainly doesn't now."

Penelope confessed, "You are correct. Daniel never would have had a chance to defeat Antonio if Nancy and I hadn't helped him."

"You betrayed your own husband?" William was genuinely appalled.

"I was a much different person back then," she confessed. "The truth is, I couldn't resist the temptations. Antonio was a Master Magi of the highest integrity. Yes, he used the power and influence of the Inner Circle to shape his version of world history during his time, and he certainly used his power to live a life of luxury and comfort. And he did much good for the less fortunate, too. He was a good man that way. But I wanted more. Daniel wanted more. So I agreed to help him in...what you might call a partnership of convenience."

"And what was Nancy's part in all of this?" he asked.

Penelope continued, "As far as Nancy's involvement goes in our little coup, it's no secret that she's been romantically involved with Daniel off and on for a very long time. I think she's convinced herself she genuinely loves him – as if that word has any meaning to a heart as dark as hers. I saw Daniel only as a means to an end, and I wasn't with him for very long, something I still regret to this day. Besides, when it all happened, I had told myself that I'd already lost one husband. Losing another one would not hurt as much."

That comment really stung William.

He said softly, "I really am sorry, Penelope. For everything. I was very ignorant back then of so much. You have to realize that. I've thought many times that things might have been very different between us if I'd better understood what you were going through and what it all really meant. The good as well as the bad, and how it all worked."

"Do you honestly think you would have even *wanted* to know?" she asked him. "I could tell it all frightened you. And because it did, you didn't want me anywhere near Sasha." She let out a heavy sigh. "All I can say to you now is that I can understand how you felt, and that's why I let you both leave together. I had the power to force you to stay."

"I appreciate that, but I would like to think I would have wanted to know the truth," he replied. "But who's to say? That was then and this is now. We are who we are because of the paths we've chosen. We don't get to un-ring all the bells in our lives." He flashed her sincere smile. "But hey, at least we did one thing right."

After an awkward pause Penelope dared to ask, "How is she?"

William smiled at the thought of Sasha. "She's doing quite well in her life. I'm very proud of her, and you will be, too. But you'll get to ask her all about those kind of things yourself tomorrow."

Penelope shivered at the very thought of seeing her precious daughter again after twenty long years. What would she be like? What would she *look* like? The last mental image she had of her daughter was that of a nine year-old little girl with a ponytail and bangs. Under the present circumstances, despite their mission and the audacity of challenging the Inner Circle, nothing could have made her more nervous. What if Sasha didn't want to have anything to do with her? Would she be afraid? Would they both be?

As Penelope started to close the gap with the truck, William advised her, "Better back off and give him a little more space. You're supposed to be five minutes back, coming to the rescue only if there's trouble and he calls for help."

"Right." Penelope slowed down and let the truck move on ahead into the night mists. When last they glimpsed it, the truck appeared to be picking up speed and heading in the direction of the highway. There weren't many serviceable highways where they were traveling, so the notion of the truck getting lost wasn't a real worry.

Several minutes later William asked her, "Any specific idea where he's headed now?"

"No, not really," she said. "But we seem to still be headed east. So, I suspect that if they have changed plans about delivering the device to the

Syrian militias, then we can only assume it's now headed into Iraq. Who knows, maybe Baghdad."

William nodded. "And if so, then logically, that would mean that the new leadership of the Inner Circle has betrayed the Sunnis and have now decided to bet on the Shi'a."

Penelope frowned and said, "Yes, which is simply a polite euphemism for working with the Persians, who, despite all their propaganda to the contrary, won't bother testing the device merely to make a political statement. They'll take it straight to Jerusalem, Tel Aviv, or Haifa and kill two birds with one stone."

William nodded. "It'll kill a lot more than two birds. But even if that's true, *our* plans don't have to change. We still want to intercept the device right when it reaches its buyers. We may have different buyers now but we still have the same objective."

She looked at him and asked, "So then what do we do about Allister, Sasha, and her friend Travis?"

William thought about that for a moment. "Good point. It doesn't look like having them drive up and meet us in Damascus in the morning is going to make any sense. I'll call Allister and leave a message for him to have them wait for us in Tel Aviv until we need them."

"If you really think about it, we may no longer need them at all," she noted. "The Inner Circle is obviously divided now. Burke is clearly out of the picture – not that he was any worry to begin with. Nevertheless, it's not likely we'll find them all gathered in one place anymore and have to confront them as a group. Which means this little turn of events may be a most opportune gift to us."

His brows rose with interest. "A little divide and conquer?"

"Exactly," she said.

"But just you and me alone?" he asked.

She nodded, "Sure. Why not?"

William warily shook his head. "Actually, if your suspicions are right about Nancy, I'd feel a whole lot better if we at least had Allister with us. I can summon him."

She said, "Okay, that's fine, but let's at least try to figure out exactly where we're going first."

"Agreed," he said.

Penelope suddenly said, "Grab my phone out of my purse and call Daniel. His number is in my Favorites."

"Why?" William asked.

"I have to report what's happened to Burke. It's the only way I can maintain this charade with what's left of the old Inner Circle. They may still have access to information we need."

"I understand."

William found her bag behind her seat and pulled out her iPhone, holding it up for her so she could unlock it with her fingerprint. He made the call, which was answered on the second ring.

From the speakerphone Daniel's sleepy voice came through with a bit of static due to poor cell reception. "Penelope, my love. I trust all is going well on your journey?"

Her voice was grave. "No, Daniel, it's not."

His voice grew anxious. "Why? What's happened?"

Penelope matter-of-factly announced, "A few minutes ago Alexey has apparently taken Burke's breath away, broken his heart, and then to make matters worse, he's taken the device as well."

"*Quoi?*" came the cry of disbelief from the phone.

After a long pause of silence, she asked, "Your instructions?"

Daniel seethed, "Follow the truck to wherever he is taking it. Then eliminate him and anyone with him. Take care of them all, burn them to ash if you have to, and then recover the device and return it to our buyers in Damascus as quickly as possible. I'll contact them straightaway and let them know there has been a slight delay."

"Understood," she said, making a slicing motion with her finger across her throat for William's benefit. He understood her gesture and promptly ended the call.

William smiled at her. "You should have told him that we were intending to do that very thing all along, with the exception of also safely disabling the device."

"What in the *world*?" she exclaimed, putting her foot on the brake.

"What's wrong?" William became alarmed.

Penelope pointed straight ahead. "Isn't that our truck?"

Parked in an abandoned gas station stood the Egyptian military transport, dark and silent. The rear doors were standing open. Clearly it was empty.

William handed Penelope her phone. "Wow. I did not see that one coming." With a half-laugh he said, "Looks like you get to call Daniel back with another update."

Chapter 30
Alexey

On the Outskirts of Damascus, Syria

Hiding in the shadows of the abandoned gas station's office and peering out a broken window, Alexey Borochenko watched the Range Rover slowly approach the back of the military transport truck and come to a complete stop, its headlights illuminating the open interior of the empty cargo compartment.

A white transfer van with the device now safely loaded and secured inside its cargo bay stood only ten yards away, in one of the gas station's dark, garage maintenance bays – completely hidden under a large tarp. His men who met him there at the prescribed rendezvous spot, and who executed the swift vehicle swap, were already gone. The whole vehicle swap took less than two minutes, executed exactly as planned.

What Alexey found most telling was the fact that he'd received no call from Penelope on the walkie-talkie. Surely she had seen Stephan Burke's body lying on the side of the road. That was the purpose of the test – i.e. to see where her allegiances truly lie. The good Archbishop Renaldo Vasquez was certain that she would remain loyal to Daniel. The probability of that was high. Everyone knew of their past together.

Penelope had been directly responsible for Daniel DuMonde taking the reins of leadership of the Inner Circle several years ago. There were rumors that at one time there may have been some romantic involvement between them as well, despite Daniel's ongoing and very public relationship with his American consort, Dr. Nancy Thompson. So, there was very little chance that Penelope would betray Daniel. And if that were the case, despite the fact that they could sincerely use Penelope's talents, then the Inner Circle would need to grow even smaller.

However, attending to that loose end would have to wait.

Alexey observed that Penelope didn't tarry very long before speeding off in the direction the military truck was still facing. A natural assumption on her part would surely be that however the device was now being transported, it couldn't have gone too far. She'd give chase for a little while, but would be sorely disappointed. And that was all the time he needed to be long gone.

On the other hand, and much to Alexey's alarm and surprise, all was not perfect. As the Range Rover passed the abandoned truck Alexey saw it. It was just a brief glimpse from the illumination of dashboard lights. But there could be no mistaking it.

Penelope Angelucci was not travelling alone. There was definitely a second individual in the passenger's seat beside her – a man with what looked like long gray hair and an almost white beard. That description fit only one person he could think of.

So the Archbishop may have been wrong after all. It now looked like Penelope was neither loyal to the old Inner Circle nor to the new one. That could be a problem.

Alexey raced to the cab of the white transfer van, fired up the engine, backed it out of the garage, and headed back in the direction from which he originally came. He checked his watch. Yes, he felt comfortable that he would make it to the Israeli border an hour or two before dawn. He had all the proper paperwork to safely and discretely cross the border from Jordan. He dared not try to cross directly from Syria, where the military security was the tightest.

Alexey pulled out a satellite phone and dialed.

Archbishop Vasquez answered promptly, "Do you have it?"

"Of course," Alexey replied.

"And Burke?"

"Done."

"Miss Penelope off your scent?"

Alexey thought again about what he believed he saw. Yes, he was sure it was true. "Yes, she is still heading east. *But...*"

"Excellent," came Archbishop Vasquez's enthusiastic reply, sobering into, "But *what*?"

"But there may be a complication," Alexey noted.

"How so?"

He sighed, "She wasn't alone in the chase vehicle."

"Who was with her?" Vasquez demanded.

Alexey huffed, "I'm not certain. But I think I have a very good idea of who it might be."

"Who?" Vasquez demanded to know.

"Let's just say that I think Daniel's absolute confidence in the recent untimely demise of our good friend, Dr. Vil'hel'm Turner, may have been greatly exaggerated."

CHAPTER 31
SASHA, TRAVIS AND ALLISTER

BEN GURION AIRPORT
TEL AVIV, ISRAEL

Despite the fact that Allister McKenzie had paid for first class seats on the El Al flight from England to Israel, Sasha was completely exhausted, as tired as she could ever remember feeling in her entire life. Travis didn't look or feel much better. With all the flight connections, from Austin to Detroit, to London, and now to Israel, plus layovers, they had been travelling for almost twenty-four hours straight, and very few of those hours involved any truly restful sleep. It was a wonder they could still stand – which is about all they were able to do, with both of them patiently waiting at the baggage claim.

Travis glanced at his watch. It was just before noon.

Allister walked up behind them, putting his phone away. "Sasha, I received a voicemail from your father. Must have called last night. He's has asked us to put everything on hold and just wait here in Tel Aviv until we receive his next call."

"When will that be?" she asked.

He shrugged, "The message said it could be a matter of days."

"We're not going on to Damascus in the morning?" She was confused.

"No," he shook his head. "Not now. It seems circumstances on the ground have changed and the meeting that was to take place there has been cancelled."

Travis wearily spoke up, yawning as he said, "So what are we supposed to do here in Israel?"

Allister shrugged. "We'll collect our things, clear customs, and settle in at our hotel. You both look like you can barely stand. I think a little nap would do you both good. You need to recharge, get over the jetlag. With no energy, you are not very helpful to anyone."

"That sounds like a great idea." All Sasha could picture was a long, hot bath and a king-sized bed with her name on it.

•

Allister didn't disappoint. He had booked rooms for them at the Ritz Carlton in Herzliya, only about fifteen minutes from the airport, right on the Mediterranean coast. Sasha barely noticed all of the fine appointments of her room, rather she headed straight to the bathroom, saw the inviting garden tub, and immediately began to run hot water and get undressed.

Sasha was asleep less than thirty seconds after easing into the delightfully warm water and leaning back to relax. She awoke over an hour later, shivering in cold water. With bleary eyes she was able to crawl out of the tub, dry herself off, find her way to the bed, slink beneath the covers, and collapse for several more hours of blissful unconsciousness.

•

Travis never made it as far as a leisurely bath. After he dropped his suitcase and backpack inside the door of his room he took off his contacts, grabbed a quick shower, dried off, and then collapsed on his bed, face down, not stirring for several hours on end as well.

But unlike Sasha, Travis' sleep was not entirely peaceful. His thoughts and dreams were troubled by a recurring vision of fighting evil sorcerers and a great red dragon.

CHAPTER 32
TRAVIS AND NANCY

ONBOARD THE LIBERTINE
AT HERZLIYA MARINA
NEAR TEL AVIV, ISRAEL

Just after noon, local time, the captain of Daniel DuMonde's yacht smoothly docked the ship in the marina adjacent to the Ritz Carlton in Herzliya. Daniel had given him urgent orders in the middle of the night to sail for Tel Aviv from Cairo as soon as his people had learned the travel itinerary of Dr. Guillaume Turner's daughter, Alexandra.

DuMonde was no longer as furious as he had been from the wee hours of the morning the night before, i.e. after Penelope's initial reports of Alexey's apparent betrayal and the tragic loss of Burke, compounded by the devastation of the loss of the device. No, he was no longer as angry because he had come up with quite a different theory about what must have happened, and what they now had to do about it.

In Daniel's mind, Penelope had merely assumed, since she neither saw nor heard anything from Alexey, that he was the culprit of Burke's assassination and theft of the device. But wasn't it just as likely that Alexey was also missing and perhaps dead as well? Penelope confirmed that he wasn't answering his radio any longer. And Daniel himself had not heard anything directly from Alexey either.

Furthermore, who else had the power to take on two of his Inner Circle members, and would dare to do so with Penelope not far away? Why, it could be none other than the elusive Dr. Guillaume Turner. Yes, somehow he must have mysteriously beguiled them in Athens with his well-known talent for illusion and trickery and subsequently escaped.

Daniel knew electronic searches for Turner would continue to yield no fruitful results. No, he was too good at hiding his tracks. But that didn't mean that others couldn't lead him to him. The Interpol Chief Inspector that interviewed him the previous week was hot on Dr. Turner's trail. So it could therefore be no coincidence that the affable Allister McKenzie just happened to be on the same flight from London to Tel Aviv as was Turner's daughter Alexandra. Clearly he was following her. And just perhaps, she was on her way to meet with her father.

That was how they would find him once more, and finish the task they started in Athens. It wasn't an option, because Daniel also knew that as long as Dr. Guillaume Turner still drew breath, he would be a threat to them all and to all of their ambitions.

However, Daniel also learned one more important detail: Alexandra Turner was not traveling alone. The passenger manifest of her flight showed a companion traveler with her, identified as one Travis Gardner. His background check revealed that Gardner and Turner's daughter worked together at the University of Texas in Austin. In fact, Gardner worked directly for Miss Turner as her teaching assistant. So it was very likely that he was well aware of everything that was going on and exactly where Dr. Turner, along with Daniel's stolen device, might be hiding. Confirming all his suspicions, a hotel reservation search revealed exactly where Miss Turner and Mr. Gardner could be found at that very moment: at the Ritz Carlton hotel he was currently staring at, right there next to the marina.

Daniel DuMonde checked his watch. It was almost half past four. He sat down at the dining table on the upper deck of his yacht and spread a fine linen napkin across his lap. He smiled at the beautiful redhead seated across from him, dressed in a white two-piece bathing suit, covered by a sheer wrap. She was enjoying a late afternoon early dinner of *duck a' l'orange*, expertly prepared by Daniel's personal chef. He nibbled on a fruit plate, not terribly hungry that early in the day.

Daniel toasted her with a glass of red wine. "To you, my dear."

Dr. Nancy Thompson nodded her thanks, swallowed her bite, and stabbed her fork into a stalk of grilled asparagus.

"You know exactly what to do?" he asked.

"Of course," she replied. "Give me a few hours and I'll find him. Whatever can be known of their plans, will be known."

"I'm counting on it," Daniel grinned. "Happy hunting."

•

Travis' jetlag made him feel like he had been hit by a truck. He could barely move. It was late afternoon, almost 5:30 local time, and he found himself blissfully reclined in a lounge chair by the pool, clad in the one bathing suit he bothered to bring on the trip "just in case." Only a few other bathers were in the pool area. The sun hung low in the western sky over the sea, but was still bright and hot.

Sasha was still hard-down crashed in her room. Allister told them that he had no idea how long they would be parked there at the hotel waiting on hold in Tel Aviv for Dr. Turner's call. Travis thought about perhaps making a touristy excursion the next day down to Jerusalem and Nazareth and checking out all the historical sites and famous holy places. But the bottom line was, at least for the time being, they had nothing to do but sit tight and kill time. Admittedly, that wasn't much of a hardship. The hotel resort was a truly beautiful place, so there was no good reason not to enjoy a little of it while they waited.

Travis had wanted Sasha to come with him down to the pool, perhaps have a little fun together, swim, maybe grab a beer, but no, she was completely out of it, and might be fast asleep until sometime the next day. He had no desire to just sit alone in his room and stare at his computer or watch TV, and so he elected to at least recuperate in the beauty of the Mediterranean resort atmosphere. The Ritz was located right on the beach, with a vast marina right next to it filled with gorgeous boats and beautiful people.

Speaking of such, a beautiful woman with long red hair, wearing a stunning white bikini took off her sheer wrap and laid it down on the lounger right next to Travis'. He wondered how old this woman might be. She could have easily passed for being in her thirties, but her hands looked a little older. He wasn't sure.

She gave him a disarming smile and asked, "Is this seat taken?"

He involuntarily shook his head, and said, "Oh, no, it's free. Help yourself."

She set a small canvas beach bag beside the chair, sat down, and swung her long, shapely legs onto the foot of the lounger. Travis watched her with some degree of interest as she pulled a tube of suntan oil out of her bag and went to work lubricating all of her extremities, face, neck, upper chest, stomach, and sides.

Travis blushed when she abruptly turned her back to him, pulled her long red locks out of the way, held out the tube of oil to him, and looked over her shoulder to ask, "Do you mind?"

"Umm, no problem, sure." He told himself he was just being helpful, right?

It felt strange taking the tube from her, squeezing a little of the oily lotion onto his fingers and then touching her creamy white skin. He dutifully rubbed the oil into her upper back, then below the swimsuit strap down to her waist. Her skin was flawless, so soft and smooth. He didn't really want to stop. She felt almost as soft as—

But he did stop, and handed the tube back to the woman.

She turned once more to face forward toward the pool. "Thank you very much. I really appreciate it."

"No, problem." He politely held out his hand. "I'm Travis."

She shook his hand. "Pleased to meet you Travis. I'm Nancy. So where are you from? I'm guessing you're here on vacation. Ever visited the Holy Land before?"

"I'm from Texas," he said, feeling unusually nervous. "Austin, Texas. And, no, this is my first time here."

She nodded with recognition. "Ah, yes. Austin, the live music capital of the world."

He smiled. "Yes, ma'am. That's the place. We all do our best to keep it weird."

"You sure do," she said. "I've been to South by Southwest a couple of times. It's always a lot of fun."

"So are *you* here on vacation?" he tentatively asked, just trying to keep the conversation going with this beautiful woman. It sure beat sitting around bored. Not that talking to pretty girls was in any way an onerous task for him. Frankly, he was still so tired, he didn't know what to think. But having someone to talk to was definitely enjoyable.

"A little business, a little fun. You know how it is," she said.

One of the hotel's uniformed servers approached them and politely asked. "May I get you two anything from the bar?"

The sultry redhead looked at Travis, flashed him a perfect smile and asked, "You up for a margarita, Travis? I'm buying."

He shrugged, thinking a margarita didn't sound half bad. "Sure."

Nancy ordered, "Two Patron margaritas, please. Rocks. No salt. The big ones."

The server nodded smartly. "Perfect. Coming right up."

Travis asked her, "So where's home for you?"

She said, "New York. In the city. It's busy and can always be a lot of fun. But it's nice to take a break and get away from it now and again."

"I can imagine," he said, trying to keep his glances at her as discreet as possible. "What kind of business are you in?"

"Would you believe me if I said research?"

That was interesting. "What kind of research?"

"Nuclear physics." Her head was resting against the chair back, eyes closed.

Travis' eyes took a quick visual tour of the woman from head to toe. This was clearly supermodel material. He said, "Wow. Nuclear physics would not have been my first guess."

She laughed. "I'm not sure what your first guess would have been, but I'll choose to take that as a compliment."

"Please do," he said. "It was meant that way. I would certainly have believed you if you'd said you were a fashion model or a fitness expert. But a scientist was definitely not what I was expecting."

She playfully pouted. "Why? You don't think smart girls can look like me and go to exotic destinations and have fun?"

Travis could sense he was about to be in a lot of trouble if he didn't get out of this hole he was digging. "No, I don't think that. I mean, it doesn't matter what you do for a living. Anybody can go wherever they want and have all the fun they want. Isn't that what freedom's all about?"

Nancy's eyes opened slowly as she turned her face to him, tipping her sunglasses down a bit on her nose so he could clearly see her sparkling green eyes. "Exactly. Just here for the freedom and the fun. And, you know what, I get the distinct impression that we're going to have a lot of fun today. Right, Travis?"

Travis involuntarily shuddered.

He pictured the image of Sasha's face for but an instant. And for some strange reason suddenly felt like he didn't want Sasha to know where he was – or who he was with.

CHAPTER 33

FROM THE JOURNAL OF WILLIAM TURNER

A MEETING OF THE MINDS

All Magi naturally gain some level of mastery of manipulation over the physical world with Magic. This is most commonly referred to by mortal folk as the Art of Telekinesis.

However, the much more useful faculty of the Magi functioning in the physical world is the ability to discern and know that which is hidden and to communicate when one cannot be heard.

This skill is what is commonly referred to as the Art of Telepathy.

At its most basic conceptual level telepathy is the art of inaudible communication between two sentient beings (i.e. souls). This can be very helpful when two Magi need to communicate but do not wish to be heard by anyone else. This function can even happen over great distances, but like everything else, it has its limitations. One mechanism to increase its effectiveness is the depth of the relationship bond between the two parties. A parent and child is one of the strongest bonds, as is that between a husband and wife, two best friends, or lovers.

The mechanism for establishing this communications link and exercising it is to first picture the target as your focus thought, and then in your mind, call out their name. If the distances between parties is too great, then of course this will not work. But within reasonable ranges it will.

Yes, indeed, there may come a day in your life when a dire cry for help can only be heard telepathically by a loved one not too far away. So this is an important skill to master.

Secondly, a Magi's telepathic skillset has another very useful function, which is to read another person's thoughts. This is quite easy to do with mortal folk, but much more difficult to do with fellow Magi. Suffice it to say that if a superior Magi doesn't want his thoughts read, it shall not be done. Conversely, if a superior Magi wishes to read the thoughts of an inferior Magi, there is little the inferior can do to stop it.

This procedure is called "Cognosco," or a "Reading."

There is one important functional element, or procedure if you will, to consider regarding this particular type of Magic. The Reading of mortal folk or an inferior Magi most effectively occurs via direct physical contact. To wit, the Reading Magi's hands must be placed on either side of the target's head, with his palms over the ears, fingers stretched as wide as possible.

The focus thought is: "Open your mind and let me see."

It is best for the reader to close his own eyes during a Reading, lest it become very confusing. For what is to be read is not words written upon a page; rather, it will be full blown memories, full motion images, sensations, sights and sounds.

Now, while it is absolutely true that a Reading allows you full access to a person's entire library of memories, it isn't practical to see and read them all. Unless you are reading a small child, there is simply too much information to sort through. Instead, what you most typically have access to is what the person is thinking about or experiencing at that exact moment, or from a more practical perspective, the answers to very direct questions. The target cannot lie, for they don't even need to offer a verbal answer. Just the asking of the question will cause their memory to recall the topic and its associated truth as they remember it, and it is these images and sounds you will be able to vividly see and hear.

However, you must be extremely careful with this process, for it is an invasive act. The mind of mortal folk is very fragile and it does not take very much to damage it, sometimes irreparably so, sometimes past the point of effective Healing Spells.

For a Magi, their minds are understandably much stronger than mortal folk and can withstand a more invasive and aggressive Reading. But everyone, whether mortal folk or Magi, has their limits. Should you detect an uncontrollable tremor in the target, or worse a seizure, it is time to cease the Reading, lest you do great neurological harm.

A third manifestation of telepathy is the most difficult one of all, and difficult at best even for true Masters. It is referred to as "Visendus" or a "Viewing." Some Magi call it by its more formal term: a "Remote Viewing."

Its simple explanation is the ability to see using someone else's eyes.

When light enters the lens of the eye, it is registered on the back of the eyeball on a cluster of nerves called the macula, which is directly connected to the optic nerve leading into the brain. Essentially, the eye is like a video camera, and what it records gets translated into electrical signals that are passed into the brain. That electrical signal is quite literally a form of communication, just like a data stream. And as such it can be tapped into by a Magi to see exactly what you are seeing in real-time, as opposed to prerecorded memories via a Reading.

Fortunately, this process isn't invasive when employed remotely, meaning it is not involuntary. Without physically touching the actual viewer, the source viewer must voluntarily open up their mind to a receiving target, and the receiving target must voluntarily "take the call" you might say. When that connection is made, then the Remote Viewing can take place.

From my own experience I can attest that this is far from a seamless crystal clear process. It can come through as single images, or snippets of scenes, as well as blurred shapes and colors. But for Magi working together, this is a most useful utility.

CHAPTER 34
THE DRAGON

THE RITZ CARLTON HERZLIYA
NEAR TEL AVIV, ISRAEL

Sasha awoke a little after seven in the evening—starving.

She managed to clean herself up, get dressed, and then head down to the lobby to forage for some food. When the elevator deposited her on the ground floor she walked past the registration desk and made her way toward the Herbert Samuel restaurant. The brochures in her room said it was supposed to have world-class fare, and kosher to boot—not that kosher food was a big deal for her personally. She was Catholic. On the other hand, a great big BLT sounded awesome at that moment, but she seriously doubted she would find one on the menu. However, before she found the restaurant, she spotted a familiar face sitting in the lobby lounge.

It was Allister.

"Hey there," she croaked, her voice not yet fully up to speed. She managed to get herself into a fresh pair of jeans and a floral top, but her road-weary face and hastily brushed hair still betrayed that delightful "just got out of bed" look.

Allister was slowly stirring a cup of hot tea and reading something on his phone. "Ah, Sasha, my dear. You're awake."

"Barely." She took a seat on the barstool next to him. There were only a few other patrons at the bar at that moment. Although, the main lobby was fairly busy with arriving and departing guests. In the background a relaxing orchestral piece played softly on the hotel's sound system.

A handsome young bartender came over, having noticed that Sasha spoke English. "What can I get for you, ma'am?" His English was perfect, with an ever so slight Hebrew accent.

Sasha asked him, "Can I get food here at the bar?"

He nodded. "At this hour, you can order anything you like from our dinner service at the restaurant. I'll get you a menu. And what will you be having to drink?"

She pointed to Allister's cup. "I'll have some of what he's having."

"Of course," the nice young man smiled warmly, put an English menu on the bar before her, and set about making her a cup of hot tea.

Sasha looked down at the menu. Everything on it sounded good, lots of delicious-sounding seafood and sushi dishes. She looked back at Allister. "Have you heard anything else from my father?"

He frowned. "Not yet. Nothing after he reported losing sight of their quarry in Syria last night. I expect they've been up there in Syria and Iraq searching all day today."

Sasha spied a tuna steak on the menu that came with an orange vegetable puree and red pepper oil that sounded delightful. When the cute bartender returned, she decided she'd go with that. In fact, she didn't want to wait. Sasha looked over to the bartender and focused on the thought: *Come to me.*

The young man quickly brought the cup of hot water and tea bag over to her. As he approached, Sasha closed her eyes and sent forth her thoughts to him: *I'll take the tuna steak.*

He stopped abruptly and set her teacup down. "I'm getting the strangest impression that you just might prefer the tuna tonight. Am I right?"

She gave him a friendly smile. "*Yes*. That's amazing. It's like you can read my mind."

Allister chuckled, even though he was still nose down in his reading on his phone.

"I'll get that order in for you right away," the bartender said.

Sasha was about to ask Allister what was so interesting to read when she was hit by a very strange and uneasy feeling. Her head began to pound, as though it was a sudden migraine attack. And for no discernable reason, she suddenly became very anxious about Travis.

She pressed her fingertips to her temples, closed her eyes, and asked Allister, "Have you seen or talked to Travis lately?"

"No, I haven't," he said. "I assumed he was as fatigued as you were, and was getting some much needed rest. Why do you ask?"

Sasha shook her head and tried to shake the ominous feeling away. "I'm not sure. I've just got a weird feeling all the sudden."

"About Travis?"

"Yes. Like something…I don't know…was *wrong*. *Very* wrong." She looked at Allister's phone. "Can you please call the hotel switchboard and see if they can ring his room? I think I'll feel a whole lot better if I know he's all right."

"Certainly." Allister did just as she asked while she sat there patiently waiting, but clearly he could see she was in some kind of distress. In a few moments the phone was ringing. It rang several times but with no answer. After a few more rings Allister ended the call. "I'm sorry, my dear, but it appears he's not in his room. Or if he is, he's not answering his phone. Perhaps in the shower?"

"Maybe. Or, could he have been so tired he'd not hear the phone?" she said, more wondering aloud than asking a real question.

"You know him better than I," Allister said. "Do you know him to be a light or heavy sleeper."

She gave him an odd look. "No, I *wouldn't* know that."

The elderly gentleman held up a defensive hand. "Oh, no, I didn't mean to imply anything improper, my dear. I just meant you might have observed his sleeping habits on your flight over."

"Sorry," she shrugged. "But I have no idea. I think I nodded off more on the way over here than he did."

Sasha!

Sasha's hands suddenly flew to the sides of her head again as a bolt of searing pain flashed behind her eyes, which were now clamped down tight. It was much more intense this time. The image of large dark-red scales, like that of an alligator or crocodile, flashed in her mind.

Sasha! Hear me! Sasha! Help me!

"What is it?" Allister sat forward in alarm.

Through clenched teeth, Sasha groaned, "It's Travis. He's in trouble. I can *hear* him. In my mind. He's screaming and screaming in pain and crying out for help." Now she could see a ravenous maw opening to reveal rows of sharp jagged teeth. The image began to thrash back and forth, looking left and right, past the rough scales in front of her. Objects became visible. It was a room. A hotel room. A window. Outside the window was a vista of the sea and boats far below parked in neat rows.

Sasha! I'm here! Find me! Help me!

"Where is he?" Allister implored.

"Somewhere high up." Sasha strained to see and comprehend the flood of images and sensations suddenly pouring into her head in a blurred torrent. "Definitely somewhere close...here in the hotel."

She saw the image of a large hotel suite with a contemporary styled sitting group.

"A big suite, could be a penthouse, I think, maybe..." she stammered.

A scene of a recorded memory suddenly played in her mind, but it was not one of her memories...

•

"I really shouldn't go in," Travis' voice said to a very pretty redhead wearing nothing but a skimpy white bathing suit with a sheer wrap around her shoulders. They appeared to be standing in a foyer before two double-doors.

The woman said to him, "Travis, you have to see this place. Just take a quick tour. Then you can tell Sasha all about it when she wakes up. Because I'm telling you, I've stayed at lots of fancy hotels in my day, but this suite will blow you away. I swear, it's bigger than my apartment back in New York. When I checked in, they told me that every sitting US President, with the exception of the current one, of course, has stayed in this suite ever since the place was first built."

As Travis' gaze panned over to a brass placard which read: Presidential Suite, his voice said, "Well, maybe just a quick peek."

His eyes moved forward through the double-doors into a small inner foyer. Just to his left was a small bar and beyond it a kitchen, which opened into a formal dining room that seated ten people. To his right was a half-bath. Moving further inside was an elegant living room with a gorgeous view of the Mediterranean. Beyond the living room, to his right was the master bathroom and master bedroom. He had just stepped into the bedroom when something hard and black grabbed his shoulder and spun him around.

The mesmerizing face of the redhead was gone. He was now staring into the blazing yellow eyes of a monster.

•

"No, not just a penthouse, it's the Presidential Suite. That's where he is. And he's in great pain."

Sasha! Please!

"Let's go!" Allister pocketed his phone and quickly took Sasha by the hand, led her to the elevators, and pushed the "UP" button.

"Can't we do something a little more...*expeditious?*" she asked.

Allister nodded. "Yes, as soon as we're out of sight. Popping out of here from the bar might attract a bit of undue attention."

"Right," she agreed, as the bell chimed and the elevator doors opened. Thankfully the car was empty.

As soon as the elevator doors closed behind them, Allister hugged Sasha close to his body. A high pitch whine grew in intensity and then...

FLASH!

The elevator car was empty.

Sasha's next conscious sight was standing in front of the set of double doors in a contemporary appointed hallway foyer with a brass placard next to them which read: Presidential Suite. She knew she didn't need a key. Travis's voice in her head grew even louder, screaming in horror for help.

Sasha! Help me!

Her hands thrust forward as if she were pushing over a large object. The double doors flew open before them, banging hard against the walls inside the suite. Allister and Sasha bolted forward, abruptly stopping inside the living room area when they saw no one.

A muffled whimpering could be distinctly heard coming from what was undoubtedly the master bedroom of the nearly 2,000 square foot luxury suite. Sasha ran through the bedroom doorway and saw it first, recoiling in revulsion, her forearms clenched tight against her chest, fists pressed in front of her face. Allister burst into the room and stopped cold as well, gasping for breath, his elbow lifted up and pointing forward, hiding his grimace behind the back of his hand.

Travis was indeed in the bedroom, seated on the foot of the king-sized bed. Standing before him, or rather, towering over him at about ten feet in height or more, was a hideous, dark-red reptilian creature, covered in thick armored scales, with a long barbed tail swishing back and forth. Black leathern bat wings were folded tight against its sides. A row of sharp spikes ran down its entire spine from head to tail. Its forelegs were much smaller than its powerful hind legs, but its forepaws sported long, sharp, gleaming, onyx-black talons, which at that moment were holding Travis' head on either side, covering his ears.

Travis' body was trembling uncontrollably in a violent seizure. A froth of spittle coursed down his chin and dribbled in a thick viscous tendril into his lap. His eyes were locked open, milky and terrified.

"Travis!" Sasha screamed in horror.

The beast's head turned from its task on a reticulating serpentine neck to address the intrusion to its business. Its large burning yellow eyes with reptilian vertical black slits for pupils locked onto Sasha's terrified eyes. The creature began to inhale deeply and a burning glow illuminated in its upper chest and throat.

Allister half jumped in front of Sasha, half pulled her behind him, then locked his forearms in an "X" in front of his face, commanding with great authority, "*Ergo Praesidium*! We are protected!"

The Protection Spell radiated over Allister and Sasha in a perfect sphere, undulating and rippling, just as the reptile's head struck forward like a viper and a torrid blast of fire shot forth from its carnivorous maw, only to quickly dissipate in the cloud of Allister's spell. Allister stood firm. The beast blasted its jets of fire at the intruders yet again, and then a third time before reeling back and roaring at the ceiling in frustration.

The ineffectiveness of its attack enraged the beast to its core. It prepared to attack again. Its chest and throat began to glow red and yellow once more as it drew and another long breath. Yet, when it saw Allister bringing both of his hands to his chin, and blowing into his palms, it abruptly released Travis' head, and leapt headlong for the open balcony door. Its wings unfurled as it made its escape, soaring high into the early evening sky.

Travis fell forward into a heap on the floor.

Sasha rushed to him, pulling him into protectively into her arms and cradling his head. "Allister, he's not breathing!"

PART 3

THE MASTERY OF MAGIC

"The world is full of obvious things which nobody by any chance ever observes."

Sir Arthur Conan Doyle
The Hound of the Baskervilles

"Greater love has no one that this, than to lay down one's life for his friends."

John 15:13

CHAPTER 35

ALLIES AND ENEMIES

Dr. William Turner ended his call with Allister McKenzie and put his phone back in his shirt-pocket. Penelope could tell by the look on his face the news wasn't good. The road they were on was deserted.

"What is it?" she asked, hesitant to hear the answer.

William pointed ahead. "We can't spend any more time looking for Alexey up here in Syria or in Iraq. We have got to get back to Tel Aviv as quickly as possible. There's been an attack."

Penelope's eyes went wide, demanding to know, "Is Sasha all right?"

"Yes," he nodded. "She's fine. But not her friend Travis. He's been hurt pretty badly."

"By whom?" Penelope accelerated the Range Rover down the barren highway. She knew if she pushed it and drove all night they could be in Tel Aviv sometime early the following morning, perhaps by eight or nine o'clock.

"Apparently it was our good friend Dr. Nancy Thompson," he said, "in her more colorful, fire-breathing, and dangerous form."

"I told you she was a dragon," she snapped.

"I believed you," William said. "But I had no idea she or anyone else could possibly know where Allister, Sasha, and Travis were."

"Actually, I'm not surprised," Penelope said. "You know they have full access to any and all travel records and all online data, as much so if not more than Allister does via his Interpol connections. I'm sure they've been keeping an eye on Sasha for some time because of you, and especially of late. But a brazen ambush on them makes no sense. It would seem to make a lot more sense to lie in wait for you to come and meet with them, or follow them should they intend to come to you, that is, if they truly see you as their primary threat."

William shrugged and said, "Maybe it does make a little sense, at least in terms of how they found them. In fact, it could very well accidentally be Allister's fault."

"Why do you say that?" she asked.

He explained, "You said he paid a visit to Daniel last week claiming to be looking for me, even though he was really trying to track down all the other members of the Inner Circle. So that means Daniel knows Interpol is trying to find me. So he simply begins to track Allister. Allister travels to Israel, my daughter is on the same flight, data filters spot the correlation and flag it. The next thing you know, Nancy appears and attacks Travis at their hotel in order to find out everything they know about me."

"What did she do to him?" she asked.

"From what Allister described, she was Reading him—to the point of no return." He shook his head in sadness. "Hard to say what the full extent of the damage is."

Penelope let out a long sigh. "If that's true then Nancy now knows that Allister, Sasha and Travis were all originally planning to come up to meet you in Damascus first thing in the morning, and that your intent was to stop them from delivering the device in Raqqa at midday. Plus, she also now knows anything else Sasha and Allister bothered to share with him about you. But, on the positive side, they may know very little about my involvement thus far in helping you."

He agreed, "I think it's safe to make that assumption. With Travis unable to defend himself, Daniel's thinking may be for he and Nancy to now separately attack Allister or Sasha next with superior numbers. Which if true, makes me believe we need to get to them quickly, and get them to a much safer location."

"Before the dragon returns," she added.

William thought out loud as they drove over the featureless countryside. "So who is on whose side? Clearly, Alexey is no longer working with Daniel."

Penelope noted, "If he's taking the weapon to the Persians, then I would say he's more likely to be in league with Archbishop Vasquez. He's the one who desperately wants to start World War III by doing grave apocalyptic-level harm to the Israelis as a catalyst."

"So General bin Faisal is probably also in that camp," he mused, "as I'm sure he has no great affection for the Israelis."

"Another safe assumption," she said. "I may be wrong about them, but I'd be extremely surprised if Walter Stephens and Frank Donaldson weren't still solidly aligned with Daniel and ready to support him. I don't see either of them as End-of-the-World supporters. I see no motive for them to betray Daniel."

William calculated, "Okay then, of the remaining six of them besides Daniel, three stand with him, and the other three are the renegades. But, Daniel also still believes you stand with him."

"As far as I know he does," she agreed.

"So that's five Magi against three in his mind," he concluded. "Which is still acceptable odds. And Daniel will never yield to an insurrection while he still has the stronger hand."

"Of course not," she said.

William said. "But you must realize that all that matters at this point is stopping the weapon from whatever Alexey and company intend to do with it. And to do that we still have to find Alexey. *Someone* must know where he is and where he's going."

Penelope nodded, "And if I had to wager, I believe that someone is most likely going to either be General Mohammed bin Faisal or his Excellency Archbishop Vasquez."

"Exactly," he concurred. "And either of them or both of them just might be easier for us to find rather than Alexey at the moment. And then they'll lead us straight to him."

"How?" she asked.

William pulled his phone out again and began to redial Allister. "We do it the same way Daniel's people found Sasha and Travis. Allister has just as many data assets at his disposal as they do, if not more. If they've bought a plane ticket, checked into a hotel, used an ATM, or even bought a meal on a credit card, we'll know that very quickly."

"I hope you're right," she said.

Chapter 36
Alexey

Ben Gurion Airport
Tel Aviv, Israel

It was just after dawn, about fifteen minutes after sunrise, at precisely 6:03 a.m. to be exact.

The white transport van made its way to the top level of the long-term parking garage and stopped amid a few other vehicles. The van was nondescript, much like thousands of other delivery vans used prominently all over the city. No one would pay this van any special mind. Alexey Borochenko threw the van's keys in the glove box, knowing he'd never need them again. He got out of the van's cab and went to the rear of the vehicle, unlocked the doors and opened the cargo compartment.

There it was.

Inside the cargo bay stood the wooden crate bound in chains. Inside the crate was a device about the size of a hotel room refrigerator, which was in reality a 1.2 megaton warhead, plutonium-based, of Pakistani manufacture. Such products were very reliable, if operated properly. It took him several minutes to manually unchain the crate and open it. He knew he couldn't use any magic anywhere in the immediate vicinity of the device, so everything he did was done manually. Thus, just as instructed by Dr. Thompson, he connected the power supply, activated the arming triggers with two brass keys turned in unison, and then entered the arming security codes.

Only one step left.

Alexey set the detonation timer for twenty-seven hours away, which was roughly 9:07 a.m. the following morning, give or take a few seconds. Detonation would occur during peak morning rush hour, both in terms of the volume of flights and cars on the highways. That amount of time would also be more than sufficient for him to catch his flight to Amsterdam later that morning, and then make a connecting flight to Kiev and be far, far away when the device did its earth-changing magic.

For good measure Alexey reached down and pulled the two brass keys out of the arming triggers and stuffed them in his pants pocket. He concluded his task by reciting a sacred Shiite prayer for victory in battle. With eyes closed and reciting the ancient Arabic lines by rote, his memories wandered far back to the long and arduous path that brought him to this momentous day of vengeance and triumph.

In his mind's eye, he could see the face of his father.

Alexey's father, for whom he was named, was eastern Ukrainian, a very hard-working factory worker from Kharkov, which was Ukraine's second largest city. However, Alexey's mother was Persian. She was a strictly devout Muslim who came from a very poor family in Tehran. His parents had first met in Kiev shortly after his mother had fled from Iran to Ukraine in the late 1960's when it was still ruthlessly ruled by the Shah, and in her estimation the culture had begun to become more westernized and vulgar. Alexey's father initially took the beautiful young refugee woman into his home as a servant girl out of pity, but within a year he married her so she could remain in the country and not be deported by the Soviets. The following year Alexey was born.

Alexey's mother made the decision to return to Iran with her young son soon after the news of the Islamic Revolution in 1979. However, his father, an Eastern Orthodox Christian, flatly refused to go with her. It was for that reason, as she patiently explained one cold winter day to her seven year old child, why it was necessary for the faithful to slay the infidels and to become part of the revolution. He watched her cut his father's throat as he ate his dinner that night—the very night they left for Iran.

Alexey never saw Ukraine again until his first year of University, when his mosque's Imam told him that he felt Alexey could be of much greater service to their cause if he returned to Ukraine and blended into the culture of the West. Alexey spoke fluent Russian, Ukrainian, English and Farsi. He was told that in time he would be called upon to do a great act of service for Allah. But for many years after he returned, no one ever contacted him nor asked him to do any great act of service.

However, it was while working for a large computer firm in Kiev that

Alexey had a chance meeting with a wealthy Italian businessman named Antonio Angelucci. It was Antonio who recognized a rare talent in Alexey that he had no idea even existed. But it wasn't long before Antonio became Alexey's Master and began to train him in the Art of Magic.

Like most gifted young Magi, Alexey progressed quickly, but before Antonio could complete Alexey's training, he was murdered by three of his Magi subordinates: a Frenchman named Daniel DuMonde, who was in league with Daniel's two mistresses, an American named Nancy Thompson, and Antonio's very own wife, Penelope Angelucci. Daniel DuMonde subsequently usurped Antonio's leadership position in the secret group to which they all belonged known as the Inner Circle. It was then that Alexey chose to make it his top priority to also become accepted in that group and one day find a means to exact vengeance for his Master.

Five years later, when Archbishop Renaldo Vasquez, another powerful Magi and member of the Inner Circle approached Alexey about making the arms deal for the nuclear device with the Shiites in Iran instead of the Sunnis in Syria, and especially when he realized doing so also meant the overthrow and imminent deaths of Daniel, Nancy, and Penelope, Alexey was only too happy to join the coup. However, if the truth be known, it was primarily due to Alexey's personal contacts with his old Grand Imam in Tehran, a very well-connected and influential Mullah from his youth by the name of Farshid Sassani, that set all the wheels of the current operation in motion.

Thus, for Alexey, this grand operation had nothing to do with gaining riches, but was both an act of his faith and also an act of holy vengeance on all those who deserved it most. Plus, the Tel Aviv airport was a perfect target location to do what needed to be done. For not only would the airport be totally destroyed, along with most, if not all of Tel Aviv and the Little Satan's infidels, but it would also take numerous international flights with it, directly impacting the citizens of many nations all over the world. World outrage would never be greater. And, naturally, angry people are the most prone to take violent action, especially in a rage of righteous indignation and a blood lust for retribution.

Yes, the Day of Retribution was at hand.

Tomorrow morning would, at last, mark the beginning of the great retribution prophesied centuries ago. Imam Sassani had told him so only a few months ago, when they were joyfully reunited for a planning meeting in Tehran with Archbishop Vasquez. The Imam explained to him how this was truly his fate, his destiny, his holy role in the events that were soon to come to pass.

A tear of pride and joy trickled down Alexey's cheek.

It was time to fulfill his final duties.

When the crate and the van were re-secured, Alexey fetched his overnight bag from the cab of the van and headed for the garage's stairwell and then made his way down to the street level. From there he casually walked toward the departing flights concourse, like all of the other travelers at that hour. He checked his pockets for his passport. Actually, it wasn't his own Ukrainian passport he had with him to use on today's flights, but that of the late Englishman Stephan Burke. So before making his way to the ticket counter to check in, he stopped by the men's room.

Alexey had to wait a few minutes for a few other travelers to do their business and vacate the restroom before he had it to himself for a moment. However, a brief moment of privacy was all he required.

He stood at the row of sinks looking into the mirror. A thoughtful glance at Burke's passport photo was all he needed. As he closed his eyes and concentrated, Stephan Burke's face became his focus thought.

And then it happened.

Alexey opened his eyes. The round, bearded face of Stephan Burke was staring back at him. He laughed, "Stephan, I always thought you always were such a handsome devil."

CHAPTER 37

ONBOARD THE LIBERTINE
HERZLIYA MARINA
NEAR TEL AVIV, ISRAEL

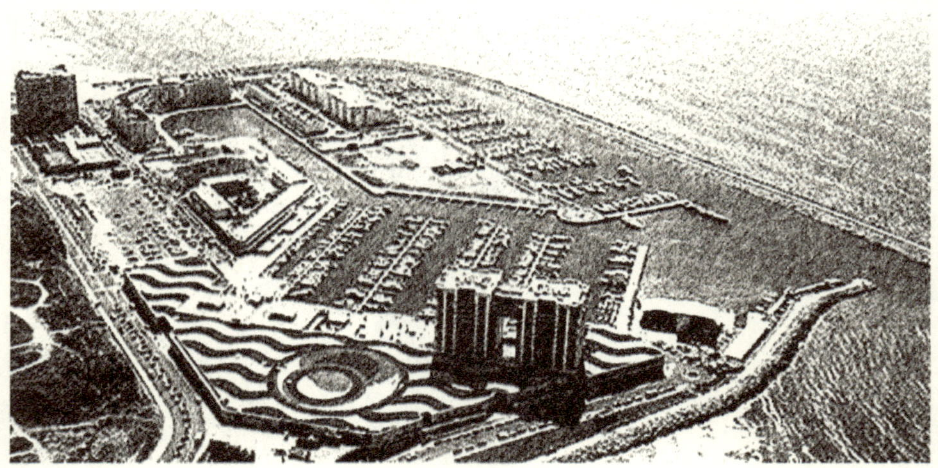

Daniel DuMonde stood on the bow of his ship in the morning air, astride a large section of green artificial turf. Near the starboard side of the section of turf a two inch length of half-inch diameter white rubber hose, as is commonly used at most driving ranges, served as his golf tee. Daniel put another golf ball on the tee, took his driver and proceeded to smash the ball over 300 yards out into the Mediterranean.

Judge Frank Donaldson applauded from a seat near the rail. "Nice one, Daniel."

Daniel gave a nod of thanks to Frank, and then turned to Dr. Nancy Thompson, who was sitting on a chaise lounge a few feet away, no longer in her reptilian form, but once again the becoming redhead attired in tasteful beachwear.

Daniel asked her, "So if I understand you correctly, then Dr. Turner could very well be on his way here to see *us*?"

"That's right," Nancy said.

"Splendid." Daniel grabbed another ball.

"Plus, the Interpol Chief Inspector you met, Allister McKenzie, turns out is in reality Magi, a close compatriot of Dr. Turner's, and, in fact, he is William's Master, if you can believe it."

"And how powerful of Magi are his daughter and the young man you read last night?" Daniel smacked his golf ball far into the shimmering blue sea.

"How do you do that?" asked Donaldson. "Skill or magic?"

Daniel just gave Frank a knowing wink.

Nancy answered, "Travis Gardner is not that strong. He shows promise, but needs a few years of seasoning. He believes Sasha Turner to be much further developed than himself, but she is still learning and growing. Neither will have supreme confidence in their powers at this stage, and that will be their primary weakness. The young man also has strong protective feelings for Turner's daughter, and deeply romantic ones as well. That will surely be useful to us."

Daniel returned his driver to his golf bag and gestured for Frank to take a turn. Frank selected an iron from Daniel's bag and prepared a ball on the tee. Frank was dressed casually that day, in khaki cargo shorts, a navy blue Ralph Laruen polo shirt, and tan leather huarache sandals.

DuMonde asked Nancy, "And what of our dear Penelope?"

Nancy shrugged, "He didn't know much of anything about her. They've never met. He did believe that Penelope is Sasha's true birth mother, and that Sasha just learned that Penelope is alive and not dead as Sasha was told by her father as a young child."

Frank hit his ball, slicing it rather severely. He swore under his breath and grabbed another ball from the wire bucket.

"Any possibility she might be working *with* Guillaume?" Daniel asked. "I knew of her first marriage to him a very long time ago. But my understanding was that it wasn't a very amicable divorce. They didn't communicate at all, not even about the daughter, and rarely on any Inner Circle business. My understanding from her was that she despised him."

"All I can tell you is, if they have managed to reconcile somehow after twenty years of no contact, and she is now helping him, then the young man was completely unaware of it." Nancy took a long sip of her Bloody Mary. "We both know what Penelope was willing to do for you and for the Inner Circle. I think she's earned a little benefit of the doubt. As far as I know she is still completely loyal to you and right now is still out searching for Alexey and the device. If she has contacted William at all, then it might be to track him for you. Or in this case, perhaps even to bring him to you."

"That would be most convenient if she did, and much appreciated." He paused and then laughed at a strange thought. "Although, under the circumstances, until the device is located, assuming Guillaume doesn't have it himself already, having Guillaume and his coterie search for it, might actually be quite beneficial."

•

The device, at that very moment, was parked less than ten miles away. It's timer read just under twenty-four hours remaining.

•

After the morning driving session on the ship's bow, Frank Donaldson returned to his stateroom for a quick shower. But before he stepped into the luxurious marble, walk-in shower, his phone on the dressing stand played the chime of an arriving text message. He grabbed his phone and looked at the incoming message.

It was from Archbishop Vasquez:

Alexey going home. Package delivered. Exit now.

Frank understood. It was time to leave, and do so quickly. Alexey had done his part, as had Frank done his: i.e. to ensure that Daniel DuMonde and Nancy Thompson would be close enough to the blast radius to not only complete their sacred mission to cleanse the planet, but at the same time to usher in the new leadership ascendancy of the Inner Circle, and do so without the need of a formal challenge by combat against a maniacal borderline Master, who also had a dragon at his disposal to call upon as personal champion if needed.

It was a perfect plan – which is why the Archbishop and the General were in such enthusiastic support of it. And why Frank himself was about to become the new high leader of the Inner Circle.

CHAPTER 38
WILLIAM AND PENELOPE

THE RITZ CARLTON HERZLIYA
NEAR TEL AVIV, ISRAEL

William and Penelope pulled up to the entrance of the Ritz just after 9:00 a.m., local time. They been driving all night, and despite being delayed by traffic and a few construction zones, they made all haste to get to Tel Aviv and find Allister and Sasha, who were both to be found in Travis Gardner's room at his bedside.

Sasha startled when she heard the knock on the hotel room door. A quick glance through the peephole revealed the worried face of her father – a face she'd not seen in-person in almost three years. She flung the door open and threw herself into her father's arms.

Dr. William Turner held his daughter close for several moments, feeling the wetness of her tears against his neck. Her arms were squeezing him nearly to the point of pain. "We're here, honey. It's going to be okay."

He sincerely hoped that was true.

Through her blurry tears, Sasha saw her father wasn't alone. A very beautiful woman with long black hair, as black as her own, stood a few feet away. A tear was coursing down the woman's face as well. But it was the woman's eyes themselves that told Sasha the truth. She knew those brown eyes well – despite not seeing them for twenty years, those were the eyes she could never forget. A flood of memories washed over her. Those were the eyes that oversaw Band-Aids on skinned knees, that looked expectantly as she held up flash cards to learn her multiplication tables, that sparkled with mirth when they made cupcakes for bake sales, that cried when she sang at the kindergarten Christmas program, but mostly those eyes were the last thing she saw at night as a child when she was kissed goodnight and tucked into bed.

Neither of them knew quite what to do or say. Sasha wanted to throw her arms around her mother, too; and Penelope felt the same; but they both just stood there staring into each other's eyes, motionless, afraid.

William broke the spell. "Sasha, this is Penelope Angelucci. And yes, she is your mother." He glanced at Penelope. "Penelope, my dear, this is your daughter Sasha."

That was sufficient to prompt both women to rush to one another and hold each other tight.

William gave them a moment of intimacy and tears before he spoke up, interrupting their awkward reunion, "I know you two have much to talk about, and that's understandable, but we're here to help Travis right now, if we can. How is he?"

Sasha pulled herself away from her mother's grasp and replied, "Of course. Come this way."

Upon entering the hotel suite William embraced Allister warmly, introduced him to Penelope, and then asked him, "What's your prognosis? How bad is it?"

Allister's expression was grim. "I won't lie to you, William. If we hadn't interrupted the process when we did, he'd already be dead. Right now he's in a coma-like state. Basically, his mind has been scrambled, completely devastated. If he can make it back at all, he's got a whole life's worth of thoughts to put back in proper order."

Penelope asked, "Have all the healing spells been tried?"

Allister nodded, "Repeatedly. His body is sound. It's up to him now, and whatever Providence offers as his destiny."

Sasha sat down on the bed and took Travis' hand in hers. "Come back to us, Travis. We *need* you. *I* need you." A fresh rivulet of warm tears ran down her face.

"Can he be moved?" William asked.

"I think so," Allister said. "As I said, physically, he'll be all right."

"Good," William replied. "Then here's what I want you to do. Check out of here and take Sasha and Travis to the Sadot hotel. It's right by the airport. I'm assuming your Interpol connections can help you get rooms under a clean alias so Daniel DuMonde's people can't locate you so easily again. And, if I need you all to travel on a moment's notice, you'll all be ready to go. I've got to continue the search for Alexey."

Allister looked at bit embarrassed. "I can certainly manage a good bit more discretion from here on out." He then added with a bit more cheer. "We do have one bit of good news. Signals department has got a couple of solid hits on the General and the Archbishop."

"And?"

"And you're not going to like it," Allister smirked.

"Try me."

"All right. It appears they are indeed in league with the Persians, just as we suspected. So much so, they are in Tehran as we speak. We have their full itineraries and know where they're both staying."

Penelope asked, "Do you think they might have instructed Alexey to take the weapon to them there?"

Allister shrugged. "I suppose it's possible. But it's far more likely that they wouldn't have wasted any time and effort to transport it hundreds of miles across an unstable Iraqi territory, only to send it back across the same hazardous route aimed at a target in Israel. For all we know it could be sitting right outside as we speak."

"No, I don't believe it is," said William. "I'm guessing if they really want the shock and awe value of targeting Israel to start their world war, Jerusalem is much more likely the target. That's why I recommend that you stay further north here in Tel Aviv, where, worst case, I think you'll be safer for the time being. But get away from this particular hotel. Nancy and Daniel know you're here."

•

It wasn't true, of course. The device wasn't sitting right outside the Ritz, nor was it anywhere near Jerusalem or Haifa. It was still just a few miles away, parked at Ben Gurion International airport.

Its timer now read just under twenty-three hours until detonation.

CHAPTER 39
THE FALCON

TEHRAN, IRAN

"What a triumph of worldwide ecumenism we have here, my esteemed and honored friends!" proclaimed Archbishop Renaldo Vasquez to his two luncheon companions, which were his colleague General Mohammed bin Faisal, and the Ayatollah's chief foreign minister and senior cleric, Farshid Sassani. The Catholic priest laughed heartily and joked, "So a Sunni, a Shi'a and a Catholic walk into a bar..."

The Muslim cleric joined his laughter, "Ah, but we have no bars in Iran! Allah forbids it."

The General from Saudi Arabia huffed, "The same is theoretically true in my kingdom. But for the right price..."

They all laughed all the more.

If the truth be told, despite the strict Islamic prohibition of alcohol in Iran, it was the third greatest consumer of alcoholic beverages of all the

Muslim majority countries, following only behind Lebanon and Turkey, where alcohol consumption is perfectly legal.

All three men richly toasted to their imminent success with a savory sip of Remy Martin's Louis XIII cognac, which had been discretely smuggled in from Kurdistan, of course.

Archbishop Vasquez tempered his mirth as he shared with the Mullah, "We are most pleased to inform you that we have just confirmed with our colleague that the package is on target, in country, and properly prepared for its destiny."

"And this is someone you trust with so great a responsibility?" Sassani asked.

Vasquez smiled and said, "Yes. As do you. It is none other than Alexey Borochenko."

Sassani nodded his approval, "Ah! Alexey. Yes, he is like a son to me. I cannot think of another faithful soul I would trust more."

"Which is why he was chosen," the general added.

Sassani said, "Then you may be assured the appropriate wire transfers to Switzerland will occur this afternoon, one third in good faith, and the remainder as soon as confirmation of full consummation of the event is received. You will then be able to withdraw full payment in bullion at your discretion."

Vasquez and bin Faisal shared a look of satisfaction.

The general was privy to all the financial details of the transaction, since it was his connections with the Pakistani Inter-Service Intelligence service, or ISI, that made the entire deal possible. Five billion in gold could get a working device from Pakistan, which was originally to be acquired by the Syrian militant jihadists for double that price. They certainly had the money, as their oil revenues continued to accumulate in direct proportion to the oil rich lands of Syria and Iraq they continued to conquer and plunder.

The Iranians, on the other hand, whose eyes were fixed solely on fulfillment of ancient prophecy and the realization of their eschatology, had no problem paying a hundred billion for the single working device. They had spent far more than that figure in their own inept pursuit of a uranium enrichment and nuclear weapons program. So, in reality, it was a fantastic bargain for them – a simple buy versus build decision.

Besides, if the logic of their gambit was correct, they would only ever need the one weapon. The Persians invented the game of chess, were masters of the game, and were supremely confident that what they were planning was certain to be the checkmate move for which they had been praying for generations.

The three men sat outside at a table located on the 8th floor balcony of the elegant Divan restaurant, which was situated above the Sam Center mall, right in the heart of the city. It offered a magnificent view of the northern neighborhoods and the northern mountains. The entire balcony section had been exclusively reserved that day for this very private meal and official government meeting. The view really was spectacular, noted Archbishop Vasquez as he watched a red-necked falcon riding the air currents high into a cloudless sky. A most majestic bird, he thought to himself.

"Where exactly will the most holy event take place?" Sassani asked.

Vasquez replied, "Only Alexey knows."

"Is that wise?" the Iranian asked.

General bin Faisal answered, "Extremely. Not even we have been told of its precise placement. We just know that it is already somewhere within Israel right now, and ready to go. So even if tortured, we could not reveal its location, and thus it cannot be stopped at this point. Its destiny is certain. Plus, we trust Alexey to ensure that a most opportune and effective location has been carefully chosen. We guarantee you shall not be disappointed."

"But what if *he* is caught?" Sassani asked most urgently.

The Archbishop shook his head. "It can't happen. It's too late. He is far away by now on his way back to Europe. And by tomorrow, he will be well beyond anyone's reach to make any difference."

The red-necked falcon caught Vasquez's attention once more, flying a bit lower, a little closer to the building where the priest could make out more of the bird's exquisite colorings.

Sassani nodded yet again, even more pleased. "Yes, yes. Excellent. And how long do you believe shall we wait for the blessed event?"

The Archbishop smiled, "For that question, I can be much more precise. We guarantee that it shall come on the morrow before the setting of the sun."

The general laughed, "Which is why my charter flight to Thailand leaves later this afternoon."

The Iranian asked, "Do you really think the retaliation of the west will be so swift? Or do you think we are in any danger here directly from the device itself?"

The Arab military officer replied, "This weapon is relatively low yield. Only one-point-two megatons. The primary impact radius will be about twenty kilometers or so. Complete incineration and annihilation. The secondary blast wave will be a zone of fifty to a hundred kilometers away, knocking down anything standing. And I also suspect there will be lethal radioactive fallout, an evil wind you might say, that could ride the Mediterranean breezes across Jordan, into parts of Syria, and perhaps as far as western Iraq, but likely no further. But don't doubt for a moment that if any of the Israeli Defense Force remains intact, their military response will be exceedingly swift and most severe."

The Mullah smiled, "We're counting on it. We have our Press Release ready to dispatch on all the major wire services, taking full credit for the scourging of the unrighteous two hours after the confirmation and satellite damage assessments have been completed."

The men toasted to their success once more as Vasquez watched the falcon he'd been admiring circle yet closer, and on its next pass, alight on the balcony rail several yards away in his full line of sight. The Mullah's back was to the bird, and it sat perpendicular to the General's view.

"Oh, my!" the prelate exclaimed with genuine pleasure. "Look. Do you see the beautiful bird there? The falcon. If I am not mistaken, I believe it is a red-necked falcon. Such a majestic auburn head and golden markings on its face. Incredible."

"Are birds an interest of yours?" Sassani asked, turning around to give the bird a token glance, clearly not terribly interested in it himself, but endeavoring to be polite to his honored guests.

The general likewise took a brief look to his left. It was indeed a handsome animal, nothing like the dirty scavengers that frequented outdoor eating establishments looking for fallen crumbs and table scraps.

"Why, yes," Vasquez replied. "Ornithology has always been a special interest of mine, ever since I was a boy. I especially took a keen liking to the larger raptors. So free. So powerful. Amazing creatures."

"Such birds of prey are common in these lands," Sassani remarked.

As if on cue, the bird spread its wings wide in an impressive show and shrieked at them. Curiously, the bird didn't immediately take to flight again; rather, it just calmly stood in its place on the railing. Its head tilted back and forth to give its incredibly powerful eyes the best perspective of the three large animals sitting nearby.

And then it happened.

FLASH!

Vasquez was first to see the brilliant flash of light, momentarily blinding him, leaving him with a trail of yellow spots dancing and floating before his eyes. The general was vaguely aware of the flash of light to his left, but was all the more alarmed by the look of shock on Vazquez's face. Sassani could see the look of fear on the eyes of both his companions. He spun around with a jerk.

The bird was gone.

Standing next to the railing was a man – a man Sassani didn't know – with long gray hair and a long white beard, dressed all in black from head to toe. Just as Sassani was about to shout for his security detail, the strange man extended his palm directly toward the entire group. A cold wind flooded over his entire being and he suddenly felt that he couldn't move. He was frozen in place, terrified.

In similar fashion, Sassani then saw the man hold up his other hand, his palm facing toward the balcony door, and with a voice of authority, in English said, "No one may pass that door."

The air in the doorway seemed to visibly blur.

In his peripheral vision Sassani could see his guards suddenly aware of an intruder, but inexplicably unable to come to his aid. It was as if the glass door was mysteriously locked somehow. In fact whenever anyone dared touch it, a yellowish-orange light flashed and they recoiled in pain.

The man stepped forward.

"Hello, General, and your Excellency," Master Magi William Turner greeted the two frightened Novice Magi with a forced smile. "I'd say you gentlemen have created a great bit of mischief that we desperately need to correct."

Sassani said nothing, frozen in his chair by both fear and magic.

The Archbishop spoke up, defiant and stern, "I would hope you know by now, William, that I am not afraid to die for what must be done. Don't you understand that?"

"I understand completely, Renaldo, and, indeed, you shall presently have that wish fulfilled," William said. "But before I deal with you, you are going to sit there Iced in that chair for the next few minutes and watch me Read our friend Mohammed here of everything he's ever known – and most importantly, the whereabouts of Alexey Borochenko."

"You're too late," Vasquez spat.

"That remains to be seen," William snapped.

Sassani sneered at William. "It doesn't matter if you find him. Alexey is one of the faithful. He will die before he tells you anything."

William chuckled at the hubris of the Persian as he walked behind the Arab general and placed his hands on either side of his head, covering his ears with his palms. He then turned his gaze back to Sassani. "Sorry, but you have that backwards. Alexey will tell me everything I want to know *before* he dies. That's how this works."

General bin Faisal's face went pale.

"And when I am finished with these two and take my leave," William continued addressing Sassani. "I want you to go tell your masters that if they *ever* contemplate conspiring in this evil manner again, I will know of it, and I *will* be back. And when I return I will hunt you down first, and what you're about to see happen to these two men is what I will do to you." William then directed his attention to the general. "But first, old friend, let us discuss where our elusive colleague Alexey has gone."

•

In Tel Aviv, Israel, in a white cargo van parked on the upper level of a parking garage at Ben Gurion International Airport, a timer continued to count down toward zero.

It currently displayed just under twenty hours remaining.

CHAPTER 40

FROM THE JOURNAL OF WILLIAM TURNER

THE POWER OF PROVIDENCE

The more I delved ever deeper into the Magic arts over the years, no matter how much more I learned, and no matter how much more powerful I became – I honestly confess that I also became somewhat discouraged. It was due to seeing and experiencing more and more of the ugly side of Magic. The dark side. The evil it was capable of unleashing.

Where were all the good Magi?

Most all of the Magi I knew had all succumbed to one temptation or another, and thus to one degree or another were consumed by their own base appetites and temporal ambitions. There is simply no denying the truth that power corrupts, and absolute power corrupts absolutely.

I asked my Master about this, and he conceded that, undeniably, the good Magi were far outnumbered by the evil ones, and it wasn't likely for that reality to ever not be the case. It's a function of carnal human nature. However, he was able to help me cope in this area. And he did so by teaching me a great truth; in fact, it was the most important insight I needed to know about the true nature of good and evil.

Conceptually, good versus evil are but moral constructs we assign to the favored over the prohibited. Little did I realize that good and evil are actually the opposite poles of the sentient universe's true form.

Once again: physics.

It's true: Magic is real.

What is also true: the Universe is alive.

And not only is the universe truly alive, but I use the word "alive" in the sense of a living, conscious being that is self-aware. All that exists is made of it, both the good and the bad. Moral perspectives are subsequently shaped by exactly how that energy manifests itself and how it impacts the world we are conditioned to perceive around us.

I know this may be a hard idea to grasp, so let me give you an illustration. Picture a simple sine wave (if you can't picture one you should have paid more attention in geometry class).

Here's one:

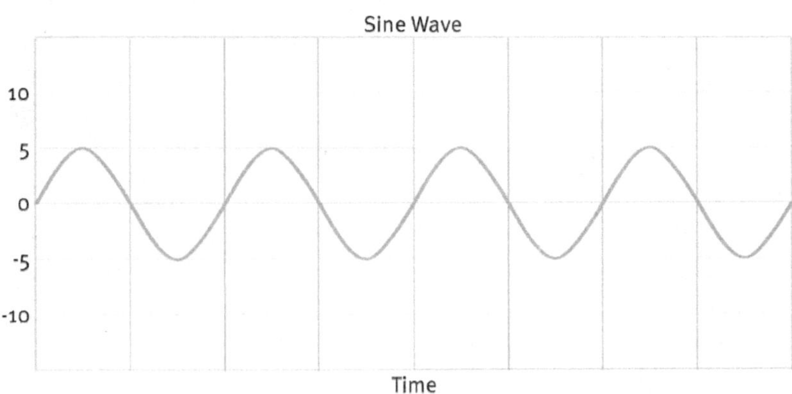

Now imagine this energy wave is a moral construct whereby when the amplitude (i.e. the height) of the wave is greater than zero (the upper half of the waves), some people are taught to call it good energy. But when the amplitude dips down below zero (the bottom half of the waves) it is thought to be bad energy.

The reality of it is, the energy wave is just a wave, and is neither good nor bad. It doesn't know or care where zero is, because morally speaking most zero points are arbitrarily assigned. Zero is just a baseline, simply a reference point.

For instance, on the graph above, if the baseline reference point is instead said to be where negative five is currently on the chart, then the entire waveform is above the reference line and therefore good and nothing about it is bad. Conversely, if the baseline is reassigned to where positive five is located on the graph, then all of the waveform is bad and nothing is good.

If you think this idea of determining good and evil this way sounds nonsensical, you would be correct. It is. And it is also why so much that is culturally ascribed as good versus evil in the world is often little more than a difference in baseline perspective.

But let's get back to the idea of a living universe.

Magic isn't an impersonal power like fire or electricity.

You may have been taught that anything supernatural functions on a spiritual plane of light and darkness, good and evil, life and death. This too is but a moral construct or meme intended to explain that which is nearly impossible for mortal folk to comprehend. But that doesn't change the fact that Magic is, in fact, our ability as sentient beings to tap into the living energy of the entire universe, and then shape and mold that energy into new creations and use it in a myriad of functions. Those functions, and the infinite possibilities they represent, ultimately lead to only one of two ends: to Create or to Destroy.

Creative Magic creates all that is good: life and joy, wisdom and knowledge, prosperity and comfort, courage and valor, health and vitality, and yes, even love – each and every one of the true virtues in life. Said another way: there simply are no true virtues in life devoid of Creative Magic, regardless of whether anyone notices it or accepts it as true or not.

Destructive Magic ultimately seeks to undo Creative Magic, which is all it can do, for nothing can be destroyed that doesn't first exist.

So this is why these two types of energy are continually in fierce opposition. It is also why even good Magi must sometimes avail themselves to Destructive Magic on occasion to thwart even greater Destructive Magic. It's a counterintuitive idea, but there are specific occasions when a wrong is necessary to thwart a much greater wrong. That's not to say that the end justifies the means. Rather, it is a recognition that sometimes there are few virtuous alternatives available to achieve the best outcome, and sometimes every available alternative is patently undesirable on its face, but at least one of the lesser of evils is absolutely necessary.

For example, most people rightly shun war and would prefer living in a world of nothing but enduring peace. But many a foe take that option off the table as long as they are left unrestrained and unvanquished. And therefore, many a brave soul has gone forth to battle to fulfil their duty for a just cause.

It was only after I began to grasp these concepts that my Master told me I was now ready to take the next step in my magical development – to embrace the Creative light of Magic and to reject the darkness.

You see, the living universe is not only self-aware, it has the ability and the desire to communicate and actually have an interactive relationship with the sentient members of its own creation. If you still your mind and quiet your heart, you can indeed hear the Voice of the Creator.

Now you are free to call this Voice by any name or label you like: It might be what you conceive of as Natural Law, or Mother Nature, The Great Spirit, or the Creator or Creation's God, the Gods or just plain God. You're just conjuring up differing labels for the exact same basic metaphysical as well as truly physical concept, and there are countless more name variations to be sure.

An obvious philosophical question you might be wondering at this point is: If all in the universe is essentially God, does that include all of its evil too?

The answer to that question is: If God were the only sentience – the only soul or psyche in existence – throughout the whole universe, then yes, He would be solely responsible for it all, all the good and all the bad. But by God allowing new sentient souls to be created and nurtured throughout the annals of time, souls numbering greater than all the stars in the heavens, and giving them each a free will to use their Magic to both create and/or destroy, then each individual soul bears the responsibility for what they have conjured into manifested form, whether that be good or evil, and ultimately to be judged on whether or not they ever voluntarily came out of the shadows of darkness into the light and learned what it really means to truly be alive.

But to be clear, I'm not describing any form of pantheism or infantile environmental worship. That's a vain delusion. I'm talking about the ability to physically connect to a truly Supreme Being that exists everywhere at once, in an eternal moment of infinite singularity, and is not confined to the environs of this planet nor to its flora and fauna, but permeates all planets, all solar systems, all galaxies, the entire universe.

You have my utmost sympathies if you consider that a lot to try and get your head around. I was for me too.

Yes, admittedly, in the context of many traditional dogmas, creeds, doctrines, and countless religious orthodoxies the world over, such ideas as I'm discussing here might easily be deemed blasphemy of one sort or another. But if I recall my own Sunday School catechism correctly, it was Christ himself who told his disciples that the Kingdom of God was within them, not something to be externally sought though outward displays of good works or empty ritual. And he also told them that with a little "faith" they could say to a mountain to be cast into the sea, and it would obey them. Or they could tell a tree to be uprooted and plant itself in the sea, and likewise it would magically obey.

My life experience to this point, especially over these last few years, has taught me that he knew exactly what he was talking about, and was not speaking in riddles, metaphors or allegory, but simply speaking the plain truth to whomever had an ear to hear.

Moreover, he did his best to get first century mortal folk to understand many profound truths, most of whom were poor and uneducated, who lived under the chains and scourge of a brutal Roman occupation, but at the same time, from birth, they were all completely indoctrinated in their own four-thousand year old cultural milieu and contrived religious traditions. So that was a tall task.

How exactly does one tell a poor shepherd, carpenter, or illiterate fisherman living in the Iron Age with no form of mass communication yet invented that they have the power to change the entire world by means of a living, conscious energy that can be found within their own hearts – and not be considered a madman? With respect to the enormity of this challenge, I can empathize completely.

Nevertheless, as always, please don't put your trust in my words. See for yourself. As I said, in the stillness of the mind and in the quietness of the heart, there is a Voice of Creation waiting to be heard. And if you'll humble yourself and heed that Voice, it will direct your path. Sometimes this Voice is explicit and detailed. Other times it is subtle and manifests itself as a conviction of conscience, allowing you to know confidently in your heart of hearts what the right thing is to say or do.

Needless to say, the more mortal folk there are in the world who recognize their own desire and genuine opportunity to become true Magi, those who choose to open their hearts to that Voice of Creation and discover their own unlimited resources and powers of creative Magic, the better and brighter this world can be.

Conversely, those who would use Magic only for their own selfish ends, they condemn the world to a path of ever-growing darkness.

CHAPTER 41
DANIEL AND PENELOPE

ONBOARD THE LIBERTINE
HERZLIYA MARINA
NEAR TEL AVIV, ISRAEL

"Penelope, my love, it's so good to see you again."

Daniel DuMonde met Penelope at the stern platform as she walked across the gangplank from the marina dock to the gleaming white ship trimmed in oiled teak and polished brass.

She kissed Daniel on the cheek and gave him a brief hug. "I came as soon as I possibly could. I can't believe you tracked down William's daughter here in Israel."

Daniel took her arm and escorted her up a winding staircase to the upper deck salon, proudly explaining along the way, "Yes, we did, my dear, we did indeed."

Penelope stopped cold when she saw Nancy Thompson sunning herself on the upper deck. All Penelope could picture in that instant was Travis' body lying almost lifeless in a hotel bed a few miles away. Just as William had instructed before he left for Iran, she, Allister, and Sasha had taken Travis to the Sadot Hotel near the airport and checked in under false names. When last she saw Travis, at least he appeared to be resting comfortably. Sasha never left his side.

It was at the new hotel that Penelope got the bright idea to not wait to be hunted and instead become the hunter, or at a minimum a master spy. Thus, she had called Daniel again that morning, informed him she'd crossed the border into Israel from Syria, and updated him on her lack of any progress in finding Alexey. Predictably, Daniel took the bait, and brought her up to speed on their good fortune in locating Allister and Sasha. He also gave her the highlights of everything Nancy had learned from her Reading of Travis. That phone call culminated with Daniel's invitation for her to join them on his yacht, conveniently docked at the marina next to the Ritz Carlton, which was only fifteen minutes from the airport.

Penelope glanced at her watch. It was almost 4:00 p.m., local time.

"Hello, Darling," Nancy gave Penelope a half-hearted greeting with a flutter of her fingers, not bothering to get up or even to open her eyes hidden behind her oversized, tortoise shell Jackie-O sunglasses. "Glad you could join the party."

Penelope glanced around, but didn't see anyone else present. "Didn't you say Frank was here sailing with you as well?"

"He was earlier." Daniel busied himself pouring Penelope a glass of white wine, as well as one for himself and one for Nancy. "But I'm afraid he was called away on some personal business. He's promised to join us for brunch in the morning around ten."

"Delightful," she lied.

Daniel handed Penelope her wine and added, "And Walter will also be joining us. He said his flight arrives in the morning from Sydney at around eight."

"Perfect." Penelope took a sip of the wine, exquisite as usual. "Have you heard anything at all from Renaldo or Mohammed?"

Daniel took a seat next to Nancy, obviously taking a moment to admire her bathing suit, which was a gold metal flake number that left little to the imagination. Although, Penelope had to admit, Nancy's exceptional figure did it justice.

Daniel said, "No, I've not heard a single word from them, and nor do I expect to. I've not had any contact with either of them since our meeting in Cairo."

"Then you believe they are the ones working with Alexey?" Penelope felt a strange tingling in her ears. It was only then that she noticed Nancy rubbing her temples as though she were tired.

Oh, no you don't.

Penelope knew immediately that Nancy was trying to peek into her thoughts. An ever so slight Protection Spell, applied with a brief stroke of her chin, made the tingling stop. Nancy's eyes came open, looking directly at her. Penelope resolved that if Nancy tried to touch her, she was going to have to fight. And that wouldn't be pretty. She just smiled back at Nancy as sweetly as she could and took another long sip of her wine.

During this exchange Daniel answered Penelope's previous question, "If Alexey himself is still alive, then yes, I'm convinced they are working together. But even if he's not among the living, then the answer is still yes, as those two are clearly involved in some form of betrayal. As I said, neither of them are answering any of my calls or texts. But, it's no matter, we've endured coup attempts in the past. I'm sure this won't be the last time in my tenure we'll need to quench such fires. But rest assured, their fates have been sealed and won't be among our number for very much longer."

"Any sign of William?" Penelope asked.

Daniel shook his head. "Not yet. But that's surely just a matter of time. The perfect bait for him is now in our grasp. I can't imagine that his daughter, or the gentleman who we've learned is his Master, the good Chief Inspector Allister McKenzie, has neglected to inform him of Nancy's contact with the other young man in their party and the potential peril they all now find themselves in."

Penelope smiled inwardly to herself. If that was Daniel's thinking, then that meant they didn't yet know that their bait had already escaped the trap, nor the little fact that Dr. William Turner had already come and gone.

"So what happens now if you are correct and Alexey was in fact dispatched by William and now *he* has the device? Can he not just disable it or destroy it?" Penelope really did want to better understand Daniel's thinking.

"No, he can't harm it in any way," he insisted. "Nancy, would you mind explaining?"

Nancy obliged, "This is the little secret he doesn't yet understand. Although, for someone in his field he should. It's the plutonium in the device. It is a powerful quantum energy source that is totally incompatible with his magic, and ours too for that matter. It is like the two similar poles on a magnet. The dark energy of the nuclear fissile material repels the magic of light and is immune to it. Conversely, if dark magic is used to try and destroy the device, that would only act as a trigger itself and start the chain reaction that detonates the weapon. It can only be stopped by manually disarming it, of which I'm fairly certain William isn't terribly well-versed in doing, as I am."

Penelope played devil's advocate, "But what if, on the other hand, you're mistaken and Alexey is still alive and has taken the device himself, and William doesn't have it?"

"Then William shall be so kind as to retrieve it from Alexey for us," Daniel said very matter-of-fact.

"And why would he do that?" Penelope asked.

Daniel laughed, "Because, knowing him, he will have no other choice but to promptly turn the device over to us if he has it, or go get it for us if he doesn't, in order to make his *ransom* payment."

"A ransom payment? For what? What are you talking about? Are you planning on kidnapping his daughter from the hotel?" Penelope was getting confused, and very worried. She could feel her heart racing.

Nancy Thompson sat up and stretched her arms, blithely announcing, "Heavens no, dear. We know they've all gone from the Ritz. And we know you were directly involved in taking them away. But don't worry. We have no interest whatsoever in anything unpleasant happening to your daughter or her friend."

Penelope gasped under her breath, trying not to look as shocked as she suddenly felt.

Nancy added, "Yes, that's right. We are well aware that Sasha Turner is your daughter, too. However, we no longer need any of them to get William to come to us and then get him to do what we need him to do." She smiled and took off her sun glasses, looking Penelope directly in the eye, her eyes flashing yellow and black. "Because now we have *you*."

Daniel added with a harsh quip, "And the only way he sees you alive again is when I get my device back."

Penelope's head was starting to spin. She suddenly felt sick to her stomach and the images before her eyes began to blur. It was at that moment that it occurred to her that neither Daniel nor Nancy had bothered to drink from their own wine glasses. Penelope's wine glass slipped from her fingers and crashed on the teak decking below her.

The last thing Penelope heard before losing consciousness was Daniel telling Nancy, "A most effective potion, my sweet. Most effective."

•

The timer on the device read just over sixteen hours remaining.

Chapter 42
William and Alexey

Kiev, Ukraine

The sky was overcast and brooding in the early evening hours, which on the positive side helped the temperature feel a bit more comfortable in the summer months in Ukraine. The smell of imminent rain hung heavy in the air. The gray pall overhead made the entire city feel colorless and bland, like living in an old black and white film. It wasn't fully dark yet, as sunset at this time of year wasn't until after 9:00 p.m.

It was only a little past 7:00 p.m.

Kiev (properly pronounced with one syllable, rhyming with "Leave," not like the two syllable word used to refer to the rolled and breaded chicken cutlet dish) was a very old city, formally founded in the late ninth century. However, it had served as a major commercial center on the Scandinavian-Constantinople trade route since the late fifth century. Now it was home to almost three-million people, the eighth largest city in all of Europe. Kiev was a unique mixture of old world historical charm, bland utilitarian former soviet concrete squalor, and modern western-styled urban development rivaling the leading cities in the world. High-rise cranes dotted the skyline as massive new construction continued to strengthen the vitality of the city growing ever more cosmopolitan each day.

Situated on the banks of the Dnieper River, in many ways Kiev has become the true demarcation point between the East and the West, no longer Berlin after the Wall came down in 1989. Russia and its predominantly Russian speaking Ukrainians sit to its east, and Poland and the rest of Western Europe are to its west, with western Ukraine primarily inhabited by ethnic Ukrainian speaking people. It is said that the ethnic Ukrainians in the west feel much the same way about the Russians as many of the Irish feel about the English.

Dr. William Turner wandered around the expansive, meticulously tended grounds of the Lavra, which began as an ancient cave monastery centuries ago and had served as the center of the Eastern Orthodox Christian church, its "Vatican" if you will, ever since the mid-eleventh century. It was established after the Eastern Orthodox Church's center was relocated there from Constantinople after the city's fall to the Muslim armies in Turkey, which was then renamed and became the city of Istanbul. The most prominent feature of the Lavra complex was its massive four-tier Bell Tower and Domitian Cathedral, all crowned with golden spires. The Lavra was also home to another eight churches on its grounds, in addition to the monastery.

William had been diligently searching throughout the city for Alexey Borochenko for most of the day but with no luck. From his Reading of General bin Faisal he had learned that Alexey was headed back to his home here in Ukraine, which consisted of a modest flat right here in Kiev, but the clever Ukrainian was not to be found there. With exhaustion setting in, William decided to come to the Lavra to find some quiet time for his troubled mind and to let his heart be at peace.

He placed his hands on an ancient stone wall, letting his gaze wander. It didn't take long. There it was: the face of an elderly woman. Her eyes were filled with sympathy and compassion. Perhaps pity? After a few seconds the mouth turned ever so slightly into a smile. William closed his eyes and breathed in deeply through his nose, holding his breath for as long as he could, and then releasing it slowly through his mouth. These walls had been witness to so many centuries of life and death, war and peace, famine and plenty. There was so much life force energy to be found here. After the seventh long cleansing breath he felt himself begin to relax and to feel refreshed. A warm sense of peace and strength began to flow through his veins.

He opened his eyes. The face of the woman was gone – but instead of seeing something else, he heard something.

I can help you.

William certainly wasn't expecting to hear what he was certain he just heard. But it wasn't audible for anyone else to hear. The Voice was coming from deep within his own heart, a message reserved for him alone. Several tourists wandered along where he stood, a few giving him odd looks, presumably thinking anyone holding onto a wall was most likely inebriated. He certainly didn't wish to attract any undue attention. It was time to move along.

Solace – was the next word he heard from within.

He understood. William made his way to the Church of the Savior at Berestove on the Lavra grounds and entered the old sanctuary. He was immediately struck by the vivid iconography and multicolored frescoes adorning the walls and the high arched ceiling. He found a quiet alcove away from any other visitors and bowed his head, again taking long slow breaths in and out.

That which you seek is hidden.

"I know" William whispered softly. "That's the problem."

All things hidden can be made known.

"Show me." He closed his eyes. "Please."

William expected to be shown a physical place, hopefully the location where Alexey was hiding. Once he knew of a specific location, he could teleport there in a matter of seconds and do exactly what needed to be done. Instead, what he saw in his mind's eye was initially very blurred and fuzzy, but then it slowly came into clear view. It wasn't a person or a place, but a thing.

It was a machine, some complex electronic device.

He gasped with a sense of recognition. He was looking at *the* device. Undoubtedly, at that very moment it was sitting somewhere in Israel in a heavily populated area. Yes, this was the "hidden thing" he was ultimately seeking.

The row of red LED numerals of the timer came sharply into view. It read hours, minutes, and seconds, 14:32:09 and was counting down one second at a time.

"Oh, no," he whispered. "Is that all the time we have?"

Yes.

"Then it's been armed."

Yes.

"Where is it?"

The one you seek must show you.

"I know. That's why I seek him."

He waits for you.

"I imagine he does."

He is not alone.

A pang of apprehension shot through William. He had wanted to take Alexey by surprise, and find him all by himself. Alexey was a Practicing Magi, a lot stronger Magi than the archbishop and the general. Confronting the other two together in Tehran was no great challenge. But Alexey and another strong Magi with him could potentially be problematic.

"I think I can handle two."

There are three. One is secretly a Master. And together the three are united to protect him.

William's heart sank. He was now convinced that he couldn't do it alone. He would have to leave Ukraine and return right away with at least Allister and Penelope, if not Sasha too. He seriously doubted Travis would be in any condition to do much of anything helpful.

He looked at his watch and remembered the image of the timer. Only a little over fourteen hours remained. That would put zero hour at a little after nine o'clock the following morning.

"I'll be back with help," he said.

The path ahead will be difficult.

"I know."

Trust, and I will guide you."

"I will."

In William's mind he pictured the room he once occupied at the Sadot Hotel in Tel Aviv near the Ben Gurion International Airport. He took another deep breath as the high pitched whine filled the air.

FLASH!

In the next instant Dr. William Turner was no longer in Ukraine.

•

Over 100,000 screaming fans leapt to their feet as the ball hit the back of the net, scoring a goal for the Ukrainian national team. They led Poland three to nil entering the last ten minutes of the match.

In the gleaming new stadium, built fairly recently for the World Cup games, Alexey Borochenko stood by the bulletproof security glass window of the luxury suite, high above the action on the pitch below. The suite was the size of a small apartment, complete with tiered stadium seating closest to the glass accommodating up to twenty guests. Behind the seats was a full living room area and dining room set, plus a very well-stocked kitchenette, a wet bar, and a private bathroom. A seventy-inch flat-screen television adorned one side wall, displaying the game in real-time as it was broadcast on both national and international networks. All the Ukrainian and Russian oligarchs, the well-placed politicians, senior military officers and all their families had such suites, which ringed the state-of-the-art sports complex.

Judge Frank Donaldson from San Francisco added some ice to his glass and doused it with his favorite Nemiroff Lex vodka. He had only recently arrived at the stadium from the Boryspil airport located just east of downtown Kiev on the opposite side of the Dnieper River. His flight from Tel Aviv was thankfully uneventful. "Sorry, I'm just not that into soccer."

"Football," Alexey corrected him.

Frank huffed, "That, my friend, is *not* football. The Forty-Niners is football."

"You do know, Frank," Alexey pointed out, "that more people around the world watch our form of football than yours, right?"

"They're both rubbish!" insisted Walter Stephens. "Can't use your hands or arms. Stupid. And the Americans are all covered with body armor like a sissy. Ridiculous. Now *Rugby's* a man's game. Real bumping, tackling and thrashing about, blood and bruises."

They all shared a laugh.

Alexey gave a nod of appreciation and thanks to both of his companions for being there to help protect him. "It is good that you both are here to help. I thank you both very much."

Frank gestured toward Walter, but spoke to Alexey, "Walter has been here all day waiting for your arrival. I came as soon as I got the bad news about Mohammed and Renaldo."

Alexey asked, "Is the deal still on?"

Frank nodded. "The senior representatives of the Ayatollah's Council were most distressed at the loss of life in their midst. And their foreign minister, the Imam that you know, is said to still be hospitalized in a state of shock and hasn't spoken a word since he was admitted. But I have personally assured them that nothing of a material nature has changed. Despite the setback, the operation is still on course and will endeavor to proceed as planned. They are willing to wait to see the results tomorrow, despite the fact that William is apparently still attempting to get in the way and abort our efforts."

"Daniel assured us Vil'hel'm was dead," Alexey spat.

Frank nodded. "And, obviously, he was wrong. And such serious mistakes are why Daniel is no longer fit to lead. And why…" He looked at his watch. "In less than twelve hours from now, he'll be gone, our Persian friends will have their bloodbath, and we'll be positioned to come in and rule over what, if anything, remains of that part of the world as we stock the entire region with more and more nuclear products."

Walter mused aloud, "There really is no viable alternative. For anyone. These nasty things are the world's destiny. The Persians and the Arabs all recognize that now. We must too. Nothing personal. It's just business."

Alexey finished the last sip of his own cup of green tea. "But he *is* coming to find us, isn't he?"

Frank gave him a sober nod. "Undoubtedly. Most likely later tonight sometime, assuming he makes it here at all. And if he does, I trust he won't be alone."

Walter's phone rang. He pulled it from his pocket and looked at the caller ID. "Well, mates, speak of the devil!"

He showed his companions the contact name: Daniel DuMonde. He raised his eyebrows questioningly to Alexey and Frank. They both nodded at him, indicating he should take the call. Walter swiped the screen to answer it.

"Daniel, good evening, good sir," he said.

Walter's jovial smile faded into a mask of seriousness as he listened very carefully for almost two full minutes before replying. "I understand. No, don't wait. Press any advantage you might have before he has a chance to reinforce." A pause. "Right. And if there's anything left to clean up in the morning, you know Frank and I will be there to help you." Another pause. "Got it." He hit the End button and popped his phone back in his pocket.

Frank sipped his drink and asked, "So what's Daniel up to now?"

Alexey walked to the bar and refilled his cup from the white porcelain teapot, then stirred in two small straws of sugar.

Walter said, "Well, for starters, it's a good thing he still believes we're in league with him and is still sharing information with us."

Frank just laughed. Alexey did too.

"But it seems our soon-to-be former leader and his pretty pet dragon have decided to take matters into their own hands with respect to dealing with our meddlesome Dr. Turner. And that may be to our benefit."

Alexey spoke up, "How so?"

"He says they've apprehended Penelope, who they now realize was in league with William all along, just as Alexey suspected, and they are using her as bait to get William to give them back the weapon."

Alexey took a hot sip from his cup, frowned and said, "And how is he going to do that? He doesn't have it. We do. And no one besides me knows where I put it."

Walter said, "Daniel's under the odd notion that William has the weapon in his personal possession, after he killed both you and Stephan and then hijacked the weapon from you."

Alexey just shook his head in wonder.

Frank lifted his glass in an impromptu toast, "Well then. This is good news, gents. To Daniel. May he soon vanquish our common foe, the persistent and seemingly indestructible Dr. William Turner. And may he do so on this very night before the Sword of Persia then smites him, Penelope, and the dragon the first thing in the morning!"

CHAPTER 43
TRAVIS

THE SADOT HOTEL
TEL AVIV, ISRAEL

In the midst of the dark, churning clouds and momentary flashes of lightning within their billowing and undulating swells, came a soft glow of light. The light grew brighter and brighter until it illuminated a large object floating in space.

A box.

No, not just a box, a perfect six-sided cube.

The image grew larger, filling most of the field of vision.

The cube was divided into smaller cubes, stacked three-by-three to a side. And yet what initially looked like a common neutral color for the cube diverged into six distinct colors on the exposed faces of the smaller cubes: red, blue, green, yellow, white, and orange.

How amusing: A Rubik's Cube.

Another peal of thunder rumbled in the depths of the cloud.

Urgency. Okay.

The cube was scrambled, not solved.

Pick a color to start. Blue.

The cube began to rotate as the center cubes with at least one blue side were positioned over the corresponding fixed center cube of the adjacent faces. With those four steps done, the correct blue faced corners were positioned so as to match not only the blue side, but the two adjacent corner faces, which also matched the proper center faces. In a few moves, the first level was solved. The cube inverted such that the solved first level with blue side complete was on the bottom.

The next step was to get the middle pieces of the second level in their correct positions. Start by finding the piece needed from the third level and place it atop the fixed center piece so that if it were tipped over into the second level position it would be right. The manipulation to do that takes eight steps. So in 32-40 turns, level two is complete.

Now for the top cross. Another complex manipulation, but performed two or three times, and the top green face opposite the blue side of the cube on the bottom is done.

Now to get the top level corners in their right places. They don't have to be correctly oriented just yet, but they must be in the correct corners. That manipulation is more complex, but works almost always the first time.

The next step is to then get those corners in the right orientation. That manipulation just takes a little patience, as it may need to be done several times to achieve the desired result.

When that's done, all that is left to complete the top layer is to get the center pieces in the right place. The green face is complete, and one of the side faces as well, but the other three top-center pieces are out of place. They must be rotated around to get them in their proper locations. This manipulation is the most complex, and if it doesn't produce the complete solution the first time it's tried, it must be done again until all is where it should be.

Ah, there.

The cube was solved.

The dark clouds began to part. A ray of sunlight cut through as blue skies emerged.

Travis Gardner's eyes popped open.

He gasped for air and sat up straight in bed, his lungs heaving for air.

•

It was just past midnight. Only nine hours left.

Dr. William Turner stood at the balcony rail of the suite at the Sadot Hotel that Allister had reserved for Travis Gardner, who, when last they checked on him, was still resting comfortably. Allister and Sasha sat quietly at the patio table a few paces away.

It was Allister who had originally taken the disconcerting phone call a few hours ago that he thought was coming from Penelope, but turned out to be from Daniel DuMonde using her phone to inform them of Penelope's capture and their nonnegotiable demands for the return of the missing weapon – along with, of course, William's unconditional surrender by dawn of the next morning.

"Surely they have her on Ice," William mused out loud to the night. "We'd never be able to attack the ship, try to find her, and also deal with Daniel and Nancy, plus has a full crew of mortal folk, very likely heavily armed, before they had time to kill her."

"Well, we certainly can't consider the alternative of giving a man like Daniel DuMonde an armed weapon of that type." Allister also pointed out, "And you know if you dare to bow the knee to Daniel in the morning you'll never see another sunset."

"It's not me I'm worried about." William spun around to face them, clearly frustrated and starting to sound desperate. "Besides, right now we don't have a weapon to give him, even if we wanted to. And to find the missing one, we're still going to need to go to Ukraine very soon, find Alexey, and get him to tell us where it is. And I'm betting that when we get there, we'll also find our two remaining Inner Circle friends, Frank and Walter, right there as well, ready to fight right alongside him. Which means Penelope has to come with us, lest we walk into a Magi firefight with no clear advantage. And to add a degree of difficulty, just to keep it all interesting, all of this has to happen in less than nine hours from now. Make it eight hours if we really want any chance to actually disarm the weapon after we find it."

"What makes you so certain Frank and Walter are with him?" Allister asked.

"Process of elimination, literally. Mohammed and Renaldo are no more, and I know in my heart Alexey is not alone. He is with two others. Other than Alexey himself, they're the only two members left of the Inner Circle. Daniel, Nancy, and Penelope are all here in Israel with us." He bowed his head and ran tired fingers through his long locks of hair, no longer bound into a single braid down his back.

"Are you really so hesitant for just the three of us to take them on?" Sasha asked. It was a legitimate question. "You're both Masters and you know I've been getting a lot better? I'm strong, I promise."

Allister nodded, "She's right. She's *very* good."

William shook his head. "It's not that. I'm sure she'll do fine. It's that under the circumstances, we can't afford to fail. It's simply not an option. I know the day may come where I might have to lay down my life in battle, and perhaps each of you will too, but today *can't* be that day. If that thing goes off *anywhere* in this country untold millions will die in an instant, and a hundred-fold beyond that would perish as the world implodes upon itself in the aftermath. I'm certain that we'll need at least four of us to tip the odds in our favor. As long as we have at least one more than they do, each of them is vulnerable."

"So then four of us you shall have," came a strong and determined voice from the doorway.

All eyes instantly went toward the sound, each shocked to see a healthy and alert Travis Gardner standing in the doorway. He was fully dressed in faded blue jeans and a burnt orange University of Texas Longhorns polo shirt. Everyone stood slack-jawed for nearly a full minute before Sasha could collect her wits, scream for joy and run over to wholeheartedly embrace him.

CHAPTER 44
PENELOPE AND SASHA

ON BOARD THE LIBERTINE
HERZLIYA MARINA
NEAR TEL AVIV, ISRAEL

All she could feel was an oppressive sense of cold and numbness. Her eyes could move and her lips and tongue, but little else.

"Hello?" Penelope Angelucci tentatively called out in the darkness, but received no reply. She was alone.

Was she standing up or laying down? She couldn't tell. The Icing Spell on her was very strong. It had probably been enhanced chemically with whatever Daniel and Nancy had put in her wine to knock her out. Whatever it was, it had to have been extremely potent, for her own magic was normally more than strong enough to overcome any of the more common sleeping or paralysis potions.

Since she was planning on spending the night aboard the ship anyway, to either collect more information or to find an opportunity to strike a blow against Daniel or Nancy with the element of surprise, it was very likely that no one with William even knew of her predicament yet. If only there was a way to let them know...

Of course!

Her body might be paralyzed, but not her mind and spirit.

Penelope closed her eyes and began to take long slow breaths, in and out, in through her nose, held for several seconds, then out slowly through her mouth. After the seventh one she could feel the energy welling up within her. She began to imagine a face—no, not William's—her baby's, Alexandra. Her sweet Sasha.

"Sasha. *Sasha*, hear me..."

•

With their midnight snack from Room Service almost finished, it was nearly 1:00 a.m. Time was growing short. All four of them still sat around the balcony patio table, knowing they had to renew their strength and plan carefully for what awaited them that very night.

William and Allister were very impressed with Travis. In no time they were thoroughly convinced that he could indeed help give them the tactical flanking advantage they needed when they arrived in Ukraine to face Alexey, Frank, and Walter.

And then it happened.

Sasha abruptly dropped her fork, still heaped with a piece of poached salmon. It clattered onto her plate. William, Allister, and Travis all halted their conversation and looked at her.

"Honey, are you all right?" William asked as a pang of fear shot through him. He meant it when he said that if he were ever called upon to lay down his life he'd gladly do it. But he would never consciously let anything happen to his daughter if he could possibly prevent it. If this emergency didn't require her to go with them, he would have forbade it – Icing her until he got back if he had to.

Sasha was staring straight ahead, her eyes vacant and glassy.

Travis was worried. "Sasha, what is it? What's happening to you?"

Sasha's index finger came to her lips and she softly shushed them, whispering, "I need to hear her."

They all sat in silence for several moments. Then Sasha whispered, "I understand. And don't worry. We *will* come for you."

And with that, she shook her head and her eyes cleared after a few exaggerated blinks.

Allister reached out and laid his hand on her arm, with a look of deep concern on his face. "What is it, girl?"

She met all of their gazes. "It was my mother."

William looked surprised. "Penelope was successfully able to connect to you?"

Sasha nodded. "Yes. And she told me there's something you don't know that you *have* to know before you go after the weapon."

"What is it?" he asked.

"It's about the weapon itself," she said. "Your magic won't work on it. Good magic is repelled by it and dark magic will set it off. It has to be disarmed manually, or it won't be disarmed at all."

William said, "I'm not so sure about that. But I promise you, I saw exactly how Nancy showed Alexey how to arm it. Presumably the opposite procedure disarms it."

"But you're *not* certain?" Allister asked. "What if the wrong procedure sets it off? What if a different security code is required?"

William conceded, "That would be a dangerous possibility, but a real one to have to think about. It could very well have a failsafe mechanism to ensure it does its job. But it doesn't matter. We at least have to try. There's no alternative. If we do nothing, then we know it will go off. If we try to do something to stop it, assuming we can ever find the thing, then either we fail and it goes off, or it works and we stop a global holocaust. I'd rather play fifty-fifty odds than a guaranteed zero."

"All right. Let's think this through carefully. It's abundantly clear that priority number one for us is to find the device," Allister noted. "But to do that we know we must first find Alexey Borochenko and make him tell us where it is."

"So then, if we get him, we can't hurt him," Sasha said. "Right?"

William said, "Not exactly. We just can't do anything too severe to him until we have what we need to know from him about how to turn the thing off."

"But you *do* intend to terminate him?" Travis asked.

William paused for a moment, looking Travis in the eye. "Should any of us falter in our quest, the Inner Circle *must* be broken. If even one of them remains, the group will reconstitute itself and continue its reign. I trust everyone is prepared to do their duty if called upon to do so."

Sasha stoically asked her father, "What about my mother? Must you terminate her as well?"

William cast his eyes down. "I'm reasonably certain she's no longer a member of their fold. She's changed. I believe that."

Sasha and Travis exchanged a wary glance. Neither of them had ever contemplated the idea of casting a Death Spell, nor knew if called upon to do so if they could actually do it.

"So what is the next step?" Allister asked.

William stood up. "Now that we have sufficient numbers to engage, the next step is for me to take a few moments of solitude to listen to my heart. It will show me the right path."

Chapter 45
Alexey, Frank and Walter

St. Andrew's Church
Kiev, Ukraine

At 3:00 a.m. in the morning, the mid-eighteenth century baroque church, built by renowned Italian architect Bartolomeo Rastrelli, was deserted and securely locked for the night. While incomparably ornate and gilded inside and out, the small church building stood on the high ground of Andriyivska Hill in the Podil neighborhood of Kiev. However, its secured doors were no real obstacle for three Magi in search of sanctuary.

Alexey was still skeptical about their plan. "Do you really think we can just run out the clock on Vil'hel'm?"

Frank Donaldson nodded. "I do. I am comfortable with the calculation that we can combine our strength and focus it on a united Protection Spell for this sacred place, fortify it as a Persistent Spell, and that spell will be sufficient to hold against anything and anyone for at least ten hours. By then it will be too late for William and any of his compatriots to stop what is coming."

Walter gazed around in awe at the elaborate artwork and detail of the church's interior, highlighted by the massive three tier iconostasis at one end of the sanctuary. An iconostasis is an elaborate stand-alone wall or partition, covered with religious icons, which acts as a screen to separate the most sacred part of the church sanctuary at the far end from the main public area the church.

Walter commented, "I believe there's a special energy in this place that can serve us well. We would be wise to infuse ourselves with as much of it as possible before we begin."

"A good thought," Frank said. "But we dare not tarry too long." He looked at his watch. "It is three-fifteen. At four, we engage our Protection Spell and hold fast until well after nine in the morning. If we stay strong for one another, William can bring all the heavenly hosts he can find and they'll not touch us. And that's assuming he ever finds us at all."

Alexey asked. "But what then? What if he just waits us out? The fate of the weapon notwithstanding, he still wants our blood."

Walter added, "And if we've spent most, or nearly all, of our energy on the Protection Spell, when it falls, we'll be defenseless."

Frank wasn't sympathetic. "Then I suggest you pace yourself, and take in as much reserve energy from this place as you can in the next forty-five minutes."

Alexey pulled out a Beretta nine millimeter semi-automatic pistol out of the waistband of his pants near his spine and said to Walter, "And that is why, my friend, magic is not always the answer to all problems. Some battles must be fought the old fashioned way."

CHAPTER 46
PREPARING FOR BATTLE

THE SADOT HOTEL
TEL AVIV, ISRAEL

The Sadot Hotel was located just to the south of to the Assaf Harofeh Medical Center; and just to the south of the hotel was a vast expanse of various types of agricultural fields. It was in one such field that Dr. William Turner was walking at 3:30 a.m., alone with his thoughts, quieting his mind, stilling his heart, and listening to the melodic songs of wildflowers in the field.

He glanced down at his watch. There just didn't seem to possibly be enough time with only five and a half hours left. A desperate feeling of futility was seeping into his soul, tempting his heart to race. The deep cleansing breaths were getting so much harder and harder to release past his clenched teeth.

"I need your help," he whispered.

Yes, you do.

"I know they are in the ancient city on the Dnieper."

Yes, they are.

"Unfortunately, that great city covers over three-hundred square miles, and time is short."

Yes, it is.

"How do I find them?"

You must see the world from their eyes.

"Surely they are well-defended by now behind a Persistent Protection Spell, working in league. They would deny me such vision."

Not their physical eyes. From their perspective. Walk in their shoes. What would they do? What would you *do if you were in their position?*

"I would seek sanctuary. Something defensible. Public, but small, so I could control the venue to my best advantage."

As have they done.

"Where?"

High ground.

William wracked his brain trying to remember all the high points of Kiev, Ukraine. There were many of them to consider. The main part of the city was on the western banks of the Dnieper, built among steep hills and bluffs along the river. The eastern side of the river was predominantly flat, mostly farmland.

"In the midst of the main part of the city is the highest ground."

Yes.

"I was at the Lavra. No. It wouldn't be there. Too expansive. Hard to defend with only three."

Yes, but a sacred place of high energy is wise.

"St. Sophia's?" No, that didn't feel right. "St. Michael's?" No, too big. "St. Andrew's?" He pictured the picturesque baroque church atop one of the highest points in all of Kiev. "Ah, yes, St. Andrews. That is where I would choose to make my stand."

Yes.

"But as I said, it will certainly be completely enshrouded with a very powerful, Persistent Protection Spell of three Magi, one of them a Master. Their reinforced magic could last many hours before it wanes. Hours we don't have to wait."

Yes.

"So how can we reach them in time to stop the slaughter? How do we get to Alexey and learn what he knows?"

By exploitation of limited perspective.

"What perspective?"

The perspective of simple men who can only see their world in only two dimensions, not three.

William thought about that for several moments, then whispered aloud, "I don't understand. If they extend their joint Protection Spell around the entire church, it is absolute, secure from any side, even from above. A complete dome."

Yes. But to protect a building does not necessarily lay claim to its foundations and its land.

"We don't have time to tunnel." William was starting to feel very frustrated and frightened. There didn't seem to be any viable approach to achieve their goal.

You don't need to. The passageways are already there.

Images of long, brick and concrete pipes came into his mind. "The sewers?"

Yes.

William Turner suddenly knew exactly what they had to do.

CHAPTER 47

FROM THE JOURNAL OF WILLIAM TURNER

CLOSE YOUR EYES AND SEE

By this time in the development of your Magic you are undoubtedly encountering complex details and technical nuances of magical functions that require much further elaboration. I shall endeavor to add as much additional insight as I can, while I still have opportunity to do so.

When it comes to the Praesidium Cantamen, or the Protection Spell, the rules are as I've previously stated: A Protection Spell is only as strong and the Magi who casts it. It remains intact until it is revoked by the Magi who cast it, or revoked by a greater Magi

This logic of this practice must all seem very straightforward, but there are other considerations. Such as: What if an inferior Magi knows that a superior Magi intends to revoke his Protection Spell. Can anything be done to prevent it? Yes, something can be done.

Multiple inferior Magi may pool their magic as one to provide a much stronger Protection Spell, such that a single superior Magi does not have the power to revoke it. Likewise, multiple superior Magi may revoke the Protection Spell of multiple inferior Magi.

It really is a cumulative contrast that will always prevail. Whether we're talking about one Magi or more than one, whichever side has the greater accumulation of energy will have their will made manifest.

Does this mean that the inferior Magi will always be at the mercy of the superior? Most of the time, yes. But not always. There is another scenario, and that is the possibility of what's called the Adsiduus Cantamen, or the Persistent Spell.

This is a situation where the Magi who casts the spell, alone or in league with others, remains in a constant state of casting the spell, again and again, even if revoked. This puts the onus on the opposition to continually attempt to revoke it. Even if they are able to do so, a stalemate of futility ensues, like a game of Tic-Tac-Toe. In such a confrontation, the Magi or group of Magi with the greater stores of energy would ultimately prevail. Although, such clashes might very well last for many hours, and possibly even days before a clear victor emerges.

Additionally, realize that Magi who are in the state of casting a Persistent Spell are extremely vulnerable, which is why the Protection Spell is so important. Woe be it to a Magi who believes themselves safe behind a Protection Spell only, who is in a state of persistent casting, and then is encountered by an enemy. Other than the case of a personal Protection Spell, for example, if you are protecting a room or a house, should a Magi enter into persistent casting, he would be wise to have an ally stand watch over him and be prepared to defend him, for the Magi in the Persistent Spell state will not be able to readily defend himself.

Beware of illusions.

One of the most effective manifestations of true Magic is the art of waveform transformation – especially manifested in the range of the visible light spectrum as it behaves for the perspective of the human eye. Essentially, anything a Magi can imagine can be projected in three-dimensional space, much like a three-dimensional hologram, with the deliberate intention that any viewer would perceive the illusion as reality.

Often this is done for intimidation purposes. But it can also be done purely to confuse or deceive. So do not always trust all that you see with the naked eye.

Trust your heart. And in doing so, this means sometimes having to close your eyes to what you perceive as reality and instead see what is truly before you with the purity of your heart, not your eyes.

This may sound like a romanticized notion, but it is not. It is a literal function. This is not vain imagining of what you hope to see, but a true reaching out with a new sense of perception, using your magical senses, and thereby perceiving what truly is, not what another would wish you to see and attempt to make you believe, which may be of itself nothing more than a conjured illusion.

A Note on Death Spells.

As noted, some particular Death Spells require the Magi to make some form of physical contact with the enemy. The energy released from the Magi in the moment of this contact is what inflicts whatever lethal blow is being cast. In that moment, a great deal of sentient life force energy leaves the attacking Magi and is transferred to the target. In virtually all cases, it is this overwhelming volume of invasive energy that the target cannot contain and therefore bodily damage is the result.

However, in the next moment after the invasive energy is cast, it is then immediately reflected back. Think of this like bouncing a ball against a wall, or throwing a boomerang. It leaves, then it returns.

But here is where the note of caution comes in.

There are two possible dangers to be aware of.

First, the reflected energy may contain much of the native energy of the target. From a pure energy standpoint there is no issue with that concept. But from a magical perspective, if the target is consumed with evil and darkness, then some or all of that dark energy may reflect back into the attacking Magi and stain the heart, corrupting the soul, and weakening resistance to temptations.

It is technically possible to filter this dark energy, but it is not easy to do and, in my experience, only done consistently by very experienced true

Master Magi. Thus, a Practicing Magi need to be most cautious when gaining expertise with Death Spells.

The second possibility is of even greater danger.

This would be the instance of a failed Death Spell, which occurs when the target is more powerful than the attacking Magi and is ready for the attack.

In this scenario, the energy that is released by the attacking Magi to inflict the lethal blow is successfully contained by the target and not reflected. The result is a much more powerful and energized foe and an attacking Magi low on energy and now vulnerable to attack himself. Think of this like throwing a knife at an enemy, only to have it caught in midair and your enemy is now armed with your knife and you are now unarmed.

This is why Death Spells are so dangerous and to be avoided at all costs unless no other option remains.

Tandem Teleportation is possible.

For a Magi to teleport, along with an additional person or inanimate physical object, the Magi must be in direct bodily contact with it - not merely in contact with a light touch or holding hands, but full torso contact. If it is a person, they must be embraced completely. If it were an inanimate object like a sword, the sword would need to be clutched tightly to the chest.

Failure to do this could leave exposed portions of the other person or thing outside of the teleportation perimeter, resulting in a truncation. In the case of humans, that could easily equate to amputations and dismemberment.

So if you wish to teleport with a passenger or any sort of baggage, keep them close and safe.

CHAPTER 48
ENTERING THE BATTLE

ST. ANDREWS CHURCH
KIEV, UKRAINE

All three Magi knelt together on the cool stone floor in the center of the main area of the church, directly beneath the icon covered rotunda above them. Each kept his elbows at his sides, hands extended toward one another, palms up, eyes closed, lips softly chanting the Persistent Protection Spell incantation, over and over without ceasing. They were spaced approximately two meters apart in their joint triangle.

It was nearing 5:30 a.m.

The vigil was well into its second hour, with three and a half more hours to go. Alexey Borochenko knew energy drain was not a major issue for any of them so far. Each was strong and determined to see the quest through to the end. Shortly after 9:00 a.m. the deed would be done.

Surely Imam Sassani would have his spies positioned far enough away for safety, but close enough to confirm whether or not there was a devastating blow against the Little Satan in either Jerusalem, Tel Aviv, or Haifa. One of those cities would be the only acceptable targets.

Nevertheless, Alexey Borochenko was the only one on earth who knew the exact location of the white transfer van parked on the top level of the parking garage at the Ben Gurion International Airport in Tel Aviv. If need be, he knew he would have to take that information to his grave. He wished to avoid that fate if at all possible, but was willing to face whatever came to strike this mighty blow for Allah and his servants.

Alexey paused for but a second, opening his eyes to check on his two partners. Walter looked fine, persevering through the endlessly repetitive process of the Persistent Spell. The same was true of Frank. He looked strong and confident. It would be interesting to see how the Inner Circle would be reconstituted with Frank as its new high leader – especially since he had recently attained his Mastery level of Magic. Daniel had been a most selfish leader, always preferring to take his own counsel over anyone else's. Admittedly, he was amply ambitious, but could be most myopic, petty, and obtuse at times. They needed a more visionary mind at the helm. He sincerely hoped that Frank did not disappoint.

A tiny movement in Alexey's peripheral vision caught his attention.

Scurrying along the edge of the wall, moving in the direction of the iconostasis was a gray rat. Alexey shook his head to himself in dismay, not entirely surprised. Despite the sanctity and prestige of the venue, mice and rats probably represented a greater population in the city than humans. So why wouldn't they wait until the humans departed to emerge from the safety of their nests and hiding places to forage for crumbs?

The rat stopped his diligent sniffing and lifted his head.

Alexey was almost certain the little rodent was looking directly at him. Maybe he was. Was he surprised to see people still in the church so late at night? Was he frightened? Was he about to run for cover?

And that's when it happened.

•

A little over thirty minutes earlier two flashes of light blinked in the early morning hours behind St. Andrew's Church in Kiev, Ukraine.

William was still holding Sasha tightly against him, as was Travis clinging closely to Allister. Travis ventured to open his eyes. He was still trembling. A moment earlier he'd closed his eyes standing in his hotel room in Tel Aviv.

"You know what to do," was all William said to the other three as he made his way toward the storm drains on the map he carried.

The maps they needed in order to properly plan their operation were not easy to come by in so short a time. Allister had to call in many favors via Interpol in the dead of night, to the point of waking up several senior officials at museums in Vienna, Italy to get the right documentation they needed scanned and sent to them in Israel. But within the hour they had the two and a half centuries old schematics of St. Andrew's Church, as drawn by the original architect, Bartolomeo Rastrelli, himself. The most current city sewage and drainage documentation was from the soviet era, but not a lot had changed in that department for Kiev since the collapse of the Soviet Union.

William found the particular manhole cover he sought, and with a wave of his hand it rose from its position and quietly alighted on the sidewalk nearby. He cautiously looked around, but saw no one in the immediate area. With a decelerating Levitation Spell, he stepped into the blackness and floated slowly to the bottom of the vertical concrete access cylinder that connected to the horizontal main sewer drains. It was wet and dark and reeked of foulness and filth down there.

It was time.

FLASH!

Another bright white flash of light erupted from the open manhole.

The wet, debris strewn base of the wide sewer pipe was now much closer to William's eyes. The smells assaulted his nose all the more, making his whole head twitch in a slight sneeze. His eyes could see everything. On all fours now, he moved forward quickly in the direction of the church. He remembered that only three turns would be encountered before he found the right access pipe to take him upward into the facility. That final pipe was only going to be three inches in diameter, but at the moment, that wasn't going to be a problem.

•

Back outside, Allister, Sasha and Travis each moved around to the main entrance. And there they waited.

At one point Travis moved toward the door and, despite Allister's warning to the contrary, he tried to touch it. A dull yellowish-orange glow pushed his hand back. He recoiled in no small measure of burning pain, like being stung by a wasp.

"I told you," Allister just shook his head in dismay.

Sasha sounded hopeful. "At least we know we're in the right place."

Travis retreated from the door, rubbing his slightly wounded hand. "How will we know when it's time?"

Allister said, "If he successfully makes it inside, trust me, you won't have to guess."

•

William had encountered his first obstacle in the form of a partially clogged drainpipe. Water was still able to make it past the obstruction, but the three inch pipe now only offered a single inch of clearance. It took him several minutes to chew through the hair, grease, organic material, and dirt before he could manage to squeeze his body through the narrow opening.

The second significant challenge encountered was the S-shaped trap half filled with water to prevent the sewage smells from entering the room above. This entailed a few inches if swimming underwater, but he managed without getting stuck and drowning.

The last obstacle he needed to overcome was the small steel circular grate over the top of the drain in the shower stall located in the dressing area of the administrative offices where he had found himself. William's mind concentrated on the two metal screws holding it fast. One-by-one, with a little Levitation and Propulsion Spell, they began to turn counterclockwise until they fell over and rolled away. He pushed the grate away with his tiny head, and by some unknown instinct, shook his entire body side to side, like a wet dog determined to dislodge anything and everything he could from his fur.

His ears twitched, moving forward and back, searching the air for any sounds. There was one detectible sound, faint but audible, off in the distance. It was human voices, chanting. His nose and long whiskers twitched again. Yes, he could smell them, the pungent scent of human body odor. All four of his feet quietly plodded off in that direction.

Down a few hallways and squeezing under a door, he felt he was getting close. All was going well. That is, until he saw the cat.

•

"What's taking so long?" Sasha was getting impatient.

Allister shrugged, "Hard to say. I doubt he's ever attempted to gain access to a building before in the current manner, so it's not inconceivable that he may get turned around, run into an obstacle or two. We must give him time."

Travis glanced at his watch. It read 5:28 a.m.

•

William froze in place.

He didn't intend to, it was just a natural reaction, hoping that perhaps the cat had not seen him. He wasn't so lucky. The cat's ears at first swung toward him with great interest, then slowly pinned them back as its eyes narrowed in the dim light with a look of recognition and it began to slowly creep forward—stalking, ready to pounce at the first sign of any sudden movement.

William's eyes scanned left and right, searching for the most attractive escape route. He could sense the energy in the cat increasing, its heart beating faster. He could feel its instincts kicking in, its mind calculating the length and force of its leap. Its lips began to curl back revealing its pointed carnivorous teeth. The sound of a low gurgling growl softly pierced the room. He could now even hear the ever so faint scrapes of its claws beginning to emerge from the end of its toes.

If he didn't do something to defend himself in the next few seconds, William knew that in his current condition the cat could very well kill him. He couldn't really blame the cat. It was probably its job to police the sanctuary at night, to find and eliminate small invaders like himself. He got a simple idea. He was still not close enough to see the humans, nor they him, so he took a chance.

FLASH!

The cat's eyes instantly went wide and it hissed in fear, staring now into the face of a snarling Doberman five times its size. The cat wasted no time effecting a full retreat, bolting from the hallway and disappearing from sight.

FLASH!

The floor was much closer once again.

William scampered forward along the edge of the wall leading into the main sanctuary and toward the iconostasis, keeping an eye on the three chanting men the entire time. As he carefully drew closer and closer, one of the men spotted him. He froze in place, again more by instinct than conscious decision.

The man was staring at him.

It was his quarry: Alexey Borochenko. That meant the other two men, Walter Stephens and Frank Donaldson, were now expendable.

One of the two was a Master. But which one? There would be no way to make that determination except in battle.

It was time.

FLASH!

CHAPTER 49
DANIEL AND PENELOPE

ONBOARD THE LIBERTINE
HERZLIYA MARINA
NEAR TEL AVIV, ISRAEL

"What time is it?" Penelope Angelucci asked Daniel as she awoke and saw him sitting on the sofa in her stateroom, He had obviously spent the entire night guarding her and watching her sleep.

Penelope was in one of the ten luxuriously appointed staterooms aboard the ship, no longer bound in an Icing Spell, but still held captive by Daniel's Protection Spell sealing the stateroom from the outside, effectively making it a prison cell.

"It is very early in the morning, my dear," Daniel DuMonde said. "Almost five-thirty. Your beloved Guillaume is running out of time. If he isn't here to surrender and give me what I want very soon, then I am very sorry, but a heavy price will have to be paid by you."

"He'll come," she said matter-of-factly. "Just give him time. He'll make it."

"I trust he will," he said. "And if he doesn't then he'll be spending the rest of his life mourning you and attempting to keep his daughter safe from me."

"What happened to you, Daniel?" she asked, almost with a note of pity in her voice. "You know, I used to care about you and believe in you, in what you did, in what *we* did."

"I've not changed," he insisted. "Maybe it was *you* who did."

She nodded, "Perhaps."

He smiled, "I do have a little surprise for you."

She skeptically angled her gaze at him, "Oh really?"

"*Oui*," he said. "While your fate remains in Guillaume's hands, you will not be here when he arrives."

Penelope studied his eyes, wondering what he was up to now, but said nothing.

Daniel continued his thought, tossing his long hair with a roll of his eyes, "Oh, come now, *mon chéri*. We all fully expect him to attempt to rescue you, and come here with whomever he has to help him, his cavalry. But he can't save you if you're not here."

"So where am I going?" She really wanted to know.

"Very soon Nancy will be escorting you to the airport," he explained. "You have a nine o'clock flight to New York with her – first class accommodations, of course. If Dr. Turner comes through on his obligations this morning, then when you arrive in New York, Nancy will be notified, and you will be released unharmed. And there I will wish for you to stay. That is, on the other side of the world if you wish to remain alive for years to come. You will not return to Rome. You can go to Texas and live with your daughter if you wish. I'm sure you have a great deal of catching up to do. However, if Guillaume does not do what he has been instructed, then Nancy has been instructed to take care of you. It's that simple." He added, "Oh, and if it comes down to Nancy taking care of you..." he paused for effect, "...it will be by fire."

"I see," Penelope said, hoping and praying inwardly that William, Sasha, Allister and Travis would come through, as promised.

CHAPTER 50
THE BATTLE

ST. ANDREW'S CHURCH
KIEV, UKRAINE

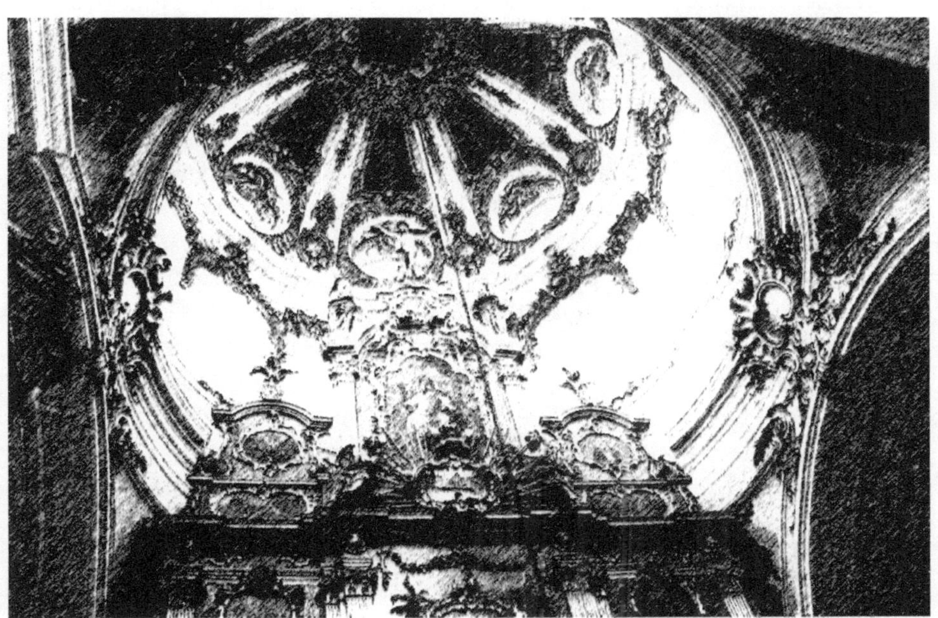

The flash of light where the gray rat was just standing momentarily blinded Alexey, like a harsh camera flash. Yellow and white dots spotted his vision. Frank and Walter had not noticed it, as both were still kneeling, with eyes closed, lost in the trance of their chanting and disciplined breathing. When Alexey's vision did begin to clear, his heart leapt up into his throat. Running full speed at him was a tall man with long gray hair and a long white beard. There was only one person the world it could be.

Alexey reached for his gun.

•

William threw the first energy pulse directly into the face of Alexey Borochenko, sending him toppling over backward, clearly stunned and gasping for air. He did the same with Frank, who was the furthest from him, achieving the same result.

Alexey rolled over and frantically pointed something at William. A red and blue flash winked from the object at the same instant a thundering explosion shook the room.

A hot, burning sensation creased William's left shoulder.

Walter came out of his trancelike state with a startled cry.

William reached for Walter, who was closest to him and grabbed him by his arms and lifted him up ready to take his breath away and break his heart. Instead, Walter's chest exploded in dots of blood as the object in Alexey's hand kept erupting fire and thunder.

A gun.

With a wave of William's hand the pistol jammed, then crumpled in Alexey's hand like an empty beer can. With another thrust of his hand toward Alexey the Ukrainian stood frozen in William's strongest Icing Spell. A final gurgle and gasp slipped past Walter's lips as William dropped his bullet-riddled body on the stone floor.

A fresh wave of William's hands were thrown toward the grand front doors of the church's entrance, as William shouted, "*Praesidium Riscindo*!" followed by, "Doors Open!" The Protection Spell on the church was revoked and the two massive wooden doors burst wide.

Allister, Sasha and Travis raced inside, each activating their own personal Protection Spells as they entered.

Frank Donaldson struggled to get to his feet, both shocked and momentarily disoriented.

William directed all of them toward Frank, "Over there, get that one! I've got to read Alexey!"

Sasha, Allister and Travis attempted to fire a unified Icing Spell at Frank. They didn't have much luck.

Frank was wary enough to beat his own chest with a Protection Spell the instant after he felt the energy pulse hit him and he heard the sharp pops of gunfire ring out. The Icing energy of the intruders just deflected off Frank's Protection Spell, completely ineffective.

Allister shouted to Sasha and Travis, "We have to revoke his shield. *Praesidium Riscindo,* all together in unison."

Unfortunately, at that very moment Frank Donaldson was nowhere to be seen.

William shouted, "Where is he?"

Travis turned to William. "I'm sorry, we lost him."

Allister spoke to Travis. "We don't know that for certain yet, my dear boy. If he managed to teleport, then, yes, he's gone. If he's just invisible, then he's still here somewhere. Be ready!"

All four of them were sufficiently protected for the time being by their own personal Protection Spells, just in case Frank *was* still there and contemplating a counterattack – which in the case of Sasha and Travis would likely work, at least in terms of revoking their Protection Spells and subsequently hitting them with an energy pulse of his own. Although, they also all knew that if he dared to do so, then they would then have some idea of his physical location. For even while a Magi was himself invisible, any offensive energy pulse cast disturbed and blurred the air enough to be visible and therefore traceable to its source.

William commanded, "Search for him, just in case. Throw very light pulses. Do no damage, but look for deflections." He moved behind Alexey and wrapped his hands on either side of Alexey's head. "This is the one we came for. This should only take a few seconds."

"*Nyet*!" Alexey screamed and then started reciting something in Arabic over and over.

"He'll reveal nothing!" shouted Frank's voice from somewhere nearby, echoing through the church.

And then it happened.

A hot red blur of energy, a swirling mixture of hot fire and light, drew a four inch thick blast, as if sprayed from a firehose, starting from a spot about ten feet away from Alexey to strike him in the middle of his chest, which immediately burst into flames and spread rapidly over most of the rest of his body. William defensively let go of Alexey's head and reeled back from the hot flames a full pace.

Alexey screamed out in horror and in tortured pain. If there was any mercy for him, it was William's Ice Spell still being in place. At least from the neck down, Alexey wouldn't be able to feel himself being incinerated. However that wasn't true for his head.

As for Frank, the cumulative energy drain of the initial Persistent Protection Spell on the church, plus the Combustion Spell to silence Alexey, plus an Invisibility Spell and a Personal Protection Spell were all now draining him well beyond his limits to the point of exhaustion and vulnerability. His spells were beginning to fragment and his image was starting to reappear in intermittent glimpses.

Sasha saw it, recognized it as a moment of weakness, then pointed and shouted, "There he is!"

Six combined energy pulses, two each from Allister, Sasha and Travis all converged upon the spot in the next instant, colliding into a massive shower of sparks and twisted twigs of light. The floor shook beneath their feet. The chandelier's hanging from the ceiling above shook on their chains. Even the iconostasis trembled from the shock wave.

Frank Donaldson fully reappeared and slumped to the floor, wheezing, barely conscious. Knowing their foe's vulnerability might only last a fleeting moment, Allister raced over to him. He grimaced at the thought of what he needed to do, but didn't falter. He reached down and touched Frank's neck, releasing a lethally powerful burst of dark energy.

It was the first Death Spell that Allister had cast in many, many years. Frank's last breath oozed between his lips as his lungs collapsed and heart tore in two. It was all Allister could manage to filter the putrid wave of darkness that flowed back at him in the energy reflex. He was genuinely shocked a single soul could possess that much pure evil. A wave of nausea hit him and he doubled over, vomiting and retching on the stone floor.

Allister could feel his mind darkening. He no longer felt any revulsion at taking a life. No, he wanted to do it again. And again.

Both Sasha and Travis immediately came to Allister's aid, laying hands on him and formally rebuking the darkness they could see flooding his eyes. At first he resisted them, slapping at them and trying to push them away, but they wouldn't be deterred. Bright white light shone from their palms, increasing in intensity, driving the darkness away. Finally, with a hoarse wretch, Allister coughed up a cloud of what appeared to be microscopic insects, like a swarm of gnats, that swirled around his head and then flew away, evaporating into the air.

All the while Allister, Sasha and Travis fought and put an end to Frank Donaldson and minister to Allister, William dared to lunge forward once more against the flames and grab Alexey's burning head. Cruel tongues of fire licked up Alexey's body and wrapped themselves around William's hands and forearms, setting his shirtsleeves on fire.

William strained to see inside the man's mind, reading anything and everything he could. Yet, the only images coming through were those of intense pain and suffering. At one point, William couldn't discern whose pain it was, Alexey's or his own. His hands and arms were being cooked right along with Alexey's entire body. Portions of Alexey's flesh were starting to melt off his bones. The screaming had stopped, and it was nearly impossible to believe he was still conscious.

William cried out to Alexey while he still had a shred of consciousness left, "Don't be a monster, Alexey! *Where* did you put the device?"

A lone image shot into William's mind: that of an El Al flight landing on a modern runway, as seen from an outside vantage point, high atop a multistoried structure. In his peripheral vision stood a white cargo van. And then everything went dark.

William leapt away, his hands and arms singed and scorched bright pink, red and black. Some places were charred and blistered. The pain was so intense his vision blurred and he feared he was about to faint. Alexey's body crumpled to the floor, continuing to burn until there was nothing left that was recognizable.

With help from Sasha and Travis, Allister rose quickly to his feet and came to William's aid, and the three of them lay hands on his wounds and gently healed them, as well as patting out a few remaining glowing embers and smoldering patches on his shirt. In a few minutes time of the group's ministrations, the charred and singed flesh began to heal and return to its normal hue.

When all the commotion had subsided and the flames of what little remained of Alexey died out leaving a pile of ash behind, Sasha said to her father, "Please tell us, after suffering through all of that, that you got what you needed to find the weapon and stop it."

William gave them a curt nod, whispering through the pain, "I think so. I recognized the airport. You were just there. But I'll have to go see for myself to be certain."

Travis said, "Then we're coming with you."

"No, it would be better if you stayed here," William said. "This is far enough away to stay safe."

It was Allister's turn to pipe up. "No, we're all coming, too, William. If the seconds draw nigh to destruction, then we'll all leave again, and that means you included."

William was too tired to argue with them all. He could tell it would just be a waste of time. He reluctantly nodded in agreement and then looked at his slightly charred watch face.

It was almost 5:45 a.m.

They had a couple of hours left to find and deal with the weapon. Unfortunately, Penelope supposedly only had until sunrise. And in Tel Aviv at that particular time of year, which was in the same time zone as Ukraine, the sun rose around 5:45 a.m.

It was time to take a chance. He pulled out his phone and called a number he'd not dialed on his own behalf in a very long time.

No one in the room noticed that in the smoldering pile of ash that was once Alexey Borochenko was left a charred belt-buckle, a zipper, a watch, a gold ring, and two brass keys.

Chapter 51
A New Deal

Onboard the Libertine
Herzliya Marina
Near Tel Aviv, Israel

"You're late, Guillaume." Daniel DuMonde sat on the upper deck of his yacht, enjoying the beautiful sunrise. A uniformed steward placed his breakfast down before him and left.

Dr. William Turner's voice came though quite clearly over the speakerphone sitting on the marble-top dining table as Daniel neatly placed his napkin on his lap and lifted his knife and fork.

William simply asked him, "Do you still want it or not?"

"You still have it, do you not?" Daniel asked somewhat rhetorically. "Why are we quibbling? You know my price for it."

"Sorry to disappoint you, old friend, but I *never* had it," William insisted. "Alexey stole it in Syria, working along with Renaldo, Mohammed, Frank and Walter. It's taken me this long to finally locate its hiding place and be in a position to retrieve it. Right now I am standing in a lovely little church in Kiev, Ukraine, and I'm just now on my way back to Israel to find the device where Alexey left it."

"I find that rather hard to believe," DuMonde quipped.

"If you still want the device then you had better believe me. You see, Daniel, whether you can accept it or not, all of your remaining members of the Inner Circle that I just mentioned sold you out to the Persians. Other than Nancy, you're on your own now." William almost sounded pleased at that idea.

"The General and the Archbishop I might believe were traitors. But not Frank and Walter. They are joining me here on my ship later this morning."

"Unfortunately, they can't come see you this morning, Daniel. Because all of them are dead. I've seen to that personally. Mohammed and Renaldo were taken out in Tehran, and now Frank and Walter and Alexey here in Kiev. I'm looking at what's left of them as we speak. But regardless of whether you believe me or not, you do need to realize one important thing, and that's that they *all* wanted *you* dead," William explained. "Which is why the weapon is not only located in Israel, right there in Tel Aviv with you right now, where it's been all this time, but it is armed and preparing to detonate this morning. It's probably very close to where you are sitting. It's so close in fact, that you couldn't sail away under a full head of steam and expect to escape its wrath before it goes off."

"You're lying," he spat.

"Are you willing to test that theory?" Before Daniel could answer, William added, "No, Daniel, it's the truth. The device is set to detonate at around nine o'clock this morning."

"Why should I believe you?"

William said, "Because if I'm lying or if I'm just wrong, then you have nothing to worry about. But if I'm right, you are in grave personal danger. So tell me, what are you going to do?"

Daniel DuMonde looked at his watch. It read 6:12 a.m. If Guillaume was telling the truth, then there were perhaps only between two to three hours left at most. It would take at least twenty to thirty minutes to get the ship underway. Steaming away at twenty knots per hour, he might get fifty kilometers away before it went off. That wasn't far enough – and teleporting wasn't something he had mastered yet.

"So what do you propose, Dr. Turner?"

William's voice took on a more amiable tone. "Well, Daniel, under the circumstances, I think we should consider a new deal arrangement. Such as, you agree to let Penelope and I live, I figure out how to stop the weapon and let most of the world live, which would also include you and Nancy. Sounds fair to me."

Daniel was enraged, "*No!* I paid five billion dollars for that device! It belongs to *me*!"

William shouted back, "Then you're welcome to go find it and turn it off yourself."

Daniel spoke without thinking, "Nancy can disarm it."

"I'm not letting her get anywhere near it until *after* I have Penelope back safely with me," William spat back. "Sorry, old boy, but I'm you're only hope at this point."

After a weary pause Daniel DuMonde said, "Then you are also going to be Penelope's last hope as well. Oh, yes. You see, she and Nancy are on their way to Ben Gurion as we speak for a flight to New York. If you fail, then she dies with you."

"You mean, with us *all*," William corrected him.

"If that's to be our fate, Guillaume, then so be it. But unless I get the device back in working order, all you'll be doing is delaying the inevitable. Penelope will die today by Nancy's hand, and you will die by mine on the day that I find you."

The line was quiet. Daniel could tell Dr. Turner was taking quite a bit of time to think this impasse through.

It was a stalemate. If he finds and disarms the weapon and then gives it up they all live, but if he doesn't give it up then everyone—potentially millions—all die.

Finally, William said, "All right, Daniel. You win. If I'm successful in disarming the device, I'll call you, and then you can have Nancy deliver Penelope to me. As soon as I have Penelope, then Nancy can pick up the device. At least I know it wasn't your intention to sell it to the Persians. Agreed?"

Daniel swallowed a fresh piece of honeydew melon. He smiled at the thought that this whole sequence of events had serendipitously served to eliminate the traitors in his organization, and he was still poised to make his sale for double his money, just a few days delayed. His Syrian buyers would forgive him that slight inconvenience. And if he had any more good fortune, he would ultimately find a way to put an ignoble end to both Dr. Turner and Penelope Angelucci before everything was said and done.

Daniel said, "You have a deal, Guillaume. And good luck with your task. I sincerely mean that. For all our sakes."

CHAPTER 52
THE CORE

BEN GURION INTERNATIONAL AIRPORT
TEL AVIV, ISRAEL

"You can't possibly consider giving him that weapon," Sasha said to her father.

"Of course not," William replied. "But I had to say that to buy Penelope some more time."

The four of them stood on the top level of the parking garage at Ben Gurion International Airport next to a nondescript white transfer van. It had only taken them about twenty minutes or so to track the van down after teleporting from Ukraine back to Tel Aviv, reappearing behind a cargo hangar at the airport.

It was 6:20 a.m. they still had a little bit of time.

William lifted the padlock on the back of the van and touched the tip of his finger to the keyhole.

Nothing happened.

That was odd. He concentrated harder and eventually the tumblers inside the lock slowly clicked into place and the lock popped open. He removed it from its hasp and lifted up the rear cargo door. Inside the van stood a wooden crate wrapped with heavy stainless steel chains. A few minutes of work later the chains were loosed and the crate stood open.

Inside the wooden crate was the device.

The bright red LED timer William had seen in his vision continued to tick down seconds. It now read 02:27:14. Just under two and a half hours to go. That was more than enough time to teleport clear if they failed, along with the entire group, but it would consign untold multitudes to a horrifying death. If there were any way to prevent that, William was going to find it.

He looked at the device for several seconds before announcing, "We may have a big problem."

Sasha stepped up and looked over his shoulder. "What's wrong?"

He explained, "The original arming sequence involved pressing this ARM button right here and then entering a security code on this keypad, followed by the simultaneous turning of the two arming keys – a form of two-factor authentication. Standard nuclear protocol would be for separate individuals to each have a key, thus a weapon could only be armed by two trusted people working in cooperation, not one person acting alone. Although, if one person had both keys, it could be done on a device as small as this."

"So what's the problem?" Sasha asked.

Travis saw it first, and said, "Where are the keys?"

William shook his head, "They appear to have been taken, perhaps by Alexey after he armed it, to ensure it couldn't be stopped. And without magic, we can't unlock those tumblers of the triggers."

Allister was alarmed, "So it can't be stopped?"

William ran weary fingers through his hair. "Unfortunately, it doesn't look that way."

Travis leaned over and looked more closely at the device himself, and then suggested, "If we can't stop it, why can't we just move it? Like teleport it out into the middle of the Mediterranean or maybe even the Atlantic and let it sink to the bottom before it goes off? Maybe just kill a bunch of fish?"

William nodded, "Good thought, but not with this weapon."

"Why not?" asked Travis.

Sasha answered the question, "The same reason we can't magically unlock the arming triggers. The presence of the plutonium. As my mother said, the good magic, like teleporting or levitation, won't work around it. And if we try to destroy it with dark magic, that energy will trigger the nuclear fission and then it goes boom in a big way."

Travis said, "Okay, this is sounding more and more like we're all screwed along with a few million people within a hundred miles or so of here."

If thine eye offend thee, cut it out.

A most ingenious, but incredibly dangerous idea suddenly popped into William's head. He abruptly said, "Perhaps not."

Allister desperately hoped he had come up with something viable. "How so, William?"

He smiled. "We just might be able to change the ground rules in our favor."

•

Inside the passenger concourse Nancy Thompson received an urgent call from Daniel DuMonde. She listened carefully before saying nothing more than, "I understand."

Penelope asked, "What is it?"

Nancy smiled, still invisibly holding Penelope on a strong Icing leash, enhanced with her rare poisons and hallucinogens. That is, Penelope was still lucid, but most compliant to everything she was ordered to do.

Nancy replied, "There's been a change of plans."

Penelope felt slightly inebriated, but did manage to catch the gist of what Nancy was saying. "How so?"

Nancy rolled her eyes and said, "Well, it appears your gallant knight in shining armor has finally shown up to collect you. And when he does, we get our prize."

Penelope's heart leapt. "Where is he?"

Nancy shrugged. "Unknown. But somewhere around here at the airport. He has consented to trading the device for you."

Penelope's face lit up with a dreamy smile, "I *knew* he'd come."

Nancy grabbed Penelope by the arm and guided her toward the exit.

CHAPTER 53
CASUALTIES OF WAR

BEN GURION INTERNATIONAL AIRPORT
TEL AVIV, ISRAEL

The group of Magi stood several yards away from the van, far enough away from the disarming effects of the plutonium radiation, discussing their game plan.

William explained, "Inasmuch as I theoretically understand how these weapons really function, essentially all of its electronics, other than its basic housekeeping functions, are just a big switch to ensure that it is difficult to arm such a weapon, couldn't be done by accident, and can only be done by the right people. When the switch is thrown, it activates a detonator of conventional explosives and then the big boom."

"Okay..." Sasha prompted.

He continued, "Otherwise, all you have is a core of fissile material, plutonium in this case, an isotope made from highly enriched uranium. Outside of this fissile core is the detonator, which is a larger sphere of conventional explosives. The electronics of the weapon, when detonated, sets off the conventional explosive which, in turn, starts a chain reaction in the fissile material, causing atoms to split, and then the split atoms cause other atoms to split, exponentially releasing the unimaginable amounts of energy and radiation of the fissile isotope. In a word: Boom!"

Travis asked, "So how does that help us?"

William asked them all, "Well, what do you think would happen if we could remove the fissile core?"

Allister nodded and said, "Then the entire device becomes nothing more than a conventional bomb. Might destroy a building, but not much else. Limited casualties and collateral damage."

Sasha added, "And it would also be a bomb that *could* be teleported if the plutonium were no longer around."

William smiled. "Exactly."

"Wait, wait, wait," Travis interrupted. "I've read a lot about the first atomic bombs, *Fat Man* and *Little Boy*, about the work Oppenheimer and his team did in the creation of the Hiroshima and Nagasaki atomic weapons. I guarantee you that much of that device's internal architecture is layers of lead lining, lead that is shielding the radiation of that core. You can't just snatch it out of there. We'd all die in a pretty gruesome manner in a matter of hours, if not minutes, from extreme radiation exposure."

Sasha added, "And you wouldn't be able to use a Protection Spell to shield yourself from it. The radiation would repel it."

William bowed his head in silence for a moment, then lifted it and looked into Allister's eyes. "I am strong. You know that. I can withstand far more bodily damage than any mortal folk, and most Magi. Take Sasha and Travis with you into one of the fields nearby, far enough away from this thing such that you can use your magic, and dig a good sized hole several feet deep. I'll go as fast I can. If I can get the core out, I'll run it to you. Travis is right. You all will need to be standing a safe distance back away from the thing, with your Protection Spells active. Once the core is in the hole then we bury it. Cover it with large stones if need be. If we all get out of this alive, then we'll go tell the proper Israeli authorities where it is and let them properly dispose of it." His eyes found Sasha's. "And if I'm not too far gone, all of you can help heal me like you did before."

Sasha had a lump in her throat and a dark pang of fear in her heart. What he was explaining seemed to make sense, but something felt very wrong about it. *Very* wrong.

Allister frowned and said, "Wait a second. I have an idea that might help a bit, but perhaps only a bit." He reached into his jacket pocket and pulled out a worn pair of leather driving gloves.

William chuckled at him, "I don't think those will provide me with much protection."

Allister smiled, "Not these. No, not as they are." He balled them up in is hands, and projected a transmutation thought of energy into them. He opened his hands as the gloves grew a bit larger and turned gray. He held them out to William. "A little touch of alchemy. They now have a little lead lining."

William took them, not really believing they would do much good, but appreciative of the gesture. "Thank you, good sir."

•

The procedure itself wasn't that difficult. Although, William was limited to using conventional hand tools instead of magic. To get to the device's guts, the front panel of the crate had to be removed. A heavy, lead-lined external access plate on the front of the device was removed revealing the internal bomb-works. When that was done, William was immediately hit by a wave of warm air and heard the soft hum of a cooling fan.

The spherical outer charge, which was about the size of a beach ball, also had a five inch in diameter convex access port on it just below its equator, secured by several finely threaded screws. Removing those screws revealed the circular access port, which was actually a three inch deep and four inch in diameter cylinder leading to the central core compartment. At the other end of that access cylinder he knew would find the plutonium core resting in the center compartment. Removing the access cylinder would then allow the core to roll out due to its own weight and thus be extracted.

William knew the fissile core would be about the size of a softball, or more accurately, a small eight or ten pound cannonball, and look as though it were made of chrome or polished silver. That was the prize. However, a cannonball was typically made of iron or lead, not plutonium. This one would more likely weigh the better part of a hundred pounds, much heavier than even pure gold.

It was time.

He removed the last screw of the access cylinder. As the cylinder began to release a rubber O-ring was breached and a trickle of liquid nitrogen began seeping out and evaporating on the floor of the device's case, causing a dense cloud of fog to fill the air. William did his best to wave it away. He'd forgotten about the cooling process of the bomb, which was needed to keep the core from overheating and going critical mass all on its own. Yes, it surely would have had a trickle circulation system of liquid nitrogen continuously flowing all around it and plumbed to a small cooling unit, effectively a radiator with a tiny compressor to release the accumulated heat. That explained the warm air and fan inside the device.

There was no more time to hesitate. William knew full well what the risks were. He took several deep cleansing breaths...and then pulled the cylinder the rest of the way out.

Following the cylinder was the silver cannonball.

William grabbed the ball wearing Allister's alchemy gloves. It was heavier than he could believe was possible for an object so small. And even through the dense glove he could tell it was extremely hot to the touch. For that reason alone he was thankful to have Allister's gloves.

No time to tarry.

Cradling the hot, heavy, silver ball as best he could manage, William jumped out of the back of the van and ran to the edge of the parking garage. Spying a landscaped bed of shrubs below, he let the core drop. No sense being close to the accursed thing a second longer than absolutely needed.

He ran to the stairwell.

Emerging from the stairwell at ground level William ran at a full speed to fetch the silver ball from the bushes and make a bee line toward the spot where he'd seen Allister a few moments earlier from the top level of the garage. It wasn't far, perhaps only a hundred yards, safely away from roads or any potential civilian interaction.

As he ran, his stomach began to churn with an unexpected wave of nausea.

William grit his teeth and tried to run faster. A dull ache started to swell in all of his joints: knees, ankles, hips, shoulders, elbow, wrists.

He couldn't move quite as fast as normal, but he knew he had to.

He could see the fresh pile of dirt next to a hole in a fallow field. There, Allister stood close by covered in a Protection Spell. Sasha and Travis were safely standing back at a distance, also covered by their own Protection Spells. The closer William drew to Allister, the more Allister's Protection Spell began to dissipate.

Only twenty yards or so were left to reach the hole.

William could feel a wetness on his upper lip and wiped it away with his right shoulder only to see fresh blood on his shirt.

His vision began to blur.

Slowed to a quick walk, he was still determined to make it. His last thought before his eyes closed was to thrust the heavy weight forward with both hands directly at the mouth of the hole with all the strength he had remaining. Dr. William Turner lost consciousness and fell to the ground about two paces shy of the hole.

CHAPTER 54

FROM THE JOURNAL OF WILLIAM TURNER

MORTALITY

A pertinent question I thought to ask my Master was how long Magi normally live. With everything I had learned about the Magic of healing and self-defense, it seemed logical that Magi could be practically immortal. The answer I received wasn't as infinite as I'd hoped.

Unfortunately, my Master told me that once the level of Master was achieved, Magi did tend to outlive most mortal folk, on average. But we were still very much mortal creatures, subject to physical suffering and even death. Granted, a strong, well-trained, and disciplined Magi is hard to kill, but "hard" doesn't mean "impossible."

Harvest a Magi of all his energy, he will be as vulnerable and weak as any mortal man. Cast a Death Spell on an inferior Magi, even a Master if he is weaker, and surely he will fall in battle.

Magi are also vulnerable to conventional weapons if no Protection Spell is in place to prevent it. Cut a Magi with a knife or sword, and he bleeds. Shoot him in a vital organ, and if he's not promptly healed, he dies. Hit a Magi with a strong enough Energy Pulse, you can knock him over as effectively as a strong punch to the face. And yes, punches to the face can still cause pain and bodily damage.

This lesson just reinforced a concept that my Master had been trying to get through to me from the beginning. And that is that we Magi are not so different from mortal folk. We all started our lives as mortal folk, but through study and experience became something more.

What singularly distinguishes the Magi from mortal folk is our accumulation of knowledge and experience, which together give us access to awesome power readily available to all, if they likewise knew what we know and do what we do.

The rest is just practice.

So don't let access to power deceive you into believing that you are invincible or immortal. You're not. I'm not. Magic can indeed help protect you, but it can never take away all of the vulnerabilities of the flesh.

Chapter 55
The Spoils of War

Ben Gurion International Airport
Tel Aviv, Israel

The very first image that William Turner saw when he awoke was that of his daughter Sasha leaning over him, with a pained look of concern and fear on her face. He could feel the warmth of her hand holding his. He could tell she had been crying.

Sasha turned to Allister, "The healing, it's working. Don't stop! He's waking up."

William was sore from head to toe, as though he'd been severely beaten for hours and hours on end. Perhaps at the cellular level that was a lot more true than he wanted to believe. He saw that he was still lying prone on the bare ground, but not near the hole Allister had created for storing the radioactive plutonium core. They were gathered much closer to the parking garage. And he was laying on his back.

His voice was a hoarse whisper, "The core?"

Allister smiled at him. "All taken care of, my lad. You did it. Your last, seemingly desperate, but accurate, throw sent the shiny ball into the bottom of the hole and the deed was done." He then amended, "Although, I must say, a lot of the dirt had to be pushed back in the hole by hand until the core was covered up enough so as not to interfere with our magic. Which, in turn, also made it unnecessary to have to carry you over here."

William asked, "What time is it?"

Travis checked his watch and told him, "Almost seven-thirty."

"Help me up," William instructed. With great difficulty he regained his feet. His stomach was still nauseous, his joints were still aching and sore. He leaned heavily on Allister's shoulder, doing his best to clear his head and think about the tasks at hand.

Time was growing exceedingly short.

He asked them, "Does everyone still know what remains to be done?"

Sasha nodded, "We do. Are you going to be able to do your part?"

William nodded through the pain and forced a wan smile. "Feeling a little better with every second that goes by."

•

Nancy Thompson didn't have very far to walk with Penelope to reach William and company at the top level of the parking garage. The climb up all the stairs wasn't terribly pleasant, but they managed. The call from Daniel had come about fifteen minutes earlier. Nancy was actually relieved to learn that William was so close by.

At long last, she spied him standing at the rear of a white cargo van. He looked a mess, his long gray hair was matted down with sweat, his white beard unkempt and soiled. His face was red, as though he were sunburned. His black shirt sleeves appeared to have been torn, if not burned away. His trousers were filthy, as though he'd been crawling around in a sewer. There was a tear in his shirt on his left shoulder, revealing a graze of dried blood, along with a smear of fresh blood on his right shoulder.

His eyes looked weary and glazed.

An elderly man stood next to William – in fact, he appeared to be holding William up. That was curious. He must be the Master, Allister McKenzie. She'd only seen him once before, the night they came to find Travis in her room, but only for a moment before she made her hasty escape. A very lovely looking young woman with long dark hair, presumably William and Penelope's daughter, and a young man stood on either side of the van. Four against one were not good odds for any kind of Magi confrontation, even if William was operating at less than a hundred percent.

Despite William's disheveled appearance, the group looked more than ready for her.

William, in particular, looked genuinely happy to see Penelope alive and unharmed.

When Penelope began to move toward him, Nancy touched her arm, "Not so fast, my dear."

Penelope stopped in her tracks. She knew the spell Nancy had cast on her was a combination of an Icing Spell mixed with a Death Spell. That is, as long as the spell was active, if Penelope moved more than a few feet away from Nancy, she'd die. It was the same logic as the invisible fence for dogs, only with much more lethal consequences.

"Hello, Nancy," William pleasantly greeted her. "Let's all do our best to avoid any unpleasantness, if you don't mind. Allister is a true Master, as am I. Our other associates aren't mortal folk either. So just let's get this over with, shall we?"

Nancy gave him her best pretend smile. "Good morning, William. Rough night? You don't look so well."

William didn't bother to answer her. Instead he looked at Penelope and asked her, "Are *you* all right?"

Penelope replied in a sleepy slur. "I've been better. She has a spell on me. I can't... I ... I can't..."

Nancy finished for her, "She can't leave my presence alive. Show me the merchandise and let me leave with it, then I will release her to your custody."

"Fair enough," William gestured toward the open cargo door. He had replaced the front panel of the wooden crate. Only the top portion of the decide was visible once more.

Nancy stepped closer, wary of any kind of ambush. She gingerly stepped up into the back of the cargo bay. Outside the truck both Sasha and Travis turned and laid their hands on the side panels of the van and began to whisper softly. Stepping further into the van, Nancy looked inside the open wooden crate.

Indeed, there was the device. Its red LED timer read all zeros. The ARM button was dark.

Nancy turned to William, looking puzzled, "You managed to disarm it yourself? How?"

He said, "Let's just say Alexey told me everything I needed to know."

She glanced down again. "Where are the keys?"

"What keys?" William innocently asked.

Her poor imitation of a smile faded to a stern scowl. "The keys for the arming triggers."

"Ah, those keys." William shrugged. "Sorry, but that's my insurance policy. Those keys aren't here, but will be sent to Daniel separately, once I know all this is done and everyone is safe."

Nancy huffed, "Clever thinking, William, but irrelevant. I have one of the spare sets with all my equipment on the ship. Nice try, but you can keep your set as a souvenir."

She turned around and climbed out of the rear of the cargo van. William followed her and then signaled Sasha and Travis.

Sasha came around and reclosed the van's cargo door.

Travis spoke up, "You will need these keys." He pulled the van's ignition keys out of his pocket. "They were in the glove." He tossed them to Nancy, having no desire to ever get within arm's reach of her ever again.

Sasha reattached the padlock to the van's rear cargo door.

Nancy gave Travis a disingenuous smile. "Why thank you, Travis. And might I say, you're looking well today. Much better than when last I saw you. No hard feelings about the other day, I trust?"

Travis' face remained stoic and he said nothing.

Nancy abruptly turned to Penelope, touched her cheek and said, "You are free."

Penelope staggered forward, shaking her head to clear it. The clouds in her mind were quickly clearing as well.

"Thank you, Nancy. I believe our business in concluded." With a slight wince, William turned his face to address Allister. "Allister, if you will?"

"Of course." Allister promptly stepped forward and held his arms out to Penelope. "How about a hug, my dear?"

Penelope practically collapsed into the older man's arms. The high pitched whine filled the air.

FLASH!

Allister and Penelope were gone.

Without another word, William, Sasha and Travis stepped back and watched Nancy get in the van's cab, back it out, and drive away without incident.

Sasha noted, "That went about as good as can be expected."

William said, "I agree."

"How long do you think before she finds out?" Travis asked.

William looked at his watch. It was just past 8:00 a.m. "I'm guessing not for at least an hour. And that's all the time we need. I'll meet you both back at the hotel in a few minutes. One more task left to do."

Travis said to Sasha, "Apparently we did the illusion perfectly."

She smiled. "I know!" She took him by the hand. "Let go."

Travis was very pleased to be holding Sasha's hand. As they headed toward the stairwell to descend one last time he said, "I swear, when we practiced it before she showed up, I really thought it looked like the real device."

Sasha replied, "Let's just be thankful she didn't try to touch it."

Indeed, Dr. Nancy Thompson was at that very moment driving back to Herzliya Marina with an empty crate in the back of her van.

Just inside the parking garage, under a large canvass tarp found in the back of the van was the real device. Its timer was still ticking.

It read 00:52:18.

William Turner closed his eyes and the high pitch whine ensued.

FLASH!

CHAPTER 56
THE CONSEQUENCES OF WAR

ONBOARD THE LIBERTINE
HERZLIYA MARINA
NEAR TEL AVIV, ISRAEL

"You did it, my dear," Daniel enthusiastically complimented Dr. Nancy Thompson with a toast of champagne.

She clinked her glass against his, took a sip, and said, "But William and his band of merry Magi are still out there and need to be dealt with. I'm sorry, but I didn't have an opportunity to take care of those loose ends today. There were too many of them."

The dock began to slowly move away from them as *The Libertine* used its bow thrusters to move laterally into the channel and slowly depart from the Herzliya Marina. The morning was absolutely glorious as the sun proudly announced itself to a cloudless blue sky.

Daniel nodded. "*Oui*, they are still an issue for us. But clearly it was necessary to execute a strategic retreat for the time being. We had no choice but to get the device back. Closing that first transaction on that product in Syria is what will provide us all the necessary capital to capture this new and emerging market in this part of the world. And with all the other disloyal members out of the picture, it will be fantastic for us. Less bounty to have to share."

She asked, "Can the deals with the Russians even still be done without Alexey?"

"I trust so." Daniel sipped his glass. "If not with the Russians, we'll have a chat with the Chinese. For a communist country, they always seem to be most eager to turn a profit."

Daniel asked her, "By the way, where did you put it?"

Nancy pointed back toward the Marina. "It's in the parking lot right over there. It's been in a parking lot at the airport all week, I assumed it wouldn't hurt to sit in plain sight for a day or two more waiting for the client to come pick it up."

Daniel threw a nervous glance toward the parking lot beyond the rows of boats in the marina. "I don't know. I think I'd prefer it to be in a locked warehouse guarded by dozens of very scary men with big guns. Did you at least put a Protection Spell on it?"

She shook her head. "I couldn't. You know very well the plutonium in it negates all magic anywhere near it."

"Right, right, right. I'm sorry. I forgot." Daniel looked uncomfortable. After a moment he said, "No, Nancy. I don't like this. No, not at all. I'm worried. I really would like it to be taken to a warehouse or some other safe location. Not just left out in the open like this."

The long, stately ship cleared the outer rows of the marina at idle speed and cruised toward the open Mediterranean.

Daniel instructed her, "Please. It won't take long. Go and guard it for a short time. I'll make some calls. I promise, I'll shall have someone come within the hour to collect it and take it to safety. Then you come back to the ship. I know you can fly, and shouldn't have a problem finding us."

And that's when it occurred to Nancy.

Inspector Allister McKenzie was able to successfully teleport away with Penelope in his arms. He shouldn't have been able to do that in such close proximity to the device.

She stood up in a mild state of alarm. "All right, Daniel. I will go see to the van. Besides, there's something about it, something important, that I think I need to check on."

"Excellent," he stood as well and took her unfinished glass from her hand. "I'll go make those calls."

Nancy's eyes flashed yellow as her Invisibility Spell masked her transformation into a massive flying reptile. She took to the skies and soared back to the parking lot where she'd parked the van. Assuming her human form and then becoming visible once more, she approached the rear cargo door of the van. She disintegrated the padlock with a touch of her finger, and then flung the door open wide with nothing more than a simple levitation thought. None of that should have been possible around the device.

"Let's have a look in here, shall we?"

•

William needed to make two trips to Daniel's yacht to ensure he got the teleportation coordinates correct. Teleportation only works when traveling to a place that can be visualized accurately in the mind. He was running very low on both energy and time, so he couldn't afford a mistake of any kind.

The first trip he was able to appear on the ship's rear deck, which he could easily see from onshore. That was a bit of a risk, since he didn't have enough energy to both teleport and cast an Invisibility Spell simultaneously. But after a few moments of rest, crouching behind a canvass covered wave-runner, and taking in a few long slow breaths, he was able to proceed with his mission. Once invisible, he surreptitiously made his way below decks and found the engine room.

There wasn't a lot of open space available in the engine compartment. The room was dominated by twin diesel engines that looked like they could power a small town. Between them was a small walking space for the ship's mechanics. And just behind the engines were the dual fuel tanks.

Perfect.

•

On his second teleport to the ship, now able to visualize exactly where he needed to go, William appeared with the device cradled in his arms. With no plutonium present he was also able to use a basic levitation spell to support its 500 pound weight, mostly weighed down by the layers of lead previously shielding its former core. With great physical difficulty and still suffering in intense pain he carefully maneuvered the device into the small open space between the engines and flush against the main fuel tanks. He glanced one last time at the red LED timer.

It read: 00:04:32.

Less than five minutes. He thought that should be enough time.

His upper lip felt wet again. A swipe with his finger revealed fresh blood. He was almost done, and determined to make it – even if it was the last thing he ever did. He only needed enough magic to make one more teleport. Just a little more energy.

"Help me," he whispered.

Fear not. They are here for you. Take comfort in them.

In the textured flooring at his feet he saw them.

Faces. Seven of them, all looking him in the eye with pained expressions of sadness. William took the time for seven slow breaths, in through his nose, held momentarily, and slowly out through his mouth. It would have to be enough.

•

The Captain of The Libertine approached Daniel DuMonde, who was both composing an email on an iPad and simultaneously was also on the phone completing the arrangements for the an armed security detail to come take the van to a secure location.

"*Monsieur, DuMonde?*" interrupted the Captain.

"*Oui?*" Daniel pulled the phone away from his ear.

In French, the Captain urgently said, "Sir, there is a problem."

Replying in his native French, DuMonde snapped, "What kind of problem?"

"An intruder alert," the Captain said. "A few minutes ago we detected a secure hatch alarm, on the engine room, but our video surveillance detected nothing."

"So what's the problem?" DuMonde asked. "You get false alarms from time to time."

"The alarm has gone off again, sir. Only this time, on our surveillance cameras we can see there is a visible intruder down in the engine room. Security guards have been dispatched."

"Description?" Daniel snapped.

The Captain answered, "He is a tall man, with long gray hair and a long white beard."

"Excellent, Captain!" Daniel jumped to his feet and raced down the stairs and gangways toward the engine room door. He shouted, "Have all hands stand back and secure the lower deck. No one approaches him but me. He's mine!"

•

William let out the seventh breath slowly and deliberately. He could feel the energy begin to swell inside him. The high-pitched whine in the air started softly then grew in intensity. Just a few more seconds and it would all be over.

And then it happened.

The energy pulse hit William in the chest and sent him tumbling backward head over heels. He struggled to regain his feet, desperately trying to see through his blurred vision. By reflex he thrust his palm toward the direction of the attack, focusing his thoughts on: *Be Still!*

In that same moment, another wave of energy hit him, only this one was not a second body blow, but a wave of cold – ice cold.

William Turner was paralyzed from the neck down.

As his eyes cleared, he could see Daniel DuMonde standing in the doorway of the engine room, trembling and, just like himself, was also frozen in place. Daniel's countenance was a macabre mixture of defiance and rage. Apparently, William's Icing Spell had likewise immobilized Daniel DuMonde. Their magic must have been cast at each other in the exact same instant.

This scenario made for an odd stalemate.

But was it a stalemate, William wondered? He was a Master, Daniel was not. It was time to revoke Daniel's Icing Spell and leave while there was still time. He said aloud, "*Glacio Riscindo*!"

Nothing happened.

William was still frozen in Daniel's Spell. He couldn't believe that he was so weak he couldn't break the Icing Spell Time was short. From where he now stood, in his peripheral vision he could just make out the red LED timer.

It read 00:03:27.

"*Docteur* Guillaume Turner, you are my prisoner at *last*," Daniel seethed. "I knew Providence would not let you escape me again."

William could barely remain conscious he was in so much pain. But with the bravest face he could muster, and with all the energy he could summons just to speak, he forced a crooked smile and said, "It seems I have you at the same disadvantage you have me, old boy."

Daniel laughed defiantly, "Your spell on me will break as soon as my guards put a bullet in your brain."

"It won't matter, Daniel," William taunted him "We'll all be dead very shortly. Look behind me."

It was at that moment that Daniel noticed the device on the gangway between the engines on the floor just behind William.

He gasped, "*Mon Dieu!* What have you *done?*"

William's smile was absolutely genuine as he thought about the irony of his fate in a few minutes. "I kept my promise. You said you wanted the device in exchange for returning Penelope to me safe and sound. You did that, and now I'm just keeping my word."

"You gave the device to Nancy!" he shouted. "She verified it."

"Sorry, old boy. She saw what I wanted her to see. I didn't trust her. I've never trusted dragons. They're an unpredictable sort. And besides, my agreement was with you, not her."

"So now you wish to play the martyr? You kill us both? You kill the millions of souls you wanted to save?"

Another glance: the timer read 00:02:53.

"The millions are safe, Daniel. The device is no longer nuclear. Just conventional. But still more than strong enough to take this ship apart in less than three minutes from now. Can't be disarmed. Too big, too heavy, and too far to go for your crew to throw it overboard. So then, with you and Nancy taken care of, even if I have to die with you, my work is done. The Inner Circle will be no more."

Daniel was smug, "No, you're wrong. You have failed, Guillaume. Nancy is no longer here aboard this ship. And as long as she lives, I can assure you she will hunt down Penelope and Sasha and cause both of them, as well as all those in their lives around them, more pain and suffering than you can ever possibly imagine."

William's heart sank. This was supposed to be the end game move, checkmate, regardless of what happened to himself. But in his heart he immediately knew Daniel was right. Until each and every last one of the Inner Circle was destroyed, then all good Magi would always be hunted. He closed his eyes and did his best to quiet his pounding heart.

The timer read 00:02:07.

Don't let perfect be the enemy of good.

William's eyes came open a the sound of the Voice in his heart. A new idea quickly formed in his mind. Daniel would lie and say anything to save his own hide. That was the key. Maybe there *was* a way out of this.

He said, "Then I'll make you one final deal, Daniel."

Daniel could see the timer as well. It read 00:01:56.

"Is there still time for any deals?" DuMonde was almost afraid to ask.

William proposed, "If we both revoke our Icing Spells on one another, I can teleport us both out of here. You don't want to die today. Neither do I. So the deal is, if I get us free from here, then we call for a lasting truce. You and Nancy get to live. Sasha, Allister, Travis and myself get to live. No vendettas. Live and let live."

Daniel's eyes were locked on the timer: 00:01:33.

"If I agree to release you, what prevents you from just leaving me in Ice and teleporting away and just letting me die here?"

William replied, "My word. Unlike yours, Daniel, my word is still worth something. I don't ask you to trust me, just to believe me. *Ergo Glacio Riscindo*. I release you."

Daniel suddenly was free and could move.

"Your decision, Daniel. Stay and die or go with me and live."

00:01:07.

"*D'accord*," DuMonde shouted. "I agree. *Ergo Giacio Riscindo*. I release you. Do it. Quickly while there is still time."

The cold sensation evaporated around William and he could move once more. He staggered forward a step.

00:00:55.

"What do I do, Guillaume?" Daniel pleaded with William as he rushed over to him. "How does this teleportation magic work?"

William gave Daniel a big smile as he began to take in long breaths, holding them momentarily and releasing them. When he felt his energy was sufficient to make one more jump, he said, "It's very easy, Daniel. You simply take my hand. Hold tight, and don't let go."

Daniel reached out his right hand and firmly grasped William's open hand.

"Perfect. Now close your eyes, and then we leave."

The high-pitched whine filled the air.

00:00:12.

FLASH!

•

Nancy came roaring out of the back of the van - literally. Behind her, the wooden crate was shattered and still burning. No longer in her human form, and to the utter horror of many marina patrons, she was fully visible for all to see. The dark red dragon took to the skies, climbing higher and higher, roaring and shrieking in blind rage. She could see the long white ship, *The Libertine* cruising about half a mile from the marina.

And then it happened.

The red, yellow, and orange fireball tore the rear third of the ship to shreds. A dense black and charcoal gray mushroom cloud billowed up from the hungry flames toward the sky. A secondary blast from beneath the surface sent a tower of water soaring into the sky. The ship's bow pitched high into the air, before all of what was left intact of *The Libertine* – its brilliant chrome, its polished brass, its oiled teakwood, its glistening marble, all of it – slowly slid backwards into the warm embrace of the waters of the Mediterranean and disappeared below the surface of the sea.

The red dragon flew to the site, circling, searching, and still shrieking in anger and anguish.

The surface of the water eventually calmed, but was littered with large chunks of debris, some of it still burning and smoldering.

After four more laps in the sky around the debris field, the enraged dragon soared off toward the north at great speed. She'd make it to Turkey in a couple of hours, and there she would resume her human form and take more conventional transportation back to New York.

But what then?

They were all gone. The Inner Circle was no more.

No, that wasn't true.

She still remained.

As long as at least one legacy member of the Inner Circle remained, the group and all of its powers could be reconstituted. New Magi could be trained and groomed. Certainly the most current leadership weren't its original founders. No, the Inner Circle had been around for over a thousand years. And so it would revive itself and live again.

And she would be its mother.

CHAPTER 57
DESTINY

THE RITZ CARLTON HERZLIYA
NEAR TEL AVIV, ISRAEL

This was the second time Sasha, Travis, and Allister had been in the Presidential Suite of the Ritz – but on this occasion it seemed to be under much more pleasant conditions.

FLASH!

Sasha's father had returned.

William looked far more tired and weary than Allister had ever seen him, barely able to stand.

Allister, Sasha and Travis all recoiled in unison from the ghastly sight of what William appeared to be still holding in his right hand. It was a dismembered human hand and forearm, complete with a 1939 Patek Philippe watch with a dark brown leather band on the wrist. The severed arm appeared to have been bloodlessly cauterized just above the elbow. William let it slip from his grasp and drop to the floor with a meaty thump.

Responding to all the blank questioning expressions staring at him William pointed to the arm and said, "That ghastly thing is what's about to be all that's left of Daniel DuMonde. He confronted me in the engine room. I was fortunate to make it out. That's all of him that did."

Allister quickly moved to William and embraced him, "So then the deed is done?"

William checked his own watch, which still had some dark soot on it from Kiev. "Any second now."

They all moved to the plate glass windows overlooking the panoramic view of the Herzliya marina and the Mediterranean sea.

"There it is," Travis pointed to the enormous white yacht heading out to sea.

•

Daniel DuMonde lay on the floor of his engine room going into shock. He couldn't grasp the reality of the sight of his missing right arm or the intense pain radiating all over his entire right side. He cradled the severed stump of his arm against his chest with his trembling left hand.

His eyes watched the timer go from 00:00:01 to 00:00:00.

And then it happened.

•

The ship was perhaps half a mile out from the marina when the concussion of the explosion could be felt slamming against the plate glass before them. Everyone cringed back, arms defensively flying up to protect their faces, but the glass held firm.

Sasha watched the black smoke billowing up into the air as a second explosion thundered, sending a tower of water into the air as the bow of the ship started to rise straight up out of the water, exposing the foremost part of the hull. The rear part of the ship was simply gone. And then what was left of *The Libertine* began to gradually slide backward, gently swallowed by the sea. Sasha's finger tips were on her lips, utterly aghast at the horrific sight. Yet part of her also felt greatly relieved.

"So you got him?" Allister asked.

William nodded, glancing momentarily at the severed arm lying on the floor at his feet. He coughed and rasped out a, "Yes."

Travis turned to William and said, "Then that's one more of them gone. So what about Nancy? Other than Sasha's mom, she should be the last one. Was she onboard the ship too?"

Before William could even venture a guess, they all saw it: the dark red dragon soaring over the marina and swooping low over the site of the destroyed and sunken ship. Around and around the beast flew until at last it shrieked as if wounded and in great pain and then soared off toward the north.

William coughed again, winced hard in his own pain, then cleared his throat and said, "I want all of you to remember... as long as even one of them is left, you can never lower your guard. And in time, you will need to find her and do what must be done. Otherwise, the disease just continues to replicate and spread."

Penelope echoed his sentiment. "He's right."

Sasha asked him, "What will she do?"

William answered, "The same as all who came before her over the centuries. She'll find and create other Magi susceptible to temptation and reconstitute her evil little clan. And that's why it means that as long as their kind exist, they'll still be hunting our kind. So stay strong and grow in power."

Allister added, "It's how it's always been for our kind. And how it is likely to ever be." He pointed to Sasha and Travis. "But you two are our next generation. You will carry on the light of good magic."

Sasha and Travis traded a goosebump-laden glance.

Penelope looked at William with grave concern on her face. "William, are you sure you're all right? You look terrible."

He just waved away the question and gave her a pained smile. "Gee thanks. Perhaps Nancy was right. I did have a pretty long night last night. Tell you what, after today, I promise to go take the longest shower of my life and then sleep for at least a week."

William staggered a couple of uneasy steps and Allister caught him before he fell down. A wet, strained coughing fit sent William urgently sitting down on the edge of the sectional sofa, clearly having difficulty breathing. There was blood on his hand again. He opened his fist and looked at two teeth in his palm.

He barely whispered, "Oh no. Not now." He seemed to speak to no one in particular, rather to some unseen member of their company. "Just a little more time. Please?"

Sasha rushed to his side and cried out to Allister, "What's happening to him. I thought we healed him."

Allister came and sat beside Sasha. His voice was grave, but filled with a note of compassion. "No, my dear. I'm sorry. We were only able to slow the process and provide him with some temporary relief."

Her desperate and confused eyes flew around to his.

Allister told her plainly. "But, unfortunately, the process could not, and cannot, be stopped."

"What are you *talking* about?" she shrieked. "We have *magic*!"

William reached out to his daughter, found her hands, and rasped, "That's just the problem, sweetheart. The levels of radiation I was exposed to, specifically its gamma rays in such high concentration, they don't just neutralize or repel the magic of light. They destroy it. There is no greater example of dark and evil energy in all the universe than gamma radiation. At the level and duration of exposure I've received, my body can no longer heal itself, not with its own natural magic. That magic, that *capacity* within me is gone. And with no natural organic magic to amplify, I can't heal, nor can anyone else's magic help me now."

Sasha suddenly grew quiet, her voice stern and accusing, "You *knew* this would happen. Didn't you?"

William coughed once more. His eyes were starting to get milky, his skin was going from a sunburned looking shade of pink to a darker shade of red and beginning to blister. He said, "I knew it was a possibility. But I hoped for the best. There really was no choice in the matter. Now was there?"

"Of *course* you had a choice," she insisted, hot tears rolling down her cheeks.

William shook his head. "No, honey. If we had let that thing go off, millions and millions of innocent people would have died. Maybe billions in its aftermath."

"Why didn't we call the Israeli authorities hours ago?" she demanded "We had a couple of hours."

"It wasn't enough," her father told her. "It wasn't enough time to be sure."

Allister said to Sasha, "Rest assured, we'd actually discussed that idea, but had no basis to think that we would have even been believed, and risked being locked up as part of an official investigation, ensuring our mission's failure."

"So what happens now?" Sasha looked to her mother.

Penelope's face was wet with her own tears. She held out her arms to Sasha, who promptly ran into them sobbing on her mother's shoulder.

William looked up and caught Penelope's gaze, and silently mouthed: *"Thank you. Take care of her."*

Penelope nodded.

William ran his trembling fingers through his long gray hair. Large quantities of it pulled out into his hands. He looked up, scanned the eyes of everyone in the room, and with his waning strength proclaimed, "I wouldn't want to have spent my last moments of this life with any other people in the world." He coughed and winced once more. "You all may not realize it now, but in time you just might be able to come to understand more fully…but if not for what we did today, there might not be much of a world left for anyone to ever try and save. We stood at the precipice of oblivion, and prevailed."

Sasha spun around and faced her father. "So this is good-bye?"

William nodded. "I'm afraid so, my dear. I may very well last another few hours here, depending on how long it takes for my organs to shut down. But I don't want any of you here to see me like this. Please grant me that small dignity. I can assure you it won't be very pleasant. Besides, at the rate the damage to my cells is advancing, in a few more minutes, it won't matter. I doubt I'll still be able to speak, or hear you, or see you."

There were tears in everyone's eyes.

After a long moment of silence, Sasha stood tall, dried her cheeks with the backs of her hands, and then walked over to her father. She sat next to him again, and gave him one last long hug and kissed him sweetly on both cheeks and softly on the lips.

William Turner watched his daughter rise to her feet once more and stand before him. He didn't know what she was doing.

"What is it, my sweet?" he asked.

Sasha spoke to him ever so tenderly with a completely stoic expression on her face, "I'll not leave here knowing you spent your last hours on this earth in great suffering and all alone."

"It's okay," he assured her.

William was perfectly ready to face whatever pains and horrors came in whatever time he had left. He'd done his duty, saved untold multitudes, and knowing that was enough for him to face whatever came. A tender, welcoming Voice in his heart told him the time of his Destiny was near.

"You have to go now," he told her. His words were barely audible.

Sasha nodded, "I know. I *am* going now. And as much of you…as there is still left…is coming with me."

William didn't understand, until the instant her soft fingers touched his warm, blistering sweat-soaked forehead.

In that brief instant of time, Dr. William Turner drew his last gasp of air right before his lungs collapsed and his heart cleaved in two. His last physical, intellectual, and spiritual sensation was all the energy of his life rushing forward through four delicate fingers into a very bright white light.

Chapter 58
Penelope and Allister

In the Countryside
Near London, England

Allister McKenzie lived a very comfortable life for a man who worked for the government. Then again, as he taught his apprentices, wealth just seems to flow toward the Magi. His country estate sat on fifty forested acres. The manor house offered twelve bedrooms, and was once owned by a British nobleman, the Duke of Something-or-Other. The man was actually a wealthy pig farmer in his day, but he did have a title, and five hundred years ago that mattered a lot more than it did today.

Although, Allister McKenzie was not without some political resource and fortitude when needed. It had taken him only a few days to clean up the unfortunate incident at the Herzliya Marina: the accidental fire and explosion onboard a yacht killing a wealthy French businessman, along with twelve of the ship's crew members. The Israeli government had no choice but to confiscate many smartphone pictures and amateur video of what appeared to be a real-life flying dragon near the site of the tragic marine disaster – quashing the story in the press as a hoax, and forcing all witnesses to sign criminally binding nondisclosure agreements.

Interpol was invaluable at helping to smooth over the recovery of the nuclear core buried in a field near Ben Gurion International Airport. The Israeli government was none too happy about the potential danger it represented to its citizens, but were somewhat appeased when they realized that they could keep it for the benefit of their own arsenal and no one would be coming to claim it, certainly not the Pakistanis, who had been paid handsomely for it.

The Iranians were likewise none too happy about the loss of a non-reversible wire transfer to a bank in Switzerland of just over thirty-three billion dollars. But what could they really do? Anyone they might wish to appeal to for a refund was dead.

Dr. William Turner was never found, and to this day he remains on Interpol's ten most wanted list.

•

"I'll sincerely miss him," Allister confessed. "He was the best Magi, nay the best *man*, I ever knew."

Penelope Angelucci sat with him on his rear terrace overlooking his manicured gardens and fountains, enjoying the four o'clock tea time. They were both still grieving. It was something made a bit more bearable to do by being together.

She said, "Sasha shows great promise."

"Indeed, she does," Allister agreed. "So when are you planning to go see her?"

"I promised her I would make a trip to Texas at least three or four times a year. We'll have to see how long I can keep that promise." She sipped her delicious chamomile tea, with one sugar and just a dash of fresh cream. "You know, I still have an active medical practice to support in Rome. I'm needed there. I can't be gone all the time.

He noted, "Yes. You're right. Austin is a long way from Rome."

She gave him a frown. "I told her it works both ways, you know. She's welcome to come see me as often as she likes, too. Money is no object. She knows that. William left her more in her trust than she could ever hope to spend in a lifetime."

Allister huffed, "She *will* come to Rome, of that I have no doubt, my dear. Yes, she'll come, both her and that nice young boy who's head-over-heels in love with her."

"Yes, Travis obviously worships her," she said.

Allister set his empty cup down and poured himself another from the antique china tea pot decorated with wildflowers. "Do you really think she knows just how devoted to her he is?"

"I would like to think so," Penelope said. "She's a very clever girl. But who am I to know such things? I once thought William wouldn't mind being married to a witch."

Allister chuckled.

Penelope added, "Fortunately, they're both Magi. That's good. She needs someone like herself in her life now. And so does he. They need each other."

"It *is* important," Allister noted.

She said, "What's more, I'll have you know, I do approve of him, should his intentions become more serious toward her, and should he ever do me the courtesy of asking me how I feel about his intentions."

Allister grinned at her, "He might just do that. And perhaps much sooner than you might think. I like him a lot, too, and I can assure you that he comes from a very fine family."

Penelope returned his smile. "I would expect nothing less."

CHAPTER 59
SASHA AND TRAVIS

THE BLIND PIG
AUSTIN, TX

Sixth Street in Austin, Texas really is the live music capital of the world. Stretching several miles, from the far west side of downtown Austin going east past Interstate 35, bars and nightclubs line both sides of the street. It's said that on any given Friday or Saturday night over 600 live bands are playing in Austin.

And live music isn't only happening down on 6th street. Just about any and every eating establishment in town features someone playing music, be it a singer-songwriter with a guitar, trios, quartets, or full-on rock-and-roll bands, jazz, rock, dance, country, metal – music is everywhere in and around Austin.

The Blind Pig is one of those small bars nestled on 6th street, just a couple blocks east of Congress Blvd. It's a long and narrow establishment with its main bar just to your right as you walk in. A small stage is downstairs, nestled under the stairs on your left, used primarily for the one or two musician acts. The bigger bands play upstairs on its second floor. And when they do it's hard to even hear yourself think. But downstairs, it's not so bad a spot to hang out and relax.

In fact, that's where Sasha and Travis were at that moment, seated at the bar in The Blind Pig. It was happy hour, a little after five o'clock on a Thursday afternoon. The upstairs bands wouldn't get cranked up until eight or nine that evening. The guitarist downstairs played an acoustic guitar and took requests. He was playing *Brown Eyed Girl* for about the third time in the last hour. No one seemed to mind.

A month had passed since Sasha and Travis returned from Israel. They'd stopped off in London for a week on the way back, to decompress and to spend some quality time with Allister and Penelope. Allister's country home certainly had plenty of spare guest rooms. Penelope had promised to come to Texas for Thanksgiving, and Sasha had promised to spend Christmas in Rome. When Travis graduated in December he was only too glad accept Allister's offer to come to London for two months of advanced training in Magic. Travis was really looking forward to that. For Sasha and Travis together, it seemed life these days was...

It was weird.

For the last twenty years Sasha lived with no mother in her life, believing her mother to be long dead. Now she had a mother in her life. In that same period of time she saw her father infrequently, maybe once every few years. They had chatted on the phone and Skyped every now and then, but didn't spend a lot of quality time with each other. Now she'd never see him again.

That was just weird.

Sasha still saw Travis almost every day at school. He was still her teaching assistant until his graduation, and the Fall semester wasn't that far away anymore. There were a lot of preparations to make, new material to get ready, lessons to plan, and whatnot.

That was kind of weird too.

After everything they'd been through, everything they'd learned, everything they now had the power to do – just going back to everyday life on a college campus was just...

Weird.

If fact, the past six weeks had taught them both just how insulated a life they lived in the artificial bubble of academia. Information and knowledge was important, as well as the debate and exchange of new and profound ideas – but it simply wasn't the real world. The world was a place of risks and consequences, filled with a continuum of souls from the most noble and loving to the most wretched and evil. All people weren't good deep down inside. Nor were all people permanently lost and unredeemable. Everything wasn't always what it appeared to be. There were illusion and deceptions. But the world didn't have to accept a dark fate of victimhood in the face of evil: because there was Magic.

Yes, Magic *was* real.

Sasha broke her zoned-out stare of ruminations and noticed Travis amusing himself trying to get the label off his beer bottle all in one piece.

He asked her, "Do you still take it out and read it?"

She nodded. "I have to. It's one of the most important things I really have left of him." She put her hand on her heart. "But I still feel him in my heart. His light. His energy. Sometimes, when I'm quiet and still, I believe I can even hear his voice, deep down, guiding me and trying to help me."

"I can believe that," Travis said, and then asked her, "But, seriously, have you read the entire journal yet?" The crinkled label of his beer bottle fell to the bar top, leaving a naked brown bottle in Travis' hand.

Sasha snapped her fingers and the discarded label flew back up to its previous home, flattened out perfectly and reattached to the bottle as if it were new. "There. Fixed it for you."

He frowned. "I wanted it off."

She playfully scolded. "You were making a mess."

He hooked a thumb over his shoulder toward the bartender. "They would have thrown it away."

She chided him, "So why are you making messes for other people to clean up?"

He cast his eyes down, and set the empty bottle gently on the bar. "I'm sorry. I didn't think of it that way."

Sasha playfully pushed him. "I'm just teasing you, silly. Man, lighten up! And no, I haven't read all of it yet. It's pretty thick. But I'm working on it. It's like the unending bowl of pasta. No matter how much you consume, there still seems to be a lot left."

At that very moment Sasha's eyes saw it in the woodgrain of the bar near her elbow: it was a face.

It was a most familiar bearded face. Her eyes got glassy as she reached out and touched it with the tip of her finger, closed her eyes and breathed in deeply, held the breath for a moment, and then let it out slowly. Feeling better, she turned to Travis and smiled.

He returned the smile. "You saw him again, didn't you?"

She just smiled even bigger and gave him a little nod.

He asked, "Well, if you're doing all this new reading and learning, have you mastered anything new lately I don't know about?"

Sasha nodded again, "As a matter of fact, yes, I have. If I can find all the right ingredients, which might be hard to do, I think I can make a magic potion that will make you fall hopelessly in love with me."

Travis looked away, clearly embarrassed. "Stop it. Don't tease."

Sasha leaned over and with her index finger pulled his chin back around to face her. She looked deeply into his eyes and told him seriously. "But hey, I would never really do that because it would be a total waste of time. Right?"

He looked wounded. "Why? You don't think I could ever love you?"

Sasha tenderly took his cheeks in her hands, laughed out loud, and said, "No, silly, because I know you already do."

And with that she pulled his lips to hers and kissed him long and deep. When she let him go, she could see he was in a mild state of shock, which only deepened when she added, "I've wanted to do that for a very long time. But I didn't want to scare you off, since you were my teaching assistant and still a student. Cause if you report me I could get fired. But after everything we've been through together, I'm betting that getting a surprise kiss isn't going to be the scariest thing that's ever happened to you."

"Not by a long shot," Travis whispered as he leaned forward and kissed her again. It wouldn't be the last time.

CHAPTER 60

FROM THE JOURNAL OF WILLIAM TURNER

MY EPILOGUE

I am afraid, dear Reader, that this is going to have to be my last entry in this specific journal. If all goes well for me, then I fully intend to start a new one in a few months. But if things bode badly on the road ahead, then this will surely be my last contribution of knowledge to you herein. But fret not, this isn't the only journal I've ever kept, and certainly not the only one since my discovery of Magic. In this one, I've endeavored to concisely consolidate what I felt was most essential for mortal folk to grasp the basics of Novice Magic and to inspire them to want to delve deeper into the life of a Magician. If you do choose to explore further, then heed what you have learned from me wisely.

By way of update: I have successfully been welcomed into the trust of the Inner Circle for some time now, and am learning quite a lot about them. I know who comprises the leadership of the group and where they are all located. The entire group is a total of about twelve or thirteen in number. Each member governs a geographic region and has an array of underlings, i.e. minions who are comprised of a combination of both Magi and mortal folk.

Their plans to acquire a weapon of mass destruction and market it to some Middle Eastern radicals appears to be on track. The high leader of the Inner Circle is personally overseeing the operation. So I don't have much time to act to stop it. And it must be stopped, even at the price of my covert mission of infiltration, or possibly even my life.

However, I don't believe I will be alone in my quest. I will personally seek out Penelope, who is in Rome, and see if I can turn her to the light. She loved me once in life. Perhaps that is still worth something. Plus, in a month or so from now, if needed, I will also be dispatching my Master to America on my behalf to marshal yet more assistance.

Strength in numbers is always good policy.

In fact, that is the main reason why this must be my last entry in this particular journal. For tomorrow I shall be packing it up and sending it to my lawyer in Texas as a contingency plan, which I fear has little chance of being avoided.

The symposium here in Geneva starts in three weeks. One of the Inner Circle members, an important French Finance Minister, will be here. My new mission shall all start with him. It will be quick. I'll take his breath away and break his heart. That should send a clear signal to the others that I'm soon coming for them, i.e. coming to stop their madness. Hopefully, a little intimidation will give me the advantage while their numbers are so strong and united against me.

However, should anything untoward happen to me, someone must take up the mantle and soldier on. The stakes are too high to shrink from battle. Therefore, I can think of no one better suited for the task than my daughter, Alexandra, someone who I believe would at least do me the courtesy of listening to what I have to say, and with any good fortune, to act upon it. She shall have this journal to guide her.

I pray Godspeed to her efforts.

If she doesn't choose to follow in my footsteps, then I fear all may be lost. But who am I to say? Magic has a way of persevering and prevailing. I have to believe that more and more mortal folk will discover it, somehow, and awaken it in themselves. They have to, or we are lost.

This was my Master's vision. This was his quest. And now it is mine as well. If my daughter joins in the quest, then I believe that high magic and the Magi will survive for at least another generation.

I've often wondered just how many souls are really out there who have inadvertently seen the Faces in the Stones with no realization of the power that waits for them there.

I promised you I'd explain the faces a little more one day. And that day is today. For the truth is, the Faces in the Stones that you see are all Master Magi, departed from this physical life, commissioned to seek out promising mortal folk and to continue to inspire and energize the younger Magi on their journeys through life. So whenever you see them, don't neglect their energy, or their wisdom, or their direction.

They only wish to help you.

Your path will be exceedingly difficult. How could it be otherwise? But remember the Song of the Flowers. They will refresh you when you are weary.

Lastly, to my beloved Sasha, if you are ever reading this, and I am no longer with you in this world, please know two things:

1. First and foremost, I love you and will always carry you in my heart, as I hope one day I have the opportunity to fill yours with bright white light; and

2. **Magic is real.**

ABOUT THE AUTHOR

ROBERT E. GELINAS

Bob Gelinas lives and works in Austin, TX. Born in Blytheville, AR in 1960, he has lived all over the United States, as well as in Europe. The Magician's Guide, is Bob's seventh published novel.

Outside of his writing career, Bob is a successful startup entrepreneur and an accomplished businessman. He has spent over thirty years in the Information Technology (IT) industry, and serves as CEO of an International software company, founded in 2012. He also serves and Publisher and Editor-in-Chief of ArcheBooks Publishing, founded in 2003. He is a decorated veteran (1980-1987), and just for fun, plays drums in a local Austin Rock-and-Roll band, called Suburban Whiskey.

www.ingramcontent.com/pod-product-compliance
Lightning Source LLC
Chambersburg PA
CBHW021508240626
47154CB00002B/543

* 9 7 8 1 5 9 5 0 7 2 6 7 2 *